What the Moon Saw

What the Moon Saw

D.L. Koontz

TULE
PUBLISHING

Dedication

To my mother, Mary Audrey Stanley Koontz. Thank you for encouraging my creativity, and for taking your little girl—more often than you wanted—to visit the mystical, magical Bedford Springs Hotel. I felt you reading over my shoulder from Heaven as I penned this story.

Acknowledgements

First, and foremost, thank you to my readers. You—my friends, and soon-to-meet friends, and perhaps-destined-never-to-meet friends—are incredible. You have encouraged, nudged, and sometimes outright nagged me to produce another book. Thank you for the inspiration.

To my family, sister-cousins, friends, and other loved ones (you know who you are), I cherish you all. Thank you for your love and support, for understanding all the alone time I need to write, and mostly for having faith in my ability to spin a yarn.

To my literary agent Cyle Young, thank you for being my cheerleader, sounding board, counselor, and therapist. Your advice is always spot-on.

To the folks at Tule Publishing, thank you for letting me join your incredible family of talented authors. *What the Moon Saw* came to life under the creative guidance and skills of Sinclair Sawhey, Meghan Farrell, Michelle Morris, Sarah McDonagh, Marlene Engel, and Voule Walker.

And finally, to God be the glory for all the many blessings I have received in this crazy, wonderful life.

"History is not merely what happened: it is what happened in the context of what might have happened."

~ Hugh Redwald Trevor-Roper, Baron Dacre of Glanton

People have been "taking the waters" at the springs in Bedford, Pennsylvania for centuries. The Native Americans—*e.g.:* the Tuscarora, Iroquois, Shawnee and Lenape (Delaware) Indians—were the first to discover the miraculous healing powers of the local mineral waters, assigning them references that, in English, mean "Big Medicine," "Medicine Spring," and "Medicine Water."

The practice of using natural mineral water for the treatment or cure of disease is known as "balneology." Soaking in highly concentrated mineral water is believed to have many health and life-sustaining benefits, such as increasing body temperature, thereby killing harmful germs and viruses, eliminating toxins, increasing blood flow and circulation, increasing metabolism, and absorption of essential minerals.

Native Ballad

Legend sings of a maiden lost
In hope, in love, in time,
Winds whisper, trees turn away
As water roars, "She is mine."

Valley echoes with wails of the loss
Sky fists clouds in despair
Beasts cry out, "Where has she gone?"
Water alone knows where.

I am that maiden, floated and wafted
To another time on a distant shore
All that was me has been taken away
Help me find what came before.

<u>Chorus</u>

Where have I gone?
Where could I be?
I think of your face
As it looks back for me.
The past engulfs me
The future no more
I don't know
What I was before.

Prologue

1760

T HE TALL CHESTNUT'S rider slid the horse to a stop in front of what was left of the smoldering cabin. The pre-dawn morning unfolding around him would have been peaceful, almost serene, had it not been for the contrasting horror before his eyes and the rasps of despair emanating from behind the charred remains. Neighbors had arrived before him, and he could discern from their screams that the cabin's owners were dead.

Or worse—*please God, no!*—still alive.

Scalped, but left alive to suffer an excruciating death.

And, if that were the case, what would be the most humane thing to do? Was it murder to end their suffering? This dilemma loomed before them—him and the other settlers in the area—much too often lately.

It could have been his family. What was it about this senseless, random selection that always left him—as he suspected it would tonight also—sobbing like a baby on some hidden spot of his family's acreage, feeling both a depraved sort of gratitude and a sickening guilt his life had been spared?

But this…this was worse. He'd been in charge of patrol last night. A tip had taken him and his men four miles east of here. He should have ignored that unsubstantiated tiding. Guilt

1

washed over him, coursed into his blood.

Pushing the self-reproach aside, the rider vaulted to the dirt and darted to the destruction. Mixed odors of burned wood and flesh filled his nostrils. With wobbly legs and a stomach that threatened to empty itself on the spot, he tripped up what remained of the steps. The dead body of Neil Macay draped across a barrel on the farthest corner of the porch, eyes still open and forehead split wide, courtesy of the thrust of a tomahawk.

A loud sob escaped the rider's throat for the proud Scotsman and his family. Pushing up, he looked away and struggled through the doorway, its frame smudged with streaks of blood.

Too late again.

An hour later, five mutilated and burned bodies lay side-by-side in the dawning light, awaiting burial. Neil and Martha Macay, and three of their four children.

But, eleven-year-old Elisa, the oldest daughter, wasn't there. She was, it was concluded by the stunned few who whispered the unfathomable, a captive. Taken by the Lenape or Shawnee Indians, no doubt to replace one of their own that was lost through fighting or disease.

As the scattering of neighbors examined the bodies, sobbing and retching at the horror placed before them, he formed a plan, knowing full well what he had to do, given that the girl had no other family and no one to carry out justice for them.

He, Nathan McKenzie, would find and bring her back, no matter where it would take him, no matter how long. He had to. It was his fault. *Wasn't it?*

His betrothed, Anabelle, would understand. He was certain. What if she had been taken instead? She would want someone to come after her.

So he left…
And searched…
And endured…

1765

FIVE YEARS LATER, five revolutions of the sun, five frigid winters and backbreaking summers in the desolate western New York and Canadian territories, he returned with the girl, now a young woman, to the land they had once called home. He was no longer a settler named Nathan McKenzie, but rather an adopted Mohawk re-named Broken Arrow; and she was no longer Elisa Macay, but rather, Morning Meadow, his wife. They rode bareback on a stolen white mare with gray spots, and ate nuts, dried beans, and stale jerky out of a deer-hide satchel that crisscrossed his back.

He was now twenty-two, and she sixteen, both wizened and fractured beyond their years with scars that would never heal, and hardened in places that others would never touch. Yet, the understandings they voiced through their shared language and experiences worked liked a balm, enough to convince them they could, whether by choice or desperation or pure survival, keep on keeping on.

Together.

You can't go home again, a distant voice called, as it had every mile of their journey, insisting they were daft to even try. They'd changed too much. Experienced too many of the wrong things. He'd spent ten months searching. Another nine being tortured, beaten, and forced to work like an animal, before being traded with her to the Mohawks in the French colony called Montreal. Later, he'd had to run the gauntlet to stay alive. To save her. To claim her. Next, came acclimation, acceptance, then years later, rejection when his red-skinned brothers were caught in a lengthy war that involved the British and the French. He and Morning Meadow left, banned from returning.

Outcasts.

They'd changed in that time, no longer fitting in anywhere, with any group. Only fitting with one another.

No, they shouldn't return.

However, *one* could return the voice reasoned. *One* could restore life to what it was and adjust to the future. *One* could deny, refute, disown what had actually transpired.

But not *two*. *Two* would always serve as a visual and inescapable reminder of the ordeal, the past never leaving. With *two*, truth would lurk in every corner, hide around every turn, ignite every time they fielded a question by the well-intentioned who would awkwardly support them and the sanctimonious who would stalwartly shun them.

He had continued with her anyway, sitting behind her on the lone horse, ignoring the voice, sleeping on the earthen floor twenty-one moons before seeing the familiar terrain that marked their homeland, the country for which his heart yearned—the unusual copse of lofty trees, the gurgling streams of mountain water, the crooked line of the ridges that swept up into hills he'd climbed in childhood, all unchanged.

They were near home. Back in the Appalachian foothills of the western Pennsylvania frontier territory. Just another hour's ride to his family's home, beyond this open stretch of meadow, past the distant grove of dense woods, across the Juniata River, and through the steep gap.

He reined in the horse, deciding to delay their return until the morning. He wanted one more night alone with her. One more night not thinking of past or future. The departure from their Mohawk family could not be altered. The future with the frontier settlers would bring what it would. They would face it, together. Tomorrow.

"Home in the morning." He whispered in their new language. Kanien'keha. *Mohawk.*

He watched her shoulders drop as relief washed over her. He knew of her concern. Recognized she was grateful for this reprieve.

"Niá:wen." *Thank you.* She hesitated and repeated the word in English, their original language. One he'd tried to keep alive between them by reading to her at night from a book of Shakespeare his Mohawk brothers had taken from a white man, just moments after killing him.

The sentiment in her 'thank you' was strong. Delivered with a warmth and a trust that made his heart swell. But the pronunciation was weak, delivered in a halting manner as though the word no longer came easily to her.

How he loved this woman! Cherished her. They could weather anything. Together.

She placed her palms on the side of his face. "You give me strength, my husband. You are my air. My water." She hesitated, donned a determined look, and continued, this time in broken English. "Where you go, I go. Always together." She finished her delivery with a tenacious nod as though to punctuate her resolve.

Once again, he was captivated by her eyes. One green, the

other green with almost a quarter of it blue. While with the Mohawks, he'd learned that her unusual eyes were the reason the Lenape had allowed her to live. They believed her to hold special powers or blessings from nature. Selfishly, he'd often teased her that because he had blue eyes, her blue speck represented the inevitability of him becoming a part of her. "Ohonte, oròn:ya," he reminded her again. *Green with blue. Together.*

Later, after they'd eaten and watched their fire burn low, he pulled her close and promised that they would survive re-entry into the settler world.

She turned to him. Despite the amber glow of sunset fading quickly into dark shadows, he could see concern about the morrow etched on her face again. He stroked her neck and planted a kiss on her shoulder. Her eyes were averted but he felt her shiver and make a noise of pleasure. She turned to face him. The light was too dim to see the disparate colors of her eyes, but he could see that her frown had softened to a smile.

"Morning Meadow." His voice was hoarse. It was all he could say before she lifted a hand to his face and drew his mouth down to hers.

He took her in his arms. A groan rose from within her, and he broke the kiss only long enough to murmur, "You are my life," before descending into the physical expression of what dwelled in their hearts.

By mid-morning the next day, from atop the mare, they spotted the first sign of the outmost settler boundary, the territory they would soon call home again—a split-rail fence.

"What is past is prologue," she quoted in English. He appreciated that she'd chosen both the language and the quote at this moment to please him, a sign she accepted their destiny, this return to a long-forgotten people and way of life. What was past was now gone and had led them to this new life. She moved her hands to his forearms and leaned back against his chest as though needing his fortitude and protection. *Like she had last night.*

But in that trenchant and ironic way that fate takes the reins when least expected, hope fled at the crack of a musket sounding from the east, and he felt a *thunk* reverberate through her with the force of an axe hitting wood. Her torso slammed back into his. The impact shuddered up his core, choking off any ability to talk. He felt her body go limp.

Terror slithered across his nerves.

Reining in the horse for a frenzied dismount, he cradled her in his arms, and dropped to the ground, tumbling and landing hard but taking the brunt of the impact, her blood smearing onto his breechcloth and fringed deer hide leggings. After easing her to the grass, he wrenched his gaze toward the east and saw a man sitting atop a sturdy mount, rifle pointed at him. A second shot rang out striking his chest with a thrust that knocked him backward. He fell, and his head hit a rock, the impact driving spikes into his skull, cutting off the light.

He opened his eyes. The sun had moved, now glaring at him from the west and hinting that several hours had lapsed since he last saw it. Skewers of pain stabbed at his chest and he clenched in agony, his hand moving to the source of pain. The feel of the fabric confused him and he looked down to see he'd been wrapped with a muslin bandage.

He remembered—he'd been shot.

So had Morning Meadow!

7

He groaned. He must save her. He summoned strength he heretofore didn't know he had, rolling to his side and sitting up. Dizziness made him nauseous.

She was no longer beside him.

Panicked, he twisted, looking into the distance, north, east.

"I have her."

The voice came from the south so he turned and hand-crawled in that direction, blinking in rapid succession and lifting a throbbing hand to his brow to blot out the sun's rays.

An old woman stood beside his horse, the young woman draped like a corpse across its top. He noted the old woman's high cheekbones and coal-black hair, a braid trailing from beneath her hat and down one side of her face and chest. Her face was in shadow, so he could not see her well. She wore gloves. She was short, yet looked strong, capable, and wore a crude version of a man's clothes, but made of buckskin, with a feather draping from her hat.

"You will hurt," she called to him, "but you will live." She gestured with her head toward the young woman. "You cannot help her now."

Fifty paces lay between them, but he heard her voice as though she were at his side. It was a firm voice. A reassuring voice. A voice that neither boomed nor whispered. Still, he had strained to listen because of the words she used. She spoke English to him, but it sounded garbled, like it wasn't her original language.

The woman turned and walked south away from him, reins in hand, horse following.

Certain he had descended into a horrible nightmare, he opened his mouth to respond but his voice wouldn't work.

How could he scream, "Stop!" when he couldn't even whisper? He wanted to beg the old woman to have mercy and keep them together, because Morning Meadow—*his wife!*—was dying, probably already dead.

She was his life! Their souls were destined to be together, weren't they?

It couldn't end this way. Not after all they'd been through to stay alive. *To stay together!*

His chest tightened as if a merciless hand were squeezing his heart. Tears that held unimaginable grief welled in his eyes, blurring his already tainted vision. Standing was impossible, but he tried anyway. He needed to go after her, but pain gripped him and he fell back. He reached a hand in her direction, but throbbing and despair washed over him, dropping him into dark nothingness where there were no Indians or longhouses, no gunshots or pain to add another mark to his body, or to a memory he'd have to blot away.

Later, he awoke to nighttime. For a split second the moon seemed to peer from behind a cloud before frowning and tucking away again. Broken Arrow found himself alone in the vast, forbidding darkness. This time, the tears turned to sobs as the pain of losing Morning Meadow collided with the pain of a life without her. He was certain he wouldn't survive it.

Because there was no life without her.

She had been his life. Now, she was gone.

Chapter One

June 2016

L OOKING BACK LATER, Libby Shaw would swear her life began the day of her death.

She should have known. Should have grasped it. If only she had paid better attention.

But, she'd been looking in a different direction—at the present, right where all the philosophers, talk show hosts, and MEMEs on Pinterest and Facebook advised one to focus.

The ponderous revelation that changed it all was divulged on an unusually sultry evening in mid-June in one of Georgetown's finest restaurants. The kind that delivered five-star service seconds before conveying a bloated bill. After that, everything in Libby's life had become one baffling, tumultuous whirl.

Earlier, that afternoon and into evening, she had sat at her desk at FBI headquarters in Washington D.C. tethered via headphones to a recording machine. Listening. Translating into English what she could.

Voice One: "People go missing all the time. It's *luronchelavyek.*"

Voice Two: "No, *Scrakoheu* will not want *grubpemry* carried out this way. Killing her is only part of the solution. *Davryemya* wants a more permanent *ludpanyat.*"

Libby pressed the cold plastic of the headset tighter to her ears and leaned in to hear the perplexing words better, which was pointless of course because the volume was fine. The language too. As a linguist, Libby had full command of this foreign language and eight others.

The problems were the unusual accent and the speakers' baffling tendency to use an unfamiliar term every few words. If she didn't know better, she'd guess they were using a cipher or code, or perhaps select words from a language that was either so new or so old it would make sense to a handful, if not only these two. Regardless, she didn't want to meet them, particularly Voice One. His chilled tone carried a sinister edge to it.

Voice One: "But this will solve everything. She is predictable. She will *felvzyat*."

Voice Two: "Only if you *kipmaiteu sarinzvya.*"

Libby groaned, hit the stop button, and yanked the headphones from her ears. She slouched back in her chair, her gaze darting to the scenic poster above her desk featuring a lone, rustic cabin set amidst a range of mountains. Emblazoned above it were words that taunted her daily with advice she had yet to achieve: *Seek a Simpler Life*. "Yeah, right," she mumbled. Her shoulders ached, head throbbed, stomach growled. Despite her long day, she harbored hope of finishing the audio translation before leaving the office.

She sipped her coffee and grimaced. The pot must have sat on the burner all afternoon, and now it was bitter. She pulled open her middle desk drawer and pushed aside camping brochures, hiking trail maps, and packets of herbal supplements, to find packets of sweetener. This coffee was her only hope of making it through these tapes.

After the attacks on September 11, 2001, the Federal Bureau of Investigation switched its primary focus from criminal investigation to counter terrorism and domestic intelligence, which prompted an increase in translation and interpretation jobs. Libby and the other linguists analyzed and translated thousands of pages of foreign materials each year, and provided several hundred hours of vocal translation. The translations had proven astonishing, shocking, even threatening at times, but never had they been more puzzling than this case. It was one of the few that didn't involve Islamic radicalism. Even more confounding, the bureau suspected a mole.

Libby looked at the time on her computer screen, 6:09 p.m., then swept a gaze behind her, around the large office space. As she suspected, her co-workers had gone home.

"Country Roads" sounded from her cell phone. She smiled when she read the caller ID. *Andrew Grey.* "Hello, handsome. You have perfect timing." Melting into the back of her chair, she wondered why, after four weeks of titillating moments and outings together, her skin still goose bumped when he called.

"Hey beautiful. You still at work? We have reservations at eight-thirty, you know."

Libby groaned. "I should work on this…."

"Still that same project?" His tone sounded annoyed. "Must it be done tonight? That investigation has been going on for years."

She picked up the folder detailing her part of the assignment. Case 2157, the 'Matryoshka Project.' *Hmm, Matryoshka, Russian for nesting dolls. Remove one and there's still one there.* It was marked "high priority," but not "urgent." No further details given. Not surprising, since she was often given portions of important investigations. The sensitive parts generally were provided on a 'need to know' basis only. Her role was simply to listen, translate, and develop a transcript.

Fine then, she would pick up the task tomorrow. A fresh perspective was best for the job anyway.

"I'll be there. Don't worry." She grinned. "I'd still like to know what's so important about tonight."

He had selected one of the finest restaurants in Georgetown, La Cicia, and urged—practically begged—they talk *that* night.

"You'll see." His tone had grown serious, a startling change to his warmth when she answered the phone earlier. "Hey, babe, I better go."

With a sigh, she clicked off the call and turned her thoughts to the horrendous rush-hour traffic awaiting her.

✕

"WHY TONIGHT?" LIBBY'S roommate and co-worker Colette Ma yelled from their living room.

They shared a two-bedroom apartment in Old Towne Alexandria, on the south side of the nation's capital. Colette was two years older than Libby's age of twenty-nine, and a six-year bureau veteran, whereas Libby had been recruited only a year earlier. When they'd met, Colette wasted no time convincing Libby to become her roommate.

"Why is he so insistent?" Colette continued, having returned moments earlier from her latest assignment, a job she'd described as "tedious," and "child's play." Her plan was to repack and head out for a birthday surprise for her widowed mother on Maryland's Eastern Shore.

Libby could hear her traipsing around the living room, the sounds of luggage and paper bags being shuffled from the front door to her bedroom.

Finished changing, Libby rubbed make-up concealer on the puckered scar that marred the skin beneath her collarbone. Her aunt Isabel had told her not to be ashamed of it, that it simply meant she was stronger than what had caused it. Libby had never really bought into that concept, given that she didn't remember what produced it anyway. She checked herself one more time, then strutted into the living room with an exaggerated catwalk and posed provocatively.

Colette moved her gaze from her bags to Libby, taking in the four-inch heels and black silk dress with its daring slit up the right leg. Libby had piled her unruly shoulder-length auburn curls atop her head, leaving little tendrils loose around her face.

A Cheshire grin grew on Colette's flawless face and Libby caught the familiar bright alertness in her narrow gaze. There was nothing fainthearted or indecisive about her roommate. Colette threw her shoulders back, parked a hand on her waist, and with the index finger of her hand, traced the air. "Girl, you are rocking that LBD."

This attempt at humor was so out of character for her staid, hardboiled friend, that Libby rolled her eyes. "I'd rather be in jeans. And, don't ever accept an assignment as a Valley girl. You're not convincing."

"Yeah well, I'm not a professional shopper either, but I pulled that one off." She pointed toward the door where four department store bags sagged to the left of the threshold, each brimming with colorfully wrapped presents. She'd worked undercover in New York City and D.C. for the past two weeks on a push to bring down a counterfeit designer handbag operation with ties to human trafficking. "There's three more in the bedroom."

"What is all that stuff?"

"For the senior center." Colette shrugged. "I got side-tracked. No big deal."

Libby walked closer and perused the purchases. "Took your directive seriously, eh?"

Colette waved a dismissing hand. "When in Rome." Grabbing her stack of unopened mail from the dining table, she folded her tall, lithe body onto the arm and back of their couch in a pose of graceful exhaustion, her long black flowing tresses and chestnut-colored skin further paling the honey-colored upholstery beneath her.

Her roommate hailed from a long line of FBI agents, her great grandmother Tillie having started the tradition in the early 1900s, long before the FBI officially acknowledged women on its books. Tillie had married a man while on an "undocumented" assignment in China, and a recessive gene remained hidden through subsequent generations of marriages to tall, white Americans and one Swede, before materializing on Colette, awarding her with a beautiful and unique look: East-Asian features mixed with blue eyes and freckles across the span of her cheeks. Sharp, feisty, acerbic and top of her graduating class in martial arts, Colette was part of the bureau's Specialized Weapons and Tactics team and, therefore, often involved in high-risk situations.

"Colette Ma, you've got a big heart."

"Pffft, keep it on the QT. It'll ruin my image." Colette flicked each piece of mail into one of two piles, a bored look on her face. Without looking up, she said, "Don't change the subject. I'm still waiting for an answer, Libs."

"About what?"

"Why Creases—"

"Please stop calling him that," Libby scolded for the umpteenth time. Colette had nicknamed him *Creases* because he was persnickety about his appearance and always meticulously tailored, with perfect pleats on shirts and pants.

Colette continued without a blink, her gaze fixed on the mail. "—is so adamant about dinner tonight? You've been each other's shadow from the moment you met. Why the big deal now?" She groaned as though she'd had a thought, and slumped further into the cushion. "He's going to propose."

"What? No." Libby rejected the suggestion, shaking her head.

"You sure?"

"We've only known each other a month, for pity's sake." Still, the question took root in Libby's mind, and as she fumbled for another denial, Colette looked at her with a worried expression in her eyes.

"See? You wonder, too."

Libby pumped both palms at her. "That's not it. We agreed to take things slowly." She turned away, emptying items from her shoulder bag into a clutch purse, and cringing at the realization that, for the first time in her life, she had defined herself as part of a "we."

When had that happened?

Oddly enough, she liked the classification.

Oh. My.

The instant Andrew and she met four weeks earlier, following his lecture at the bureau on advanced digital forensics and incident response, Libby learned attraction has no logic. Their gazes had met and held a moment.

Then another.

She'd found it harder to breathe.

As they shook hands, she'd been awash with a sense of reconnecting with a part of herself she had lost long ago. A jolt of recognition, but not from a memory. The air thickened and her chest tightened, and in a daze, she had agreed to dinner. That began four weeks of a frenzied romance. Each time, she was left feeling addled. Distracted. Anticipating the next date.

Colette's voice cut through Libby's thoughts: "Slowly? The vibes between you two were thick like pea soup from the get-go. Don't forget, I was there."

"That's silly. Besides, he—"

"Only has eyes for you, and you know it. I hear you tiptoe in, at the early hours of the morning. But hey, I get it. He's older, handsome, smart, down-to-earth." She lowered her voice to a murmur. "If you can tolerate his short stature and stuffy personality."

"Short stature? He's five-nine, an inch taller than me. We're a good fit. Besides, we can't all be five-eleven like you."

"Ever heard of short-man syndrome?" Colette quipped.

Libby ignored her. "Furthermore, he's not stuffy. You just said he was down-to-earth. How could he be both? He has an old-world demeanor. It lends a gravitas to everything he says and does." He certainly had the suave manners of a man several decades beyond his age of forty.

"Please." Colette dragged out the word. "Gravitas? He prefers Andrew, not Andy. Always the proper language. Tailored clothing. Carries a pocket watch. It's like he's from another time...or planet. Tell me something normal about him."

Libby tilted her head to think. "He loves cars...and he reads."

"What does he read? *GQ?* Comics? *Pokémon Go* guides?"

"The classics. Dickens. Tolstoy. Melville."

Colette kept her face pointed toward her mail, but rolled her eyes upward long enough to shoot Libby a gaze that said, "Are you serious?"

"He likes the old stuff." Libby kept her tone flat, hoping to sound indifferent. "That's part of his charm." Despite her words she weathered a cringe. Her feminine dander *did* rise when he acted too stuffy. But, that was his only flaw to date. Well, that and the fact he was a little obsessed with finery and abhorred camping, whereas she loved being close to nature and roughing it.

She had hoped their sense of connection would abate as they got to know each other. That they would do more to disillusion one another. But, it hadn't happened.

Colette pressed her lips together like she was holding in a barrage of disparaging comments, then looked up from her mail. "There's just something off, don't you think?"

"He's distinct. That's all." Libby's tone grew softer. "Why do you dislike him so much? Are you afraid I'll move out?"

"Have you done a background check?"

"Col, why would I bother when the bureau did one already? Relax, it's not like my skills are going to take me to the head of the bureau one day, so I doubt he has a nefarious intent."

"True…about your skills, I mean. Not the nefarious intent. That's still questionable."

Libby smiled. She wasn't insulted by Colette's honest assessment. Libby was average in almost every agent ranking, except languages and target shooting. For some inexplicable quirk of her DNA, she excelled at both. Particularly languages. Nine, to be exact, including several from Asia: Russian, Chinese, Arabic, and Farsi. After her parents' deaths, she'd traveled in third-world countries with her aunt Isabel, a physician, in a type of doctors-without-borders program. She didn't remember much of those years except discovering her aptitude for languages. Given that translation was the only unique skill she brought to the bureau, she doubted she would see many opportunities to demonstrate her competence. That was fine. She was happy to have a more balanced life and excel below the radar. Colette could be the one who rose to the top.

As Libby studied her roommate now, she felt a warm rush of affection. "You worry too much."

"You don't worry enough."

Their gazes locked, silently acknowledging a stalemate.

As usual, Libby gave in first. "Just give him a chance. For me?"

Colette frowned, and reached for Libby's hand. "You're right. You, my dear, are falling in love."

Love? The word burned in Libby's mind and gave her a start. Hearing it from Colette's mouth, it resonated differently in Libby's head than anytime she had posed—then flatly dismissed—the sentiment to herself.

Was it true?

But, marriage? No, too much, too soon. If ever. All he wanted that night was for her to meet his family or discuss where they would go from here.

Didn't he?

Chapter Two

2016

A HALF-HOUR AFTER the prim, stiff-backed maître d' seated Libby, she still wondered about Andrew's intent. She studied him from across the table—clean-shaven, olive-skinned, and a stalky kind of muscular. He appeared a patron relaxed, a man enjoying where he was at the moment and in life. His dark curly hair topped an alert face with thick, level brows and wide eyes hidden beneath gold wire-rimmed glasses.

But, as an agent, Libby had been taught to read people. If she gauged him correctly, he acted anxious, almost fretful. One knee bounced up and down, and he kept checking his pocket watch. She sat back in her chair, doing her best not to let him know his demeanor unnerved her.

And, what was with the table he'd reserved? Uncharacteristically, he'd selected one near the wide front window. She didn't like such placement because it was hard to secure situational awareness with so many patrons continually in and out the main entrance, and intense people scurrying by in every direction seeking their versions of thrills and nightlife. She preferred sitting more strategically, her back against a wall and some distance between her and any threat that might come at her.

He had dismissed her confusion over their placement with

a wave of his hand and a trite, "It's something different." His momentary deer-in-the-headlights look had left her wondering. Still, he made a stab at normalcy, discussing random things— the weather, the restaurant, the problems with the Metro that morning.

Despite his restlessness, she enjoyed listening to him talk, like always. His voice was smooth and deep, like James Earl Jones, yet his words always settled over her softly, like snow touching down. Furthermore, the way he looked at her with those chocolate-colored eyes—such adoration and appreciation. All of him, his whole package, struck her again as familiar, as though she had known him for years. Wasn't that a sign of a poetic gravitation, a promising match, perhaps even destiny?

Sometime between the appetizer and the soup, he checked his watch again. Libby was about to question him on it when he reached across the table seeking her hand. His hands were strong and uncalloused, and she anticipated him squeezing and letting go, but instead he gripped securely. Their gazes locked. He swallowed. "Libby, you are so beautiful. You must know that I've fallen in love with you…"

The tone in his voice suggested something elemental was forthcoming. With a start, she drew in a nervous breath and straightened her shoulders. Her senses blocked out the mingled smells and the murmur of conversations that lingered around them.

He swallowed again. "…but, I'm not who you think I am."

And there it was. A whisper of dread unfurled in her stomach. Her mouth opened, posing the retort, "I knew this was too good to be true." But she remained quiet, remembering her agent training: *Don't assume. Don't jump to conclusions.*

Still, her mind raced as she studied him, trying to gauge his sincerity and the direction of the conversation. Nothing in his carriage or disposition appeared false or untoward.

No, he hadn't toyed with her this past month. His pleasure in their time together was too genuine. Then again, he was an agent. Like her. He could hide his true self when necessary. She assessed his face, hoping to read signs of teasing.

None.

With dismay, she slumped in her chair, and parked the soup spoon in her free hand onto the saucer. She was on a runaway train with no perceptible way to get off. She had to follow this rocky ride of a conversation to its inevitable, probably hurtful, collision.

She started to pull her hand from his clasp, but he clutched tighter.

"What? You're not Andrew Grey? Not a computer forensics expert? What is it?" The clipped questions hurled from her like flying bullets.

He cringed. "No, I am all that. I—"

Frustration got the better of her and she rushed ahead, seeking the damaging facts. "Married? Bisexual? Transvestite? Which is it?"

Andrew's head jolted back like he had been struck. "No, none of that. Let me explain." He leaned forward again, a dark curl falling carelessly over his forehead. He spoke slowly, as though choosing his words with care. "I told you I was forty. That's true. I have lived forty years, but ..." He hesitated and his gaze intensified. "I wasn't born forty years ago."

"So...when?"

He shrugged a stalky shoulder. "Add a century...or two."

Libby blinked as a warning bell tolled in the deep recesses of her mind. Insanity? A fountain of youth? Perhaps he'd been unknowingly hypnotized on assignment? Yes, that was it. Should she extract herself from this madman, bolt, and run while she still could? She dismissed the questions as absurd.

"Go on," she whispered, dread blossoming into extreme foreboding in the pit of her stomach.

He thrust a frustrated hand through his curls. "I'm not explaining myself well. I've rehearsed this for months but—"

"Months? We just met four weeks ago. What are you talking about?" This time she did jerk her hand free. Who *was* this crazed man and what kind of a ruse was he pulling?

"Okay, I'll say this quickly. Hear me through, Libby, I beg you. Then I can answer your questions."

The back of her neck prickled, but she bit back a rebuke and swept an impatient hand for him to proceed.

"I *am* Andrew Grey and I *was* born...well, a long time ago. When doesn't matter. What *does* matter is that I began to feel ill several years ago. In another time. At first it wasn't anything I couldn't handle, but I kept deteriorating. At times I could barely walk. The pain was unbearable. I tried doctor after doctor. Nothing helped—"

He broke off as a waiter arrived to top off their water glasses, unknowingly adding to the stiltedness that already lay between them.

Andrew watched him leave before gazing back at her. "Finally, I sought the medicinal benefits of mineral water."

"Water?"

"At a place called Bedford Springs. Previously, I'd only vacationed there, but for the first time, I paid heed to the medicinal reputation of the water."

"Water?" she repeated, this time with a mixture of irritation and sarcasm in her voice.

Andrew continued nonplussed. "After taking the water a few times, I showed improvement, but each time, in quick manner, my symptoms returned—"

He'd hit her limit. "This is crazy. Do you expect me to—"

"Libby, please." His tone grew hard. "Listen. It's important."

She studied him, before bobbing her head in defeat.

"One night, summer solstice, I was in severe pain. Half out of my mind. I decided death would be more welcome. But first I wanted to give the water one last effort. I waited until dark. Around midnight, I hurried to one of the springs. The Crystal Spring. In desperation I immersed myself in the water. It was frigid cold but I decided I was going to either die there that night, or leave a restored man."

Despite her internal BS meter pinging loudly, Libby found herself leaning in and asking, "What happened?"

"I left the next morning. Cured. But I walked into the year 2022."

He stopped and studied her, giving her time to adjust to this latest bombshell.

She tried to flat-line her voice, but failed. "You're saying you time-traveled into 2022, a year that, by the way, hasn't even happened yet." By the time she was done with her retort, she was practically hissing the final word. She exhaled a shaky breath, "You do realize how absurd this sounds? How old are you anyway? And how—"

"I'll answer your questions later." He looked at his watch

and his dark brows came together in a grim line, alarm etching his face. "Right now I have to tell you certain things before 9:26, and it's 9:12 right now." His voice rang with a maddening resolve that startled her.

"Andrew, you're scaring me." She thumped both hands flat on the table. "What…" she lowered her voice, "…is going to happen at 9:26?"

He leaned forward again. "There's going to be a car accident. Directly outside this door. Senator Woodbine. His driver will lose his right leg. The senator will be hospitalized in intensive care overnight. Tomorrow, at 7:21 a.m., he will die."

Libby's face locked in a stare. Her lips parted but she could not find words. After a moment, she lifted a shaky hand to cover her mouth, an unconscious reminder that she had control of something, or to cover the scream within. Perhaps both.

He continued, speaking hurriedly. "I know this because in 2022, I downloaded databanks of key events. International. Domestic. Even developments about agents within the bureau. I have them for each year for a couple dozen years. Back to when computers were first refined. I was determined to return. To go back in time…back closer to my own time, and I thought I might need proof along the way. At the next equinox—"

"I thought you said solstice."

"I did. Solstice, equinox, both seem to work. They're both astronomical events and tied to the seasons of the year."

"So you're saying, four times per year this can be done?"

"Solstices are the longest and shortest days of the year, and on equinox, night and day are about the same length." He looked at his pocket watch again. "Some cultures believe it's when mystical things occur. When the visible and invisible worlds overlap. Indian lure says this is when the past and present collide." He swiped an agitated hand across his chin. "It's pure nonsense, of course. But Libby, the influence of the water is not. I experienced all the power of nature pouring forth into the spring at that time."

She recalled her aunt Isabel being preoccupied with the changes of the seasons and the rhythms of the universe. Libby had never paid it much attention. Impatience brewing, she said, "So what about the next equinox? What happened?"

"I tried, but it only took me back to 2020. However, I learned several things. One is that anything tangible from the future can't be carried into the past. But, anything stored in cyberspace can still be accessed because it's not real. Do you understand? It's digital. I had figured out how to store and retrieve information from the future. Eventually, I tried again and I ended up here, in 2016. I accessed that databank from the future, and from it I know that there's going to be a crash any moment."

"If that's true then we've got to stop it." Libby stood, tossing her napkin on the table. With that chivalric reflex of his, Andrew leaped to his feet also, cringing, and she wondered if his look of annoyance was at her or that right 'trick knee' he complained about from time to time. He grabbed her arm and pulled her eye to eye.

"No, Libby. You can't. You mustn't interfere."

She yanked her head back in defiance. "That's ridiculous. A man is going to die and you're going to sit there? Why wouldn't we stop a tragedy if we can?"

His gaze darted around them. "Please lower your voice."

He pulled her down, back into her seat. "We can't do anything because we can't use our knowledge to change history."

"But—"

"We can't play master of the universe. Besides, if you save Senator Woodbine, then you'll prevent his successor from taking the position. A position, I might add, that lands him on a senate select committee that leads to his work with the Food and Drug Administration in the Department of Health and Human Services. That effort, in turn, ushers in a new drug that saves the lives of tens of thousands of women suffering from a rare form of uterine cancer."

Libby looked at him, flabbergasted. A taut silence fell as she wrapped her arms in an embrace against a sudden chill and turned her head to eye the front door. She imagined herself running through it, across the sidewalk, and into the street. She'd beg someone in a car to block the road. Or, she would create a commotion that would cause the vehicles to slow down to avoid hitting her. But, the faces of tens of thousands of women saved from cancer came to mind and turned on her, shaking their heads as though they knew she could have done something to help them.

"Why…" Her voice was hoarse, so she took a hurried sip of water and tried again. "Why are you telling me this? Why now?"

Andrew reached for her hand. "Because you need to under-stand that I know what is going to happen." His words came out harsh, urgent, and he inched closer. "Libby, babe, you are going to die in a couple weeks. It's in the databank. An inoperable brain tumor. And there's nothing I nor any doctor can do to stop it. Not in this medical age or even into the foreseeable future."

Stunned, Libby stared at him, a chill roaring through her. No words would come.

He fidgeted in his pocket, pulled out his wallet, and began fumbling through it. "I have that card somewhere," he muttered *sotto voce*. "Yes. Here it is. Dr. Kuzmich." He tucked it into the clutch purse she'd left lying on the table. "He's helped the bureau on several cases. Has security clearance. He'll see you on short notice. Or, use your own doctor. Just have it verified. Please."

Libby whimpered and sucked in her breath, but he continued, rushing his words and grabbing both her hands again as if in a vice grip. "Summer solstice is Monday. It will be our last chance to save you. You can take medical treatments and hope for the best for the next couple weeks or you can journey in a few days to a new beginning with the help of the water. Libby, I want to give you a new life. But I promise, I won't give up until I travel in time to be with you."

An unmistakable hint of foreboding and certainty had crawled into his voice, a sense of someone who had seen life unfold in a crystal ball. He struck Libby as desperate, unhinged. She was shocked into momentary silence.

Before she could respond or even think about an exit strategy to get away from this madman, the sound of tires screeching on pavement drowned out the classic tunes on the restaurant's sound system, followed by a stomach-churning crunch of metal on metal. Andrew released her hand.

Around them, patrons screamed and hurried to the front window, many spilling into the street, but all Libby could do was sit frozen in her seat, stunned. It would be several minutes before she realized she had grabbed Andrew's forearm in a white-knuckle grip. The commotion continued around them. Sirens wailed, EMTs arrived, and people screamed "Woodbine" into their cell phones, but Andrew and Libby sat still, their gazes locked, as though in an ulterior dimension.

Then, the revulsion and the horror and the food in her stomach mixed and swirled at such a rate that she grabbed her purse and dashed to the ladies room.

Chapter Three

September 1769

THE THICKET WHERE Nathan McKenzie crouched was damp from dew and pocked with brambles. His muscles twitched for movement. But, he followed the orders: *Be still. Wait for the signal.* It was imperative if they wanted to work united to seize the garrison and free their compatriots.

Others waited too—farmers, homesteaders, restless explorers like him—spread out in a long line west of the Juniata River in the Western Territory of Pennsylvania, in a strategic gap in the mountains called "the narrows." Each sported a long rifle, shirts swathed around the locks to prevent mist from dampening the priming.

To the east, the dawning September sun cast stretched shadows along the ridge and, a quarter mile in the distance, on their target: Fort Bedford.

From behind the copse of trees and piles of underbrush, Nathan listened. The slightest of breezes wafted through the Alleghany Mountains causing the tops of the timbers to moan with the voices of ghosts who dwelled there, urging him to avenge their deaths.

He shook his head to dismiss the thought, and lifted one hand off his long rifle to brush it over his face and hair, scrubbing a new focus into place. The effort loosened a few tendrils of his shoulder-length hair from the leather strap that held it out of his way. Like the Indians and the other colonists, he had no patience for the ridiculous powdered wigs the British sported.

When he pulled his hand back, he noticed several things in the dim light. First, were the callouses that had made Anabelle, his ex-fiancé, grimace. Rough, hardened skin from a lengthy familiarity with wooden plow handles, hewing axes, and the coarse iron grips of hoes that were necessary on a backwoods farm. But it was what he saw between the creases of toughened skin that captured his thoughts anew—smudges of the black grease and red paint that covered his face.

Anabelle had scowled when she'd seen him. He thought now, with dismay, of the conversation they exchanged the evening before. She'd walked to the log cabin he shared with his family, several hours after supper, bringing apples her father harvested from their small orchard. She would exchange them with Nathan's mother for one of the quail his brother shot that afternoon or perhaps some of the hominy his sister pounded in the stump mortar.

She shouldn't visit like that. She had to know it was awkward now. He had courted her. Even proposed. In the end, she agreed to wed a British officer. A safer, more reliable option. One that would provide a future and stability unlike Nathan could provide. Once she'd heard that arrogant British soldier, Richard Wallace, talk about the opulence of London—gowns the ladies wore, china for dining, carriages that sported them about town—she'd decided she wouldn't settle for anything less refined than one of the more civilized tidewater villages of Baltimore or Philadelphia. She certainly didn't want a life here in the hard-scrapple western frontier.

No, truth is, she hadn't used any of those words. She'd been kinder when she'd told him she accepted Wallace's proposal. But, that's what Nathan had inferred, and in the end, it amounted to the same thing.

"Nathan, no!" she had scolded him mere hours ago when he opened his family's cabin door and she saw him dressed in scant Indian buckskin clothes and moccasin boots, his face and arms blackened with soot. "Not again with this foolishness."

He hadn't known she was outside. He would have exited out the back to avoid her seeing him like that.

Nathan shut the hand-hewn door behind him, hurried across the splintered porch and stepped over the grain sacks they'd placed there in case of rain, then jumped to the ground to stand beside her. She was a half-foot shorter than him and smelled of flour and butter. He imagined her humming as she baked an apple pie, and the pleasant thought annoyed him.

"Anabelle, you shouldn't be out alone. Do you have a weapon?"

"Of course not. Why would—"

"I can't talk now." He draped the leather strap of his rifle over his head and shoulders, then bent to retrieve the knife he had tucked into his knee-high wrapped moccasins. He handed it to her. "Carry it at the ready. Now, go home. Forget you saw me." He brushed past her.

She reached out and touched his arm to stop him. A wave of longing rolled over him at the sensation of her touch. He turned to her.

Taking his hand, she turned it over, and returned the knife to his palm. "I don't need it."

"Anabelle—"

"You're determined to get those boys out, aren't you? Why can't you let it alone before someone else gets killed?"

His stomach clenched and he returned the knife to his moccasin boot. By "someone" did she mean the British? In particular, her betrothed? Or, her own kinsmen, the colonists? Two of her cousins were being held. Like him, they were part of the settler movement known as the Black Boys, so-called because they blackened their faces when they took action, rebelling against British policy regarding Indians. The settlers wanted to live in peace with the natives, but the British were intent on allowing tradesmen to sell arms and ammunitions to the Indians and inciting them to kill. It was nothing more than licensed murder.

The area had become a cauldron of competing interests: Indian, imperial, colonial. The struggle between France and England for domination of America had ended and the British were in control. A westward surge of settlement and business was underway.

In 1764 the Indian uprisings had reached a crescendo when four Lenape Indian warriors entered a settler's log schoolhouse in the mountains less than twenty-five miles east of where Nathan's family settled. Enoch Brown, the schoolmaster, had pleaded with the warriors to spare the children. Nonetheless, he was shot and scalped. The warriors tomahawked, scalped, and killed nine of the children, and took four others as prisoners. Miraculously, two other scalped children survived to describe what transpired. What's more, the day before that, the Indians had encountered a pregnant Susan King Cunningham, Nathan's cousin on his mother's side. They beat and scalped her before cutting the baby from her body. Others disappeared too, all assumed to have been captured by the Indians.

The British cracked down on the savagery and kidnappings. *Briefly*. But no sooner had the savage war parties fled the area than the strangest of paradoxes occurred—the settlers witnessed merchants' wagon trains carrying arms westward for sale to the same Indians who for years had destroyed their homes, murdered and scalped their neighbors, raped their wives and daughters, and captured their children.

The settlers desired peace, but arms in the hands of the Indians thwarted that peace. So, using Indian raiding tactics, the Black Boys took action to stop the supply wagons. Earlier this year, the British had taken some of their band as prisoners, holding them in Fort Bedford.

Anabelle urged again, "Let it be."

He raised a brow, puzzled. "How can you ask that," he challenged, "when your own kin may die in there?"

She huffed away the scrutiny. "Richard promised nothing like that would happen."

He bristled at her naiveté and thoughtlessness. "Are you willing to risk their lives on that promise?" Grabbing both her upper arms, he shook gently. "Can you live with more guns in the hands of the Indians? Think of the children they've killed. Of Susan."

"Susan was selfish. Walking around all by herself like that—"

Anger coursed through him. "Like you're doing right now, you mean?" As though he were being burned, he abruptly let go, dropping his hands to his side.

She scowled, squared her shoulders and raised her chin, but

didn't say a word. Nathan suspected pride prompted her posturing, but that doubt drove her silence. Talking with her was futile. She demanded too many words anyway. He preferred action to conversation.

Anabelle reached up to touch his cheek, speaking in a softer voice. "Nathan, I just want you to live." She smiled. "I want to dance with you at Clara Miller's wedding on Saturday."

Nathan suspected Richard wouldn't be at the wedding. Wouldn't be welcome. "You're betrothed to someone else," he reminded her, removing her hand from his face. "You can't have it both ways."

"Nathan McKenzie," she said, stomping her foot, "you have no right to talk to me like this. If you hadn't left on that foolish little mission to rescue Elisa Macay years ago, we would have been married for years now and you know it. So it's your fault." She softened her voice before adding, "Besides, it's just a dance."

Were all women this fickle in their feelings? No, he'd known women who weren't. His sister often looked lovingly at her husband, and his mother and father still held hands despite years of hard labor, failing crops, and the loss of two children. And, then there was *her*—Elisa...*no, always Morning Meadow to him*—the woman between his relationships with Anabelle. *She* had loved him unconditionally. And he had loved *her*.

But, *she* was gone forever.

No, not all women were driven by self-indulgence and greed.

Nathan reined in his thoughts. "I must go." He stepped past her again but stopped in his tracks at her next words.

"Please don't hurt Richard just to get back at me."

He stiffened, icy tendrils wrapping around his heart. He'd done nothing but try to protect her and her family through the years. He turned back to respond, but was saved from it when his mother spoke from the porch. He hadn't heard her come outside.

"Isaiah's 'round back, Anabelle." Her voice was stern, her brows furrowed in concern. "He can help you."

Anabelle looked at Nathan a moment, her eyes filled with things unsaid, things he suspected she would never say again.

Finally, turning to his mother, Anabelle nodded. "Yes, ma'am." She headed toward the back.

Nathan's mother hitched the flow of her dress to step off the porch and move to his side. "So it's tonight?"

He nodded. "Dawn."

She wouldn't try to stop him. They had talked about this several nights before. His parents fretted, but understood what needed to be done. His father had said, "If you capture the fort and free our men, it will be the first time colonists have seized a garrison from the British. It will prove we can unite and rise up against their tyranny." There was no censure in his tone, no dread. In fact, Nathan thought he heard a hint of controlled hope.

His mother exhaled a resigned breath, studying his Indian garb. "God speed, my son." Her eyes watered. She embraced him, kissed his cheek, and stepped back.

Roiling with emotion, Nathan looked at the ground, shifted his stance, and returned his gaze. "Ma, if I don't come back—"

"You will." She offered a determined smile. "You were already taken from us once. Not again. You'll be back."

This was the first his mother had mentioned that torturous absence since his return. Five years lost between him and his family. Five years spent trying to bring Elisa back, just to have her shot in the end. He stared at his mother a long moment before nodding, his heart swelling with love.

She blinked thrice, as if fighting tears. "You'll never know how proud I am of the man you've become."

He visualized now his mother's face when she'd sent him off. The love he'd seen there. So much like the way Elisa had looked at him years ago. And, that quickly, her face filled his mind.

They never had a chance.

Then, Elisa's vision faded, replaced by that of Anabelle. The difference startled him.

If he survived this morning, he'd have to find a new way forward, a way to dam up the grief of the past that continually poured forth. *Now* is what mattered. Not the past. *Now* had to be dealt with. *Now* would take all his strength. He had to muster up and meet it.

Chapter Four

1769

"FOG'S ROLLING IN." The whispered voice of Ned Paxton tugged Nathan out of the past and dropped him smack in the present.

Nathan remained still. The weather was a non-concern, the comment demanding no response. He and the others had memorized what lay beyond the veil of gray, and in the darkest of caves they could pull the stoppers out of powder horns with their teeth, prime by habit, find the locks and triggers of their rifles, and retrieve their knives on the first reach every time. James Smith had trained them well when he'd formed the Black Boys.

He heard the command, "Prepare," come down the line. In moments, the soft pad of moccasins sounded through the silence as he and the others moved to the concealed rendezvous point and crouched. The river, over the ridge behind them, made more noise than they did.

Rufus L'Enfant, a Black Boy they all teasingly referred to as Frenchie, fished under a log and pulled out the small iron kettle he'd hidden there hours before. Fingers dipped in, scooping out black grease and daubing it to freshen the stain on their faces. The purpose of the subterfuge was simple: Look enough like Indians to gain the element of surprise. It could be the difference between victory and death in a chance encounter on some forest trails.

While they finger-painted themselves, Nathan listened to the other nineteen men whisper their advice on applying the stain. Several spoke with accents. Most were Scots-Irish like him, but others were German, Dutch, French. He wasn't even sure of their collective origins. One was a free Negro, two were dark in color with last names that were as long as his first and last put together. Their faiths included Puritans, Huguenots, Calvinists, Catholic, but by far, they were Protestant. Some were agnostic going into battle, but men of faith coming out. Yet, they shared a bond, born of freedom and a quest for self-sufficiency. They were varied: farmers who'd moved west from eastern counties, village craftsmen turned pioneering entrepreneurs, immigrants from small European villages, freed redemptioners who had traded their freedom for seven years to pay their sea passage to the New World, where a man could sweat and dig and chop and saw his own homestead out of woods and fields.

James Smith whispered, "Ned, you've been to the fort?"

"In it last night, Jim, deliverin' that gelding they demanded," Ned said. "They're ready for the Black Boys. They got more'n three dozen men on night guard, but they think it's all a joke."

Nathan wasn't surprised at the Redcoats' reaction. Several days earlier, the Black Boys staged and dawdled around the local villages and trading posts acting drunk, strutting like confused ducks, bumping into cabin doors, singing and answering questions loudly. To anyone that would listen, they'd bragged, "We're goin' acrost the ridge to flop the

Redcoats on their blasted heads. Goin' to take Fort Bedford."
Smith had counted on word of their behavior trickling back to
the fort. He wanted the commandant to think they were a joke.
Hiding behind trees, Smith explained, is not the only way to lay
an ambush.

One of the newest Black Boys, a fellow named Andreii,
asked, "Do they know where we are?"

Nathan cringed at Andreii's question, but didn't know
why.

"Nossir." Ned chuckled. "They got word we'd camped at
the northern ridge. They figure we can't get to Bedford before
high noon, even if we're sober enough to chance it. They're
layin' odds we don't come within five miles o' the fort."

Amos Warren spoke next. "I been watchin'. Gate's closed
every night, but they open it at dawn. If they're so sure of
themselves they'll likely open it today, same as always."

"Their guns?" James directed the question to Amos.

"Stacked together. 'Bout forty paces from the front gate.
We can get to 'em first if they're in back eating. And, if we're
fast."

James nodded. "Remember, if I go down, Nathan is next in
command." He smiled, ear to ear. "Are we ready? Let's set our
boys free."

They spread out like they were trained, moving left, scrambling over the next bank and lying down just below the sod
brink. They stopped to prepare their long rifles, fingers cud-
dling the slim riggers.

Climbing to their feet, but remaining stooped as low as
possible, they moved, inching closer, dropped and listened
again, then repeated the process until they got within two

stones' throw of the fort. The white mist that swaddled the terrain had looked thick but offered no resistance.

Nathan could see the stockade and the blockhouse roof.

As Amos predicted, the gate was open. Nathan counted three sentries on the wall, but the other Redcoats were gathered on the far side of the stronghold. He signaled 'three' to the man on his left and trusted it would be passed down the line.

At Smith's signal, the Black Boys lunged up, clawed, scrambled and sprinted full force to the fort. Smith and Nathan crossed through the gate at the same time, one dashing right, the other left, as practiced. Redcoats screamed and one rang a warning bell. A few shots rang out, but in the noisy confusion, Nathan couldn't tell if the shots were from their long rifles or the Redcoats' muskets.

Within seconds, the Redcoats threw their hands in the air as though cognizant they were too unarmed to fight, even though it was quite clear they outnumbered the Black Boys by more than two to one.

At Smith's command, the sentinels scuttled down from their posts and ducked into the huddle of red tunics, their hands raised also.

Nathan didn't see Richard Wallace among the group. Just as well. Richard wouldn't have been able to recognize him in the Indian garb, but still, he didn't want his family identified with this in any way. Maybe Richard had been spending the night with one of the barmaids from the local tavern, where rumor often placed him. The thought made him sad for Anabelle.

James Smith issued orders. Pointing at Levi, he said, "Find an ax to smash the guardhouse door." Turning to Solomon he directed, "Take the flints out of those muskets. Put 'em in your pocket." The Black Boys understood James pointing rather than calling them by name: he didn't want to jeopardize their identity.

"The strong box," Will Chatham reminded their leader. It had been seized by Indians from new homesteaders, the Lauers, who had moved into the area several months earlier with their life savings. The Indians had exchanged the box of currency— sparse English coins, Spanish-milled dollars, rare gold pieces— with the British for ammunition. The Redcoats refused to believe the money belonged to the colonist family; now that the trade was over, they didn't want to be without the money *and* the ammo.

James nodded and turned to Nathan. "Search the officer's quarters while we free the men."

"I'll go with him," Andreii offered and hurried after Nathan.

Nathan bristled at the man's offer, but didn't break stride. He preferred to work alone.

Within minutes, Nathan found a small tin box in the commandant's desk. It matched the homesteaders' description so he lifted the lid and confirmed it still contained the amount and variety of currency the Lauers described. Snapping it shut, he turned to tell Andreii he'd secured it, but instead looked directly into the barrel tip of a pistol.

"I'll take that, brother," Andreii said, his voice cold, his free hand outstretched. His eyes were invisible in the shafts of shadows that crossed his face in the dimly lit room.

Startled, Nathan stiffened as Andreii pulled the box from his hands and tucked it in a deep pocket on the inside of his sleeveless moleskin vest, hidden from view.

Andreii grabbed Nathan's rifle. "You won't be needing this either."

Nathan swallowed. "Andreii, why? You won't get away. If you shoot me, the others will be here directly."

Andreii shrugged. "But you will be dead. You want to take that risk?"

"But why? If you need money—"

"I do not need your help. Now move." Andreii motioned his head toward a door that exited into the back of the fort.

"This is foolish. There's only one way out of here."

"Wrong again, my friend. There is a narrow door in the back, off the kitchen. Cook uses it to dispose dishwater. It is bolted and secured from the inside which, of course, works for me, does it not?" He shoved Nathan to move faster.

As they proceeded, Nathan tried to reason with him even as his gaze cast about looking for anything to grab as a weapon. "You side with the British?"

Andreii smiled. "I side with myself."

"You won't get far. They'll hear you. They'll know we're missing."

"In that chaos?" He gestured toward the front of the fort. "No, by the time they search for us, they won't find anything."

They'd reached the back, their movements all the while blocked from view by walls. Andreii lifted the wooden bars that secured the small door, pushed it open and shoved Nathan through hard enough that he fell to his knees.

Climbing off the ground, Nathan twisted and leaped at Andreii, but his opponent was ready and smacked him in the face with the gun stock, the blow so hard it knocked him back to his knees. Pain and dizziness surfaced. Instinctively, Nathan touched the damage.

"Get up! Over there." Andreii pointed toward a forested grove about a hundred paces from them. "I have horses waiting. Move!"

"Horses?" That was all Nathan could say. When he'd spoken, a spasm of pain rent across his face again. He was rather sure his nose was broken and his right cheek split open, because blood now covered his hand.

Andreii chuckled a strange hysterical sound. "You did not think I would be unprepared, did you? Paid a town kid a king's ransom to put them there before sunrise. I hoped this opportunity would present itself."

Despite the pain, Nathan's mind raced. If he yelled, Andreii would shoot him. He quickly surveyed his surroundings, but didn't see another person anywhere, just trees. Perhaps he could overpower Andreii. After all, the man was short and stalky, whereas he was six feet tall and limber. But, executing the pull of a trigger was faster than executing a tackle any day.

In moments, they reached the grove and stumbled in another twenty paces, where the canopy of colored leaves overhead prevented the sun from reaching. Nathan saw two saddled horses tethered to a tree.

"Get on." Andreii pointed to the black-colored one.

Nathan plotted. He could probably bolt once he was on the horse. Could maybe dodge behind the trees, but then Andreii would still have the money, and the Lauers needed it to build a future.

Seeing no recourse, Nathan complied, deciding he'd seize an opportunity to overpower Andreii as soon as he could. He just hoped his vision didn't get any worse and that he wouldn't lose too much blood before he had his chance.

They rode around the outskirts of the town, cutting south then west, staying in woods most of the distance. Nathan watched at least four miles of ground sweep by beneath the horse. Finally, Andreii stopped and dismounted, ordering Nathan to do the same. He tethered Nathan's rifle to the saddle, but kept the pistol pointed.

Nathan wasn't familiar with the area, but from what he saw, it was deserted. Hushed. Probably not a cabin within a mile.

"This is the end of your trip," Andreii spat.

Although Nathan had fought losing consciousness on the horse, clarity hit him now. Andreii couldn't let him go. He had to know Nathan would report what he'd done. No, Andreii planned to kill him. He probably even planned to return to the others and tell him that Nathan had deserted, taking the money with him. That's why there had been two horses waiting.

Nathan moaned and bent over, grabbing his head and posturing severe pain, which was mostly true anyway. Sensing that Andreii hadn't expected such a move, he grabbed the knife with his right hand, and bounded up and forward in one fluid movement. His intent was to stab Andreii in the chest, but his opponent was too fast, stepping back and kicking Nathan. The knife entered Andreii's knee and they both fell to the ground struggling. Nathan heard the pistol fall, but Andreii got to it first, rolled over, and aimed at Nathan, still prone beside him on the ground.

The gunshot was so loud Nathan felt the ringing in his ears before he felt the pain. Due to the way he'd been lying, one bullet pierced his left hand *and* entered his belly. He screamed in agony and curled into a fetal position, pressing his other hand against a wound that he had learned, from having spent time in battle, generally proved fatal.

Andreii struggled to his feet, his leg now bent at an odd angle. "You fool," Andreii glowered, pain etching his face. He spit grass from his mouth. "I was going to shoot you in the heart so you would die quickly. But with that stunt, I will let you here to die the slow death you deserve."

Despite Nathan's blurred vision, he watched as Andreii removed his rifle and jammed the stock one hard and fast thrust into Nathan's wounded stomach.

Nathan wailed in pain.

Andreii limped to the horses, grabbing the reins of one and hobbling onto the other. Blood covered his damaged leg.

Nathan vaguely heard Andreii ride off with the horses, then everything went black.

Chapter Five

2016

AFTER ESCAPING THE restaurant, Libby learned over the next few days that there's an obscure and intimate chasm of anger and denial one must cross between accepting the horror that one's life is going to end, and embracing the hope that life can start anew somewhere…*sometime*…else.

After climbing off the ladies' room floor at the restaurant, she had exited through the back door without saying goodbye to Andrew. By one a.m. he tried calling for the sixth time, each, she ignored, before leaving a final message saying he understood she needed time alone to come to terms with what he'd said.

With Colette already gone, Libby was left alone to prowl through the apartment, pacing then sitting, and pacing again, her eyes searching the ceiling, the walls, the floor, as though she were a caged animal seeking escape.

You are going to die. The words echoed again and again like a dominant chord.

She plopped onto the couch and bounced back up, repeatedly. By candlelight, she poured wine, brooded, and paced some more. She wandered into the kitchen, stood staring into the refrigerator for a moment, decided she couldn't bear food, and closed the door. Drifting to the bedroom she opened her jewelry box and pulled out the few items she owned that had any value. To whom should she give them if death truly were imminent? With a burst of anger, she grabbed the pieces in one fell swoop from the dresser top, plunked them back into the box, and slammed the lid.

Preposterous! Andrew was wrong. He'd gone mad. His story was impossible. Asinine. Pure science fiction.

And yet, through the sulking and indignation and denial, Libby waited.

For 7:21 a.m. ...*at 7:21 a.m., he will die.*

She glanced at the clock on the wall for the thousandth time, and, for the thousandth time, followed it with verification on her cell phone. Each change of the digits taunted her, as though the numbers held on out of stubbornness, or fear of being replaced by the next ones.

At 7:02, she stepped onto the balcony and breathed in the familiar odor of exhaust fumes and distant garbage. Ugh, city life. Why had she settled for a profession that hadn't fulfilled her, and which required her to live in a city? She looked east and watched daybreak arrive slowly, nudging through the gray pallor of tall buildings, one begrudging sunray at a time as though toying with her, knowing she was anxious for time to pass. She eyed the eighteen pots of herbs and medicinal plants that adorned her balcony. Her passion and hobby. The plants needed to be pinched and deadheaded. But, what would be the point? *Fat lot of good they had done for her health.*

At 7:18, she stared at her laptop, willing herself to turn it on. That emotion warred with the determination to wait, knowing the news media needed a few minutes to compose and dramatize a story. She counted, a thousand-one, a thousand-two, and so forth, a game, to see if she could count more slowly than the seconds ticked by. An effort to control her sanity.

At 7:30 she logged on, and there it was. The headline she'd denied, yet somehow anticipated, would appear: "Breaking News: Senator Woodbine Dead Following Car Crash."

She read the story, word for word.

Three times.

Then, logged off. After pacing the room twice, she logged back on and saw new headlines: "Senator Succumbs to Injuries." "Woodbine Dead After Georgetown Accident." "Woodbine Dies at 54."

Time of death: 7:21 a.m.

Libby reached for her cell phone, returned to the balcony to gulp in heaps of stale air, and called Andrew. "I need more," was all she said, her tone cold.

As though he had anticipated this, he was quick to answer, never questioning her or asking to see her. He intoned: "At 8:24, two construction workers die from a building collapse near Dupont Circle. At 10:11 an earthquake hits Nepal, killing 65. At 11:14 a freight train jumps the tracks in northern France and crashes into a government building. Six people are transported to the hospital; two of them from South Africa." He cleared his throat. "Babe, I could give you more. Things pertinent to the bureau. An agent's death in—"

She blanched and clicked off the call. Within seconds, her phone sounded. Fearing Andrew had called back, she read the caller ID. Colette. Despite wanting to ignore the call, she took a deep breath and answered. She didn't want Colette to think anything amiss.

"I made it to the Eastern Shore. Thought you'd want to know," Colette said, her voice chipper. "I decided to stay through next week so the place is yours. How was dinner last night?"

Libby forced a normal tone into her voice. "Uneventful. Did your mom like the gifts?"

"What? Oh…yeah. Loved them. Hey girl, I gotta' go. Mom needs me. Take care."

Libby clicked off and called her doctor's office. He couldn't fit her in until next week. She fumbled through her purse to find the card Andrew tucked there. *Dr. Kuzmich.* She secured an appointment for three p.m. Next, she called in sick, and laid down to await the first event, the minutes ticking by with agonizing slowness.

After seeing coverage on YouTube about the building collapse, she waited for the second calamity, then the third.

Once she verified all three online, she turned on the television and there was proof again, before her eyes: descriptions by witnesses who saw the collapse at Dupont. Families searching for loved ones among the ruins of Nepal. Twisted train cars buried beneath what was left of a building near Rouen, France. Still in denial, she switched on the radio. Again, verification proved swift.

She blamed Andrew, wanted to hurt him. Because in telling her all this, he'd hurt her. Besides, it was probably his fault. He was a computer expert; somehow, none of this was true and he was manipulating cyberspace. He was involved in some vast conspiracy, or he worked with one of their enemies overseas powerful enough to create an electromagnetic pulse that had disturbed electronic equipment.

Desperate, she tucked cash into her jeans, grabbed a sweater to ward against the crisp early summer air and walked to the closest convenient store. Halfway there she realized she was wearing bedroom slippers, but kept going anyway.

She traipsed through the store and stopped at a display near the checkout counter to study the man behind the cash register. He made eye contact with customers and smiled, the entire lower half of his face changing with the effort. Deciding he looked genuine, honest, and couldn't be an operative stationed here to deceive her, she stepped forward and asked for a pack of cigarettes. They sat on the shelves behind him, and this seemed like a good way to open communication. When he asked which brand she wanted, she stopped short of confessing she didn't smoke.

"The …" Libby swallowed and raced her gaze across the packs on the metal shelving. "The red ones." She pointed at the cartons.

Despite her impression of his veracity, she eyed him warily, as though he were part of an alien race that had taken over the earth, having placed themselves strategically to deceive her.

"Sad, isn't it?" Libby said as she fished in her pockets for the money, never taking her gaze off him. "About the Senator, I mean."

His shoulders dropped and he shook his head in dismay, his reaction too genuine to be denied. "Very sad, Miss. The country needed him. He was a good man."

She blinked, breathed slowly. "And…and the earthquake."

He bobbed his head in agreement. "Terrible. The world is falling apart. Over sixty dead. So sad."

Libby plopped the money on the counter and left, forgetting the cigarettes and hurrying outside, then around the corner before doubling over to gulp in deep breaths of air. After a few moments, she stood and backed up to the wall of a building, trying to steady herself. It was then she found herself rubbing the scar that marred her chest, a memento of another particularly bad time in her life. She wondered why she hadn't run in the opposite direction that day. She wished she could run away now.

She staggered home, her thoughts dwelling on how chance changes everything, how it can work for or against you, and when it's against you, how it shifts your entire universe from one that had been orderly and workable, into one that prompts you to see everything around you as dark and threatening.

And yet, hope is a clinging, clawing sentiment that desperately holds on. She needed something more than secondary confirmation, despite it being available on multiple communication devices. Back at her apartment building, she climbed into her car and drove, in her slippers, for thirty minutes through heavy traffic to reach Dupont Circle. Pulling the car over, she parked illegally and climbed out, walking right up to the crime scene tape that designated the perimeter. Dazed, she stood there with a mute detachment, staring at the flattened building for almost an hour while streams of people eddied past.

That was when her internal switch flipped, moving from denial, to expectation. Everything after that happened in a haze. She began to see events, even herself, in more of a series of images, as still-shots, rather than as a moving flow of life. A shot of an event. A shot of her verifying it.

Somehow, she returned home, changed her shoes and made it to the doctor's office in time for her appointment. She must have looked healthy because he contented himself with age, weight, and vitals. She lied, describing horrific headaches that landed her in several emergency rooms. No, she couldn't get those records because the incidents occurred while overseas. More lies. He sent her for blood work and an emergency MRI. His office would call when they got the results.

Back at the apartment she stepped onto the balcony, called Andrew and asked for more. As before, there was no discussion of feelings, no questions of well-being. He fed her four more events, all destined to occur by 10 p.m. A flood in western Mexico, a chemical explosion in India, a Jet Ski crash in Panama City, Florida that kills a prominent Broadway star, and a huge drug raid involving a massive underground tunnel south of Phoenix.

In a rush, he added, "One of our agents is killed on assignment in Spain—"

"No!" She didn't mean to be harsh, just to stop him. She couldn't bear learning about those tragedies happening to fellow co-workers when she was on a track to prove, then probably remove herself from, her own demise. "This is enough," Libby murmured and disconnected the call.

Sometime around 10:30, after verifying each development, she acknowledged to herself that the events were varied, not just involving technological disasters. They included manmade *and* natural tragedies. Despite her anger at Andrew, she accepted that he was innocent. He could not have manipulated or orchestrated these events to occur. And why would he? He loved her enough to be painfully honest. Overcome with exhaustion, she grabbed a blanket and reclined on the couch, giving in to the pull of sleep.

She dreamed she stood in a sea of fog when a voice called

out. Turning to it, she saw *him*, running out of a distant wooded area. She'd had occasional dreams of this mysterious man through the years, but he was always faceless, shapeless, a murky unclear presence. Almost a phantom. A suggestion of reality. But this was different, and it jolted her. Now, he was clear and vibrant and alive. She drank in this phantom man as he moved to her side. "You're my life. Please," he urged, "come back to me." Libby choked with the intensity of his emotion. Her eyes misted and she blinked. And in that blink, he disappeared. She cried out in despair, shooting upright into a sitting position, her blanket tangled and twisted around her legs and torso.

She drowsed in the dark for hours, all the while wondering: why is the past calling to her? What does it want from her? The questions hung in the silence of the room as darkened shadows shifted and changed with the movement of the moonbeams that stretched in through the glass doors to her balcony—the same moon that in mere days would watch with a front-row seat as the water claimed her.

FOR GOOD MEASURE, and from her balcony refuge, she repeated her verifications the next day. First, she called work and lied about having the flu, describing in detail alleged warnings she'd been given about how contagious she was. Next, she called Andrew. He offered more events, their times and locations, and she verified each through every means possible.

The final call that day was to the doctor's office. Yes, they'd just gotten the results back, but could she please come in to discuss them in person? Following repeated no's and pleas from her that they cut the crap and tell her over the phone, she was put through to Dr. Kuzmich. His voice was gentle, the typical doctor giving bad news. Yes, it was a tumor. Inoperable. And, by the way, she had tumors in her lungs as well. No, he wasn't surprised she felt fine. Yes, the prognosis for individuals in this situation depends upon how early treatments begin. It's not good, but there is radiation therapy. Perhaps chemotherapy. She really should give treatments a try; fight this, he urged. Give herself a chance for another few weeks of life. Besides, there are experimental treatments and medical breakthroughs every day. Blah, blah, blah.

Libby could take treatments, live a few more weeks, face the pity and goodbyes from friends and co-workers. All those pained, awkward looks and words. She toyed with the possibility one heartbeat before vetoing it. That decision made, exhaustion and darkness overcame her, and she accepted she was going to die.

The next morning, she woke up on the floor with no idea how she'd gotten there, despite being wrapped around her bed covers, her pillow cushioning her head. Sunlight spilled in through the angled slats of the window blinds, falling in patterned rectangles across the floor and interior walls. She ran a hand over her forehead and hair. It left an oily film on her fingers. She couldn't remember when she'd last showered or eaten.

When had she ceased to care?

Within minutes, she found herself lying on the plush rug in Colette's bedroom, with no memory of having gone there or why. As she pushed herself up, she noticed a familiar-looking bag under the bed. Curious, she pulled it out, pushed it back, then pulled it out again. Sure enough, it was the bag into which Colette had stored her mother's wrapped birthday presents.

Why would her best friend lie about something so minor? Was she truly in the Eastern Shore? Now that Libby thought about it, Colette had been unusually curious about Libby's comings and goings lately. With a small whine, Libby shoved the bag back under the bed and left the room. Anger raced through her. Was there *nothing* reliable and trustworthy and honest in her life?

Her next memory involved being balled up in a corner of the bathroom, her face moist and no idea how long she had been there. She began to sob, welcoming the release. She breathed in torturous gasps, as tears flowed in endless streams down her cheeks. She was powerless. Without options. She'd lost control of everything that mattered, even the thoughts in her head.

Once Libby emptied herself, she experienced a hardness surrounding her heart, and an enmity entering her brain. Climbing to her feet, she looked in the bathroom mirror. Her face appeared contorted as though the ghost of death had already begun seeping into her being. She'd never felt so empty in her life. So devoid of purpose. People who feel like that die, don't they? Isn't the will to live everything?

She touched her brows, her cheeks, her lips, and accepted that denial had to end. The tragedies Andrew told her about on the first day had barely been repeated by the news media on the second day. By the third day they were gone. Each misfortune elbowed aside for the sake of a newer one. She was running out of time. History would close over her absence even more seamlessly than it had over those tragic events.

Would she cling to her anger at Andrew, at life, at God, even in the face of her own inevitable death?

With a surprising surge of spunk—and with no idea from where it had come—Libby decided she wanted to live, and she was running out of time.

She called Andrew, this time asking, "When can we meet?"

Chapter Six

2016

W HEN SHE'D HEARD her shaky voice on the phone, her apartment suddenly felt stale and oppressive, like a crypt. Ironically, in order to confront the details of her death, she needed the warmth of the sunlight to buoy her, to bolster her to full life. So, she suggested they meet at the True Grounds Café, on the corner of King and Patrick streets, about eight blocks and countless head-clearing opportunities from where she lived.

They had first discovered the quaint 24-hour café after their third date, a Friday night spent soaking in a series of performances by jazz bands from dusk till dawn, at the river park. They'd left the concert pavilion after immersing (him explaining, her struggling to understand) themselves in what she'd considered to be random, haphazard tunes. As they headed back to her place in the limited pre-dawn light, she admitted to herself that she didn't like the improvised, polyrhythmic sounds of jazz, but she certainly liked the man who liked it. So, when he'd spotted the café and suggested they get a cup of coffee, she was only too willing to prolong their date. They had agreed to a quick cup before entering, but once inside, the eclectic décor of chrome and burlap mixed with the rich infiltration of a variety of brews proved so pleasant, they'd wandered through the café's five rooms seeking out their own corner hideaway. They had stayed for three hours.

This morning, Libby found Andrew at that same quiet corner table, his black hair mussed and dark semi-circles below his eyes. Beneath a sports coat with patches on the elbows, he wore faded chinos and a wrinkled white shirt. She'd never seen him looking so beleaguered and unkempt. Her pride conjured a vision of him pacing in his townhouse, waiting for her call, plagued with worry.

He stood as she approached the table. The effort annoyed her. Whereas before, she'd found the chivalric gesture charming, it now served as a reminder that he was from another time, and that before long, she might be describing herself in like manner.

He leaned in to kiss her cheek, but she tilted it away and dropped into a chair opposite him facing the window. Outside, the sun shot beams of a lazy, muted yellow, and pedestrians went about their business. And why wouldn't they? They would still be here tomorrow and the day after that, and…

Andrew had already purchased a mug of coffee for her. She slid it from the seat beside him to the seat she'd chosen.

His eyes revealed his hurt.

"Libby, I'm just the messenger," he said, his voice hoarse. "I love you. I want to save you."

She exhaled a deep sound and looked around, an effort to collect her thoughts. The café was busier than usual. A young couple chatted over coffee and pastries, their child played with a digital gadget beneath a neighboring table. A businessman flipped the pages of a thick document, and a frizzy-haired lady wearing a BORN TO BINGO T-shirt kept her nose in her book.

"Seigneur-terraces," she mumbled. *French for coffee shop dwellers who sit at tables a long time but spend little money.* She had explained the term to Andrew a few weeks earlier.

Andrew ignored her. "Did you hear what I said?"

Libby looked back at him. "I know you're trying to help. It's just hard to accept that I'm stamped with an expiration date." Plopping an elbow on the table, she lowered her forehead into her palm, needing the support. "This whole thing is so…unreal," she said, and it came out in a whisper.

"I'm sorry." His voice caught on the words, and she saw tears in his eyes. In that instant, somehow, his words touched her heart. He was struggling with this, too. Again feelings of familiarity with this man settled over her, just as they had when they'd met.

On their first date, he'd walked her home and at the door lifted her hand to kiss it. No man had ever done that before, and she hadn't realized how it would affect her. The simple act struck her as one of the most romantic displays of affection and respect a man could offer a woman. How did he know she would love such an endearment before she knew it herself?

At another time, he'd sent a bouquet of calla lilies, not roses. How could he have sensed that such an odd choice in flowers would be her favorite? And there were dozens of other moments as well. He practically intuited that rubbing her temples would take her headaches away, that she found foot massages the height of decadence, that her favorite color was blue, her preferred poet, Henry Wadsworth Longfellow. Always, she was left wondering if these moments confirmed the actuality of soul mates, or if the familiarity represented nothing more than a fortuitous quirk of fate that they had met.

What's more, he was right again. In this moment. He *was* only the messenger. His knowledge didn't mean he was to blame for any of this. Quite the opposite actually, he was tortured by the development, too.

Libby looked at her coffee. Fragrant steam rose from the center and she wrapped her hands around the warmth of its vessel, grasping it like a lifeline. "I had the tumor confirmed."

The edges of his lips dropped and he closed his eyes as he took a fortifying breath. "At least now you know." She heard sadness in his deep, velvety voice. Sadness, soul-deep. "Now we need to get another opinion as soon as possible."

She shook her head. "It would be a waste of time. There's so little of it left."

"But Libby—"

"No."

At her firm tone, he raised a brow. "Libby, this is crazy. You ought to—"

"No," she repeated, her voice stern, final.

It would also be a pointless loss of precious time to discuss how he'd captured forthcoming events in some digital netherworld. What did it matter now? She'd already established there was nothing she could do to change the course she was on. Assessing options would be fruitless because they both were aware she had only two: try the mineral water or die.

A sound came, a low moan, and realizing it came from her, Libby flattened her hand over her mouth. "So, what do I do now?" She choked on the words as tears surfaced. "I'm so afraid."

"I know, babe." He moved to the chair beside her, scooting it closer, and rubbed gentle circles between her shoulder blades.

She whimpered and he pulled her into a full embrace. They sat there for several heartbeats, sharing fear and sorrow without words.

When they pulled apart, he looked away and she watched him wipe an eye with the back of his hand. He hurt too, yet he was fighting to be strong.

For her.

She bit her lip, almost undone by his concern. If she traveled through time, could they find one another? Or, would this be goodbye?

"First..." He cleared his throat and started again. "First, I want you to know I've researched your condition ad naseum. There is no cure yet, and there isn't one into the future as far as I can tell." He gripped her hand. "I don't want to lose you, but I love you enough to let you go. I have to believe the water can heal you. But, it may mean altering your situation."

"By traveling to the future."

His eyebrows flicked up and down, a rapid movement that she'd come to recognize as his body's way of reacting to information he didn't welcome. "Hopefully."

"You do understand that what you say sounds like nonsense."

He nodded. "I know. But trust me, it's not. And, isn't it worth a try?"

"But how?" Libby shook her head. "How can water cure? Or transport anyone to a different state? A different time, for pity's sake."

He straightened his posture as though energized by some hope he heard in her voice, which, frankly, she hadn't intended. "It's called balneology. Using natural mineral spring water and geothermal water to cure diseases."

She repeated the word: "Balneology."

Andrew nodded. "It's been traced back almost 5,000 years. To the Bronze Age. Practiced here in the States until about the 1940s, before the pharmaceutical companies took a foothold and made chemicals and pills for instant relief of every ailment imaginable."

"Great, so this miracle water has proven less effective than drugs." She hadn't meant sarcasm to enter her voice, but it did.

Nonplussed, he ignored her comment. "Balneology is highly regarded again. It's used in Europe and Japan for treatment of diseases. Part of a holistic approach to health and well-being."

He paused as if to punctuate the importance of his words. They had once talked about the logic of approaching health in holistic ways. She preferred essential oils to pills, natural herbs over synthetic vitamins. Probably some deep-seated allegiance to her botanist mother or physician aunt Isabel.

He continued. "Back in the eighteenth and nineteenth, even early twentieth centuries, before modern medicines vied for attention, it was easier to appreciate mineral springs. To see them as the power spots in nature they are. They facilitate healing. Some say the water can even help us become more sensitive to our natural rhythms and what's right for each of us."

He sounded rote, like a brochure. She rubbed her palms up her forehead and down the sides of her face. "But how? It's just water."

"Water, yes. But natural spring water is pure. Composed of negative ions and trace minerals like sulfur, magnesium, lithium. The body absorbs healing minerals into the bloodstream. The result is medicinal to your organs. It stimulates the immune system. Produces endorphins."

He rattled on about filtration springs verses primary springs, and fractures and faults down in the earth filled with rich minerals, and glaciers and limestone deposits, but Libby's mind shifted away from the science behind it to the more pressing concern of what she needed to do.

She was running out of time.

"So, I go to Massachusetts, climb into mineral water, and violá." She splayed her hands. "Is that what you're saying?"

"Pennsylvania."

"What?"

"Bedford, Pennsylvania. Not, Bedford, Massachusetts."

"Never heard of it."

"In the nineteenth and twentieth centuries you would have. It was a popular location for over a hundred years. All sorts of dignitaries and famous people frequented the springs and stayed at the nearby hotel. Several presidents. Millionaires and billionaires as well as the poor. 'Course, the hotel's a five-star resort now." His gaze intensified and bored into her. "In answer to the rest of your question, no you won't drive there alone. I'll go along. And, yes, it is as simple as immersing yourself...*fully*...in the water."

Hope surged. "Then you'll go with me? Into the water I mean? We'll go through this together?"

His eyebrows flicked again. "No, unfortunately each person must do this alone. For full immersion." He stared at his mug, as though struggling with a thought. "Besides, I can't chance it yet. I'm still learning... it seems the water takes you to where you need to be the first time. But it fights efforts to try again."

He raked a hand over his head. "I won't lie to you. It's painful. Your body undergoes drastic transformations as it seeks a different equilibrium and works to heal itself. When I came through my first experience, it was agonizing. Disorienting. That was years ago. After that, I tried to return several times. I wanted to get back to the year after I died."

She stared at him, incredulous. Why would he want to go back that badly?

Andrew continued. "I think if you experience your death, there's no reviving you. But, you can skip over your death. So I concentrated on that. Instead, I went forward again, then back only a few years each time. Every attempt was more painful than the others, although each time was easier to restore my memory. It was like the water was determined to keep me in contemporary times. My last attempt almost...well...I've decided to wait until I learn more about the process. But I promise I will find you."

"So I'm an experiment?" Libby blazed, instantly regretting her outburst.

Astonishment crossed his face. He grabbed her hand and said softly, "No. I love you. I have helped others, too. People I felt were deserving, or still had much to offer."

"And they all disappeared? You believe they went to another time?"

He took a deep breath and exhaled, waiting for three people to pass by to another table. The interruption reminded Libby of her surroundings. Street honking trickled in through the open door at the front of the café. Pedestrians entered, laughing, their lightheartedness grating on her nerves. Even the coffee burners emitted chuckling sounds. The world pressed on, taunting her.

"No," Andrew continued. "One exited the water, healed. I gave him a ride home. He died three years ago in a car accident in Amsterdam. Another walked from the water in the same year he went in, but died a month later." He took a deep breath. "One died in the water. I don't know why. I'm not sure what went wrong. But there always is that possibility."

She bristled. "Only one was healed and continued on in the same timeframe?" Her mouth felt dry, so she took a sip of coffee, closing her eyes and swallowing the rich brew. "The ones that journeyed...to where...*when* did they go?"

"To 1798, 1848...it's varied. Others, to the future. I'm not sure of all the dates."

"Why don't you know?" Libby huffed a short syllable of frustration at her own question. "What am I saying? The better question is how could you know?"

His lips pulled in a wistful smile as though appreciating her attempt to understand. "Near the mineral springs, there's a hidden cave. Tucked in a hollow in the woods. I ask each person to carve their initials and the year into its walls. No one can steal that. But if they go forward in time, obviously I can't see that because it's not recorded yet in my time."

Carvings instead of letters. For the first time it hit her: "I can't take anything with me." No medicines, money, credit cards, bank accounts, mementos, clothes, photographs, passport, ID.

He looked down. "Just your body. Perhaps some sort of a cotton or linen shift, if it's vintage, and you go to a time after it was made."

Libby took another sip of coffee, needing fortitude. "At the restaurant, you were adamant we not change history. Yet, your presence confirms you've done that. And you want to plunk me from one time to another? That's changing history."

"It's infinitesimal. Besides, I am not doing it. The water is. Maybe it is a part of nature…of a natural history we don't understand—"

"But we're bound by the laws of nature—"

"*Perceived* laws of nature. Ever heard of the Heisenberg Uncertainty Principle? Yes, well, it was introduced in 1927 by a German physicist. He determined there is an obscureness in nature, a significant limit to what we can know about the behavior of quantum particles and the smallest scales of nature. The best we can hope for is to calculate probabilities for where things are and how they will behave."

"So?"

"Don't you see? It destroys Newton's clockwork universe in which everything follows clear-cut laws on how to act, and where prediction is easy if you know the starting conditions." He swatted a hand in frustration. "Then again, maybe it involves the space-time vortex around Earth…or perhaps the chaos theory."

"Chaos?"

"You know, that straight linearity is not realistic because events are unpredictable. Perhaps time is not linear, but instead it's like a large body of water with everything already in it. Everything happening at the same time. No past or future. It's all in how we order it in our minds—"

"Andrew, this isn't helping."

He took a calming breath. "You're right. It doesn't matter.

What's important is that I would do anything to save you. I am not changing any laws of nature. I am simply using what nature provides. For us."

He looked so forlorn that she would question him, doubt him. She placed a hand across her mouth to stop another whimper. This man's love was so strong and so real he was going beyond regular human understanding to save her.

She reached over and gripped his hand. "I do trust you. I'm just so afraid."

He squeezed her hand back, and with his other hand tucked a lock of hair behind her ear. "I know. Fear of the unknown. It's human. And, we're both too young to appreciate the transience of life." He twisted his lips. "But, when you became an agent, you accepted the possibility of the unknown. Of going to another country one day and never returning. Different cultures, different food, different languages. You've been taught to be flexible, adaptable. What is so different about this?"

"In those situations there's always hope for return. This is so conclusive." She went still. She needed to concentrate on facts, not feelings. Her scientific mother, her mechanic father, her physician aunt—they'd all taught her to deal in the concrete, the evidence before her. The fact was, she had no choice. The sooner she made peace with that truth, the better off she would be. "There's so little time to prepare."

"You don't need much time. Think about it. You're the perfect candidate. You have many skills. Like languages. You won't need them anyway because you will still be in this country. And, probably just a couple years into the future."

She made a chuckling noise, but it sounded fake. "I'll speak the language, that's my only qualification? Even the English language was different through history. And will be in the future. I'll stand out no matter where I end up."

"You can deliver a commendable accent. You could pass yourself as having spent time overseas. No one will know. When you say something unfamiliar, people will assume it's due to having spent time in a foreign country. Which is true. You should stick as close to the truth as possible anyway. It is easier to remember."

It was true that she could instinctively match her speech and accent to the person she was with. It had always been normal for her.

"What if I'm taken to a future that's awful? After nuclear war or something horrendous? Or, back to Civil War times?" She gasped. "Or Revolutionary? Or, before the country was even settled?"

He swiped his hand in the air. "The water is medicinal, not harmful." He touched her cheek. "I think it knows the cravings of the heart as much as the needs of the body. Maybe even better than we do."

She drew in a calming breath. "So it healed you. But, your knee…that happened *after* you traveled through time?"

His gaze dropped to the table. "That's correct. Look, Libby, you have no family here to miss you. No pets either. You're more prepared than most."

For a moment, her mind froze on his comment about no family to miss her. He was right. She had purposely streamlined her life and kept it simple since her days with Aunt Isabel. Oh my, how she missed that woman. Her voice. Her touch. Even her smell. Libby caught herself rubbing her scar again. It was because of Aunt Isabel she had moved on from that. She hadn't even told Colette the story behind the scar.

Colette! Libby didn't want the heartache or drama of telling her.

But what would happen when she disappeared? People went missing all the time, most by tragic circumstances, others by choice. Her situation was somewhere between the two. Unlike those others, she would disappear into thin air. *Thin air.* As in, untraceable. She must admit, as an investigator, some odd and perhaps perverted part of her was almost bewitched by that prospect. In her experience, no matter how well they hid or how clean their break, suspects' pasts always had a way of coming forth to trip them up. Hers would be one of the few complete disappearances.

But how would she explain that? As quickly as the question surfaced, the answer dawned: *She won't have to explain. She will be gone. To another time.*

Or, she could die. When she saw Andrew's shoulders slump, she realized she had voiced the thought.

"No, Libby." He embraced her again and murmured her name in the way he might say fascinating or beautiful and really mean it. "We will not let that happen."

"But you can't stop it." She pulled free as a chasm of dread opened inside her again. "There was so much I wanted to do. Have a family. Children. I've never even been married, and I—"

"Then marry me. Now."

Libby looked away. "Andrew, don't. This isn't the time."

"This is the best time." He pulled her chin back so their gazes met. "This is the only time we might have."

"Look, I appreciate what you're trying to do. It's very gallant—"

"This has nothing to do with chivalry. The practical side of this is that it is best to stick with the truth. The truth is you might go back in time. If that is the case, then no matter what timeframe you go to, women had fewer opportunities. You will have more options if you can say you are married. If it is true, then you will not cringe as you say it. Besides, I am coming after you as soon as I can. Hopefully, three months. September equinox. I want to know you will be there for me. As my wife."

He remained silent for a moment before taking her hand and kissing it. A tinge of hurt bathed his eyes. "You are everything to me. Beautiful, vibrant, intelligent, exciting. We can both pretend this did not happen. The truth is, we have not known each other very long. I have always been doubtful of immediate attraction and I tell myself over and over that infatuation is not real love…but we both know that is not the case here. We can tell ourselves anything we want, but we cannot make what happened go away. No matter where in time we live, we will remember this. Maybe it happened quickly because we are making up for lost time."

"Lost time? What do you mean?"

His eyebrows moved quickly up, down. "Time we are losing together. Time we will lose had this not happened." He took a deep breath and slowly exhaled. "I love you so much, Libby, I will find you. Somewhere. Somehow. I will not give up until I can be with you. Say you will marry me."

His gaze seemed to reach through her toward a time when they would be together. She wanted that assurance, if even for a moment. Or, the two days they had left. Could she commit to 'until death do us part'? Yes, given that it might be only two days. She could do that. Besides, wouldn't that mean he'd try harder to find her, wherever and whenever she landed?

Then again, would he help her if she said no to his proposal?

He was right. It didn't matter what mystery had joined them or how long they would have. All that mattered was this time and that they should share it together. She couldn't change the facts, so she let her heart take over. It wanted to secure some sort of fulfillment before it risked ending its beats. She nodded, forced a smile. "Yes."

He surged to his feet and scooped her from her chair into his arms as if she weighed no more than the mug he'd been holding a moment before. With a hearty exclamation, he spun her around and kissed her. She inhaled the smell of him, his presence and his fervor, trying to fix this moment in her memory before he set her back down. She wished she could match his zeal.

Around her, people stared and laughed. She ignored them. They didn't matter. In a few days they would cease to exist in her world.

They left the café, walking in silence, holding on to each other.

The courthouse was unadorned, the justice of the peace stoic, and the ceremony brief, pragmatic, and made up of "I do's," and signatures. Afterward, they headed to his townhouse where they spent the night together as husband and wife, in a cocoon of peace and a temporary suspension of all things real.

Chapter Seven

1769

NATHAN WOKE TO find Andreii gone, and darkness so complete, he thought he'd gone blind. Pain scorched through his core and spread to his limbs. He shivered, thought about trying to move, but darkness consumed him again.

DAYLIGHT. HE'D LOST track of time.

Twice he thought he heard a noise, first tromping in the distant woods; later, children laughing beyond the ridge, but he was too weak to call out.

Exhausted, he closed his eyes.

"LADDIE. KIN YE 'ear me?"

The voice sounded like it was a hundred miles away. Nathan felt a damp rag on his face. He opened his eyes. An old man, bearded and crusted with layers of dirt and dust, stared back.

A searing pain radiated from Nathan's stomach and he realized he was shaking. Fever.

"Laddie, you been hurt somethin' fierce. Iffin' you can stand the pain, I'll try to get that bullet out fer ye."

Dazed, Nathan visualized himself responding in the affirmative, but wondered if he'd spoken at all. Darkness claimed him.

✕

NATHAN HEARD THE sounds of a crackling fire. Smelled some kind of wild game cooking. "Water," he rasped and tried to lift his arms to remove whatever cloth was making him so warm. He opened his eyes to the darkness of night.

Sounds came from his right, before the face of the bearded man appeared inches in front of him. The man pulled something away and Nathan felt cooler.

"Doona move much, laddie. You got a bad fever. Done me best to get that bullet out, but…" He made a worrisome sound with his teeth and lips, and didn't bother finishing the sentence.

Despite the old-timer's advice, Nathan tried to lift his head. The man pulled a ruffsack closer and laid his arm under Nathan's shoulders to help him ease to a semi-sitting position. Nathan noticed bandages on his own left hand and lower torso. The man secured Nathan against the sack then held a leather pouch of water to his lips, waiting patiently as Nathan drained it dry. The man patted him, then moved about a yard away, to the fire.

"Me name's Duncan." He scrunched his face and coughed. "Duncan Brodie. And who might ye be?"

Nathan studied the man. The firelight flickered between shadow and light. Nathan's vision was blurred, but he could make out a head of shoulder-length hair that matched the red and gray in the man's scraggly beard. Duncan was far too skinny, and he had a long crooked nose and spidery stretches of wrinkles that testified to too much misfortune and too many years in the sun.

"Nathan." He swallowed and tried again. "Nathan McKenzie."

"McKenzie? Aye, Scottish like me, err ye? Highlands, no doubt, as tall and strappin' as ye are."

"So I'm told." Nathan's voice was hoarse. "Th-thank you for…" He cut off when a sharp pain streaked through him.

"Pffshhh, t'weren't no trouble. Now, lad, ye just rest. I doona want ye to get worse. That's gotta' hurt somethin' powerful."

Nathan thought he saw Duncan wink as the old man continued. "I got shot once meself. 'Course it was by a young lass that accidentally shot me in the arse." He laughed a deep, guttural belly laugh that shook his whole frame, but it quickly turned to coughing. When he could speak again, he said, "She took the bullet out, so I had to marry 'er. I dinna ken what else to do."

Duncan laughed again. "Cora was 'er name." He poked at the fire with a stick. "She's been gone fourteen years now. So, I finally sold me place and came 'ere. Make me living just movin' around, huntin'. Tradin' furs is good business in these parts 'cause folks're too busy tryin' to homestead."

"What…what day…?" Nathan needed to know how long it had been since he'd been shot. His family must be panicked.

Duncan shrugged. "Don't know what day o' the week, but I count the moons." Another cough racked his body. "Today makes it twenty September."

Ten days! He'd been left for dead for ten days now. But how? How could he have survived that long?

As though Duncan read the confusion on Nathan's face, he explained, "Ye been with me seven o' them moons."

Seven. This man had been doctoring him for seven days. In his dazed state, Nathan wondered if Duncan was some kind of magical wood nymph or angel in disguise. But, he decided, those spirits wouldn't cough the way this man did. It sounded menacing, as though years of illness had piled up in his lungs.

"Ye gotta wife? Bairns?"

Nathan started to shake his head, but it caused pain, so he said: "Neither."

"No? I pegged ye a homesteader."

"Always busy with something else," Nathan said. His voice was hoarse and he spoke slowly, taking breaths often. It was painful, but somehow a review of his life felt appropriate, even necessary right now. "I...spent several years with the Lenapes and Shawnees." He swallowed. "Then, the Mohawks."

"A captive?"

Nathan's mind swirled with an involved answer, but limited it to "yes."

"But you made it back."

"My body did, yes."

Duncan frowned at the response, but kept his gaze on the fire.

After a few moments to steady his breathing, Nathan continued. "Since then...four years...been trying to help my family. On our farm. Hoped to build my own one day."

Duncan chuckled, but not with humor. He coughed. "Aye,

this land will age a man quickly. Me, I had a son but he's gone too. The fever." *Typhoid*. He looked in the sky as though contemplating. "Guess I'll be joining 'em afore long."

Nathan didn't know what to say. The old-timer sounded tough, but that cough…. With a grimace, he wondered which of them would die first.

"When I was stitchin' ye," Duncan said, "I saw them marks on yer body. Those from them Indians?"

Nathan had been forced to run a gauntlet. Then ritually cleansed and adopted by a Mohawk family. To survive he had to practice tribal ways and constantly prove himself to stay alive. But that was all too much to explain. "Yes."

They sat in silence for a while. Duncan offered Nathan some meat, but it was too painful to chew, so the old-timer pulled a kettle from the fire and spoon-fed him strings of meat floating in hot broth.

"Laddie," Duncan said in a voice pitched low with concern and a palpable trace of warning, "ye ain't gonna' live much longer on broth…and ye're bleedin' stronger. I ain't gonna lie to ye. It doona look good."

When he got no response, Duncan continued, speaking in an apologetic tone. "If ye'd let me, I'd like to take ye to the magic water. Natives say it has healing power. Just a mile over two ridges. Headed there meself." He coughed again. "Problem is, I kin't carry ye. I'll have to pull ye on a travois, hitched there to me sweet Daisy."

Nathan tracked where the man pointed to an old, shaggy mule. The firelight was strong enough he could see the animal gorging on tall grass. He looked back at Duncan, guilt washing over him. He was keeping this old man from his destination.

From Nathan's time with the natives, he'd learned they had ways of tackling illnesses and injuries that others would scoff at. Yet, he'd seen some of those efforts work. He couldn't imagine what powers mere water might have. But if he said no, the old-timer might deprive himself of going.

"Much obliged," Nathan murmured and closed his eyes.

✕

BEFORE NATHAN OPENED his eyes, he felt his body being jounced and the sun warming his skin. He lifted his eyelids to find himself angled, strapped to a makeshift pallet of branches and hides, and being pulled, he deduced, by Daisy. The bouncing and relentless jerk-drag rhythm intensified his pain.

From atop Daisy, Duncan's soft warbling of a Gaelic ballad reached Nathan's ears.

He closed his eyes and thought of home.

✕

NATHAN HEARD A familiar female voice, soft and melodious like an angel humming.

Did he hear that right? No, how could that be? He opened his eyes. Mist hugged the ground, wrapping the world in cool silvery silence, and the clouds above him were gray like chunks of spent coal. Rain dropped on him. That's the humming he'd heard, the steady patter of rain. The chill of the wind found the dampness of his body. He shivered.

But, why did he think he heard the words, "Find me?"

It was the fever. That's all it was. It was killing him.

HE WOKE BATHED in sweat, and on the ground. The giant pines above him leaned into the wind, bringing the fragrance of evergreen. The sun was full, but the air brought that briskness that reminded him of autumn's arrival.

His thoughts wandered like an agitated leaf caught on a breeze, maneuvered this way and that, guided only by the frenzy of his mind. His white mother and father. His Indian family. His precious Elisa. Duncan.

Duncan! Where was the old man?

With his right elbow, he inched himself up, looked around.

There, not even ten feet away the old man lay on his back. A few yards from him, a spring gushed forth from a crevice in the rocks.

Nathan crawled to the old man, fighting against the pain. He didn't need to touch Duncan to know he was dead. The deeply etched wrinkles around his eyes were now frozen in place. The stillness of the man hushed the elements around him as though weeping for his soul and questioning the loss of the man Nathan had known only as kind and generous. Had the universe stolen his life before he could make it to his magical water? Or, had the old man chosen death, opting to join Cora and his son?

Nathan wept a tear for this loss, then another because he could not bury his new friend. Stronger and more certain than any strength Nathan could muster to lay Duncan to rest, was the truth that now unveiled itself: he, too, was moments from death.

He closed his eyes and breathed deeply, desiring to hear his own last sounds of life. He was tired. Defeated. The damage to his body, unbearable. He wanted to remove himself from the pain and tumult of his life, and go to a place where there was no agony, no uncertainties. He would go, and be with God…and *her*.

But the wind whispered louder than his breathing, whistling poignant tales spun by Indians around campfires of ancestors and creatures of the night that used the spring to cleanse and renew.

Burning with fever, he stared at the water. It looked seductive, cool, welcoming. A pleasant way to die. To honor Duncan, Nathan would make it to the spring.

He crawled. Rested. Crawled some more, leaving a trail of blood. His heart hammered. His vision dulled.

At the spring's edge, exhausted and anguished, he whispered a prayer for forgiveness and rolled, sideways, into the water.

He was sure his heart stopped beating as the water enveloped him. He felt nothing. Heard nothing. Saw nothing.

His pain subsided, and he opened himself to death.

Chapter Eight

2016

OTHER THAN A brief conversation about the process she would undergo in the water, Libby and Andrew passed most of the two-and-a-half-hour drive to Bedford in silence. She closed her eyes several times and prayed for the courage to face whatever lie ahead.

They approached the town after dusk that Monday night and Andrew began to talk about the town in a hurried pace as though channeling his anxiety into a productive effort. Bedford sits about a hundred miles southwest of Pennsylvania's capital, Harrisburg, and at least 105 miles east of Pittsburgh. Population, 3,000. Settled, 1751. For years it served as an important frontier military post thanks to the British Army, which erected Fort Bedford, named for the Duke of Bedford in England. The British used the fort to drive away the Indians and the French, the latter to ensure the new continent would be British-controlled. Other nods to notoriety included the nearby Blue Knob ski resort, and the historical claim that the town headquartered George Washington and his force of 13,000 while putting down the Whiskey Rebellion in 1794.

Much as Libby appreciated Andrew discussing the origins of the town, given that she relished history, her thoughts were fixated on the grim task of 'taking the water.' If she didn't die straightaway, she was either going to leave Bedford with Andrew that night, or experience it at a far different time in history, so what did she care about the town as it stood now? She was glad it was dark so she couldn't establish a *before* picture of the area in her head.

Still, from the house and pole lights that dotted different elevations of the mountainous landscape, and then streetlights in the sloped town itself, Libby could tell Bedford was small, quiet, and tucked strategically into its landscape.

As they crossed an overpass on Route 30 called the Narrows Bridge, which spanned a deep gorge, Andrew said the town was located beside the Raystown branch of the Juniata River, which flowed into the Susquehanna River. After a few miles through the rim of the town, they turned off Route 30 onto Richard Street and headed south, passing varied-sized and styled houses, a few businesses, and a golf course edged with a roadside billboard announcing it as the "Bedford Elks Country Club." Within a minute, they turned onto Sweet Root Road.

After another bend in the road, they drove for about a quarter-mile with shades of darkness flanking them on both sides. Andrew pulled the car to the side of the empty road and turned it off. The night was moon-drenched, warm, still, and smelled of earth and pine. As they climbed from the car, Libby inhaled a deep, shaky breath, hoping her panic would subside.

Distant sounds of a band reached her ears through the darkness, carried on the slightest of breezes. She looked that direction and saw a startling variety of muted lights in the sky.

Andrew tracked her gaze. "Bedford Springs Resort. You didn't want to see what it looks like now, so this is as close as we dare go. The mineral springs are over that incline." He pointed left into the shadows, then reached for her hand. The sensation of his cool touch against her clammy skin in the cavernous darkness brought her back to the moment with a shiver. He didn't notice, instead lifting her hand to his lips, and kissing it. "You ready for this?" His voice cracked on the question.

Libby pressed her lips together, uncertain of what to say. Ready? Did she have a choice? She had a thousand questions, but why bother voicing them? He could shed no more light on what she might experience. If she survived and went to another time, where she would end up was as much a mystery to him as it was to her. *Wasn't it?*

Andrew continued. "Did you tell Colette you were leaving on a long-term assignment?"

Libby looked away. "Something like that. Look, I don't want to talk about her in our last few minutes together."

She hadn't said a word to her roommate. It would have involved too many questions raised, concerns expressed, doubts debated. She also had left no note. She'd been too angry about Colette's lie. Besides, to leave a note would raise questions if she did return.

"We better get on with it," he said, squeezing her hand. "Midnight is approaching."

He opened the door to the back seat, and pulled out a flashlight and a small plastic bag. With the aid of the dim light, he led her a short distance from the road into the edges of a steep wooded hill, following it parallel about a hundred feet until they came to a small clearing, near a grove of assorted maples and oaks. Between the illumination from the moon and the flashlight, she could see that the trees stretched into the sky, surrounding them like church pillars. But it was the sound of trickling water that captured and held her attention. Just in front of them, water cascaded from between two rocks, about twelve feet off the ground. The water fell into a ground cavity about ten feet in diameter around which a low-slung manmade rock wall had been added to form a pond. In the dim light, it looked to be only about three feet deep.

Andrew had explained the immediate area sported seven mineral springs for hundreds of years, but that an eighth one was discovered in the twenty-first century when the hotel was refurbished into a resort and changed its name from the Springs Hotel to the Bedford Springs Resort. Among the eight were the popular Iron Spring, the Magnesia Spring, the Limestone Spring and the Sulfur Spring. However, the most popular and medicinal of all, the Crystal Spring, was purported to be made up of elements of all the others put together—limestone, iron, magnesium, sulfur, among a host of other healing elements.

He knelt down by the Crystal Spring, placed the flashlight on the ground, and began to pull what looked like fabric from the bag.

As Libby watched, an unexpected thrum of anxiety began to move along the base of her brain. "What is that?"

"A linen shift."

The low thrum turned into a roar. "How old is it?"

"A hundred and fifty years, plus or minus. Oldest I could find. Linen doesn't age well."

Sweat broke out on the back of her neck as a daunting sense of destiny gripped her by the throat. She stared at it, her thoughts clouded and vague. Before she even touched the garment, she could feel its weight across her shoulders, the pull of something uncontrollable. Her dream of *him*—that mysterious man from her dreams—and *his* voice saying, "Come back to me," skittered through her mind, disappearing as fast as it surfaced.

Andrew's expectant stare suggested he was waiting for her to put it on, so she stripped to her underwear, refusing to remove that. A huge fissure of existential dread opened inside her as she dropped her clothes beside the flashlight on the ground.

Libby reached slowly to take the shift from him, and emitted a sudden exhalation of breath as its age came to life beneath her fingertips. She donned the baggy garment and a sense of familiarity enveloped her.

She looked at Andrew, no longer able to voice her concerns, her despair. It had all been said. Andrew likewise appeared at a loss for words.

They stood like actors who had forgotten their next lines, both frozen, rigid, mute. The scene about to be executed would be—*had to be*—unyielding and unscripted anyway.

And most daunting of all, performed solo.

With the limited beam of light coming from the ground, she watched him reach for her hands and, in a gentle voice said, "Love is patient, love is kind. It always trusts, always hopes, always perseveres."

She smiled at the sentimentality, but was bereft at the blossoming of this strange awkwardness between them, and confused by his decision to quote written words rather than speak what dwelled in his heart.

He continued, gripping stronger as though to emphasize his next words. "Love keeps no record of wrongs."

Startled, Libby's head jerked back before she could stop herself. "What?" she asked, meaning, what was with his demeanor and his choice of rewriting the verse? She remembered that Bible passage differently. Why had he selected a portion of it? His answer revealed he thought she was asking about the origin of the quote.

"First Corinthians, I think."

The moment struck Libby as odd, but she said nothing, afraid she might spoil their goodbye by questioning it. She looked at their clinched hands and focused on the inevitable, that she'd need to let go. Truly let go. His hand was not a lifeline. It wasn't protection.

"I…I love you." Libby choked the words, and they sounded mundane, inconsequential, when they ought to have been delivered with passion against a backdrop of heart-stirring music like that featured in romantic films. Moisture flooded her eyes. *Ahh, yes.* That must be why he resorted to a quote.

He drew in a breath and stood straighter, like a man who was about to step into battle, then released it and closed his eyes. With a whimper he removed the arm length between them, pulling Libby into his arms as if he'd determined to hold on forever.

But he didn't. He couldn't. He pulled back, and bent over enough to catch the light on his watch. "It's time."

He held her hand again as she climbed over the low-slung stone wall like she was stepping into her own coffin. The water was cold, but the heat of the night made it bearable. She cringed as she sat down in the water and the darkness, and stretched out until she was covered to her neck. She leaned against the inside well, her gaze flicking to Andrew and back.

Without further fanfare, she squeezed his hand. The feeling of panic threatened to overwhelm again, so she took a deep breath and fully submerged into the dark water.

FOR SECONDS—FIVE, TEN, thirty?—Libby focused on the words 'heal me,' as Andrew earlier had suggested. He'd said it might help to draw her consciousness away from the current period in time. That it was her consciousness of the present that kept her rooted there and in poor health.

A mounting disorientation set in as the mineral water claimed her, and she suddenly realized she no longer cared about air. Her pulse stopped sounding in her ears, and her lungs quit trying to exhale. With that realization, an unexpected thrill of seemingly unconnected elements came together. Her body quivered and the sensation was like floating on nothing. She sensed a void around her.

As she had submerged, she'd lost hold of Andrew's hand. She began to panic. Where was he? She opened her eyes against the water but could see nothing. She reached out her hand to grope for him, and saw, to her astonishment, that her hand had lost substance.

She'd lost the anchor holding her to 2016.

She didn't remember much about the next few moments. Flashes of light. Visions of herself screaming and tears streaming down her face, despite being in the water. If she surfaced for air, she would ensure her death. But, if she stayed, would she do the same?

An odd sensation settled in her stomach. Something like

the feeling of being inside a vehicle that's moving, but watching the scenes around pass by rapidly. Inside, her body recognized it was stationary, yet visually she raced at high speed, rushing past the physical world outside. Was that movement *time*? Was it her identity being stripped away?

In the next instant, the moving stopped, but she sensed a rhythmic vibration, a steady thumping in her ears growing louder, beating an affirmation of acceptance and healing to her. The heartbeat of the earth.

Then: *Come back to me.* That voice again! *His* voice.

Next, she saw white light. Calming. Beckoning her. Time to choose. Succumb to the light and its tempting pull, filled with release. Peace. Completion. Or, fight her way to a new unknown life, living until she experienced this gateway again. *Choose.* Was that God speaking? Giving her that choice? Life and how she lived it was up to her?

She chose life. She saw herself scream into the nothingness: "Heal me!" The words became a litany, spiraling over and over as she persevered. Soon she was beyond exhaustion.

Visions swirled. Of her, with strangers. She was younger. Frail. A child? Dressed in unfamiliar clothing. An unfamiliar landscape behind her. Then, an adult placing her in water. Was she bathing? Swimming? Was this simply symbolic of rebirth? She saw a dark face. Africa? The Australian Outback? No, she couldn't go there again. Different hands pulled her out. Drenched. Naked. Crying. Then, peace, as strong arms gripped her, rejoicing in her presence.

The placidity of the visions morphed into pain. Immense pain, as though she were being punished for having experienced the visions.

The agony grew stronger. Unbearably stronger.

Every part of her body felt as if spears were being plunged cruelly, mercilessly into it. In and out. Repeatedly, relentlessly.

"No! I was wrong. Let me die!" she yelled into the nothingness.

She felt strong arms—*different arms*—lifting her body from the water.

Andrew! She'd failed him.

She'd failed herself.

Chapter Nine

2016

ANDREW KNELT BY the edge of the Crystal Spring until Libby disappeared. A tear moistened his cheek and he brushed it away.

Beautiful, vibrant, gentle Libby. His wife. Gone. He was alone again.

He should feel euphoric, as he had with the others he'd aided. But this was different. She was part of his destiny, and he'd sent her back with reluctance. He needed her. It was both comforting and disturbing that she was lost, somewhere in time. He didn't have assurance, but he did have an inkling, of *when* she landed, given what he'd learned of the water, her, and the Matryoshka investigation. It might take him a while to find her, but eventually he would.

He took a deep breath, rubbed his face with both hands, then got to his feet. Picking up the flashlight, he checked the time. After midnight. He tried to concentrate. With her gone, he needed to rethink things.

He removed his glasses and folded them neatly into the pocket of his shirt. His eyesight was excellent, perfected each time he took the water. The eyeglasses were simply a veil, a prop. People saw them instead of the eyes. In the years since going forward in time he had found the small charade useful.

For some odd reason people tended to discount the possibility that a man wearing spectacles might prove duplicitous, particularly harboring another life. He should have suggested such a disguise to Libby to facilitate her in her new life. Another regret.

Memories surfaced of their time together this past month. The outings. Her laughter. Her trust. The sweet, hot ache of glee that gripped him the first time she walked into the lecture hall had shaken him to his core. He had seen wariness and deliberation on her face, and had told himself he should take things slowly and cautiously.

But, quoting the Bible at her departure? What had he been thinking? So much for originality.

He turned and walked back to his car, listening to the unnerving voices in his head. They were always there. Waiting. There, since long before he began the journey. How unfortunate, and yet delightful, that Libby had interrupted the carefully designed and perfectly balanced order of his world. She made him want more. And desire was the most delectable force of all.

How he would miss her!

But, he had to do what was necessary.

As he walked to his car, he breathed in the fresh, mountain air and reminded himself of what so few people ever learn: the future lies in the past.

Chapter Ten

1926

LIBBY'S EYES REMAINED closed as other senses activated. Crackling. Snapping. Fire crackers? No, something sizzling and burning. Cold and dampness beneath her. Heat washed across the upper half of her body.

A fire? Yes, she smelled burning wood, the essence of smoke, mixed with an earthen mustiness, mildew. She'd been camping often enough to know the smells, the *feel* of it.

Yet, something was different. Not just her surroundings, but something more encompassing had changed. Perhaps lost, and she ought to be looking for it. But, her brain was listless and she couldn't grasp the answer.

She forced her eyes open, then clenched them closed again, recoiling from an onslaught of blinding light. No, not blinding. It was muted and flickering, wasn't it?

The movement prompted a spastic pain in her head, consuming the frontal portion of her brain. Her stomach churned, threatening upheaval as a rancid taste surfaced in her mouth.

She cracked one eyelid halfway open and surveyed her surroundings. She was on her side on a flannel blanket on the earthen floor, back-dropped by unequal, unordered, knobby rock walls. A cavity etched into the earth. A cave. Positioning her hands beneath her, she slowly pulled herself into a semi-upright position. The spike of pain in her brain lanced stronger.

A voice spoke. Someone talked to her from some space-less, timeless zone, urging her to do something. Wasn't it? She registered no words but was sure there was a voice. She inched her head toward it, fighting against the pain.

A form huddled by a fire. A man. His face sat in shadow on wide shoulders. Slowly, Libby's eyes adjusted and she could see him better. His mouth moved and she suspected words were being shared but she couldn't catch them, not in any way that made sense. She couldn't hear anything above the roaring in her ears. She didn't know him, did she? She should be concerned, perhaps scared for her life. But she wasn't. The pain made her not care and she voiced what she felt with every fiber of her being. "Please, I want to die. I can't stand this pain."

She dropped back to the ground, her mind emptying to blessed oblivion.

✖

SHE SWAM OUT of her fog enough to discover she was crying. But, from what? Loss? Fear? No, perhaps the pain. The intense, unbearable, pounding and throbbing and certainty that knives—razor-sharp and penetrating—were being jabbed repeatedly into her body.

She screamed again, heard it echoing and returning to her, mocking and denying. Make it stop, she begged.

Arms encircled her. She heard a voice murmur as though she were a child afraid of the dark. She clung to the figure that offered the voice, sobbing and begging for release, not caring what she said or how desperate she was. She felt a cloth dabbing at her face as she alternately shivered and perspired. Over and over the voice whispered for her to "hold on," and "fight it" because "the pain will stop in a while."

Her whimpers subsided, her breath slowed, and everything went black again.

✕

WHEN LIBBY NEXT awoke, she pushed up on an elbow before thinking about the repercussions of the action. Her surroundings swirled into darkness and she braced her hands to keep from falling back. Her head pounded with pain as though it were rolling around on her shoulders, and her arms ached, startling her with their weakness. Still, she pushed until she sat upright. Her pulse raced as she struggled for reason.

The man was gone. The fire, a low glow of embers. She stared into the shadowy corners of the cave for a minute or two, or ten. She had no sense of time. Or place. Or why she was here. Frogs called out from somewhere outside.

With a push, she tried to stand too quickly and, again, the spinning darkness engulfed her, but she refused to slump back and, instead, hovered on hands and knees. She drew in shaking breaths until the spike of vertigo lessened.

After a few moments, she tried again, and had to reach out for the firmness of the dank, earthen wall. She felt the fuzziness of lichen and moss.

Taking a deep breath and gritting her teeth, she willed herself to take a step, fighting the urge to drop to the ground. She managed to stay erect, wobbling like a surprised infant attempting her first steps.

Memories of the man by the fire surfaced, and fear set in. Who was he? And, what did he want? Why was he here? Where was her husband? She had one...*didn't she*?

That's when it hit her with certainty, there was no longer a husband. Somehow—she didn't know how—but somehow she also discerned it wasn't 2016 anymore.

This was absurd. If she knew that date, she should know more. Of course she grasped who she was...didn't she? But the harder she tried to seize the information, the more it scampered out of reach.

That realization, combined with fear of the man in the cave earlier, buoyed her to action. With tears clouding her eyes, she turned and exited the cave, her heart thundering with desperation to get away and go...*where*? She didn't know, didn't care. What *was* she trying to escape, or outrun?

It was dark, but moonlight grazed the tops of the forest, casting a dim beam between the canopy of trees to the ground. In the unlit pockets of the terrain, the woods gaped like black open mouths. With a spike of adrenaline, she stumble-ran, hurrying as much as her bare feet and weak legs would allow. She tore through a screen of brambles and nettles, stubbed her feet on stones and fallen logs, but still, kept moving. The desire to fall to the ground was intense, but she managed to keep going by clinging onto a branch here, an outcropping of rocks there.

Tripping. Grabbing. Moving.

Over an incline, then down into a ravine.

Stopping to gulp a breath. Clinging to the girth of a young tree, then a protrusion in the rocks.

A slight breeze activated the sounds of the forest. Branches clacked together, loose leaves and vegetation rustled. Spooked, she moved on. Up, down, around, wherever the moonlight illuminated a path.

Over an incline, then around another.

Was she running to, or from? She wasn't sure.

She stumbled to a halt and gasped, throwing her hands over her mouth, but too late. Three men stood in front of her and they'd heard her. They were dangerously close, and while two of them looked startled, the third one—a startlingly thin, scruffy-bearded man with a black eye patch over one eye—bolted to action, coming at her. She backed away, but was brought up short by the solidness of a row of wooden barrels. He closed the five yards of space between them before she could move.

Grabbing her arm, he dragged Libby toward the others and into the light cast from several torches. His clothes were disheveled, and he was thin, reeked of body odor and tobacco, and the mangy hair on his head reached his beard. It must have been greasy too because the firelight reflected off it.

"What'r you doin' here, gal, eh?"

Libby noticed a mouth filled with crooked teeth and ruined gums before he turned his gaze to the other two, directing his next question to them. "Think the coppers sent 'er?"

One of the other two, a tall sinewy figure, spoke to the third man, his voice revealing him to be a young adult, and much older than his boyish features would suggest. "If she brung the law, we better git."

By now the bearded man had dragged her closer to the other two. Instinct—*or was it some sort of training*—blipped through her mind; immobilize him in three moves or less, then restrain him, depending on available weapons or accouterments, or run.

She had no more strength to do any of that. Besides, how did she know about disenabling an assailant?

Behind them, firelight revealed the oddest contraption she'd ever seen. A large container made of boards and sheets of metal nailed together with tubes and metal arms protruding from it in all directions. Beside the contraption sat at least a half-dozen wooden buckets and several grain bags. *A still!*

Too late. She'd have been safer if she had not seen it. A renewed fear surfaced and she dropped her gaze to the ground, panic clawing at her insides and icy wisps of fear raising gooseflesh on her arms. Still, she struggled to maintain an outward show of calm.

The third man, a portly fellow with receding hair and alert, piercing eyes twisted his rotund girth to his side and spit something from his mouth, then turned back to assess her. His belly fell over his wide rope belt, holding up dirty pants that were too short. A leather strap ran diagonally across his wide chest. Attached to it was a crude holster in which rested a large handgun. The flickering firelight revealed a look of cold displeasure on his face, but as he studied her, she could see his worry melt to amusement. "She's no copper. Probably one of them rich folks from the hotel." He spit again. "Shame she seen so much."

"What'll we do with her?" the bearded man asked. "Maybe she'd like a little fun..." His eyes raked Libby from head to toe and back again, and he laughed with a disgusting, leering nasal sound that slithered down her spine as revulsion rose in her throat. Before she realized he'd freed one of his hands, she felt it at her thigh. Felt him yank up the bottom of her shift. She tried to jerk free, but he tightened his grip. She was too weak.

The portly man scowled. "Behave, Gil. Just tie her up. Blindfold her. Later, we'll lead her outta here. I doubt she'll ever want to explain how little she was wearing when she stumbled into our little party anyway. Besides, she'll never be able to find this place again."

"There's no need for that, gentlemen."

The voice, calm and distinguished, came from the darkness behind them, prompting the youngest one to reach for a rifle and the portly man to put his hand on his pistol.

A man stepped closer, into the torchlight and walked toward Libby, holding his hands up so the others could see he carried only a lantern. Moving with the agility of a cat, his gaze remained on the two with guns.

The stranger from the cave!

Once near her and the bearded creep, he placed the lantern on the ground and gave Libby an intense look. "Sweetheart," he said in a pleasant voice. "You had me worried." He turned to the portly man and smiled. "My niece, you see. She had a bit too much..." he made a hand motion of pouring a drink into his mouth, "...so I tucked her in her room early tonight. I guess she decided to take a walk."

He reached her side and gently pulled her from the grasp of the bearded guy, wrapping his free arm around her back and resting his hand at her waist so that they stood side by side. He stood taller than her by at least four inches, and returned his gaze to the three men as he pulled her close.

Her uncle? No, the thought rang false.

This man, so confidant, so smooth, so dignified when

compared to the three hooligans, acted so cocksure of himself. His ability to step into the scene and change everything scared her. Would she be safer with three fools than this smooth-tongued intruder?

"Who the buggar are you?" the youngest man demanded, voicing the very question that swirled in Libby's mind.

As he answered, the stranger pinched the tips of his fingers into her side, a universal warning to play along. "The name's Grey." He turned his gaze to Libby and with commanding eyes, elaborated, "Andrew Grey. We're guests at a local hotel. Leaving tomorrow."

Startled, Libby sucked in her breath as warmth flooded through her. That name was familiar. But, why? And how could he know it? His fingers poked into her side again.

"Sorry…Uncle," was all she could manage, fatigue and fear making her voice weak and rough.

"Now gentlemen, if we can all agree we saw nothing, then we'll be on our way," he said, as he steered Libby around and began to lead her into the darkness. "Oh, and," he said pointing to the lantern, "keep this for your troubles. Have a good day."

He pushed Libby's back gently. "Keep walking," he whispered as they disappeared into the darkness.

And she did. For as long as her legs held her. Which, as it turned out, wasn't long. After about fifty steps, exhaustion and pain hit again, and she began panting desperately for air. Her legs felt weak and boneless before they surrendered, and she felt herself falling.

Everything went black.

✕

THIS TIME, THE return to consciousness involved a steady collection of pains: a pounding ache in the front of her head, soreness in her arms and legs, severe cramps in her stomach muscles, a dull lethargy throughout her body.

Still, the aches were less acute and much more bearable.

Smells were familiar from before—the dank odor of earth and stone walls, the scent of writhing earthworms, the fragrance of burning oak. The cave again? Wherever it was, Libby's stomach didn't like it. A tightness gripped her chest and disorientation washed through her. After a few minutes of concentrating on breathing, she opened her eyes and stared into the darkness, trying to determine where she was.

She tried to sit up. Her arms were so numb, it took three attempts. As the blood began to course again, she inched upward, attempting a sitting position. Her vision swam and pain seared in both her head and stomach. To her dismay, she began to gag. As she turned to her side so that she wouldn't vomit on herself, a hand thrust a bucket in front of her.

"Use this," the deep timbre of a familiar voice urged.

She spilled the contents of her stomach into the metal container as the man returned to the fire and poked it back to life. It was the same figure Libby had seen in the cave earlier. The one who saved her from the three grimy men.

Something roared outside, like a cannon boom that echoed over the mountains. Next came a hissing sound and a flash of light. She heard rain, growing in intensity, and the whooshing of wind through the trees. A storm.

But that's not right. When Andrew and she arrived the forecast was clear. *Andrew*! She remembered him. This man had said his name.

What else did she remember? *Taking the water!* She closed her eyes and mentally hunted for more. But, the answers capered out of reach.

She dropped the bucket to her side.

"Rinse your mouth with this." The stranger returned, handing her a metal cup with a clear liquid in it, as he hunkered down beside her, close enough that she could feel his heat, and see the outline of his firm chin and the stormy darkness of his eyes. Her hand shook and her throat burned as she drank a gulp, rinsed, spit it out, and repeated the process.

She noticed a large object, like a cloth duffel bag about a foot to her right and the opposite direction of the stranger, so she inched over, rested her back against it, and assessed her surroundings. The blaze of a torch's light cast a wavering circle around the stone walls, revealing a high ceiling with narrow cracks and fissures through which the campfire smoke could escape. Bags and assorted containers perched nearby. It appeared to be a basic cave, if such a cavity in the earth could be considered basic. It didn't appear to lead farther into the earth.

"You're shaking," he said. She hadn't noticed. He stood and walked to a large cloth bag several feet to her left, pulled out a blanket and draped it over her. Next, he picked up a jug and pulled a cork from it. He returned to her, crouched down and poured something into the cup. "This will warm you."

Libby looked at the liquid in the cup. "What is it?"

"Whiskey."

She ought to keep her head clear, but the pain was so bad she wished she were dead anyway, so maybe the whiskey, or whatever might actually be in the cup, might numb and desensitize her all the more, and help with the damp chill seeping into her. She clutched the cup with both hands, took a sip, sputtered and shivered, but managed to swallow the burning liquid.

"The worst is behind you. At least as far as your system is concerned," he said, smiling with sad apology. He remained crouched at her side. His weight rested on the balls of his feet and his arms folded across his bent knees. "You've traveled considerable distance in time, but your body is still in a confluent span of hours. No surprise it's fighting you back."

So it was true. She had traveled through time. But, how could *he* know about it?

A crashing sound came again from outside, startling her. Thunder. Or, was it those three men? Were they hunting her?

She started to speak but it came out in a squeak. She took another swig of the whiskey and tried again.

"Those men…"

"Bootleggers. They won't bother us."

Libby closed her eyes and tried to think. The effort made the pain worse, so she opened them. "Bootleggers. So it's…"

"Nineteen twenty-six."

Startled, she stared into his eyes to discern his veracity, but was caught by the warmth and intensity she saw there.

He continued. "That's what I wanted to know first, too."

He'd traveled also? And, nineteen twenty-six? What would she do now? Panic washed over her, wondering about her place in this unfamiliar tableau. Overwhelmed, dread roaring through every part of her body, she rubbed her forehead against the dull ache that throbbed there, as a thousand more questions rioted in her mind. But first, she had to remember her humanity and the kindness of this stranger.

"Thank you..." she shrugged, "for helping me. Sorry about your lantern."

Their eyes met and his attention lingered on her for a moment, providing a brief warm bond in the chilly air of the cave. "No worries. I have others." He rubbed his chin. "What about you? From what year did you come back?"

"Twenty-sixteen." Startled at her own answer, she sucked in her breath.

He twitched his lips. "I suppose we're still dealing with famine, war, and terrorism, eh?"

She nodded.

He smirked. "Some things never change."

Thunder rolled over the lamp-lit cave and bolts of lightning sent dancing shadows through the opening of the crude dwelling.

The stranger stood and returned to the fire, dropping onto a low-slung rock. Libby studied him in the flickering light. He looked to be around fifty. His clothes were tidy enough, but his brown boots were crusted with mud as was the hem of his woolen pants. The sleeves of his coarse cotton shirt were rolled up to his elbows. He looked lithe, perhaps athletic. The lines of his face were chiseled, but faint shadows hovered beneath his eyes and his hair was mussed as though he had raked his fingers through it time and again, during their stay in the cave. He must not have slept much. The thought hit her with a strange pang of guilt, and she regretted his lost rest. Despite his dishevelment, the only word she could conjure to describe him was *distinguished*.

His presence suddenly felt important. Significant. She should know him, shouldn't she? But, the answer wouldn't come. She recalled how he handled the three men, saying he was Andrew Grey so she would know to trust him. "Who are you?"

"Name's Davis Whitaker." He pointed to his left and her gaze followed to see dates and initials etched into the cave wall. "I'm the D.W., 1918."

Libby stared at the wall, disbelief and dizziness washing over her. Another memory surfaced: Andrew mentioning initials in a cave.

"Were you FBI?"

"Forensic accounting. And you, FBI?" His features reflected polite interest.

She nodded, noting as she did that the pain wasn't as intense as it had been when she awoke, and that memories were returning randomly. "When did you..." She couldn't get herself to say 'come back in time.'

"Travel? Two-thousand eight. I was Andrew's first successful traveler." He didn't say it with pride or wonder, just matter-of-factly as he poked at the fire, prompting the flames to shoot higher. "We worked together. When I learned of my imminent death, I was devastated. While others offered condolences, Andrew took action."

Talk of Andrew made her heart pound. She swallowed her sorrow and loneliness. And, her confusion. Andrew hadn't even mentioned 2008. She didn't want to share her feelings with this man, and she didn't trust him yet. She turned her head slowly to the wall again. "Who are the others?"

"The E.S. for 1848 and M.L. for 1798, I don't know. The Z.H. for 1922 is a man named Zachary Hayes."

"Is he here, too?"

"No, after a couple weeks' recovery, he left. Fancies himself the cowboy type."

"Weeks?" She said it with such abrupt dismay that her hand flew across her mouth.

He smiled, and his raised cheeks dwarfed his hazel eyes. "Yes… Miss…?"

She hesitated, flailing around in her head for her identity. She began to panic. But then it came. "Shaw. Libby Shaw." After she spoke, she remembered her name was now Grey, but she said no more.

For a moment, he looked poised to ask her something, but seemed to change his mind. "Well, Libby Shaw, you've been here four days and nights so far. We can move you to the comfort of the Springs Hotel in a few days, and then in another week or two, you'll feel normal again."

"Is that possible, to ever feel normal again?" she asked and it came out in a whisper.

He studied her with such compassion, she found it hard to breathe. "Without patronizing you, I promise things will improve. But it takes time. To adjust. To restore your equilibrium." He pushed his rolled cuffs higher and perched his elbows on his knees. "'Course, your memory may never be restored. Not fully. The body seems to heal more quickly than the mind. Your body's way of protecting you. You'll remember bits and pieces. More as time goes by. Far as I know, Zachary's memory hasn't returned fully. I suspect he left things behind he doesn't want to remember. Your improving memory may suggest you left a time you don't want to forget."

Libby frowned and took another sip of whiskey.

He continued. "The water is a curative. Like any medicine,

it seems to work differently on everyone. On some, it doesn't work at all. No two experiences are the same. Sometimes I wonder if the loss of memory isn't part of the healing too. What you can't remember can't hurt you. Sometimes it's good to forget life's heartaches and wincing failures."

She thought about that. She remembered leaving Andrew, even recalled her parents and Aunt Isabel were gone. Those were her worst memories. *Weren't they?* And yet, they remained with her. The water did indeed work differently with everyone.

She gazed at the wall again, wondering about the experiences of the others. "Why did Zachary Hayes leave?"

Davis shrugged. "Said he wanted to see the wild west while there was still one to see. Acted disappointed he hadn't gone back farther in time. It's a shame he left, really. Would have been nice to talk about the future occasionally." He waved a hand and his expression suggested nothing surprised him anymore, that he'd gotten used to people doing all sorts of things.

"So...you pulled me from the water, too. Brought me here?"

"I try to be here each solstice and equinox, but I've missed a few. Nineteen twenty-one, for one. It was a tough year at work. But," he winked, "in all these years, I never thought I'd pull from the water a young woman with cinnamon hair and the most striking eyes I'd ever seen. Green, and one with a touch of blue. Fascinating. Highly unusual."

Libby felt a blush heat her cheeks and she looked down, unable to hold his gaze. She had sectoral heterochromia wherein a small portion of one iris had different pigmentation than the rest. Heretofore, she couldn't remember anyone ever describing her eyes as fascinating. Andrew had simply called them a mutation.

She looked back at Davis. "Do you miss it? Your old life, I mean?"

"At first." He stared at something beyond her shoulder, perhaps nothing, perhaps memories. His voice had a hint of sorrow to it. "I was quite lonely. Missed my son and kid sister, what I remembered of them. You remind me of her. 'Course she's at least fifteen years older. So yeah, it was lonely." He shrugged. "But, we train for separation, don't we? Once I accepted my fate, I moved on. Now I'm as happy as I was before. Perhaps more." He smiled a private smile that excluded Libby.

She thought of Andrew, his smile, his touch. *Saudade.* Portuguese for an intense feeling of missing someone you love. Her mind went blank as darkness swirled in. She felt her body falling back to the ground.

Then, nothing.

Chapter Eleven

1926

D AVIS STUDIED LIBBY as she slept. "Why are you here?" he whispered as though hoping the universe would murmur the answer. "Why this particular moment in time?"

He'd been startled to pull her from the water, having gone there anticipating another night like all the other solstices and equinoxes he'd passed at the mineral springs. Always waiting. Waiting endlessly for that one person, *anyone*, to need from him the care he had so desperately needed, but not gotten, when he'd taken the water.

And, foremost, to ascertain what their intentions were in being there. It had been a long time since he'd been forced to kill anyone, but it was always a possibility.

Why had this woman lied about her name? She'd said many concerning things as she recovered from her passage through time, so he'd heard enough to know she had not been truthful about her past or her last name. The water had a way of bringing out all manner of truths.

He rose and checked her pulse. Steady. The laudanum he'd poured in her whiskey would keep her knocked out for hours. He pulled out his pocket watch to check the time. The town would wake soon. He could make it there and back, without her being the wiser.

It was imperative he send a telegram.

He also would purchase more supplies while there, but first, he would make two phone calls from that small boarding house beside the telegraph office. They had the most private phone in town. He needed to let his wife Darcie know he intended to stay in Bedford longer than anticipated. Then he would call work and let them know the same. Fortunately, he'd left detailed directives for his assistant, in his top desk drawer.

Thirty minutes later he pressed the pedal on the floor, shifting his 1924 Oldsmobile Touring Car into higher gear, as the motorcar barreled down the rutted road to Bedford. His hands gripped the steering wheel as he composed the telegram in his head: "There's been activity at the Crystal Spring. Might involve the Matryoshka Project. I'm concerned the lion is awake and moving. Ready to strike. I'll relocate to the Bedford Lodge and Country Club, the old Arandale Hotel. Contact me there. We may need to take action."

Action. Such a nice way to say the young woman might have to be eliminated.

He hoped it wouldn't come to that. He may not trust her, but he did like her. Cursing, he banged his palm on the oversized steering wheel. Matryoshka had caused too many problems already. Changed too many lives. Why this woman too? He liked the way she talked. Her questions and responses were direct, her tone natural, not cloying or breezy the way the upper-class women in the Twenties spoke. And thank goodness she didn't use those phrases that grated on his nerves, like *swell* and *swagger* and *good egg*. He also would not make any comparisons between her subtle beauty and the ease it took to soak her in. Such a contrast to this era's women that loved blunted hair and layers of dramatic make-up.

Then again, she could ruin everything. He had to secure the plans. Plans to finally deal with Matryoshka. To secure the future.

He would have to cater to the woman for now. Court this along. Call on his best acting skills and learn what he could.

It's such a shame that some people, who weren't even involved in certain situations, had to die simply because of what they knew.

When he reached town, he parked in front of the telegraph office, setting the brake and stopping the engine. What he wouldn't give for just one more ride in his 1965 Shelby Cobra convertible. Better still, his 1969 Chevy Camaro muscle car with its ripping horsepower and tire-shredding torque. Both antiques in his former life. Now, not even invented yet. Oh, but what a sweet ride that convertible had been. He missed that kind of speed.

After making his calls, he bounded up the wooden steps to the telegraph office and entered, a smile filling his face when he discovered Kip on duty. Kip was young, gullible, and easily bribable. For a huge tip, Kip would keep his secrets.

Fifteen minutes later, Davis emerged, puffing a cigar and holding the message he'd shortened for Kip to send, because, of course, you never left any incriminating evidence behind.

His telegram had read:

To: Zachary Hayes, Kansas City, Kansas
From: Whit, Bedford, Pennsylvania
CONCERNING DEVELOPMENT. STOP. THREAT ARRIVED. STOP. MATTER OF GREATEST SECURITY. STOP. IMPERATIVE TO CONTACT ME AT ARANDALE. STOP.

Chapter Twelve

1926

THE ROUTINE CONTINUED, conversations followed by Libby waking to find Davis across the fire from her—sleeping, tending the flames, reading by lantern light—and her wondering when she'd fallen asleep. Each time she woke, she felt a little stronger, but still had no concept of time passing as nights and days morphed together inside the cave. Davis kept her nourished and hydrated with soup and water—she assumed it was the precious mineral water—and, when nature called, helped her stumble to the outside of the cave and behind thick bushes, leaving her alone until she lumbered back in.

Once, she woke to the welcome aroma of eggs and bacon frying over the campfire. Where and when he'd secured the equipment and the food, she had no idea. Her stomach growled as though selfish and eager for the nourishment. She hoped she could keep it in her stomach.

His gaze flicked to her as she sat up. He'd changed his clothes, now wearing tweed trousers and a tan sweater cardigan, complete with brown elbow patches and leather buttons. *Old-fashioned.* No, that was a foolish deduction because she was now in the era from which that style was in vogue. His dark hair, now combed and neater, curved smoothly across his brow.

"Good morning," he said. "I thought it was time you tried

solid food. You've progressed nicely."

Libby tore her gaze from him and scanned the ceiling and the recesses of the grotto where cracks opened to the outdoors. Sure enough, the sun's rays illuminated the crevices and openings, casting long shadows across the ground, suggesting the dawning of a new day. With relief, she also noted no spider webs, no bats roosting up high, no chewed bones on the ground.

His gaze must have tracked hers to the natural illumination because he added, "We can sit outside later, if you like. You ought to get some vitamin D."

She nodded, not sure what to say. She didn't want to admit concern at this change of routine, at this inevitable next step. She drew in her knees, tugging at the linen shift to disentangle it from her calves, then circled her legs with her arms in what must have looked a defense to protect herself.

"No need to be afraid of going out," he said. "I'll help you."

She winced, then forced her lips into a half smile.

He scooped the eggs, bacon and biscuits onto two metal plates, partially stood, and stretched to hand one to her.

Giddiness and a startling desire to eat settled in. She took a bite, closing her eyes while she chewed, and savoring every sensation as her taste buds were entertained and pleasured.

She finished the eggs and bacon first, set the plate aside, and nibbled slowly at the biscuit. "Delicious," she murmured, mouth still full. The word *'shemomedjamo'* scurried across her mind; Georgian, meaning she can't believe she ate it all.

Davis had settled on his side of the fire and was bending over a metal carafe when she spoke. He looked up and smiled. "No queasiness?"

"None," Libby said. "But, even if it does come back up, the food was worth it."

He chuckled, and she was glad. She liked seeing him pleased. She owed him so much. As he continued with the carafe, she had a thought. Acting on it, she turned over her empty plate to study her reflection on the bottom. She didn't expect the limited light and tarnished metal to reveal much, but it still mirrored enough that she was appalled. Her eyes were bottomed with dark shadows, her cheeks looked hollow and pale, and the collection of days had done a thorough job of plastering her hair to her skull. It hung in uneven clumps at her shoulders. She finger-combed the strands, but called defeat quickly. With quiet resignation, she returned the plate to the ground, and focused her gaze on Davis.

He poured something steamy from the carafe into two cups. The aroma of coffee hit her and more taste buds activated. Picking up one of the cups, he stepped around the fire and handed it to her. "Arbuckles," he said. "The Starbucks of this era." He pointed to the empty plate. "More eggs? Bacon?"

Libby shook her head. "Better not." As she received the cup from him, a wave of melancholy rolled over her and she stared at the steaming refreshment. A memory of Andrew and her in a coffee shop surfaced and skittered away.

"Don't worry," he said, dropping onto the rock and taking a swig from his own cup. "Not everything is made of metal. You'll also find rubber, ceramic, porcelain, china, in this day and age. Just no plastic." He looked into his cup as he swirled it. "Synthetic plastic has been invented of course…it's out there. But, it hasn't undergone mass production yet. Doesn't become important until World War II."

She swallowed that reality; no plastic and no World War II yet. She'd have to reprogram her brain to function in this new life. She shook her head to dislodge the gloom that threatened to move in. "I wasn't thinking about the cup. I've camped a lot. Spent time in third-world countries, too. Africa. Southeast Asia. Christian missions and relief groups tend to donate supplies and products that last longer than plastic."

He nodded. "Then, why the frown?"

She didn't want to discuss Andrew, so she told a different truth. "The coffee. I usually drink it with cream and artificial sweetener. I guess the latter isn't available yet either." She made an inane attempt to chuckle at her own statement, but it sounded more like despair.

"Ah," he exaggerated the word and nodded. "I was a stevia man. 'Course you can get cream nowadays, but none of those little blue or yellow packets. You might find it easier in the long run to teach yourself to drink it black. It *is* an acquired taste."

She took a sip and was surprised to find it tolerable. But then, she hadn't had coffee in days. "Let's hope life in nineteen twenty-six is an acquired taste, too," she said.

He rubbed his forehead. "Let's hope, because, really, you have no choice."

She shivered against a chill that crawled across her skin. "I could be dead," she said with a fake hint of humor, an attempt to lighten the moment, but it sounded just that. Fake. She took another sip and looked back at the fire. Her voice dropped to a whisper as she added, "In a way I am. At least, everything I knew is gone."

"Yes, it is," he acknowledged, his voice gentle, soothing. "I found I had to blank my mind. Lay my former life to rest. That way, I know no more about this time period than anyone else out there. Foreknowledge is agony. Pure torment. When those moments hit, that's when you'll feel most alone. But, you must not intrude on history." He smirked. "I often think of Velcro and the wealth I could make by inventing it. On the other hand, I think that because we've been placed here, we can certainly use our knowledge to our own survival benefit."

"Have you?" Libby wrapped her fingers around the cup. "Used your first life to your survival benefit?"

He swayed his head side to side as though weighing his response. "I suppose I have. My wife thinks I'm a little too worried about money, but I can't unlearn what I know about the stock market crash in 1929, and the Depression ahead of us."

"Your wife?" Her tone sounded more startled than she intended and his eyes widened in surprise. For the first time she gave credence to the fact that this man would have a life separate from her intrusion on it. If she were a betting person, she'd wager he understood the ignorance behind her question, but was considerate enough to ignore it.

"Been married for five years now. I don't wear a wedding ring because men didn't much wear them before World War II. Her name is Darcie. You'd like her, although she's much older than you." He looked intently at Libby. "May I ask how old you are?"

"Twenty-nine."

He raised a brow. "She's thirty-six. Closer in age than I thought. You could pass in this period as probably twenty-one or twenty-two. I guess it's true that every generation looks younger than the last, what with modern conveniences and products." He took a sip of coffee. "I'm fifty and often mistaken for being younger. I have two children now, too." He frowned. "That's an example of how foreknowledge can be pure hell."

"What do you mean?"

"They're ages three and four. What's coming down the pike when they come of age?"

Libby's mind raced. She wanted to produce the answer, prove to herself she could identify the pitfalls to come. She cringed when the answer hit her. "World War II."

"That's right. They'll be of age when America gets involved." He continued eating as he talked. "Anyway, when I traveled back, my first wife had been dead for three years. Hit an icy patch in the road and her car skidded out of control. Died instantly. My only son was grown and on his own." He paused, and when he spoke again, his tone grew softer. "You will move on, too, Libby. You'll build a new life as well."

Libby wondered about that but forced a smile, because really, it would do no good to argue anyway. "Andrew helped you?"

He looked back at the fire. "He did."

"And you would have died otherwise?"

A shadow crossed his face and a muscle ticked in his jaw before he answered. As though he realized he'd hesitated, he hurried his answer. "Yes…that's what the doctor said. I had a rare form of liver and intrahepatic bile duct cancer. Andrew brought me to the water." He shifted as though he were uncomfortable and wished to change the conversation. For the briefest moment, it registered as odd with Libby, but his next comment made her realize he probably didn't like talking about himself. "Tell me about your past," he urged, "so we can lay that to rest and discuss your future."

It struck Libby that this was the moment they were going to become intimate in their conversations, moving from rescuer and rescued, to collaborators, perhaps friends. She owed it to him to be forthright. She was reliant on his largesse, his tolerance in helping her adapt and progress. The least she could do is trust that he knew best.

"My mother was a botanist. My father, a car mechanic."

Davis whistled low under his breath. "Unusual pairing."

She smiled to ward back a wave of sadness. "Mama had her PhD and Daddy barely finished high school. But they got along swimmingly. Daddy actually made more money than she did. He helped me learn mechanics, while Mama insisted I learn the violin. I often had to wash the grease off my hands before touching my violin."

A dimple appeared to the left of his lips. "Sounds like a diverse childhood. But, it was happy?"

"Very…at least until I was eleven. That's when my mother died. Massive stroke."

"Sorry. She sounds young to have experienced a stroke."

"Only thirty-nine. My father was terribly distraught and distracted. I was told he died shortly thereafter from a hydraulic lift accident, but I don't remember." Libby drew in a slow breath and issued a long exhale. "I traveled for five years with my mother's missionary single sister, Aunt Isabel. She was a physician. Worked with one of those doctors-without-borders groups."

Davis tilted his head. "You were allowed to travel with her? That must have been exciting, not to mention educational."

Yes, if you ignore that horrible time in Africa. Those terrible men. The attack. The deaths. My scar. Her scar! Libby gazed down at it and for the first time realized it was no longer raised and hadn't ached since coming out of the water. But, the discoloration and slight disfigurement remained.

"That from your time traveling with your aunt?" His gaze had tracked hers to the scar.

She nodded.

"You rubbed it while you were healing," he said.

"Did I say anything?"

"Not much." He looked away. "Nothing important."

She recalled the visions she had while taking the water, of herself as a girl.

He was quiet a moment, and when he spoke, he eased her discomfort by changing topics. "What happened after the five years?"

"During a stay in remote parts of Australia, Aunt Isabel braved a hunting excursion into the Outback where she defied scouts' warnings. She was attacked by a wild boar." Libby swallowed against a rising nausea before continuing. "In the saddest of ironies, my physician aunt refused medical help, insisting she could doctor herself. She died. I don't remember details of that either. I found myself shipped back to the States, and placed in foster care until I left for college. The tuition was paid courtesy of scholarships."

He stopped sopping his egg with his roll to say, "I'm sorry."

"I floundered from nursing to botany...some odd allegiance to my mother's profession, I guess...to business, before finally settling on languages. That's what I brought to the bureau. Language skills. Interpretation. Phonetic coding.

Grammatical memory. They come easy to me, as does music which depends on the same brain systems. I worked for the DOJ before the FBI recruited me."

"How many languages have you mastered?"

"Mastered? Seven, but I can speak nine, and know a little of three others. Plus, I'm a bit of a logophile. I know a bunch of random words from a few dozen other languages for which we have no equivalent in English.

"Like what?"

She tilted her head. "Ever experience that panicky hesitation before introducing someone whose name you can't quite remember?"

"All the time."

"The Scots call that 'tartle.'"

His mouth curved. "Impressive."

Libby smirked. "Thanks, but it's not such a great achievement considering it comes from a quirk of my DNA…the way I was born. I have no fashion sense, the site of blood makes me nauseous, I'm too impatient to teach, computing numbers bores me, and politics make me angry, so I didn't have many career options anyway."

He chuckled. "Still, it might serve you well as you branch out into your new life."

"Here, in rural Pennsylvania? In the Roaring Twenties? I doubt there is much need for interpreters." She stretched out her legs and cast a forlorn look at the ground.

He cocked his head as though surprised. "You don't have to stay here. The world, as they say, is your oyster."

Leave the springs? Was that possible? "Don't you live around here?"

"No." He put his empty plate on the ground, and leaned in, parking his forearms on his knees and clasping his hands. "After I traveled through the water and learned *when* I was, I decided to go to Pittsburgh. My background was in accounting. I figured the steel mills were booming in the early nineteen hundreds, and could use extra help. I was right. It has served me well. I'm in upper management now. I won't strive for a higher position because with success comes a relinquishing of privacy. People become more curious, want to know all about you. I can't afford to deal with those questions about my past."

"But Andrew said I needed to stay here. Near the water." Even as she spoke, Libby remembered Davis saying that Zachary Hayes had headed west. It hadn't registered with her before.

That tick in Davis's jaw returned and he looked away. Was that anger she saw? No, perhaps bewilderment. He stayed silent for a moment, and when at last he spoke, his tone hinted at nothing untoward. "Perhaps you misunderstood him. You should drink lots of the mineral water to complete your transition, restore your memory. But once you feel healthy again, you can taper off. You won't always be tied to the medicinal water."

"But, I didn't misunderstand him. I know for certain…" Libby snapped her mouth shut, and dropped her gaze to the ground. Davis was so kind, so helpful. Best not to change the mood of the moment. She could work this out later. She wished Andrew were here so he could explain what she'd misunderstood. More than that, she longed for his arms to be around her, to reassure her.

She looked up to see Davis staring at her. "You trusted him

very much, didn't you?" he asked, but she couldn't gage the curiosity or intensity behind his question.

Libby nodded. "Of course I did. He—"

"Became quite a good friend to you."

She wondered why Davis was so curious. "More than that," she whispered.

Davis's brows lifted, urging her to explain.

"I was his wife."

His jaw ticked, the movement there, then gone like a fleeting hint of...*what?* Anger? Dismay? Dare she interpret it as jealousy? Surely not. Yet, the vibes emanating from him were no longer those of warmth, but rather a neutral nothingness. Bewildered, she wondered about the change her comment wrought in his demeanor.

She waited for him to speak, and when he didn't she decided she misunderstood the moment. After all, she didn't know this man very well. Then again, she hadn't known Andrew very well either. "We met only a little over a month ago. A kind of whirlwind romance." She watched a look of curiosity cross Davis's face. "When he told me I was dying—"

"*He* told you?" He raised a brow, but kept his gaze on the fire as he asked his question. Libby detected no censure in his tone, just curiosity.

"That's right. From his computer files. When he told me, I had it verified by a Dr. Kuzmich."

Something passed over Davis's face again. Was it a glint of annoyance, or merely the shadows of the flames dancing that caused such a flicker?

Libby continued. "That was just a week before I took the mineral water. We got married the day before I came here."

Again, his demeanor confused her. His shoulders dropped and he formed a smile, but it didn't reach his eyes. Was he concerned about her? With a start she realized she wanted to ease his concerns, smooth her hand across his cheek and urge him to smile, tell him she was fine.

But she wasn't fine and in the next instant she fought against a wave of sadness and longing that rolled over her. Tears surfaced and she began to shake as she gave into the fear and heartache.

Davis moved to her, dropped to his knees, and pulled her into an embrace, holding her as she cried several minutes. He smelled of soap and cigars, an odd combination.

"I-I'm sorry," Libby finally blubbered. "I'm so afraid. I don't even feel married. I know Andrew will find me, but it's like I've been abandoned for now."

Davis leaned back and looked at her as he rubbed one of her arms. "I understand." His voice was pitched low with sorrow. "Things will look better with time."

"He wants to come back." She choked on her words. "He just doesn't know how to accomplish it yet. He said each time is more painful…" She broke off as she heard her own words. She'd barely survived once and couldn't imagine ever trying again. She closed her eyes and dropped her face into her hands as the reality of her aloneness set in.

Davis shifted to her side and rubbed circles on her back. When at last he spoke his tone harbored no censure, no berating. "You need to move on with your life. It's healthiest to accept that you are a widow now. Otherwise you may wait endlessly. I know I said you can go anywhere, but the truth is, I hope you stay around this area. I'm being selfish, of course. But

I would like to talk to someone occasionally, from my own time."

She pulled her shoulders back. He was trying to buoy her up, give her hope, a reason to move forward. The least she could do is rise to the effort. She shrugged a shoulder. "Maybe. I guess I could go to Pittsburgh too."

He raised a brow. "I'm not sure that's a good idea."

"Why? You think Darcie…?"

"No. It's not that. She's an incredible woman. And, she has private aspects of her life as well. When we married, we agreed we would always be honest with one another, but that if we couldn't answer a particular question, we would say so and the other would respect that. You'd be one of those questions I couldn't answer. Not yet, anyway." He rubbed his chin. "No, I'm more concerned about your safety. This may raise your feminine dander, but it's just not safe for a young woman to live alone in this period."

A renewed wave of sadness rolled over Libby at what she'd left behind.

He continued. "Let's take this one day at a time. Get used to life here, at the Springs Hotel, for a while." He pulled out a pocket watch and read it. "We can discuss this tonight when there is no sun to take advantage of."

She nodded, then remembered what she'd seen earlier reflected on the plate. She touched her hair. Greasy. Looked at her shift. Soiled. Dirty. Wrinkled. What's more the garment was so thin, it must have been almost transparent when he'd pulled her from the water. No doubt, she'd been as good as naked at that moment. "You've been very kind not mentioning how I look and smell. Do you think I could freshen up somewhere...somehow?"

Davis chuckled and stood, collecting their dishes. "Now I know you're healing. Why don't you bathe in the creek while you get some sun? A two-fer. Don't worry. You won't always have to do that. This period does have indoor plumbing and bathtubs."

Libby forced a weak smile. "I-I'm a little hesitant about submerging myself again in water."

"Ah, I see. As I recall, I was too. But you won't be in the mineral water. The creek is different, the composition of the water, the sight and sounds of it. All different. Once you're at the hotel, you may want to swim in the pool there. It's tied into another spring."

"I doubt that very much."

He shrugged. "We'll see. You might find it's the only solo form of rigorous exercise you can undertake in this period without raising eyebrows. Besides, your determination to be healed is what kept you in the water. That's not your driving force for being in the water anymore. Now, let's see..." He turned and rummaged through a couple duffel bags. "Ah, here they are." Returning, he handed her a towel. "Sorry, no Canon or Martha Stewart labels. But you'll be happy about this." He held up a bar of soap. She read the brand name, "Palmolive transparent toilet soap."

She'd never seen the soap before, but he was right that the somewhat-familiar name made her smile, although its packaging reminded her of antique markets.

"I warn you though, it's harsh stuff. More lye than lotion." He followed that with a bottle of Mulsified Cocoanut Oil Shampoo. He shrugged. "Darcie likes it. And finally, the piece de resistance." He presented a toothbrush, a tube of Pepto-Mint toothpaste, and a bottle of Listerine, each in unfamiliar packaging.

She smiled, wrapping the toiletries in the towel. "What more could a girl want?"

Davis nodded, and rubbed his hands together. "I'll take you to the creek. While you bathe, I'll head into town and get more supplies. My motorcar…eh, that's what they call them now…it's parked over the ridge in a grove of trees. I'll try to find more appropriate clothes for you, too. Shouldn't be hard. You're rather thin. Gotten thinner in the past several days." As he kicked dirt over the fire, he said, "You'll find young women now are following this ridiculous fad of looking like skinny little boys. No shapes. Just straight columns. You're a bit taller than the average woman's height these days. You may have to order clothes tailor-made later."

"You should see my roommate Colette. She's five-eleven."

He whistled. "We're lucky you came back rather than her."

If he hadn't stopped to stare at her feet, Libby would have remarked that lucky was the last thing she felt. Instead, she asked, "Something wrong?"

"Shoe sizing hasn't been standardized yet." He snapped his fingers, and said, "I know." He returned to his duffel bag and pulled out writing paper and a pencil. As he traced her foot, Libby sighed in relief that at least he hadn't pulled out a quill and ink well. She had so much to learn about this period.

As they exited the cave, a thought struck and she whirled around to voice it. "Davis, I have no money. I can't repay you for any of this."

He laughed and winked. "Money is the least of my concerns. We'll talk about that tonight, too."

With forced brightness she said, "Sounds like we'll be busy."

"Indeed. We're relocating to the hotel tomorrow. That means we've got to do a crash course about the Roaring Twenties this evening."

Chapter Thirteen

1917

NATHAN'S HEAD THROBBED with a dull, wavering pain. He groaned and rolled onto his back, eyes closed tight.

Images flickered at the edges of his memory, cavorting, as though teasing him to pursue clearer focus, to remember. *An open pasture...crystal water...a mule...an old man...*each attempt to sharpen the vision caused more throbbing. Hadn't he suffered enough?

And, for how long? Time had lost context as light and dark passed over him, an inseparable veil.

Location confused him, too. He had opened his eyes thrice, finding himself in a dwelling he didn't recognize, and unlike anything he'd ever seen. So many windows, so much sunlight, so many furnishings and things made of glass and from metals he didn't know existed. Carved and molded in shapes he'd never imagined. The odd cushioning beneath him was softer and bigger than any straw mattress he'd ever slept on.

Hadn't there earlier been an old woman spooning something into his mouth? A broth and a bitter tea made from willow bark. At other times, water or whiskey. But always, the spinning would begin again, so he had closed his eyes and drifted back to the bliss of nothingness. He'd needed to keep his eyes shut to thwart the pain.

This time, it felt like his head ached *because* he'd been lying down too long.

He opened his eyes a slit and inched into a sitting position, waiting for the dizziness to subside. The dwelling stopped spinning, and the unusual things surrounding him settled into place. Light filtered in through a faded cotton curtain and he blinked against it.

He rubbed a hand down his face and whiskered jaw. When had he shaved last? His breath hitched as the magnitude of his situation washed over him. Shaving was the least of his concerns. He couldn't remember how he got here. Or, where *here* was. He didn't know *when* it was either.

He rubbed his forehead as if pressure would activate remembrance.

He'd been on a journey. Yes, that's it. He'd been trying to get home. It had been years. *Hadn't it?*

That's why nothing looked familiar. Time had marched on, things had changed. His family... He had a family, didn't he? They must have moved and resettled here. But then, why was there no joy of anticipation in his heart at the prospect of home and familiar faces?

He dropped his hands, eased his feet to the floor, and assessed his surroundings. Nothing sparked recognition.

Music interrupted his thoughts. Sharp, tinty, but melodious and calming. Sounds that blended well together. Instruments he'd never heard before.

Nathan stood, reaching to the wall for support. He would follow the music. Someone in that group making the music might provide answers.

He stepped forward, catching an image of a harsh, weary

man in a looking glass hanging on the opposite wall. Had he always looked like that? He'd thought he was younger. Was he pale from having been ill? Lined from sleeping too long? He noted scars. *So many of them.* Scars fading into white, but still there. It had to be from a wound or two healed long ago. One scar, still raised and pinkish, sliced a crooked line along his right cheek.

It was a moment before he registered his nakedness. He looked around him. A shirt and a pair of trousers were draped across a wooden structure. Shouldn't they look familiar? These had to be a wealthy gentleman's clothes. He donned them anyway.

Dressed, but barefoot, he staggered through the next room. So large. So much space! Visions came to mind of a two-room cabin with puncheon floor, simple fireplace, and sawbuck table. None of that here.

Instead, he saw large, ponderous furniture made of mahogany and black walnut with chiseled legs and marble tops, ornamented knobs and rainbow colors of cushions. An object, ceramic at its base but topped with a fabric cylinder, appeared to be attached to the wall by way of a thick cord. That rifle over the doorway, he'd never seen anything like that. Books, *everywhere*! A ponderous black, round metal structure—a wood-fired stove? A huge basin built into what looked like a cooking area, with part of a hand pump built into it. Where was the rest of the pump and why was it inside the house?

He smelled the rich aroma of tobacco wafting through the entryway, straight ahead. The passage, leading from the cabin to the outside, had two doors. One, solid wood, stood ajar. The other, made of a wood frame and centered with fine fibers of metal molded together to create a thin mesh, offered a see-through view to the outside. He pulled it toward him, but stopped to marvel at the tiny patterned squares. A vision of different doors skirted through his mind. The first made of hides sewn together and draping to the ground. The other involved a thick batten door hung on wooden hinges, with a strong latch and an extra bar for use in time of attack. But, attack from what? The answer wouldn't come.

"Shut the screen door," a stern female voice commanded. "Keeps the bugs out."

He looked back at the door, cataloguing that term. *Screen door.*

Moving through the archway, he followed the voice, stepping onto the porch and pushing, *too hard,* the screen door shut behind him. The bang, so loud, startled a woodpecker and it leaped into soaring flight through the upper branches of the trees fronting the dwelling.

He'd been ready to utter apologies for slamming the door with such force, but instead stifled to find a lone, old woman on the porch. No musicians. No instruments in site, yet the music continued, emanating from a wooden box perched on a table near the woman. The box's lid was propped open, and something dark circulated inside.

He planted his hands in his pockets and stood firm, taking in the miracle box. The woman remained quiet and he appreciated that. He needed a moment to search for a memory, to absorb the busyness and complexity of this place he must surely call home. He found comfort *only*, and very little at that, in the dull brown color of the wood dwelling and the familiar landscape of the distant mountains.

The woman, seated in a rocking chair, turned her head. Their gazes met. As they exchanged brief nods, he noted a long black braid of hair tinged in gray, and dark eyes above a shelf of high cheekbones covered in deeply etched wrinkles and papery skin. Eyes that looked too young for the body that housed them. Eyes that struck him as vaguely familiar.

She looked back to the scenery, never breaking her measured back-and-forth motion, the wood porch floor creaking beneath the rockers. He kept his gaze on her, holding back a longing desire, a wish that he would feel a memory of her.

She sipped from a tin cup, then dragged on a cigar, her breath coming in shallow puffs. Ashes flittered on her clothing.

Did he remember his mother wearing pants? That would make practical sense for the many chores necessary on a farm. He scrutinized her hands. They were long, thick, and work-roughened, confirming she worked hard. But, why did he think his mother had a different voice and demeanor? In his mind, she was welcoming, gentler, quick to make eye contact and put others at ease. Hadn't his mother once greeted strangers with more zeal than this woman now used with her own son? Perhaps he was still fevered. Not thinking correctly.

And what of the golden bronze of her skin? His skin paled in comparison. Then again, he'd been ill.

The woman looked so old. Perhaps he too was older than he thought. He remembered the image in the looking glass earlier.

The box stopped making music and instead issued a rhythmic thumping sound as the black cylinder continued to spin. The woman leaned forward, shifted something inside the box, and turned a knob. The box went quiet.

She'd moved with an agility that belied her age.

He suspected he might make her uncomfortable if he kept staring, perhaps even sad if she realized how little he remembered, so he ambled to the rocker beside her and folded himself into it. He sat erect, keeping his chair still. She pointed to another cup on the small table between them. *She knew he would be joining her?*

He wanted to say it was good to be home, but he wasn't sure about that. And why wasn't she acting delighted? They must have shared a homecoming earlier that he did not remember. She was already used to him being there.

Instead of asking what dwelled on his mind, he picked up the cup and sipped—tea, doctored with whiskey—and said, "The music. It came from that box?"

She chuckled and looked back at him. "Good morning." She took another drag on the cigar, offered it to him, then pulled it back to rest her arm on her rocker again when he declined. "A Victor Talking Machine."

He understood her words, but the sound of them was odd, wrapped in a faint accent and a slow delivery, as though she was either in no hurry or was searching hard to say the words correctly.

He repeated the words in a whisper. "Victor Talking Machine."

She grinned and nodded, looking back at the scenery, never breaking her rhythmic movement.

Nathan waited for her to say more, and when she didn't he said the first thing that came to mind. "So many unfamiliar things. This cabin....so fancy."

"Only to you." She made a rebuffing gesture with her free

hand as she added, "To others, a shanty." Her rocking, her distant gaze, continued.

Shanty. He whispered that word also. "These clothes," he looked down at his shirt and tugged at its front. "They are mine? I don't remember owning anything so nice."

"Yours now."

He brushed back locks of shoulder-length hair that were hanging around his face so he could study the shirt more closely. He pondered the stitching, the angles where the fabric came together, the sturdiness of the garment. *Such fine work.* "You made them?"

"Bought them." Her expression did not change, betraying neither pride or embarrassment.

Nathan raised a brow. "Are we...rich then?"

The woman took another puff of the cigar, her gaze still locked on the distance, her chair still swaying back and forth. "Made in a factory. Assembly line."

He cataloged those words, too.

"You can read," she said.

How did she know? He didn't ask.

She pushed up from her chair, her joints creaking at the effort. But when she walked, she moved with a sturdiness and sure-footedness that startled him, again confirming her dexterity contradicted her looks. She grasped a book from a table several yards to her right, and returned, handing it to him. "Read when the sun sleeps." She sat back in her chair. "Work when it works."

He read the cover. "The Complete History of America, through 1900." Anxiety spread through his body like a poison. He'd thought the year was somewhere in the 1700s.

A chilled air whispered against the back of his neck. He took a fortifying swallow of the whiskey. "What year is this?"

"The year of our Lord nineteen hundred and seventeen." The woman puffed from the cigar again before adding, "Autumn. Time for harvest."

He took another sip, letting her answer settle in, feeling the enormity of it burn through him, just like the whiskey.

She sat her cigar on a tin tray between them, and returned her gaze to the distance. "What year did you take the water?"

Nathan gripped the cup tighter. Before she'd asked about it, he hadn't even remembered any water. "Seventeen sixty-nine." Both his answer and the ease with which he pulled it forth, bewildered him.

She nodded, but said nothing, and that calmed him. *She wasn't shocked. Or curious. Or concerned about his answer or state of mind.*

It struck him that time, and this woman, would be his keys to survival now.

He couldn't think about the year. It was too overwhelming. So he thought about the season. Harvest, she'd said. That meant much labor ahead. Good, he could focus on that. He understood harvest. "Should we be working?"

"Not today."

His brows drew down in confusion.

"It's Sunday. The Almighty's day. Today, we rest."

He continued to rock four, maybe five times, before saying, "You are my mother." It was a statement, not a question. If she wasn't his mother, she would set him straight.

He saw only her profile, but he watched something flicker in her expression. "I am now." She looked at him as she rocked, and gave a nod as though to reassure him.

Silence fell.

Another memory surfaced. "I had a father."

"We all had a father." She chuckled a short, breathy sound. "It's just us now."

The woman's answers were brief, yet they packed such a punch.

"What do I call you?" He expected her to say Mother or Ma or some such derivative.

Several rocking motions went by before she said, "Ista."

His gaze intensified at her answer. *Ista*. The Mohawk name for mother. Yes, that's right, he could speak the Iroquoian language. He knew Mohawk.

She asked, "What should I call you now?"

He frowned. Had he changed so much that she believed he had a new identity? He taxed his memory but could not think of his name. Finally, he said, "*Yen'a*." Mohawk, for *son*.

She studied him, a peaceful look on her face before turning away. "It will come back. Slowly." Her tone didn't impart coddling, but rather certainty, wisdom. "Best if it does not, but it will."

He shot her a look of confusion.

Without taking her gaze off the distance, she added, "Some moments should stay where they occurred. It's not good they become memories."

He nodded, but said nothing more. He leaned back and nudged his rocker into motion, moving evenly with Ista. From the corner of his eye, he saw the edge of her mouth curve up, hiding a smile.

After a while, she looked at him and they exchanged nods,

speaking an understanding that words couldn't touch.

He would read this book Ista gave him. Memorize it, if he had to. And, he'd read all the others in the house. He would observe. Listen. Learn. He didn't need a book or a memory to confirm what had already crystalized in his mind when she had voiced the date; that his life had irrevocably changed.

He had no choice but to think about the future. Logic had no place here. He could only hope for divine guidance.

Why should he waste time trying to wrestle back to life a person he wasn't certain he wanted back anyway? There was only the future, and he thought of the Good Book, of the apostle Paul's advice in Philippians to be persistent and keep pressing on.

Chapter Fourteen

1917

FOR A MONTH Ista and Nathan toiled side by side harvesting the crops, preserving food, and watching autumn bring changes daily to their front-porch view. At night he read, asked questions, read some more.

It wasn't until month two when Ista walked with him the mile into the small town of Bedford that he finally accepted what he'd read and what she'd described weren't malarkey, dreams, or magic: revolution from Britain, a war between the states, outhouses *inside* the house, motorcars, tractors, paved roads, flying machines, radios, telephones, bathtubs, stock markets, forty-eight states in the union. *So much to learn.*

The night after his first trip to town, Nathan excused himself after supper, withdrew to a dark corner of his room, and sat on the floor sobbing like a baby.

The next day he walked back to town alone, and sat for hours, observing.

That began a routine of walking to town once each week. He memorized faces, clothing, modes of transportation, streets, products, business names.

On his fourth trek, he overheard three men talking about a war that involved America. *Overseas!* Duty hastened him to the only place he could think of to go: the sheriff's office.

"It's not my decision, but I doubt they'll take you," said the sheriff, a tall, agile man of about fifty-five, with intense eyes that Nathan suspected helped him secure confessions from even the most hardened criminals. Like him, the sheriff's face sported signs of an altercation or two, and his nose bent in such a way that suggested it had once been broken. "You'll just be disappointed if you try."

Nathan didn't understand. Why wouldn't he try? He was young, willing to fight. His reflection in the looking glass that morning showed good coloring to his skin and a strong body on a capable man.

When Nathan made no response, the sheriff circled to the front of his desk, leaned back against it, and folded his arms. "First, you look like you're at least thirty. Males between 21 and 30 were required to register for military service. Did you do that?"

No, he hadn't. Nathan stood firm, but cast his eyes to the floor as he processed this. He didn't want to say the wrong thing.

"Second, you have no proof to verify who you are. How do I know you're not some foreigner hoping to infiltrate our military network? Third, you've got too many scars. Looks like you might not keep your wits about you. I doubt they'll agree with putting somebody like that in our army."

Nathan remained quiet. Frustration roared through him, particularly since the sheriff bore his own marks of controversial run-ins. Yet, he also felt gratitude to hear these insights from this modern 1917's man.

The sheriff asked, "You got a wife? Kids?"

Nathan shook his head.

"Well, that would make you an ideal candidate. No one back here to mourn you...yes, well, never mind." The sheriff grimaced and drummed his fingertips in a single staccato rhythm on the desk, then turned to pull a pencil and paper close. "Can you read and write? I'll give you the address of where you sign up."

The sheriff had been right. The office wanted identification. Verification. Proof. Nathan returned home.

The Great War ended less than a year later, 1918. By then, Nathan had recovered enough of his memory to know he had already sacrificed greatly, had already done his part to foster the development and freedoms of his country.

In that year, Nathan also established a routine with Ista. They worked together during the day tending crops or animals, but often separated in the evenings to do other things. She chose to smoke and listen to her music. He read, hunted in the surrounding mountains, and began tinkering with tools Ista pulled from a shed behind the house.

When she'd given him the tools, she'd said, "Folks without a purpose die. You will learn to use these tools." Her statement brooked no argument.

By then, he'd learned her word "shanty" didn't mean the best of dwellings. So, he practiced with the tools and began to refurbish the house to look more like the ones he saw in town. He discovered a new passion in woodworking.

Early in 1918 Nathan remembered his age (twenty-eight), full name, family, and some acquaintances, but didn't tell Ista. He'd come to care for the old woman. Other aspects of his life remained elusive.

With his name foremost on his mind, he began to take long

walks for miles in all directions from the town, first visiting the site of where Fort Bedford once stood, then looking for cemeteries. After two months of searching, he found crude headstones for his parents on the land that once belonged to his family. Although weathered and beaten by the elements, they were legible. Three weeks after that, he found a marker closer to Bedford that evoked more memories. This one read, "Richard Wallace – British officer, son, beloved husband." According to the stone, Wallace died three months after Nathan left, baffling since Wallace had been a healthy, robust young man. Was it battle? Disease?

Nathan searched another month but never found Anabelle's headstone, so he moved his inquiry to the records chamber at the courthouse. He learned Anabelle died giving birth to an infant son six months after Wallace passed away. The child survived, but no further information was available. He abandoned the search and left the courthouse. On his walk home, he shed a tear. Anabelle had never made it to her tidewater town.

IN EARLY SUMMER of 1921, Nathan caught Ista staring at him more often. Watching and studying him as though waiting to catch him crumble from inner demons or thoughts. Within weeks she returned home from a trip to town and announced she would be leaving in a couple months. She groused about having seen someone dangerous.

"Who is it?" he demanded. "I'll protect you."

She looked at him in that way he'd seen many mothers in

town look at their children. Some sort of pride and satisfaction mixed together. "This is something I must do alone."

It would do no good to argue. "Will you come back?"

She returned his gaze. "In time."

Yes, of course, in time. Everything happened in some sort of time, didn't it? He'd learned that full well.

Later, before taking the water, she shared a story with him, recounting a harrowing tale of a young woman and a young man, both harmed by another man…the same man who had harmed her, Ista. The story left him remembering more bits and pieces of his life, and fisting his hands, overcome with the desire to thrust them into a wall to relieve his anger at the man who had changed them all.

Ista shared other tales of having taken the water five times, traveling back and forth between the 1700s and present day, and detailed how she learned to make the transition easier on her body and her memory.

Before her second journey, she'd hidden coins and other valuables she expected would provide her with money to survive in the future. She told him other things as well—she was born to a Mohawk woman and a white father near a great and powerful lake (Nathan deduced it to be Lake Erie), that her husband and son had been killed by the British, that she had journeyed to the magical water alone after hearing stories about its power, and that a missionary introduced her to Christ, which prompted her to live outside the camp of her Indian brothers and sisters.

But most powerfully, she shared her wisdom, prompting a tiny tremble to grow in him. A tremble of determination, of hope.

"You're frozen," she said. "Like the lake in winter. More heavy burdens and you will shatter."

When he said nothing, she added, in a softer voice, "Stop trying to wrestle back to life a man that is long since gone."

He nodded.

She smiled. "Wait for her. Romans 8:25."

He studied her face, sensing that she would offer no clarifiers even if he asked.

She reached for him where he sat beside her in their rocking chairs. He leaned in and she kissed him on the forehead, whispering a new name for him. After a brief explanation, they nodded in agreement.

Then, she leaned back, closed her eyes, and promised he would see her again.

When he awoke the next morning, the coffee was brewing, the animals had been fed, and Ista was gone.

While he mourned her departure that autumn, he thought about her words as he continued to refurbish the house, tackling every project she'd ever voiced.

On a cold winter day in March of 1922, the sheriff stopped by. By then, he and Nathan had come to respect one another, having gone hunting, playing checkers several times, and talking about everything from science to good literature.

The sheriff found him behind the house, knee-deep in muck, in a lean-to that provided shade for the goats.

"Those scars baffle me," the sheriff said, resting his elbows on the chest-high stall divider. "I know you don't want to talk about 'em. Maybe it was self-defense. Maybe not. I know what caused mine and it was always tied to trouble." He paused. "But, I've seen you have a way with people. I've seen no malice, no deceit toward anyone. You're controlled. Observant. Honest. A straight shooter. That's commendable."

What was the sheriff's point? Nathan shoved his fork into a pile of manure and heaved it into the waiting wagon, then shoved again, with a smooth economy of motion born of years of hard work.

"I'm not honest because it's commendable," he said, without breaking his shove-and-heave rhythm. "I'm honest because lies hurt more. Especially to the person who tells them. So, really, it's selfish that I'm being honest."

The sheriff was quiet a moment. "Son, how do you tackle trouble?"

Nathan stopped and stared at the sheriff, but saw no hint to the sheriff's train of thought. He shrugged and returned to shoving and heaving. "I try to solve today's problems before they become tomorrow's trouble."

That evening as Nathan sat on his rocker, a breeze freshened the air and he reflected on the exchange he'd had with the sheriff that afternoon. He'd had no idea it was a job interview.

He looked forward to reporting for his new job the next day.

Chapter Fifteen

1924

"WHAT IS THAT? Where did you get it?" The words escaped Nathan's lips before he could restrain himself, his voice little more than a startled rasp. He had been working on updating paperwork with the department's secretary, Jean, when his boss entered the small station carrying a three by four foot painting. Having caught sight of what the painting depicted, his breath caught. He abandoned the paperwork and skirted around his desk to secure a closer look.

The sheriff startled at Nathan's tone, but continued into the building, closed the door behind him and walked to his desk. Propping the painting against the wall, he turned back to Nathan, his brows drawing down in concern. "Son, you okay? You look like you've seen a ghost."

"That painting," Nathan said studying the faces of Anabelle and Richard Wallace. "Where did it come from?"

"Seen it before, have ya?"

Nathan took a calming breath and shrugged. He needed to hold his expression in check. Too much curiosity would raise too many questions. "Looks familiar. The woman, I mean. Not the painting."

"Ah." The sheriff looked satisfied with Nathan's answer. He removed his jacket and hat, hung them on the wooden wall pegs behind his desk, and folded his form into his squeaky chair.

Jean parked her files on a side table and moved closer. Her long gray hair was always rolled into a tight bun on the back of her head. From the corner of his eye, Nathan watched the mass of hair tilt left and right as she assessed the painting. "Looks just like Gretchen Hudd," she said.

"That's the family," the sheriff said.

Jean folded her arms. "She was in my daughter's school. Dropped out in fourth grade. Always sporting a cut or a bruise. Word is, her daddy is a mean ol' son of a gun."

"Yep." The sheriff nodded. "I'm told the painting is more than a hundred-fifty years old, so the couple in it are long dead. And, that her," he pointed at the woman in the painting, "great, great, great something-or-other granddaughter— Gretchen, did you say?—bears a striking resemblance to her. They live out near Mann's Choice."

Nathan recognized the small borough as a few miles outside of Bedford, across Buffalo Mountain. A rural area full of hills and valleys where most folks tried to eke out a pitiful living farming unproductive land.

The sheriff continued. "That painting is the center of another squabble at the Hudds. You remember us talking about 'em? Hudd's a drunk. Can't hold a job. Takes it out on the family."

"Why do you have it?" Nathan asked.

"Seems Hudd hawked it without telling the missus. Instead of buying food or lumber to fix up that mess they call a home, he bought hootch. He's even too lazy to bootleg his own. Mrs. Hudd helped herself to money she found hidden in the barn and bought it back. When Hudd found out she took the money, he beat her to a pulp. He's spending the night in jail, next county over." The sheriff exhaled, closed his eyes, and pinched the bridge of his nose. "She's still in Doc Henshaw's office right now. But, he'll be giving her a ride home later. She refuses to stay longer or press charges."

Questions swirled in Nathan's mind, but he couldn't take his eyes off the painting. "If they need food, why would she spend money to get the painting back?"

The sheriff huffed a short syllable of disgust. "She's pretty banged up, so she didn't make much sense. I gathered from what she said she thinks it's worth a lot more than what Hudd got for it. Said she wanted it back so she can sell it at a better price. To buy food, and coal for the winter."

Nathan swallowed against a rising nausea. The emotion he heard in the sheriff's voice, the crack that had appeared in his usually cast-iron demeanor, suggested the situation was both tragic and destined for a catastrophic ending.

Nathan's hands fisted and his pulse raced at old man Hudd's brutality and selfishness to his family, to Anabelle's descendant.

The sheriff continued. "Guess I'll have to return it later today. If she won't press charges, there isn't much I can do."

Nathan spoke in a low voice. "Why don't she and Gretchen leave?"

Jean smirked. "And go where? Things are tough for women, ya know. We may have gotten the right to vote a few years ago, but you'd never know it in this little hick town. It's still a man's world." Jean had worked for the department two years now, having started at age forty-five when her husband died and she learned about gender inequality when it came to property and getting things done.

The sheriff shot her a look. "It certainly seems to have given women the right to speak freely."

She huffed a sound, signaling that she got the message but didn't agree. With a frown she returned to her paperwork, mumbling, "Just having my say."

"I'll take it back," Nathan said in a rush, tearing his gaze from Jean's departing form, to the painting, to his boss.

The sheriff looked surprised at Nathan's offer. Or was it from the panic in his voice? Nathan couldn't tell which, but he watched the sheriff's gaze move from his face to his fisted hands and back again.

The sheriff continued staring at him for a long moment, then brushed a hand down his cheek and across his lips. "I don't know if that's such a good idea, son." He paused as though choosing his words carefully. "Are you involved with that family in some way?"

"What? No." *Not anymore.* Nathan repeated his denial in a calmer voice, planting his hands in his pockets and standing firm. "I want to help. That's all."

In a slow, careful delivery the sheriff said, "You know, in these situations, it's worse for the women when we get involved. Mrs. Hudd could leave but she doesn't. We've told her in private that when she wants to leave, we'll help. She has a way out, she just chooses not to use it."

From her desk, Jean issued a derisive chuckle and muttered, "There's only one way out for women in that situation. From what I hear about Gretchen, she'd leave with any man that offered to take her away from this life."

"Jean." The sheriff said her name in the same way he might say, *Behave.*

Jean stood. "I'll just take these files to the back."

As she left the room, the sheriff looked at his watch. "N.C. is out sick, and I have to be at the courthouse this afternoon." He scratched his chin. "Alright, you take the painting back, but that's all you do."

Nathan nodded.

"Nothing else. But, while you're there, look around. It might come in handy one day to know the lay of the land out there. Jasper Hudd is a mean, sorry excuse of a man. His wife Sarah is wife number two. The first one, Gretchen's momma, left, or just disappeared. No one knows for sure." He turned to look at Nathan and tilted his head as though for emphasis. "Now, don't it seem odd that a woman would leave and not take her child?"

"Are you saying…she never left? That he …"

"I'm saying it makes me wonder, is all." The sheriff scratched the back of his neck as he continued. "The first time we intervened on Nora's behalf, he cracked her shoulder bone after I left, and my dog was found dead. The next time we stepped in, I learned he hit her in the face with a skillet that night, and we found the windscreen on the police motorcar shattered."

Nathan squelched a shudder. The thought of Anabelle's descendant living in that situation repulsed him. "We have to do something. Convince them to leave."

"Son, I'm telling you, you'll make it worse for the wife and the daughter." An unmistakable hint of warning crept into his voice. "There's nothing you can do if she doesn't want to press charges, and they never do. Her best bet is to high-tail it outta there. As for my dog and the windshield, I can't prove anything. But I'm sure he did it. Both times. If it makes you feel any better, I'm chomping at the bit to catch Hudd in the act."

A FEW HOURS later, Nathan steered the police motorcar down dirt backroads, his eyes darting from the road to the painting perched to his right on the bench seat. Riding horses was more direct, but he would have had a hard time carrying the picture on the horse. Besides, driving these metal contraptions was quite fun, and usually a thrill electrified him when he pressed the pedal on the floor and watched the world soar by. Today, however, his thoughts were obsessed with the task ahead. He determined to deliver the painting to Mrs. Hudd and Gretchen, then leave. Their lives had to happen without his intrusion. He couldn't interfere with history, regardless of who was involved.

As he bounced along, he watched fists of clouds move swiftly, as though scurrying away from the warm front that moved in overnight. Too bad Mrs. Hudd and Gretchen couldn't get away from Hudd's fists as easily.

He wasn't sure how many miles he'd traveled before calming his anxiety and securing a sensible train of thought. But, it wasn't long before he reached the outskirts of Mann's Choice. He shifted gears and eased back on the gas, and slowed the car to a crawl. The motorcar rolled along smoothly until Nathan spotted the ramshackle farm Jean had described. He pulled off the road and stopped altogether, just opposite a creek that ran under a weathered wooden bridge, and perpendicular to the

Hudd's gravel lane. Halfway down the lane two handmade signs hammered to trees read, "Keep Out," and "Go Away."

Nathan stared at some lazy cows munching grass, astonished at how shabby, and yet peaceful, the property appeared to be. One of the cows lifted its head and continued chewing its cud as it stared at Nathan until he pressed gas into the engine and inched across the old bridge.

He stopped the car and set the handbrake. The engine fell silent. He waited several minutes, hoping someone would come out of the house or barn. When no one did, he grabbed the painting and headed to the door. The house was worse than Ista's version of a shanty—cracked windows, gaping holes in the roof, garbage strewn about the porch, upholstery stuffing in the weedy side yard.

After knocking and waiting...and knocking again...the door opened and Nathan looked at a ghost. A barefoot young woman wrapped in a ratty dress and shawl stood in the doorframe. Her face suggested she was about seventeen or eighteen, and her disheveled hair fell below her shoulders.

The sheriff was right. Other than this girl's dirty, rumpled appearance, the resemblance to Anabelle was remarkable. Memories stirred, brief and fluttering. Anabelle's hand reaching over to touch his arm as he steered the carriage home from a church social one lazy Sunday afternoon, the smell of honeysuckle by the creek where they once shared a picnic, Anabelle's laughter when they tried to catch a butterfly.

Gretchen shielded her eyes from the sun as she looked up at him. She was so thin she looked like a stiff breeze would blow her away to a place where no one would ever find her.

Her gaze moved from the badge on his chest to his face.

"My pa ain't here."

That voice! Recollection stirred again. Nathan swallowed. "I, ah…for your mom. I'm just returning this." He placed the painting against the doorframe. "For your mom," he said, as if that fact bore repeating.

She glanced at the painting a moment, before looking back at him. She shifted her shoulders. Tilted her head. "You gotta wife, handsome?" Her voice had turned sultry, suggestive. She grinned and dropped her head to stare at him from the edges of her eyes. She reached out to place her palm on his chest.

Nathan's mouth fell open. Her voice, her features, so much like Anabelle. He was mesmerized by her looks, but puzzled by her instant change in behavior, her forwardness and flirtatiousness. She had…what was the word people used now? *Moxie.* She had moxie.

He should leave. Quickly. But her touch…

"I need to get back to town," Nathan mumbled and he turned to head back to his car.

"Please!"

Her inflection changed again, this time to a desperate whisper. Startled, Nathan whirled back to look at her.

Her eyes were misted, her voice frayed and scored with weariness. She darted her gaze to look around and behind him. "Please take me with ya." Her voice harbored a desperation, a fragility.

Stunned by this erratic duality in her manner, Nathan blinked. "I…I can't do that."

Gretchen pouted and shut the door in his face.

Once at his motorcar, he felt a chill travel down his spine. He hadn't touched her back, but he had wanted to.

FOR THE NEXT several weeks, Nathan watched for Gretchen in town. Twice he spotted her and engaged her in conversation. He always made sure she was alone, but her gaze often darted from his face to scan the streets, the buildings, the sidewalk in all directions.

Why was he obsessed with this girl? He hadn't loved Anabelle. Not really. Not like he'd loved *her,* the woman he'd lost. He wished he could remember what *she* looked like. Why would that part of his memory not cooperate?

He shrugged off the frustration. It didn't matter. He had once been prepared to pledge his life to Anabelle. Did he feel bad that her life had ended at such a young age? Guilt that he hadn't cared enough to fight for her to take her away from Richard Wallace? Or, was this just his way of grasping onto the life he once had?

Always he concluded that, despite everything, he felt responsible to ensure this young woman Gretchen survived her wretch of a father. No, he shouldn't interfere with the way history would have naturally unfolded in Gretchen's life, but then again, he'd left the past, and perhaps if he'd stayed, Anabelle's life might have been different as well.

After a month went by in which he hadn't seen her in town, he grew concerned. But to keep it official, and to ward off any impression that his behavior bordered on stalking, he told the sheriff he planned to "drive by" the Hudd property, just to "see that all was well."

The sheriff studied him. "Alright." He swiped his cheek again. "Maybe that is a good idea. To look. But, that's all. And come right back because we have that town meeting tonight."

Nathan agreed because he planned to do just that—*look*.

But, plans change.

As with his first trip, he pulled the motorcar to the side of the road and studied the farm, wishing—*and hating himself for it*—that Gretchen would make an appearance. But, like his first trip there, the place was quiet. Serene.

He pushed open his door, climbed out, and scrambled down the side of the creek bank to kneel at the edge of the stream. With cupped hands, he drank from the gurgling water, never taking his eyes off the farm. *Confound it, why was he doing this?* He removed his cap and wiped his forehead with the back of his hand. *He was being ridiculous.* Time to stop this mania, this need he had to see her. He didn't want to be *involved* in her life. He just wanted to ensure she *had* a life. He slapped his cap against his pants, sending road dust into the air, and returned to the motorcar.

He was about to pull away when the peacefulness shattered. A woman darted out of the house, followed by a large, beefy man who grabbed her arm. She slapped him across the face, and he shoved her to the ground. The strong arc of the man's shoulders reminded him of a grizzly pouncing at its prey. Gretchen followed behind them, trying to pull the man off the woman. The man turned and punched her in the face. The older woman half stood and skirted around the man to get to Gretchen, pulling her into an embrace. Together they staggered back into the house. The man followed.

Nathan scrambled from the motorcar, but stopped, remembering the sheriff's orders. He closed his eyes as his hands fisted and his pulse raced, energy coursing through him. *To interfere would make it worse for the women.* He resolved what to do: honk the motorcar's horn to interrupt them, then be available if Mrs. Hudd needed transport to Doc Henshaw's.

As he deliberated, a gunshot rang out.

Fear ripped through him. It had come from the barn. *They must have gone there when his eyes were closed!* The sheriff's warning concerned him, but his past tethered and pulled him. He raced down the lane. When he neared the buildings, he noticed a door hanging open to the barn. As if his feet surmised the situation before his brain, he steered toward it, then stopped, looking at the entry, and bracing for what he might find inside.

A twinge of alarm settled on him as he entered the unlit structure. Once inside, he hesitated to let his eyes acclimate to the dim lighting, its only source the sun streaking through the slats of wood. He stepped past a small equipment room, rounded a calf pen, and peered into the stable area. The place was empty of livestock, but he smelled the odor of dried manure.

And fresh death.

He hadn't realized it possible to smell the past, and he broke into a sweat as thoughts of his previous life streaked through his mind. All those murdered settlers he'd found *after* they were dead.

He moved slowly and stealthily, listening, looking, and sensing before each step.

Another step. Slow and cautious.

And another.

Then he saw it, a streak of blood puddling on the wooden floor, on the other side of a stack of hay. He swallowed hard and stepped around the bales. Mrs. Hudd lay there, unmoving, eyes open. Blood trickled from a bullet hole in her chest. Dead. He continued around the pile of hay, past the woman and, about three yards from her, saw a pistol on the ground.

He heard Hudd sobbing before he saw him. Sitting on the manure-laden floor, Hudd's body shook in fits as he wrung his hands together, mumbling, "Pushed me too far. Just pushed me too far." His words, his tone, his delivery, his slurred speech, all blended together such that Nathan had a hard time understanding him.

Nathan inched toward the gun, never once taking his eyes off the man on the ground. Hudd looked up and spotted him, then dropped his gaze to the pistol, before darting it back to Nathan. Hudd sported a gash over his left eye, and bloody scratches on his neck. He reeked of body odor and alcohol.

"Go ahead. Do it," Hudd snarled, a commanding tone in his voice. "You all hate me anyway. Just do it."

Nathan stood for a moment, observing Hudd. His earlier anxiety had slackened, and he wondered if he would, if he ever *could* take a life outside of war or self-defense. His curiosity warred with his inexplicable certainty that this man should be removed from the earth, that he without a doubt would forever hurt and terrorize his daughter. Anabelle's descendant was still young, still at this man's mercy. And now there was no Mrs. Hudd to protect her. A jury might believe that she had provoked her husband, or that he had shot in self-defense. Nathan should shoot this man and end Gretchen's misery of what would surely be a life of fist-poked walls, battered doors, bruised skin, and broken bones.

Hudd saw Nathan's hesitation. He sneered and ran a shaking, blood-stained hand over his face. "You haven't got the guts to shoot me."

"Maybe." He matched Hood's hard tone. "Or maybe I haven't got the guts to let you live."

Hudd didn't say a word.

Nathan swallowed, reached down and picked up the pistol. When he felt its cold smoothness, memories surfaced of the settlers' fears against the Indians and the British. Thoughts swirled in the recesses of his mind of Gretchen living in terror. He imagined her desperately clinging to hope, struggling to find safety in her own home, but living on edge hour by hour, moment by moment, waiting for the next blow to fall, the next fist to mar her skin.

When his visions cleared, he determined his next move, and realized with a start, it would forever change lives. But, he determined it was the right thing to do.

The *only* thing to do.

He emptied the pistol of all but one bullet.

Moments later, another shot sounded from the barn that afternoon, and Nathan exited, staggered a few yards, dropped to his knees, and wretched.

By that evening, the deaths of Mr. and Mrs. Hudd were labeled a murder-suicide. Gretchen was taken to Doc Henshaw's for a broken arm, split lip, and internal bruises.

After the bodies were removed from the property, the sheriff snapped his notebook shut, slapped Nathan on the back, and said he'd missed the meeting, but if he hurried he could be home in time for dinner with his wife.

"Pot roast," he said as they ambled to his motorcar. "My favorite." He tucked into the seat and, before closing the door, said, "This," he gestured toward the farm, "is best left where it happened. Tomorrow, be at the office a half-hour before anyone else arrives. We need to discuss the choices you made here today." He nodded and pulled away.

Within two days a man from the bank placed a *For Sale* sign on the edge of the farm proper, and it struck Nathan that the property began to smile with hope, as though heedless of the events it had hosted there.

After three days, the community forgot about Jasper Hudd, and any questions about his death were wafted away by colossal sighs of relief. The town seemed to agree, without a word being spoken, that there was nothing to be gained from splashing the details across the newspaper or wasting tax dollars on an investigation. The curtain had dropped, the story had ended.

In the immediate aftermath, Nathan tried to return to the rhythm of the life he'd had, but in that odd manner that life moves on and circumstances seem to fit together the way notes work together in a symphony, and one chapter closes as another begins, he received a new assignment that convinced him that what he'd done had been right and that to have taken any other action would have been wrong.

Still, guilt consumed him. Gretchen, Anabelle's descendant, had merely progressed from one life of insecurity to another. She had no family now. Despite whatever relationship she'd had with her step-mother, the news of her death appeared to have devastated her: her walk, her posture, the blank expression on her face when he'd escorted her from the Hudd house—all signaled the tenacious denial of the violently bereaved.

About a week later, Nathan sat alone on his porch one evening, wrestling with remorse and looking out past the lawn and the grove of trees beyond, when a flock of honking geese hurried into a V formation to glide across the sky. He marveled, as he always had, how geese pull together to get where they're going. *They survive by helping each other*, his father had once said.

The next morning he drove to Doc Henshaw's house where Gretchen had been staying until other arrangements could be made. Problem is, no one was coming forth with any arrangements.

When she asked him what he wanted, Nathan shrugged, as though bracing his shoulders to bear more weight, and spoke his piece.

They were married that afternoon.

The next day he waited for his restlessness to subside and relief to come, but it never did.

Chapter Sixteen

1926

"THANK YOU, DAVIS," Libby said.

The shoes pinched her feet, the dress was too short, and the cloche hat too tight, but Libby felt dressed appropriately enough in her period costume to carry off a debut in what she accepted would be a lifetime masquerade ball. Her new reality. She needed to absorb and conform in every way to 1926. The more she made herself a part of this time the less she'd fumble or stand out.

The dress was made of teal silk charmeuse, and its lines, as Davis had warned, were column-like. It hung straight from the square neck and shoulders, and gathered low on the hips rather than at the waist. Box pleating completed the lower third. The cloche hat was almond colored, rimmed with pleated teal ribbon and covered her forehead and ears, allowing wisps of auburn hair to frame her cheeks. The shoes were a T-bar heel pump of almond patent leather, and added another inch and a half to her height. Gloves, a small purse, and silk stockings completed the outfit. When he'd handed her the clothes, he said he told the saleswoman to toss in several undergarments, but that when he saw her reaching for a corset, he intervened and directed her instead to the latest fashion—a French brassiere. With a mumble and a lowered gaze, Libby had thanked him sincerely for intervening.

Davis also brought from town a pearl-encrusted hand mirror. Libby perched it on one of the duffel bags, stood back, and circled in attempt to catch as full a view as possible. Impossible. The light in the cave was dim. Still, she could see enough to know that in her own time, she would have been assumed to be dressing for the 1920s. She hoped the people who were an actual part of this period would agree.

Libby caught Davis watching her, his smile affirming he liked the change. He'd waited outside the cave while she changed and re-entered only when beckoned. Then, he'd waited patiently, seated on his usual cave rock, while she practiced walking in the stiff, uncomfortable shoes.

"Perfect," he said. "And, no tattoos to explain. That's good. Your only problem will be keeping the young blokes at bay." His words suggested he was teasing, but his voice held no humor, and the delivery, along with the inflection, carried both praise and wistfulness.

Libby shrugged. "These styles don't suit me very well."

"That's because you have a good figure. Curves. Nice gams. Trust me, these styles make women happy, but not men."

Her cheeks heated, and she suddenly felt as if she wasn't getting enough air. *He was smooth.* She ducked her head, unable to hold his gaze. She had the strangest urge to pat herself to make sure every stitch and every hair was in order under his scrutiny. Where was this ridiculous girlish reaction coming from? He was, after all, nothing more than a kindred spirit—someone who also had reinvented himself. But, would she ever experience that warmth again, after she relocated at the Springs Hotel amidst people from another time?

"Oh!" He turned and grabbed another muslin bag he'd brought back from town. "I thought you might want these. For your alone time."

She opened the bag to find a pair of jeans, two large work shirts, and a pair of felt slippers with leather soles.

The pants were ugly, stiff (no spandex!), and made for a man, but resembled modern jeans enough that she smiled. "Thank you, but why are they for alone time?"

He forced a weak smile. "You'll learn soon enough. People generally dress quite well compared to modern standards. Women mostly wear dresses. Perhaps knickers when they golf or ride horses. The exception would be the rare professional woman in the upper middle class who has become a doctor or attorney. That sort. Sometimes you'll see poorer women on farms in men's pants. But it's rare."

"So I will wear this dress every day?" Libby asked, confused.

He chuckled. "No, you're going to be among the affluent, remember? You'll need more clothes. Once you're situated at the hotel, I'll have the manager arrange for a local seamstress. She can provide you tailor-made clothing. In the interim, there's nothing surprising about repeating clothes for a few days. Even among the rich. Society hasn't yet adopted that modern American obsession with wearing something different every day."

Her stomach clenched. "You talk about money like it's no problem, but I have none."

He was still wearing the tweed jacket he'd donned for town. He reached into it and pulled a small envelope from his left lapel pocket. "You do now."

Inside, Libby found layers of paper money. Even money

was different, from the future. This paper currency featured different pictures and was at least 40 percent larger than modern bills.

"Five hundred dollars," he said. "Accounting for inflation, that would convert to about six-thousand dollars in 2008, the year I traveled back. Probably closer to seven-thousand in 2016."

"I can't accept this," Libby whispered, closing her fingers around the money and handing it back.

"You have to. You have no choice. Besides, it's a loan." He leaned in, parking his forearms on the V of his legs. "That will be more than enough to invest and pay expenses till winter. Room and board. New clothes. A cinema now and then. After that, we'll see how your investments are doing."

Libby slumped onto a stuffed duffel bag opposite him, probably looking anything but a well-bred lady. "My investments?"

"When I get back to Pittsburgh, I'll talk to my broker. Thomas St. Clair. He frequents the Springs. I'll have him ask for you. You can give him directives."

"Directives?" With shaky fingers, she pinched the folds of her skirt.

"How he should invest your money, of course."

"I don't know anything about stocks."

He tilted his head. "Yes, you do. More than anyone from this time. You have foreknowledge, remember?"

"Which you told me to be careful about using."

He brushed that off with a wave. "This is the one time you should capitalize on it. In this period...like every time in history, I imagine... money equals better health and living. You already have to get by without modern medicine, central heat and air." He broke with a smile to point at her feet, "Comfortable shoes...things you heretofore took for granted. If you had to struggle to make money in this time that is so unfamiliar to you, the limitations would be daunting. Acute. Get your finances secured first. Make that your work. You can branch out later."

Libby stared at him, dismayed. "But, investing couldn't be as simple or as certain as all that. Why wouldn't everyone do it?"

"People outside the hotel don't have the money to invest. Most have modest or insecure incomes at best. At the hotel? They don't know what to invest in. Ever heard of the radio?"

"Of course."

"How about a Jordan car, or the Heany Lamp Company, or Kirk's Jap Rose soap?"

Libby shook her head.

"See? You have foreknowledge of what will last. Radio is a good investment. The others are not. These people," he gestured toward the outside of the cave, "don't have awareness of what is going to happen. I can't tell them, and you mustn't either. Be careful what you share about the future. People will think you're odd. You'll be considered aberrant, perhaps deviant. Remember, this is still the age when female hysteria is considered real, and a viable reason to institutionalize a woman."

Libby gasped. "An insane asylum?"

His smile broadened. "Now you know why my wife loves me. She knows I have a more opened-minded view and respect for women."

Before she realized what she was saying, Libby murmured, "There are dozens of reasons to love you." *Where had that come from?* She bit her lip, regretting her words. He had rescued her. That's all. People brought together in crisis situations tended to form unusually tight—and generally short-lived—bonds. She'd learned that at the bureau.

He stood, acting nonplused. "Tell you what, while you change into those jeans, I'll build a fire. We'll dine under the stars tonight." He winked. "Spend the evening in a crash course on the Roaring Twenties."

LIBBY AND DAVIS ate slowly, sitting on duffel bags by the fire, savoring the food and the quiet dusk creeping over the mountainside around them. Davis had cooked sausage and potatoes, brought from town, and supplemented it with cheese, and a wine he said was from his own homemade brew. Libby's head was so aswarm with questions, she didn't know where to start, nor how to change the topic from the food to what waited her on the morrow. He solved the dilemma.

As he poured more wine into her metal cup, he said, "Your accent. Is it from your time overseas?"

"I can shake it if I concentrate. Do you think it will be a problem?"

He waved her words away as a non-concern. "We'll use it to your advantage. Most people will assume you've been in Europe. In that case, you couldn't be expected to know all the nuances of American life. That will help explain any missteps."

He set his empty plate on the ground and poured himself

more wine. "Fortunately, the Red Scare that gripped the country after World War I is mostly a thing of the past. Still, be aware of lingering immigrant concern. Emphasize, when you get the chance, that your parents are American."

"I'll be careful," Libby said, savoring the wine and his advice with equal fervor.

"Is it safe to assume you've studied American history?"

She nodded. "Aunt Isabel was adamant I study hard. History, geography, politics."

"Then you may remember this is an age of inventions …" He grinned as though just thinking of something humorous. "…although, ironically, sliced bread, the invention by which all other inventions are measured in the future, doesn't arrive until a couple years from now. But, other inventions abound, along with art, flamboyance, excess, satire. It's the jazz age. Expect to hear that music everywhere. Vaudeville is big, as are silent films. Next year, 1927, the first part-talkie motion picture is released."

"The Jazz Singer."

"Very good. But remember, you don't know that yet. Let's see," he said, strumming his fingers on his right thigh. "Calvin Coolidge is president. Boxing, the biggest sport. Gene Tunney captures the world heavyweight championship from Jack Dempsey later this year. Babe Ruth is an American sports hero, too, although his Yankees lose the Series this year to the St. Louis Cardinals, so you don't know that yet either. The 20th Tour de France, takes place this summer. It is the longest one in history, by the way, and—"

"The Tour de France? You have a good memory. How is it that you recall that event?"

"Ahhh, well, I love wheels and speed. Cars, motorcycles,

even bicycles. The route for this tour traces closely the borders of France. It is the first time the tour starts outside Paris. A Belgian cyclist Lucien Buysse wins." He shook himself, as though trying to remove the historic spreadsheet from his mind. "Where was I? Ah, yes, some current events. Mount Rushmore National Monument recently opened, and last year was the trial of Thomas Scopes."

Libby shot him a puzzled look.

"Taught evolution rather than creationism."

"Ahh." She nodded, satisfied. "Tennessee, right?"

"Correct. Clarence Darrow defended Scopes and therefore Charles Darwin's scientific theory of evolution. Let's see, other things you may hear in parlor talk…Sinclair Lewis and F. Scott Fitzgerald are publishing. Henri Matisse and Pablo Picasso have a following in the art world."

She closed her eyes, trying to absorb it all.

Davis continued his tutelage. "As for Hollywood, Douglas Fairbanks, Charlie Chaplin, Rudolph Valentino, Gloria Swanson, Greta Garbo, all film favorites. 'Course, Valentino dies in two months, but again, you don't know that yet. Charles Lindbergh is still carrying the mail at this point, but next year he'll do his famous solo flight from New York to Paris. But you—"

"—don't know that yet," Libby interrupted with a smile, meeting his gaze.

Davis offered a conciliatory grin. "That's right."

Libby's mind swirled with what she remembered of the Twenties, what she needed to learn, and awareness that could trip her up. She had so many questions and so few assurances. She felt like an archaeologist excavating at a dig, so enamored at the excitement of what she might find, that she forgot to secure her basic necessities.

"Am I overwhelming you?"

She looked up to see his brows furrowed. "A little. I'm grateful for this information, but right now I'm more concerned about how I'll survive, day to day."

"Of course. You can learn current events from the newspaper, can't you? Okay, let's discuss money. Always a necessity." He shifted, as though almost embarrassed by his next words. "As a woman, you will have a hard time finding good, paying work. Even if you secured something professional…say, teaching, or government work…or even interpreting if you moved to a larger city, you'll find women are not compensated near what men are. You'll have a hard time securing a safe and comfortable standard of living. The FBI, of course, was reconstituted in 1924 under J. Edgar Hoover, but is not openly receptive to female recruits yet."

"Sounds dismal."

"Dismal, but not impossible. As I said earlier, we will need to secure your finances a different way. This is an era of booming stock market fortunes. Before the war, investors tended to choose preferred stocks which paid a steady return each year. But businesses and industries are exploding with growth now, so you'll want to zero in on common stock. They pay dividends which closely reflect a business' growth and profit."

"So radio is a good investment."

He nodded, then brushed a hand down his cheek and across his lips, a pensive look. "Automobiles are booming too, so think about what goes into them. Gas. Steel. Tires. Glass.

Rubber. All growing markets. I wish I could remember other examples from my economics classes in college the way I do radio. In 1929 radio stock splits five for one and hits a high of over a hundred dollars per share. That means that a share purchased at the beginning of the decade will be worth nearly four hundred times its original cost." He added, in a tone that ringed practicality rather than smugness, "I'll be a very wealthy man." His voice dropped and he gazed into the fire. "I'm rather lucky."

She smirked. "You call this lucky?" She hadn't meant to change the mood, to sound snarky.

He shrugged, returning her gaze. "It's up to you, isn't it? You can call it a loss and dwell on anger and blame. Or, you can look at it as an opportunity." His tone grew serious, almost challenging. "I guess it depends why you came here in the first place." He looked at her expectantly.

Libby grimaced, but said nothing, instead wondering why she suddenly felt confronted.

The silence lingered, made her uncomfortable. *What was he asking?*

Davis shook himself against the moment. "Anyway, don't rely on one stock. There are other good investments. You'll recognize the names. RCA, General Motors. General Electric. The latter for example, is currently overwhelmed with public demand for generators, motors, home appliances."

"So much to memorize."

"Just remember the rules for investing in this decade." He clicked them off on his fingers. "Buy low and sell high. Diversify so that no one mistake will sink you. And, take all your money out of the stock market, and even the bank, by August

1929. That's when prices reach their highest levels. There are a couple mini collapses in the market in 1928 and early 1929, but each time the market recovers and carries on. The disaster comes in October 1929."

"The Stock Market Crash."

They spent another half hour discussing stocks and the Depression that ushered in the 1930s. By then, darkness surrounded them, save the flickering light of the fire. The sizzle and crackle of the embers was disturbed only by a distant wolf howl that carried on a breeze in the clear night air. The sound wrapped around Libby like it too didn't want to be alone, and she would have grown melancholy if she hadn't leaned back and gazed at the sky. Though the waning moon was mostly round and beige like a Nilla wafer making her wonder if that snack food even existed yet, the constellations were all in their familiar places, and that gave her a sense of momentary peace. There were a billion stars! She felt like she was trapped inside some monstrous planetarium, as there was no artificial light anywhere thwarting their sparkle.

Davis spoke, and brought her back to the moment. "As for daily life, the hotel has been electrified. Around three-quarters of urban homes and businesses have been wired for electricity. In rural areas, it's less than ten percent. Many people still live lives illuminated by the sun."

Libby tried to concentrate on her training and other basic information she might need. "What about diseases?"

"Between the shots you received with the bureau and for the countries you visited, my guess is you're safe. Cholera, smallpox, and typhoid fever have almost disappeared. Tuberculosis isn't quite the concern it used to be. Syphilis is practically brought under control, too." He grimaced. "Unfortunately, you'll find most doctors and health facilities rather antiquated in their approach to medicine compared to what you're used to. Best bet is to stay as healthy as possible. And, that reminds me, be careful of alcohol."

"Because it's illegal."

He cocked his head. "Prohibition has been in effect for more than six years now, and it's proving to be a dismal failure. It's ridiculed as 'enfarcement' rather than enforcement. Prohibition speakeasies are not quite as clandestine as what we were taught in the future. Police have learned they can't stop the illegal activity, so they've mostly turned their attention to commercial bootleggers and outlaw saloons. You'll find that if you're not flagrant about it you'll be fine. Especially around here. The local sheriff seems to look the other way when it comes to hooch. Most folks hide it by drinking from teacups. If you do imbibe, your safest bet is brandy."

He continued, dispensing tips on what to expect and advice on how to approach situations, but her head was swimming. She came out of her fog to hear him ask if she had other questions.

"Yes," she said and it came out almost breathless. "What if you had not come to my rescue?"

Despite the dim firelight, Libby saw his eyes scrunch, puzzled. He studied her. When at last he spoke his tone hinted at both surprise and conviction. "You would have managed. You have spunk and brains and charm. You'll adapt."

"I think," Libby said in a low voice as if she didn't want to disturb the nightlife in the woods, "I would have found adapting to a new time as hard as reaching this new time, if it weren't for you." She swallowed her apprehension as she looked at her companion in dismay.

"Libby, out there," he nodded his head away from them and spoke in a gentle tone, the sound stroking her like a comforting caress, "they're not aliens. True, the wealthy live in a very small, sheltered, and self-contained world, but they're people, just like us."

She thought about that a moment. "But I'm not part of them. Not part of their world."

"You are part of their world. Just a different time in history. It's important that you interact. Otherwise, you'll feel detached. A permanent observer. Being born in a place doesn't make it home. Being born in a *time* doesn't make it home either."

"Do you ever wonder about this? How is it possible?"

"What do you mean?"

"Did we create an alternate timeline when we came here?" She massaged her temples with the fingers of one hand. "I once saw this sci-fi flick about people making poor decisions. All those decisions split reality into more worlds. Did that happen to us?"

He inclined his head in thought but his gaze didn't leave the fire.

She continued. "Are we being punished? And how many other timeframes are happening at the same time as our old time? If I could live long enough, will I meet my infant self?"

"I don't think we'll ever know that answer," he said, splaying his hands. He leaned in and parked his elbows on his thighs. "In the twenty-first century, we prided ourselves on the control we had over our world, but the truth is what we don't know is vastly greater than what we do. Much of the universe is still a mystery." He wrinkled his forehead in thought. "Albert Einstein said time has no independent existence apart from the order of events by which we measure it." His lips twisted into a sheepish grin. "But I don't think he's even written those words yet." He leaned back and chuckled.

Libby stared at him a moment, then snorted a chuckle too. As though a dam had been opened, they laughed together, loud and full, unfettered by concern about the morrow. It had been a long time since she laughed this easily and comfortably, and especially with like-minded understanding.

He attempted seriousness again. "The Book of Isaiah says to forget the former things. Not to dwell on the past. Maybe we should just practice that."

The thought served only to tickle her more and she smirked. "That makes it even more complicated because our past is the future."

He laughed renewed and the sound of it warmed her.

Silence fell once more, and she studied Davis as flickers of firelight caused shadows to dance on his face. "Why do you do this? Why did you help me?"

He went still. His smile faded and he shrugged. "I admit it's a little bit curiosity, but mostly I want to make anyone else's transition a bit easier. Now, come on." He stood, stretched, and looked around. "Let's put out the fire and get some sleep." He reached out his hand to help her up.

With a faint nod of resolution, Libby took a final sip of wine and took his hand. Once she was on her feet, he let go and the loss of the physical contact left her feeling momentarily bereft, reminding her that soon she would have to proceed alone.

As she waited for sleep to come that night, her mind drifted away from Davis and Andrew, through the woods and down the road to the Springs Hotel, no inkling what the morrow might bring, but determined to meet it.

Chapter Seventeen

1926

A T SUNRISE DAVIS and Libby finished the last of the food— eggs, stale biscuits, cheese, apples, coffee—before extinguishing the fire and packing his gear. They hauled the duffel bags, bedrolls and supplies down the slope of the wooded mountainside to what appeared to be a seldom-used dirt road. After several trips, they returned to the cave where they took turns changing.

This time as they descended the hill, she wore her new dress and shoes, so Davis held her arm as they maneuvered the steep trail.

When they reached the pile of belongings they'd left there, he eyed her footwear. "Why don't you wait here while I get the motorcar? It's just up the road a bit, tucked in a ravine. Be back in about ten, fifteen minutes."

She nodded and plopped down on a bag, steadying herself, and digging her fingernails into her palms, summoning courage for the day ahead. She breathed in the evergreens and assessed the sky. It was unblemished and a perfect picture-postcard shade of blue. The woods were quiet as the morning sun buttered the tips of the mountains off to the west and filtered through the woods. "*Komorebi*," she whispered. *Japanese, for the sunlight that comes through the leaves of the trees.*

"Somebody help!"

Libby stiffened.

The voice sounded again, louder this time, carrying on an otherwise hushed breeze.

The plea persisted. "Leave me alone!"

It was a woman's panicked voice, coming from the opposite direction Davis had departed.

Go, Libby.

She galvanized into action, and sprinted around the bend in the dirt road, moving as quickly as her clumsy shoes would allow. Up ahead, a young blond-headed female struggled with a lanky man. Judging by the way he swayed and wobbled on his feet, he was a rather inebriated man as well.

The girl swung from his grasp. "I don't care who you are. I know what you did to Dulcina."

The man guffawed, and slurred out: "That little tramp? She wanted it. And so do you—"

"Let go of me!" She held an embroidered bag about the size of a briefcase and tried to swat him with it, but the man ducked and grabbed for her, his elbow ramming into her cheek before he could maneuver and twist her to grasp her around the waist.

The girl cried out and touched her cheek, dropping her bag.

He grinned, as he endeavored to hold her tighter. "Spirited little thing. I do enjoy the struggle."

Libby ran faster. "Let go of her!"

The girl screamed at the same time, drowning out Libby's warning. Between spurts of laughter the man said, "Just a little fun. Don't be such a Puritan. No one needs to know," but in his slurred speech, it sounded more like, "Jez lil fun. Don bees setch eh per tan. Nah un needsa know."

By this time, he held the girl from behind, his arms wrapped around her front. His back was to Libby as she approached. She smelled the tell-tale signs of alcohol from several yards away. Davis was right that prohibition hadn't much suppressed consumption.

The cad had a young man's strength on his side, but Libby had the element of surprise and his inebriated condition on hers.

In the noise and the scuffle, the man showed no reaction to her arrival. The first he acknowledged her was when she pounded on his back with her palm, and in her most commanding voice said, "Excuse me. You need to let go of the lady."

Libby hoped her presence might stifle his ugly behavior and they'd all walk away, but she was wrong.

Startled, he let the girl go and whirled to see what had interrupted his fun, anger etching his face. "This is none of your damn business," he growled as his fist came toward her.

Libby whipped her left arm up across her body, her hand straight and stiff, and deflected his blow. She took advantage of his shock to swing her right palm up and simultaneously kick him in the knee. Unfortunately, he shifted at the same time and her palm hit his nose and lip, rather than the chin she targeted. The moves felt familiar. Rehearsed. Like she had done them before.

His grasp for his knee, coupled with a cry of pain, gave her a quirky feeling of satisfaction, which was quickly extinguished when she realized she'd split her new dress near its hem. He collapsed on the ground cradling his leg and cursing, his face deformed with pain, his lip cut open, and blood dripping from his nose onto his shirt.

"You little guttersnipe!" he snarled between groans. "You'll pay for this." His tone made it a threat.

The girl's hat and bag had fallen to the side, so Libby hurried to retrieve and hand them to her. Libby took her by the arm and pulled her a couple yards away from the creep on the ground. "You okay?" she asked, although it was clear the girl wasn't. Color had drained from her face, her stance was rigid, and her left sleeve was torn.

With eyes round as saucers, the girl hesitated, then nodded hurriedly. Libby would have assumed she was speechless due to shock if it hadn't been for the fact she was assessing Libby like she was an alien being.

"Come on," Libby said as she gripped the girl around the shoulders and led her back the path she had come. With no cell phone to call 9-1-1 or snap a picture of the drunken idiot, it was the only wise thing to do.

"But...but..." the girl sputtered, continuing with Libby, yet repeatedly looking back over her shoulder at the guy.

"He'll be fine," Libby assured her, never breaking her stride. "He'll be able to hobble in a short time." *How did she know he'd be fine? And for that matter, how had she known how to overpower him? The FBI training?*

"But miss. That's Mr. Martelli. He's a guest at the hotel. I might lose my job."

Libby stopped and in a scolding tone asked, "Is he your boyfriend? Did you do anything to encourage his attention?"

"No, miss, I would never do that! But—"

Libby began walking again and tugged the girl along. "I

don't care if he's the president of the United States," she growled, all the while wondering if people in this day referred to the country as that or as America. "He's not allowed to attack women."

Libby led the girl back to where she'd been sitting, pulled out another duffel bag, and gestured for her to sit. "Have a seat. Davis...my uncle Davis will be here shortly. We can give you a ride to wherever you're going. You alright now?"

The girl dutifully sat, donned her hat, and tucked her bag on her lap, clutching it in a tight hold with both hands. Her right cheek had turned red and Libby suspected it would be black and blue before nightfall.

All the while the girl's wide innocent eyes stared at Libby with fascination. Finally, she swallowed. "I ain't never seen anyone do that before. Least wise, not a woman," she stammered as if in awe.

Libby forced a smile and studied her. She was a couple inches shorter but several pounds heavier, and looked to be about eighteen or nineteen years old, older than Libby originally thought. Wisps of golden curly hair peaked out from beneath an adorable cloche hat, making her drab, thread-worn brown dress look all that much blander. Her hands were calloused and showed signs of hard work, and her shoes were scuffed with marks that suggested age rather than damage from the scene they'd just left.

Libby had an urge to tell her something prescient about self-protection and the wisdom of carrying a small handgun if she had to walk this desolate road, but squelched the impulse. Libby had to learn to subdue her inclinations to comment and to offer advice based on foreknowledge or her advanced training from the future, whatever it had involved. She had to behave as if she were exactly what Davis and she rehearsed. Most daunting, Libby had to start believing it herself. As for the double negative the girl had delivered with 'ain't never,' Libby let that go, too. All that mattered was that they understood one another.

"What's your name?"

"Rosella, Miss. Rosella Morgan. But people call me Rose."

"Well, Rose, it's just something I learned through the years." Libby hoped that would put her at ease, the suggestion that she had been in Rose's shoes before. Rose appeared to relax a bit, so Libby continued, hoping her next comment would further establish her as more of a *normal* woman of this period, whatever that was. Picking up the hem of her dress, Libby said, "Besides, it clearly wasn't my wisest decision, was it?"

Rose's eyes lit up. "I can fix that, miss." She fossicked through her bag and Libby caught sight of a cloth change purse, a rabbit's foot, a maid's cap and two garments, one black and the other made of a sheer white with lace edging. From the depths of her bag Rose retrieved a pair of steel scissors, a packet of needles and thread.

It was Libby's turn to look at her with fascination. "A regular Mary Poppins bag, eh?"

Rose drew her brows together. "I don't know her ma'am. Is she a good seamstress?"

Libby's shoulders dropped. Perhaps Mary Poppins hadn't even been written yet. She'd have to be more careful. Rose's hand reached for the hem of Libby's dress, but Libby stopped her. "You don't have to do that. Your own sleeve is torn—"

"I'll fix mine later. And, it's no trouble, miss. Besides, it's the least I can do to thank ya." She scooted closer. Turning the hem to its back side, she sewed quickly, producing short, even stiches that would have competed with those of modern day machines.

As if the movement of her hands had activated her speech, Rose rattled on making Libby wonder when she'd take a breath. "That man, he's a guest at the hotel where I work. The Springs Hotel. None of us like him. Always trying to get us girls alone, he is. He already attacked another maid, he did. Dulcina. She's a maid like me—"

"He *attacked* another girl? As in, raped?"

The girl grimaced but didn't miss a stitch.

"What did the police do?"

Rose shrugged, despite the sewing. "She didn't want them to know. Can't say I blame her. Might lose her job, she might. She needs the money real bad. Got no family. Some of the girls work there hoping to catch a rich husband. Kinda loose with their morals, if you know what I mean, miss. But not me and my friends, Lavinia and Dulcina. We wanna marry for love. Someday. Right now, we work cause we need the money."

For a moment Libby was ready to respond in anger on Dulcina's behalf. To express indignation and expound on how wrong this injustice was and that it must be corrected, but Rose continued babbling with anxious release.

"Me mum lives north o' here, 'bout twelve miles, she does," Rose said. "Too far to walk every day, so I stay in a boarding house in town and walk to work. The employees' dormitory here at the Springs was filled when I started working. Mostly I clean the rooms and make the beds, but I'm the one they call when guests' clothes need to be mended." She shrugged. "I don't mind because the extra money is nice. And, sometimes I pick up an order for a hat."

She took a breath, so Libby asked, "A hat?"

"Yes, miss. Maybe you noticed mine?" She pointed to her head, blushing at her own boldness.

Libby had noticed. She studied the hat closer. Made of white straw, it was cloche style, and sported a curled red ostrich feather anchored in place by a multi-colored ribbon. Libby stifled the urge to make a quip about how Hobby Lobby and a glue gun would have made her task easier. Instead, Libby marveled that the girl didn't have those at her disposal, so the craftsmanship of the hat was all the more impressive.

"It's lovely," Libby said and, remembering her cover story with Davis, added, "You'll have to show me others. I'll need some new hats since my luggage was lost at sea."

Rose blushed. "I'd like that, miss."

"Libby."

"Excuse me, miss?"

"Libby. My name is Libby."

Rose hesitated as though not sure what the point was. "Alright, Miss Libby."

"No, I meant that you can call me Libby. There's no need for the Miss." Again, remembering her new profile, Libby quelled a cringe and added, "Besides. I'm a widow now and—"

"A widow! You're so young, ma'am."

Libby ignored how quickly she'd gone from a Miss to a Ma'am, and focused instead on Rose's reference to her as young. It was rude to put her on the spot, but Libby had to know. "How old do I look?"

When Rose's eyebrows shot up and her face turned red,

Libby said, "It's just that I've been living overseas for years. Things are quite different there. I'm just wondering how I'll fit in…with people here, I mean."

Rose relaxed her features and responded, even as she kept sewing. "Twenty-three. Twenty-four, maybe. There you go." She flipped the finished hem over and sat back, a look of pride on her face.

"You're very talented," Libby said, admiring the work. "It's perfect."

The timing was too, because at that moment a huge vehicle approached from the direction Davis had walked. *A motorcar.* It was British green with a black roof, running boards on the side, and white-wall tires. As it approached, Libby hitched her breath as once again the realities of this period hit. It had been easy to dismiss the clothing since she could still don jeans in private. But this motorcar, was so antique, and so large…and so *real*.

Davis came to a stop, pulled the brake, left the car idle, and walked around to them, eyebrows hiked in curiosity.

Libby shot him a *here-we-go* look. "Uncle Davis, this is Rose Morgan. We met on the road and I hoped we could give her a ride. She's going to the hotel, too."

For a moment he hesitated. Libby suspected his thoughts mirrored hers: they would have no more opportunity to fine-tune their story before arriving at the hotel.

"Of course. Any friend of my niece," he said tipping his hat.

Rose curtsied. "Thank you, sir."

Davis opened the passenger door for them, as a gentleman should. He gestured. "Go ahead. Get in while I load these things."

"Rose," Libby motioned for the girl to precede her.

When Rose didn't move, Libby gazed at her expectantly.

"Don't know how, ma'am. I'm all at sea with one of these," Rose whispered, her gaze glued to the metal beast in front of her. "Never rode in one before. Me mum's cousin John has a small truck, but I only ever rode on the back of it."

Libby hid her surprise. "No worries. Uncle Davis isn't looking so just do your best." With hopes that vehicles operated somewhat universally through the years, Libby demonstrated and Rose stepped onto the running board, grasping tightly to the edge of the door, then the rear bench seat before hoisting herself in, dropping with relief. She looked at Libby, a blush on her face. "Must take practice to do that like a lady," she mumbled.

In no time Davis loaded the gear and they were off. He said the motorcar was a 1924 Oldsmobile, and they were, at this moment, driving parallel to Shobers Run creek which was a spring-fed, prized trout stream, directly over the hill from the Springs Hotel. However, due to the steep hills, switch-backs, and condition of the roads, their drive would involve a distance of a couple miles. The area was made up of hills and mountains filled with crevices, dips, gullies, deep valleys and soaring peaks.

As they crawled and bounced their way down the road, Libby refrained from making a quip about the lack of shock absorbers or the atrocious mileage that vehicles must get in this period. Rose wouldn't understand the remarks anyway. Instead, she turned to look back at the girl, sitting frozen in place, wide eyes glaring straight ahead, fingers clinching her bag in a white-knuckle grip. To refocus Rose's concern, Libby asked, "Do all the maids curtsey to the guests?"

Davis moved his hand over surreptitiously and pressed on Libby's forearm, no doubt a gentle reminder of his advice the night before to learn by observation, not by asking questions. But if he thought she was inquiring about the differences between the social classes, that wasn't her intent. She simply wanted to understand the culture at this time.

"Oh no, ma'am. I'm from Wales, I am. Came here when I was seven. Me parents were in service to a British family. When they hit hard times, me folks was let go. So me father spent all his money to buy us passage to come to the Land of Opportunity."

"How nice. You have a large family?" Libby asked.

"No it's just me mum and me now. Me father couldn't get us all passage on the same ship, so we had to split up. He and me three brothers came a few days before us. We followed later on another ship. Ma and I were already out to sea and on our way by the time we learned that their ship, the Titanic, had gone down."

Davis and Libby exchanged startled glances, murmured condolences.

From the back, the girl continued. "Me family was in steerage. We reckon they never even made it to the lifeboats. Me mum's distant cousin let us move in with his family here in Pennsylvania. Mary Pearl he says—that's me mum's name—we're family and family sticks together. Anyways, Ma taught me service manners in the British way."

Libby didn't know what to offer back. To say, 'I saw the movie; it was heart-wrenching,' wouldn't make sense to Rose. "It was nice of your cousin to let you move in. That must make it crowded."

"Oh no, ma'am. Me mum and I share a room in the back. The ten of them sleep in the rest of the house."

"Ten!"

"Yes, ma'am. Me mum's cousin, John, his wife Emma, and their eight children."

"Must get a little crazy there at times," Libby said.

"Not really. It's a farm, so there's plenty o' places to get away from one another."

Davis followed the dirt pathway about a half-mile before pulling onto a road that looked as though it had some sort of manmade topping on it. Next came a bend, cut through the hills that struck Libby as familiar. Her thoughts switched from counting the limitations of the interior of the car—no radio, air conditioning, cup holder or GPS—and dwelled instead on the thought that this was the road that she and Andrew must have traveled recently. If *recently* could be considered more than a hundred years in the future.

They passed a wide building on the left called the Arandale Hotel and Libby's heart raced. She recognized it as the Bedford Elks Country Club that she and Andrew had passed.

After two more twists around rolling hills, a building came into view. No one needed to tell Libby it was the Springs Hotel. Its size and opulence alone tagged it as their destination, set as it was, apart from the local town and surrounded by immaculate lawns, flower gardens and paths, tennis courts, a golf course and club house, and rows of motorcars. The massive brick and wood structure, reminiscent of Greek Revival style architecture, was fronted with white columns, and looked to be four stories tall, stretching on forever against the curve of the hill behind it. A long two-story walkway—she would later learn it was referred to as the colonnade—led from the hotel to an elevated walking bridge over Shobers Run that crossed the road and ushered pedestrians down steps to the mineral springs. Elaborate porches and walkways were everywhere.

Before she time-traveled, Libby had read online that in 1846 a writer named Daniel Rupp had dubbed the hotel, a 'Palace in the Wilderness.' For the first time since traveling back in time, she felt a spark, although guarded, of delight. Her thoughts shifted, however, when Rose spoke from the back.

"May I be dropped off right here, Mr. Davis, sir? I must walk 'round back. To the employee entrance. Wouldn't look right if I arrive with ya. Mrs. Henderson, she's the maids' supervisor, might say I was puttin' on airs, she would. 'Sides, I don't wanna walk under that next arch. It's the thirteenth one from the door, ya know."

Davis eased up on the accelerator and wound down the window, giving a hand signal to indicate he was making a turn.

After helping Rose exit the motorcar, an effort that took a little more pushing and pulling than it should have, Libby climbed back in.

"Thirteenth arch?" Davis asked as he pulled back on the road for the rest of the short drive to the main entrance.

Libby shrugged. In rushed delivery, she told the story of how she had met and helped Rose earlier.

He had no chance to respond before they reached the porte-cochère. A uniformed porter hurried to open Libby's door. "Welcome to the Springs Hotel, Miss."

Chapter Eighteen

1926

L IBBY STEPPED FROM the motorcar wondering if it was possible for others to hear her heart thundering wildly.

People milled about everywhere, talking, strolling, and sitting under the covered walkway playing checkers or sipping drinks. She studied them while Davis discussed their limited luggage with the chief porter. The uniformed attendant was her height and stalky. She was just as tall as many of the men. They passed by, wearing suits, bowties, knickers, Oxford pants. Such a variety. Most of them wore hats—bowlers, fedoras, even a couple Panamas—which they readily tipped, casting her admiring looks and more than a passing interest. When the men removed their hats—sometimes to fan themselves or sit for a game of checkers, she noted hair styled in pompadours or parted in the middle and slicked back. Their faces were mostly clean-shaven, few sideburns and mustaches, rarely a beard.

The women, young and old, wore vivid colored dresses, heels no higher than an inch or two, and hats—wide-brimmed straw hats, berets, turbans, but most of them cloche. Most, particularly the young, wore layers of make-up, applied to look dramatic. A few carried decorative umbrellas as a barrier against the harsh sun. With dismay, Libby noticed that dental care wasn't what it was in 2016.

Davis stepped to her side, offering his arm. "You ready?"

Libby took a deep breath. "Do I have a choice?"

The details that graced the hotel's façade were impressive, but nothing compared to the opulence within. The ceiling rose well over twenty feet above the lobby, where a canopy of decorative squares surrounded a crown of crystal pendants. Behind the front desk, an ornamental, multi-layered grand staircase rose initially above a two-floor span, then opened to reveal four stories. The lobby's side walls were lined with seating and watercolor landscapes. Ornate archways interrupted the flow of walls. Colorful carpets and richly upholstered furnishings with puffy pillows were clustered to provide guests with ample lounging space. Signs propped on decorative metal tripods announced that the Pennsylvania Bakers' Association would be holding their annual meeting at the Springs that summer, with sessions to include "The Profession of Baking" and "The Campaign to Eat More Wheat."

She also noted what *wasn't* there: computers for check-in, trash bins with stretchable bag liners, artificial greens and planters, plastic "Exit" signs.

So absorbed in soaking in her new surroundings, Libby didn't remove her hand from Davis's arm until they stood at the front desk. As Davis spoke to the clerk behind the counter, Libby watched a man with perfect posture pass by two giggling young women wearing staff uniforms. With a quick flick of his eyebrows and a slight tilt to his head, he communicated something that made them stand straighter and drop their voices. When he neared Libby, his stern features relaxed into a smile and he nodded courteously to her before gazing at Davis. "Mr. Whitaker. Delighted to see you with us again."

The man was thin, an inch shorter than Davis, and looked to be early or middle forties with thinning hair and several wrinkle lines at his neck. His tweed suit, stiff collar, and perfect bow tie were in impeccable order, and his leather shoes were polished to a startling shine. His clothes did not suggest wealth, but the air of prosperous distinction he wore spoke louder than his clothes anyway.

Davis shook his hand. "Good to be back." He turned to Libby. "This is Philip Jarvis, the hotel manager, although he asks guests to call him Jarvis." Looking back to Jarvis, he said, "Allow me to introduce my niece, Libby Grey—"

"Shaw," Libby cut in.

"Uh…yes, Shaw," Davis said. "She's been living in Europe—"

"Australia." Her answer collided with Davis's.

Jarvis's brows shot toward his receding hairline. An awkward beat fell as Libby watched his face return to the grim, imposing person she'd first seen, his critical gaze taking in every detail of her appearance. She clenched her teeth, enduring his demeaning scrutiny in silence. *Careful. Maintain an air of confidence and decorum.*

Davis emitted a mirthless chuckle. "Yes, Australia. It's been a tiring morning already. Just collected my niece a few days ago." He cleared his throat. "Haven't seen her in a long time, you see."

"I see. Very good, sir," Jarvis intoned in a voice that suggested he *didn't* see, it *wasn't* very good, and it *wasn't* his business to pass judgment on guests anyway.

Davis forced a smile. "Libby, we both have rooms on the second floor of the Anderson. You'll need to sign the ledger."

He turned to Jarvis. "My niece is a recent widow. Lost her things at sea. Could you arrange for a local dressmaker to come to her room soon?"

"Certainly." Jarvis turned to Libby and offered a slight bow with his head. "Have a good stay, madam." Before she could respond, he walked away.

After Libby signed the ledger, the young man behind the desk handed her a tortoise shell mug. "It's for the water," he explained. "All the guests receive one."

Davis made quick arrangements for a porter to deliver his lone bag to his room, but he carried Libby's muslin sack with him. He led Libby toward the red-carpeted stairs, pausing long enough by a side table to pick up a thick book. He tucked it under his arm and motioned for her to proceed.

As they ascended the steps, Libby muttered, "Sorry about the faux pas back there. I was afraid there would be guests who frequent England. Andrew said I should stick as close to the truth as possible."

"I understand," he said, making a facial expression that suggested he wished they could have talked about it. "You didn't want me to say the name Grey. Why is that?"

Libby shrugged. "Same reason. I'm not used to it."

He nodded, but said nothing.

Why *hadn't* she opted for Grey? She'd have to think about that later. "Jarvis certainly over-reacted. Did you see—"

"He thinks you're my mistress."

"What!" The word popped from her mouth, a near shriek. Libby stopped, mid-step, staring at Davis. He appeared concerned, but not angry.

After waiting for another couple to pass, she whispered,

"What do you mean? How do you know?"

He splayed a hand. "What man would actually stumble over his niece's name, and where she's been living?"

Libby muttered an inane sound and covered her heated face with her hands. "They'll never accept me now. The staff, the guests…they'll all know right away. Gossip spreads so quickly."

"I doubt it." Davis took her arm and urged her to keep moving, his tone hushed. "Jarvis will not jeopardize the reputation of the hotel by repeating it. No, I think the moment will remain with him. However, I doubt he'll go out of his way to help you."

"I'll steer clear of him."

"Hard to do in this environment."

"What should I do?"

He patted her arm. "We'll talk about it later."

Libby took that to mean that they shouldn't continue talking in the hallway. Despite her concern she focused on memorizing her way through the labyrinth and stretches of long hallways, and in admiring the décor, with its intricate, painted woodwork and rich carpets. The hotel had both an elegant and an intimate feel to it, the latter due to the endless nooks and sitting rooms tucked into curving hallways. A heavy aroma hung in the air which reminded her of burning oil. She noted cords running from walls to lamps, the telltale signs of electrification, but deduced that oil lanterns must still be put into use with regularity.

As they proceeded, Davis said the hotel was more like a complex, made up of five long buildings, in this order as you walked the halls away from the first one, the Colonnade—Evitt House, Stone Inn, Swiss Cottage, Anderson House. Each was strung to the next with attached hallways, which meant guests staying in the far reaches of the Anderson House could have a ten-to-fifteen-minute walk to reach their room from the lobby. However, each structure was fronted with lengthy covered porches that provided stairwells to the grounds at both ends of each building.

Davis stopped at a door marked 208. "Your room." He handed her a long key.

"No key cards?" Libby quipped.

Davis twisted his lips. "'Fraid not. But don't worry about losing it. The routine is to give the key to the front desk when you go anywhere. Then, retrieve it when you return. You may have noticed the pigeonholes behind the desk where the staff will place messages and telegrams for you?"

Libby took a deep breath. "Telegrams," she said with dismay.

"They'll place your key there while you're out. Of course, you can wear it around your neck too, if you can find some string."

Her shoulders drooped as she stuck the key into the lock and entered. "So much to learn." She'd never gotten a telegram before. She remembered from the movies that they were always depicted as brief and expensive. With thoughts of communication on her mind, she asked, "What about phones?"

"Telephones," he offered by way of a gentle correction as he followed her into the room, leaving the door open. "They're in their infancy so the word is both a noun and a verb."

She grinned and asked again, "What about telephones?"

"We'll have to check it out later. When I first started coming here, they only had one at the front desk. Last time I was here, there were several for guests, throughout the facility. Perhaps more, by this time. Conveniences pop up every day in the twenties."

He set her small bag of clothes on the bed. It was a richly carved double, covered with a blue wool spread that matched the drapes. Other furniture in the room were a nightstand, desk and chair, wardrobe closet about four feet wide, and a low-slung armoire topped by a mirror. Although not grand in Libby's estimation, it was clean, pleasant, serviceable, and comfortable. The polished wooden floor was covered with an Oriental jewel-tone rug.

"Get settled in," Davis suggested. "I'm in room 212. I'll stop back to collect you in about an hour. We'll tour the place then head into town so you can pick up other things you'll need. You might want to make a list." He handed her the massive book.

Libby read the title and smiled. "The Sears, Roebuck Catalog."

"Thought it might be a good place for you to start learning what is and isn't available. It won't have everything, of course. There are many other products on the market. But it'll give you a good idea."

"I used to listen to old-timers on TV talk about using pages from the Sears Roebuck catalog for toilet paper during the Depression."

Davis offered a toothless smile. "Let's just make sure your investments prevent you from having to resort to that." He turned to go, but stopped. "And by the way, you'll notice you have your own bathroom. A luxury for some in this decade."

Libby smiled. "Lucky me."

"See you in an hour," Davis said, stepping into the hallway.

Libby automatically looked at her wrist. No watch. "Wait. I won't know when an hour has gone by."

"Ahh, yes, no watch and no cell phone." He stepped back into the room, crossed to the stand by her bed, and picked up a metal alarm clock. After reading the time on his pocket watch, he cranked the back of the clock to set the time, and returned it to the stand. "Be sure to wind it each day."

She nodded and mimed a salute. "Right. Wind the clock each day."

He smiled. "Add a watch to your list. They sell them in town, but they're rather pricey. Your best bet will be to get one of those ladies' time pieces that women wear like a necklace."

"That won't do for when I go running."

He rubbed a line between his eyebrows. "Libby, running isn't yet a popular activity among the ladies. Don't get me wrong. In large cities you'll see groups of women getting together to run. But I'm afraid here in the more rural areas, if people see you running they'll think someone is chasing you."

Libby dropped on the bed with a frown.

"You might want to take up tennis or golf. And, there's always swimming. The hotel has an exceptional indoor pool."

Libby ruled out golf and tennis immediately. Those activities would require another person.

She stood and walked to the small mahogany desk by the room's only window. On it, she found a fountain pen and one piece of paper. She started a list, saying each item out loud for Davis's benefit:

Stationery
Pens

Pencils
Watch
Swim suit and cover
Container for toiletries
Toiletries!

She whirled back to face him. "There, I've started. See you in an hour. And Davis," she called before he shut the door, "thank you."

He tipped his hat and left the room, closing the door behind him.

Libby dropped onto the bed again. Her new life had officially begun.

Chapter Nineteen

1926

L IBBY'S LIST OF necessities grew quickly.

From the catalog, she learned that the cheapest watch would cost her seventeen dollars and seventy-five cents. Doing a quick calculation of inflation the way Davis had shown her (prompting her to wish again for the convenience of a calculator app on a cell phone), she discovered it would be equivalent to spending two hundred and thirty seven dollars in 2016. With a little more leafing through the pages, she discovered hair dryers were available–metal, of course—but they were large and clunky, weighing in at five pounds. The least expensive one, at four dollars and thirty-five cents, would set her back fifty-eight dollars in 2016. Her only choices in the catalog for a comb and brush were to purchase them in a set with other toiletries, all metal, and mother of pearl. Probably a good idea since she'd need things like a nail file and clippers anyway, but not at the price listed: twenty-three dollars and seventy-five cents. She decided its 2016 equivalent, at three hundred and eighteen dollars, was too much to spend. Other items on her list: umbrella, underwear, hankies (because she couldn't find disposable tissues), and walking shoes. By the time her list was complete, the total came to a whopping one hundred and fifteen dollars and fifty cents (2016 equivalent roughly one thousand, five hundred and forty-six dollars), and she began to appreciate plastic in a way she never had before.

"Better be a second-hand store in town," she muttered to herself. She couldn't afford to part with that much money yet.

Twenty minutes later, a knock sounded at the door. She opened it to find a porter holding a ceramic jug. He looked like the kind, grandfatherly type with a smile that lit his face and a dimple under his lower lip. Several inches shorter than Libby, he had to lift his head to look in her eyes, and she noted that it didn't seem to bother him one bit.

"I heard you've had some unfortunate experiences with your luggage, ma'am. Thought I could at least bring you some water. You must be parched after your long trip."

"How kind of you, Mr...?"

"Oliver Kenton, but please call me Oliver." He walked to the empty water pitcher atop her dresser and poured the contents of his jug into the pitcher. "Heard you say you've been in Australia. Right envious I am, ma'am. Always wanted to see the other side of the world, but I don't think these old bones could handle the long voyage now."

"This is such a lovely place, why would you want to leave here anyway?" Libby offered, an effort to be cordial.

"Eh? Oh indeed ma'am." He pulled a hankie from his left front pocked and wiped the few drops he spilled. Turning to her, he said, "I hope to make it home again one day, but I'm content for now."

"Home?"

"Yes, ma'am. Vermont. My wife and I lived there our whole lives. Raised a family. I apprenticed as a watchmaker's assistant, but was never very good at it. So, I taught myself finish work."

"Finish work?"

"With wood, ma'am. Furniture, bookshelves, tables. That sort."

Libby liked Oliver. He had an aura of kindness and optimism about him. Foremost, she liked proving to herself that she could successfully communicate and relate to people in this period. "How large is your family?"

"Just Vera and me now." His smile faded. "Lost our son in the great war. France. A year later the influenza took our daughter."

Libby felt her stomach clench. "How awful. That must have been very heart-breaking."

"It was. Terribly lonely for us, for a long time. Didn't see the point in living. But then we realized that it's not over 'til God says it's over. So, we made changes." While he talked, he straightened her desk chair, pulled the drapes farther open, and yanked another blanket from the wardrobe and placed it on the foot of the bed.

"That's when you came here?"

"Kept traveling south. When we discovered this place, with its mineral water, we decided to stay a couple months." He laughed under his breath. "That was six years ago."

"You both like it here?"

He nodded. "What's not to like? People come from all over the country to take the water. Makes for some interesting conversation." He tilted his head and stared beyond her, a pensive look on his face. "Always wondered if that water could have helped my daughter." He shook his head, restoring his smile and his focus. "Most people stay for short periods of time.

Some all summer. A limited number of guests are here in fall and winter, so most of the hotel closes. No heat, you see. But yes, ma'am, we have all sorts stay. Writers, vaudeville stars, powerful businessmen, senators, several presidents."

"Presidents?"

"Thomas Jefferson, James Polk, Zachary Taylor, Thaddeus Stevens, several others. James Buchanan made the Springs his summer White House. While he was here, the first trans-Atlantic cable message was sent to his room from Queen Victoria in 1858. In 1855, the hotel also housed the only Supreme Court hearing ever to be held outside of the capital. Some of our more affluent guests have included Henry Ford, Jay Gould, and Henry Wannamaker." His face reddened. "Sorry, ma'am, I get a little excited about our history."

Libby liked this man. Remembering the guidance Davis gave her, she said, "Oliver, I'm American. I was born here, as were both my parents. But, due to my extended stay in Australia, I'm afraid I'm a little unfamiliar with the local culture and colloquialisms. Even the routines of life in a place like this. May I pull you aside and ask your advice from time to time?"

He stood taller, a look of pleasure on his face, as though he liked being helpful. *Being needed*, Libby suspected.

"Definitely, ma'am. You just ask and I'll help you figure your path."

"Thank you."

"I best be getting back to my duties." He nodded and walked toward the door. After stepping into the hall, he turned and offered again, "Anything. You just ask. If my daughter were alive, I'd like to know that someone would help her if she found herself in a strange place." He nodded again and left, shutting the door behind him.

✖

EXACTLY ONE HOUR after he'd left, Davis knocked on her door.

The moment Libby saw him, she said, "Did you know you can order a house from the Sears catalog? An entire house!"

"And they're quite nice too. I've seen several." The distracted look on his face didn't match his chipper voice.

"What's wrong? Has something happened? It's Jarvis isn't it?"

He held up a quelling palm. "No, all is well in that respect. I'm afraid I can't stay the night. I got a telegram. I'm needed at work as soon as possible. I'll probably drive most of the night. These motorcars don't offer the best when it comes to headlights. What would be a two-hour trip in 2016 is a four-hour trip now, even in bright daylight."

Libby's heart sank, but she stifled a visual reaction. Besides his responsibilities, the man had an aura of efficiency and accomplishment, and she'd delayed him enough. "I understand."

"I'll still take you into town. Show you how to get there. Help you tote back supplies. But, I'm afraid you'll have to dine without me tonight."

Libby took a deep breath, collected her purse, and followed him out the door.

They made a left into the next hallway where Libby saw Rose coming out of a room, a large bundle of sheets in her hand. Rose's cheek was shiny red like a tomato with wisps of purple outlining the bone.

Libby turned to Davis. "May I have a moment? I want to ask Rose about some girl things before I go shopping."

"I'll collect the motorcar and meet you in front."

The door to the next room was already open, so Libby followed Rose into it. The young maid wore a white pinafore and cap over a black dress uniform, and stopped from her work to curtsey. "You settled in, ma'am?"

"Thank you, I am. Please call me Libby," she reminded Rose.

The girl looked horrified. "I can't do that ma'am. You're a guest and…well…we're from different worlds. Different classes."

"No, Rose—" she broke off, remembering that Davis would be waiting. "We'll discuss this some other time." She paused. "Are you doing better now?"

Rose stiffened and looked around, a concerned look on her face. "Yes, ma'am, but I'd rather not talk about it if ya don't mind."

"Of course." Libby nodded. Another awkward moment passed as she regrouped her thoughts. "You're what, twenty-two, twenty-three?"

"Twenty-one, ma'am."

"You look much younger than your age. Especially for someone who must have spent time working outdoors on a farm."

"Thank ye, ma'am."

"May I ask what you use on your face?" At Rose's look of surprise, Libby added, "It's just that I've been living in Australia, remember? Things are rather different there. Different customs, different products." *Not to mention that the burgeoning cosmetics industry in this timeframe produced some rather nasty products that were dangerously unsafe.*

Rose's features softened, looking relieved at this blander topic. "Oh, yes, ma'am. Ma taught me to use a mixture of frankincense and whale oil. You can get it at the drug store in town, ya can. Oh, and always wear a hat to block the sun."

A drug store? Libby felt another spark of joy. She had used frankincense on her face every day back in 2016.

Rose continued. "Ask for Hardin Lochery. He was an apothecary in England. We're lucky to have him in our little area, we are. I hope he never leaves." She reached out to knock on the wood doorway trim.

"Hardin Lochery. Got it."

Libby walked away hoping Hardin was a pleasant person because she might become his best customer.

AS DAVIS TURNED the motorcar onto Juliana Street, the main drag through Bedford, Libby's heart thumped. She felt like an interloper on a movie set. The town looked like a colorized version of old black and white pictures that she'd once seen in a book about the Roaring Twenties. Along one side of the street stood the mercantile, and next to it a shoe repair shop with gold lettering on the windows. Farther down was a bank, a municipal building, a dentist's office, and a church. A barbershop, a haberdashery, and a bicycle shop occupied the opposite side of the street, along with a few other small businesses and two-story homes, most made of brick, although she also spotted a couple wood and stone structures. Behind them were unpainted, unadorned sheds and tiny outhouses (fortunately, most of those appeared to be abandoned), vegetable patches, and clotheslines (everywhere). In front, scattered up and down both sides of the street, were horses and wagons tethered to hitching posts, old trucks, and at least a dozen motorcars parked haphazardly.

What Libby saw changed her earlier impression of Bedford, an assumption that the town had grown up near the mineral springs simply to support the guests and activity there. However, what she saw made her realize the town had evolved regardless of the precious water.

Most of the pedestrians passing by, crossing the street, and wandering from store to store, wore shabbier, duller clothing than the apparel worn at the hotel. The people themselves looked different, too. Their postures and the creases on their faces spoke of harried, harder times than the wealthier set she'd been exposed to that morning. In town, the women's clothing tended to be longer, and fit looser, as though practicality, not fashion, was foremost on their minds. Several young girls passed by in feedsack dresses. Many of the men and boys wore patched bib overalls, or pants held in place with suspenders or twine.

After she and Davis visited the mercantile where Libby discovered she could buy everything from packaged noodles to bolts, they returned to the car to deposit her purchases.

Davis turned to her. "The telegraph office is several blocks that way. I need to send a message to work. Tell them I'll return."

It was none of her business, but Libby couldn't help asking, "Why don't you just call...err, telephone them? You said there are telephones at our hotel."

"There are. And the charge to use them is less than sending a telegram. But, the problem is privacy. I can tip the young man at the telegraph office to keep mum about my business. I can't do that on the telephone." He took her arm and moved closer, dropping his volume. "Remember, telephones are tied to switchboards these days. Those young ladies can get quite bored, so they listen to conversations. One is a county commissioner's daughter." He shot her a you-get-my-point look.

"Ahh." Libby brushed her hand in a go-ahead motion. "I see the drug store down the street. I'll be there."

Davis pulled out his pocket watch. "Tell you what, get out that fancy new watch you bought and put it to some use. See that restaurant on the corner?" He pointed beyond the drug store. "Nell's. I'll meet you there for lunch at one o'clock."

Libby grinned. The watch she'd found at the general store cost her two dollars and seventy-five cents, and was anything but fancy. Still, she had bought it because it was certainly better than the prices she'd seen on the finer watches in the catalog. "One it is."

Bells tinkled as Libby entered the drug store. It was narrow from left to right, but stretched front to back at least sixty or seventy feet. Wood shelves ran the length on both sides, and much to Libby's delight, the right counter was interrupted midway by a soda fountain. She'd seen them in the movies. Two children sat slurping drinks through straws beside a solitary man, who had parked his cap on the counter.

"Excuse me," she said to the young man behind the counter. "I'm looking for Hardin Lochery."

He pointed to a man standing by a multitude of empty glass bottles, toward the back of the store. Around him were the tell-tale signs of an apothecary—dried herbs and flowers dangling from pegs, and on the shelves: jars of oils, orange and lemon peels, bottles of cinnamon and varied beans, glass beakers, flasks, scales, and copious leather-bound books on botany.

As Libby approached, Hardin turned toward her. He didn't look anything like the men she'd seen thus far. In 2016, he would have been referred to as eccentric, or a free spirit. His salt and pepper hair was shoulder length and unkempt, and a bushy moustache edged three sides of his mouth. Wire spectacles rested on his nose, and his jacket and pants didn't match. He wore a lopsided bow tie with an artistic flair to it, but no vest. He stood at least five inches shorter than Libby, and reminded her of Albert Einstein, which in turn made her wonder if Einstein was even old enough to look like this yet.

"May I help you?" His smile was pleasant. His hazel eyes glittered a warmth she liked.

"I was told…by a friend…that you could make special mixtures for customers."

"What do you have in mind?"

"I'd like something for my face. A mixture of frankincense and jojoba oil if you can do that."

His face lit up. "Certainly. Anything else?"

She ticked her wishes off with her fingers. "For allergies, a mix of lemon, lavender, and peppermint." She paused to think. "Let's see, to ward off bug bites, could you mix some witch hazel, lavender, and peppermint?"

"Might I suggest some melaleuca in that insect repellent as well? It just arrived, from Siam."

He had melaleuca from Thailand? "Yes, of course," Libby

smiled. *Success.* She was communicating well with this man. *Then again, where, how, and when had she learned so much about plants and oils?* She couldn't remember, so she shrugged away the concern that snaked through her.

He took a few steps to his left, lifted a portion of the counter that was attached by hinges, and beckoned her to enter. "Would you like to see my products? It's such a delight to meet someone who appreciates the natural healing arts."

Libby left the drug store with a small box that contained her jars of oils and lotions, with barely enough time to make it to the restaurant. She and Hardin—he insisted she call him that and return as often as she could—had spent the time talking and comparing uses of the oils he stocked. Despite owning the entire store of mostly manufactured products, he'd made it clear the back left portion of the establishment, where he mixed his knowledge into glass jars, was his favorite. He'd offered to teach her the finer art of mixing the oils, and she'd readily agreed to stop in again before long.

As she hurried past the shoe repair shop, she noticed a crowd gathering beside an alley between two buildings, three doors from the restaurant. Two men wearing navy blue shirts, pants and caps, with pistols in holsters that crisscrossed their upper torso, stood talking to a gentleman who was busy jotting notes in a palm-sized notepad. *Police.* A vehicle marked "Ambulance," was parked nearby, along with what looked to be a body fully covered by a blanket lying on the ground. *No body bags in this day.*

Curious, Libby stopped to assess the scene, standing behind other pedestrians who appeared equally curious. Several yards into the alley, she saw a crude chalk outline on the ground.

The uniformed man talking was quite handsome, in a rugged sort of way. He stood just under six feet tall and looked to be about her age.

"That's right, Sheriff," he said, nodding his head of dark hair. "That's what Mrs. Snell said. That the victim, a Gilbert Harris, rented a room from her for three weeks now, and that he was fine when he came down for breakfast at eight o'clock. But when he didn't return with his paper by ten like he does every day, she began to worry."

The sheriff, clad in brown trousers and a tweed jacket with leather at the elbows, kept jotting notes on his notepad. Wisps of chestnut-colored hair showed beneath the edges of his brown fedora hat. Libby couldn't see his face because his head was tilted as he wrote, his features cast into shadow by the brim of his hat, a brim that attested to too many days in the sun and rain.

The other uniformed man, about five-nine in height with caramel hair, shook his head. "No signs of bullet wounds, Sheriff. Looks like a clear case of strangulation." His voice rang with confidence, and Libby got the impression he was trying to impress the other two.

Someone in the crowd gasped at the suggestion of strangulation, prompting the sheriff, without looking up, to motion for the uniformed men to disperse the crowd. The caramel-haired officer jumped into action, raising a stopping hand to the handsome officer and saying, "I got this, N.C." He stepped toward the street to shoo away bystanders and gawkers. "Folks, let's move along. We've got this under control."

Before she could stop herself, Libby felt her feet moving toward the two men that remained near the body.

"Excuse me, gentlemen," she spoke to the sheriff as she came to a stop, but noticed the handsome officer, N.C., smile and remove his cap.

"I was—" she said, but the sheriff looked up from his tablet, and the moment jolted her.

She gasped.

His face caused her such a visceral reaction, she felt disarmed, robbed of breath.

She fought the urge to back away.

His face was familiar, acutely and achingly so. Scores of confusing images of that face—in different lighting, different seasons, different moods—crashed into dozens of disorienting emotions pounding in her chest.

How could that be?

She searched her mind, trying to find something, anything that might explain this sensation.

Nothing. Visions skittered, but remained blurred and out of reach.

He appeared equally stifled. She could see it in the startled look in his eyes, the sudden twitch in his cheek, the hitch in his breathing.

Libby used the stagnant moment to search his features for some sort of memory. His hair was more bronze than chestnut, like a light coffee color. He looked somewhere between thirty and thirty-five years old. Around six feet tall. Muscular and stout, with a quality of stillness and self-awareness to his presence that daunted her.

His blue eyes pierced into hers, but it was the scar on his cheek that grabbed her focus. It twisted savagely, robbing him of warmth and stamping him with a distinctly dangerous edge.

It had to have been a deep gash once or else so poorly doctored it never healed correctly. What sort of heinous altercation had he been involved in?

The moment lingered.

Something passed between them.

Something significant. Alarming. As if her whole life had been coming to this meeting.

The reason was in her memory, she was certain, but it raced away, refusing to be caught. Then again, how could it be part of her memory?

She watched him swallow and crunch his brows before he murmuring, "Ohonte, oròn:ya." As soon as spoke it, he jerked back, shaking his head as though not understanding why it had come out of his mouth.

As dread crept through her, Libby whispered, "Who are you?" at the same time he asked it of her.

His gaze held her in a grip, as he answered the question first.

She sucked in a quick breath at his answer, throwing her hand over her mouth. That voice! She resisted the desire to turn and run. The name...had she heard correctly? "What did you say?" Her whispered tone sounded frightened, unnerved.

N.C. turned from his work and piped in before the sheriff could respond. "This is Brogan Harrow. Sheriff for the county."

But that can't be!

The name was wrong. Wasn't it?

She could have sworn she'd heard the sheriff voice a different name. Had she merely thought she heard it? Anxiety flooded through her, and she began to shake. She pressed her palms into her sides as though to grapple herself.

"Are you well, miss?" N.C. stepped closer to her but hesitated as if undecided what he should do.

She swallowed. Even though this moment had taken mere seconds, they must think her addle-headed. "Yes, yes of course, I am. I just thought…well, never mind." She pulled her shoulders back and smiled. "My name is Libby Shaw."

The sheriff's jaw grew rigid as his eyes continued boring into her. He wiped a palm over his chin as though gaining his composure. "My apologies for the confusion. May I help you?"

"What? Oh, yes…" She better collect her wits or they'd be bundling her off to the insane asylum. *Play your role, Libby.* She inched her head taller and spoke. "It's…" When her voice cracked, she tried again. "It's just that I wouldn't be so quick to jump to the conclusion of strangulation."

The sheriff blinked. Nothing on his face or demeanor changed. "You wouldn't? And why is that?"

She took a deep breath and gestured to the ground with her free hand. "Well, the chalk outline of the victim suggests a fetal position as though caused by a degree of pain or startling discomfort in the lower torso. Rather than the thrashing limbs scattered here and there one would associate with a struggle. Don't you think?" She didn't wait for an answer before continuing. "And then of course there are the facts that he ate breakfast according to Mrs. Snell, and he's not holding a paper. Therefore, death would have occurred following breakfast but before getting his paper, thus very close to breakfast. If those facts are confirmed, then together this suggests death occurred due to something ingested."

The sheriff continued to study her with such interest she

found it hard to breathe. She shrugged a shoulder and shifted her stance, moving her small box from her right hand to her left. "It's just my impression of course."

"Of course." His lips uttered the words, but as before, he made no other movement.

Again, she felt awkward under his gaze. And confused. And afraid. And like she ought to flee. Was he waiting for her to recognize him?

Should she?

As quick as the thought struck, she dismissed it. Of course she didn't know anyone from the 1920s. Perhaps they each had a doppelganger. Did people in this period even understand what a doppelganger was? Her thinking switched to the discomforting suspicion that he probably wasn't used to women speaking up, or at least, speaking out. Yes, that had to explain the moment. Ugh, she had a lot to learn. She should exit now.

"Please excuse me, I'm late for lunch."

The sheriff nodded hurriedly, as though trying to refocus. "Of course." He blinked and tipped his hat. "Good day, Miss Shaw."

N.C. stepped forward. "Miss, are you sure you're fine now? I could walk you—"

"No…no really, I'm quite fine. That won't be necessary."

As she walked away, she closed her eyes and grappled for a deep breath of air, as though she'd been held under water for far too long. She smacked directly into a solid body. A very large, solid, male body. She opened her eyes in time to discover he was surprised too.

He dropped his gaze to make eye contact, mumbling, "I'm very sorry, Miss—" His sentence died there, and Libby saw why. This was the heavy-set bootlegger she'd encountered on her first night in 1926. He stiffened as though waiting to see what she would do or say, but then N.C.'s voice called out, "Mayor Drenning, over here."

The heavy man hesitated one moment more, then responded, "Coming."

This was the mayor? As though she were tethered to him with a rope, she followed.

N.C. said something to the mayor and they walked to the body. N.C. bent down and pulled the blanket back.

Libby sucked in her breath. It was the scrawny bearded guy with the eye patch that had been with the mayor at the still.

"Never seen him before," the mayor said. His lips were thin and he flattened them, making them almost invisible, as he appeared to assess the body. "Must be a drifter. I better get to the office. Good job, men."

Libby watched, incredulous. *Never seem him before?* The mayor was lying. She opened her mouth to speak when a hand touched her arm. She turned to see Davis.

"Come on," he said and tugged her through the crowd toward the street.

She pointed behind her. "But, I was just…I have to…that bootlegger…"

"I heard. I got here in time to hear you explain to the police why the guy wasn't strangled. Impressive, but you need to stay out of it." He led her around the corner before letting go, and offered his arm instead. "Now then, let's get some lunch."

She hesitated, looking at his arm. Her sense of duty warred with the realization that she needed to stay uninvolved. *For now.* She sighed and fell in line beside him, matching his pace.

"I guess I haven't had a very auspicious start."

"What makes you say that?" he asked, his tone guarded. "This morning you demonstrated some serious self-defense moves that pitted you against another guest and will keep the maids talking all summer. Then, you gave Jarvis the impression you are my mistress. Now you've upstaged the local police and alerted the mayor to the fact that you know he's a bootlegger."

She remained quiet.

He offered a smile and, without breaking their stride, patted her hand where it rested on his arm. "Libby, I'm not sure the Roaring Twenties are quite ready for your roar."

Chapter Twenty

1926

D AVIS DROPPED THE last of Libby's purchases on her bed and turned to her. The late afternoon sun sent rays of light through the window, a stark contrast to the dark thoughts he harbored in his heart.

"Promise me you'll return," she whispered. She clamped her lips together, chin trembling.

"I will. Soon. Meanwhile, I'll send that documentation to you." At lunch he'd told her the room was paid for the month. After that, she'd have to set up an account. For that she needed identification, but Social Security cards weren't issued until 1936. He planned to have a fake birth certificate created by a discrete acquaintance in Pittsburgh, which would allow her to establish credit and obtain a driver's license.

"Thank you." Her voice was soft, laced with dejection.

"For now, keep a low profile," Davis advised. "Spend time acclimating to the place. The people. The culture. Your Australia story is a perfect cover." He gave her a reassuring smile. "It allows you to be different."

She nodded quickly. "I'm sure you're right," she said with a weak smile that suggested she didn't believe her own words.

He retrieved a small piece of paper from his jacket pocket. Two lines of letters and numbers, followed by an address. "My telephone numbers. Top is work. The other, home. But, they're for dire emergencies only; there's nothing private about them." *And, they were fake; but he could always pretend he wrote the numbers incorrectly if it came to that.* "Meanwhile, I'll call you every few days."

"I understand."

"If you need to send a telegram, ask for Kip Winders at the telegraph office. He's the young man I tip generously, and *often*, to keep my privacy."

Libby looked like she was swallowing a sob. In the next instant, she threw her arms around him, buried her face in his chest, and held on as if he were a branch suspended over a cascade of rapids in a river into which she'd fallen.

Startled, he patted her back and wished he could offer more.

After several moments, she pulled back.

Blast it. Davis reached out and cupped her cheeks in his hands, thumbing away tears. "Take it slow. You'll be fine. It will be challenging, but from what I've seen, you have the mettle for it. You're not the missish type. And, drink the medicinal water. It's important for full restoration of health and memory."

She covered his hands with her own, and nodded.

He stepped back, breaking their contact. "Now rest. Promise me you'll go to dinner tonight and join life. If you don't, all this will have been for naught."

"I suppose. It's just—"

"Libby, live in the now. If you straddle two worlds and two timeframes, you will end up nowhere. This is your life going forward. Find your horizon and start toward it."

She nodded again.

He kissed her on the cheek and exited, shutting the door behind him.

✕

DAVIS TURNED THE motorcar left from the Springs and headed to the old Arandale Hotel. It was good he was relocating, because he questioned his own objectivity at this point.

Libby had repeatedly said Andrew was coming back. Good, perhaps then they could put all the pieces together and resolve Matryoshka.

Confound it! He banged each word into the steering wheel. The woman was an enigma.

Longing swirled in his head for his Harley and the head-clearing euphoria the open road had provided him in the early 2000s. What he wouldn't give for that speed now! Instead, he pulled to the side of the road and pulled a fine Cuban cigar from his pocket. Illegal in the twenty-first century, but not now, so he imbibed in them generously. There had to be some perks to living in the Roaring Twenties. And this certainly was a fine one. Another was a good shave. In a real barbershop. In this timeframe, men received the royal treatment at a good establishment. None of that ridiculous unisex hair treatment they had in the future.

He pulled back onto the road, cigar draping from his mouth. The monstrosity of the motorcar required two hands on the wheel, so blast it with any ashes that fell on his suit. He needed this reward.

If Libby Shaw had to be eliminated, he could do it. No

problem. It's not like it would be the first time. But, it would put him in that dark place again. He hadn't been there since two years after his first wife died, when he'd fallen for Mira, that double agent in Budapest in 2007. If he could eliminate Mira, he could do the same with Mrs. Libby Shaw Grey.

Was that even her real name? She probably had more aliases than he did. Regardless, she was too easy to talk to. He'd fallen victim to the comfort of talking with someone from the future. That's all it was.

Wasn't it?

Get a grip, he admonished himself.

She said she spoke multiple languages. No doubt one was fluent Russian. And, he noticed she hadn't carved her initials in the cave. Was she defying Andrew's request? Sending a signal to someone else?

He banged the steering wheel again.

Or, perhaps she truly was innocent and just caught up in something she didn't remember. After all, his memory had suffered after taking the water.

She'd confessed to being married. To *wanting* Andrew to come back.

She'd hugged Davis, made him laugh, then cried when he left. He'd almost come to believe she really hated seeing him go.

What a fool he'd been to let his guard down. He'd actually enjoyed picking out clothes for her. Seeing her reaction.

But, she had looked him right in the eyes and lied.

"Blast!" This time he banged the inside of his car door, causing the window to rattle in a concerning way. He wasn't a bad man. But, sometimes certain problems had to be removed in the interest of national security even if they harbored no ill-intent. Sometimes just knowing the wrong thing could get you killed.

And, why had she been so quiet at lunch? She'd been nervous, distracted, almost panicky. Had something happened? Had she seen someone in town? Was Matryoshka back? Or, had she gotten a clue about his whereabouts and intent?

It was a good thing he was relocating to the Arandale for now, rather than going back to Pittsburgh. He needed a little time and distance from this woman.

But first, he would return to the cave and carve Libby's initials on the wall. That had to be done. *Immediately.*

Chapter Twenty-One

1926

T HAT EVENING, LIBBY stood in her room in front of the mirror, staring. How could she look the same as she had before this whole journey began? Mirrors were supposed to reflect the truth. Her entire world had shifted and changed, yet the woman in the mirror looked like the same one that had stared back at her in Alexandria, several weeks, *and ninety years of changes*, ago. Mirrors should show what a person carried inside.

Then again, she wouldn't want to see that reflection anyway.

She draped a thin chain of silver beads over her head, watching its length drop to below the waist of her new green skirt and blouse. From what she'd seen that day, long necklaces were the height of fashion. Perhaps this would take people's gazes away from her hair which was not in fashion at all.

Besides the chain, a small pistol, a Brownie box camera, and the many items on her list, she'd purchased several blouses, skirts, hats, a pair of ladies' trousers and boots at a women's boutique. The day had set her back forty-three dollars, but now she had a stash of mix-and-match essentials.

Thomas St. Clair, Davis's broker, had better make an appearance soon.

She had spent the afternoon in her room curled up in bed, her mind waffling between feeling sorry for herself and thoughts of Sheriff Brogan Harrow. While intriguing, and definitely baffling, the moment with him had shaken her. She *had* to push him from her mind.

Yet, when she did, her thoughts shifted to Davis and she felt even more remote and alone. She loved this man. Not romantically, but as a protector. The kind she hadn't had in years. What a fool she'd made of herself when he'd left, holding him in more of a life grasp than she had Andrew during their goodbye. But, with Davis, it was easy. She liked his kind face, his hazel eyes, the whispers of lines at the corners suggesting exposure to sun, laughter, and years of collected experiences beyond her own.

By seven o'clock she'd forced herself to climb off the bed and keep her promise.

"Join life," she repeated Davis's words into the mirror. Besides, it's what Andrew would want her to do.

In the lobby she saw no signs to designate the direction to a restaurant or cafeteria, so she headed to the front desk. Her path collided with that of Jarvis exiting through an office door.

His expression, behind pursed lips, suggested little desire to help her with anything. Still, he offered the merest bow of his head and said, "Mrs. Shaw. May I help you?"

She shot back the warmest smile she could fake. "Din—err, Supper?"

He pointed to an archway. "Take that corridor. Follow the others." Libby could hear the drag of disapproval between each word.

The long hallway had at least eight doors opening onto it.

As Libby made her way to supper, she listened to people passing by. Some of the conversations were informative, bits of them amusing, and much of them inexplicable.

"He's the bee's knees." *Agreeable? Goofy?*

"It was slick to have seen her." *Good? Lucky?*

"But it's the really swagger thing to do in the city." *Fun? Popular?*

"Sam was quite oiled." *Was Sam drunk? Dirty?*

"Trotskyite," "Bolshevism" and "Seventh imperial conference this autumn." *Too much politics in one sentence alone.*

"…similarities between Dostoevsky and Aristotle…" and "…emotional reaction to Binomial Theorem." *Two conversations over Libby's head and probably theirs as well.*

"It's a mail order service called Book of the Month Club. Thirty books for two dollars and ninety-eight cents." *Good to know.*

"… one of those Milky Way bars, from the A&P." *Candy bars and grocery store chains? Things were looking up.*

After making her selections from an impressive buffet—featuring cold poached salmon, leg of pork with sage stuffing, and several vegetables and desserts—Libby carried her tray to an unoccupied white linen-covered round table. A swift scan of the large dining room revealed furniture even heavier and darker than that in her room, and a quick calculation of the number of tables confirmed the place could hold almost five hundred people at one time. Impressive. Scattered potted palms and ferns made the room feel like a cross between a dining area and a conservatory.

Within a few minutes, a voice inquired, "May I join you? Yours is the first new mug I've seen in weeks."

Libby turned to see a pleasant-looking woman standing

beside her, fortyish in age, red wavy hair cut shorter than current fashion, wearing beige cuffed trousers, blazer, linen blouse and brown walking shoes. A look Libby imagined she might see in a 1920s L.L. Bean advertisement for the resilient outdoor adventure female.

The woman didn't wait for an answer before plopping down first her tray and then herself. She thrust out a hand. "I'm Maude Berger. Would you pass the pepper please? Phew, it's hot in here. All these bodies in one place." She removed her blazer and tossed it over the back of another chair.

Maude had an air of self-confidence and straightforwardness that reminded Libby of Colette. She missed her friend. "Libby Shaw," she said, handing over the pepper.

Maude generously coated her food. "Where're you from?"

Stay as close to the truth as possible. "Alexandria, Virginia. But I've been in Australia for several years. Just returned."

"Welcome home." Maude smiled between bites. "Must have been a long trip. Did you fly any of that?"

Trans-Atlantic flights hadn't happened yet, but were domestic passenger flights available? "No, all by ship. What about you, where are you from?"

"Cleveland. Here with a patient. I'm a doctor. How about yourself? Work? Husband? Children?"

"I became a widow recently. I've returned to my homeland to…" *How to explain?* "…start all over again."

"My condolences." She paused in a way that suggested acknowledgement of Libby's mourning. "Got any ideas what you want to do?"

"I…well, you see—"

"Smash it," Maude said and it sounded like a curse. She

leaned toward Libby and whispered. "Sorry to interrupt but we're about to be joined by the grande dame of societal convention. You might want to raise your pinkie and pull out your best posture, if that rot matters to you."

A gray-haired woman approached the table, followed by a teenage girl and a member of the hotel staff carrying a tray. Despite walking with the help of a cane, a highly decorated and ornamented walking stick tipped in silver, the older lady's posture was upright and she struck an imposing figure. Her gray hair swirled atop her head and was held in place with a pearl comb, a style Libby was sure dated from the 1890s. Neat as a pin, the old woman moved with a sense of self-importance. A cameo cinched her blouse together at the neck, and her skirt fell to near her ankles. The young woman accompanying her was waif thin with blonde hair cut in the popular blunt fashion, and wore a fashionably short dress, dramatic make-up, and a look of boredom on her face.

"We'll sit with these guests," the old woman declared to the employee, and he placed her tray at the seat she designated. The young girl rolled her eyes, dropped in a chair, and slouched.

"Good evening, ladies," Maude said with no sign that she thought the woman any more cultivated than the next person. "Libby Shaw, this is Mrs. Delilah Beachum and her granddaughter, Lena Bauer."

Libby nodded. "It's a pleasure to meet you both." She turned to Lena. "How lovely that you are traveling with your grandmother."

Mrs. Beachum sniffed. "I'm afraid Lena will not understand what you say. She is from Germany." She looked around uncomfortably as though she'd said the girl had leprosy.

Ah, yes. Less than eight years ago America fought the Germans in WWI.

Mrs. Beachum continued. "I don't speak German. Nasty language, that. And, Lena knows very little English. So this brief trip has been rather stilted to say the least. She squandered last night fiddling with that...that talking board thing." She wiggled her fingers disparagingly in the air as if the object drifted there, just over their shoulders. Libby noticed the Cartier gold and diamond watch that adorned the woman's wrist.

"A Ouija board?" Maude asked.

"Yes, that's it. Such voodoo nonsense. Does that strike you as someone mature enough to marry?"

Maude shrugged. "Well, I think they're nonsense too. Comical actually. But they certainly are all the rage lately."

"Yes, well, she leaves tomorrow to visit my youngest son in New York for a few weeks. I doubt he will let that thing in his house. My son-in-law, Lena's father, is taking a teaching position at Oxford at the end of the year so they will be leaving Germany, but Lena is determined to stay there and get married." Mrs. Beachum's body language suggested she found everything about Lena's plan distasteful.

Maude raised a brow as she peppered her food a second time. "I take it you don't approve."

The old woman pursed her lips before dropping her volume so low Libby had to lean in to hear. "She intends to marry a foreigner." Her chilled tone lowered the temperature at the table by degrees. "There's nothing wrong with being foreign, mind you..." she said, her demeanor suggesting she believed just the opposite, "...and he's from a very wealthy Jewish family. But, really, she ought to be marrying her own kind."

A chill crawled across Libby's skin. *A Jewish marriage in Germany, heading into the 1930s. A recipe for disaster.*

"She's young," Mrs. Beachum continued briskly. "Life will cure her of these naïve passions soon enough, but not before she's married I'm afraid."

Libby had a thought. If Lena believed in spiritualism, it might work. "Mrs. Beachum, I speak several languages. German being one. Would you like me to tell Lena your thoughts?"

Mrs. Beachum's eyebrows shot higher. "Oh, my dear, if you would contrive to get through to her, that would be most beneficial. Tell her she simply cannot marry this young man." She sat taller, with an imperial air about her.

Libby addressed the girl in German. "Your grandmother thinks I'm relaying her thoughts. But I'm not going to. So, be careful how you react. She is against your marriage, but the truth is, you should marry whomever you wish."

Mrs. Beachum nodded and continued. "Tell her it would be a huge mistake. That their customs and beliefs are not ours. That much of the civilized world looks down on those people."

Libby nodded at Mrs. Beachum, then spoke to Lena, continuing in German. "I have a...gift. Let's just say that traveling has given me the ability to see into the future. Your fiancé's people are going to be persecuted severely in Germany, and it will become illegal for an Aryan and a Jew to marry. A man named Adolf Hitler will rise to power and brainwash other Germans into turning violently against the Jews."

Lena sat frozen, saying nothing, eyes widened like saucers.

Mrs. Beachum blinked. "Gracious, that required a lot of

words. Tell her I emphatically forbid this preposterous union and that she will not be welcome in my home if she proceeds."

Libby stared intently at Lena. "Be extremely careful. Condition your marriage on him moving the two of you out of the country right away. Your very lives will depend on it. Now, please pretend to love your grandmother for her concern."

Lena pushed a smile onto her face, and leaned over to pull her grandmother into an embrace, kissing her cheek and patting her back, as she addressed Libby. "Thank you. I will never tell Grandmama what you said. I pray you are wrong, but I promise to think about it. I must go back to my room to write to Ephraim!"

It was clear from Mrs. Beachum's reaction to her granddaughter's fawning that she believed Lena was expressing love and gratitude.

Libby smiled, an effort to help Lena's cause, and returned to speaking English to Mrs. Beachum. "Lena said she understands and has a lot to think about. She asks permission to return to her room to rest."

As the girl let go of her grandmother, Mrs. Beachum cleared her throat and straightened the bodice of her clothing. "Yes, well, that's fine." She patted Lena's arm. "Despite that deplorable public display of emotions."

Again, in German, Libby said to Lena, "You're excused, if you wish."

The table grew quiet after Lena left, and from the corner of her eyes, Libby noticed Maude bite back a smile.

The rest of the meal involved discussions of the varied activities at the hotel, until Maude called to someone beyond Libby's shoulder. "Leon, how are you getting on with the crutches?"

Libby followed her gaze to discover the man that had attacked Rose. Their gazes collided, and he stilled her with an artic glare before hobbling closer to Maude.

Nonplussed, Maude continued. "Ladies do you know Mr. Martelli? He injured his knee this morning playing tennis. Dr. Fitch, the Springs's medical director, wasn't available so I administered aid. Leon, this is Delilah Beachum and Libby Shaw."

"Ahh, yes," Martelli said, his tone droll, "I've had the pleasure of meeting both these…ladies." His last word came out the same way one might say *hooligans*.

He gave a stiff nod and an icy acknowledgement to each of them. "Mrs. Beachum. Mrs. Shaw." He turned back to Maude. "Tell me, Dr. Berger, how it is you came to be seated at this table? I realize the doctor trade is little more glamorous than that of plumbing, but I would think you'd have a better caliber of people with whom you could dine."

Libby heard Maude suck in shock simultaneously with her, but apparently Mrs. Beachum wasn't as startled or daunted by the young man's insults.

From her pocket, Mrs. Beachum extracted a ruby-encrusted lorgnette and used it to assess him with a disdainful look. "Mr. Martelli." She smiled sweetly, stiffening her already straight spine. "I wish I could say this is a pleasure, but it never is. Like your discourse and your apparel," her gaze dropped down his body and back up, "your rudeness is both tacky and tasteless, once again. Furthermore, it's not your place to *have* an opinion about my caliber, let alone to express it."

Martelli's face grew red and his hands fisted on his crutches, but he let go of one support to bow in exaggerated fashion to her. "As ever, madam, your display of pomposity and your antiquated bastion of formality never ceases to disappoint."

"Oh good," she responded with a smirk. "I do so hate to disappoint." She placed her lorgnette beside her plate as though punctuating she was done with him.

Martelli huffed a short syllable of disgust and hobbled away.

"Who put thistles in his socks?" Maude said, still wearing a startled look, "Bugger that. I guess we're quite on his wrong side."

Libby rolled her eyes. "I don't think he has a right side."

"The cheek of it!" Maude's shoulders dropped. "My apologies. I wasn't aware you both knew him."

Libby said, "I caught him attacking one of the hotel maids this morning. That's how he hurt his knee. She said he has attacked another girl as well. Unfortunately, the other girl did not get away."

Mrs. Beachum was quick to add, "Oh, dear. For years I've watched that rake belittle the porters and show disrespect to everyone, from the maids to Jarvis to the most elite guests. Last year a guest caught him stealing, but it was one man's word against another, so he was never brought to rights. He's a cheat, a lecher, and a gambler who can't hold his liquor or his mouth."

Silence descended, each woman caught in her own thoughts. After a moment, Maude knitted her brows and gesticulated with her fork. "Doctor trade?"

Libby quickly added, "Better caliber of people?"

Mrs. Beachum joined in. "Pomposity?"

The three chuckled, and Libby bit back an urge to howl out loud. After Lena had left, she hadn't been so sure she liked Mrs. Beachum. Now she was quite sure she admired the old lady. Further, it felt good to discover she could relate to people from this timeframe.

When they departed from supper, Mrs. Beachum headed in one direction, and Maude and Libby another.

As they traversed the long hallway toward the lobby, Maude said, "Libby, after medical school, I studied psychiatry. In Germany. Later, I joined the Red Cross efforts in France during the great war. I didn't learn German well, but I learned enough to know that what you told Lena wasn't what her grandmother said."

Libby remained quiet, wondering what Maude had understood and what she planned to do about it.

"Don't worry," Maude stopped and turned to her. "Your intent back there is safe with me. And, I applaud you. But…"

"But?"

"I heard you mention time and travel together. I don't want to know more, but the last person who made such conjectures is now living in the Trans-Allegheny Lunatic Asylum. She claimed to have tried to commit suicide in the mineral water…in 1831. Ninety-five years ago. She looks twenty-five, tops. 'Course, she had a whole host of other issues too, but…well, I thought you might want to know."

Libby opened her mouth, an automatic denial forming on her lips, but hesitated. She liked Maude. This exchange had turned them into more than fellow guests. There was a bond between them now. "I understand. Thank you."

"Good." Maude sounded relieved. She pointed to a door to

her left. "This is my stop. I'm meeting a gentleman in the piano lounge. Say, do you golf? Ride horses? We should do an activity soon."

✕

IN HER ROOM, Libby kicked off her shoes, flopped on the bed, and stifled a sob. If this were the future, she'd traipse to the kitchen, pull a half-gallon of ice cream from the freezer, and eat it out of the carton. *Comfort food.* But, that was no longer an option. So many little things she'd taken for granted!

As she stared at the ceiling, the melancholy sounds of a jazz band filtered through her open window, carried on the slightest of breezes. *Rhapsody in Blue.* From a gramophone? Radio?

Libby's insides clinched. The source didn't matter. It was the music itself that grabbed her attention, drawing a new memory to mind. She and Andrew at the all-night jazz concert in Alexandria. Him trying to explain the music, her convinced she never would understand. She pressed her palms to her eyes, overcome by the hard longing to have that time back. To ponder jazz, rather than *be* jazz. Because she was. She was now like the very music she disliked, all free form, taking the rhythms of her life where they might lead, no particular destination in mind, no inkling as to how her song would end.

She rolled to her side, and looked out her window at the moonlit sky. It appeared silvery and cold, and the moon seemed so remote and distant, so disinterred in her now. Curling into a fetal position, she sobbed. She loved music. How would she ever survive with no more George Strait? No Eagles. Or Beatles, or Josh Grobin, or Adele, or Abba, or CCR, or Jimi Hendrix?

No Rock and Roll. Or Blues. Not even Disney songs!

The music that soothed her, motivated her, anchored her, entertained her, would no long filter through headphones as she went about her day. She'd lost many things and opportunities and understandings in this new life. She'd have to sacrifice and adjust, but to say goodbye to familiar music...this left her with none of her adored routines to look forward to, to organize her continued existence around.

It was more than not merely being able to download and listen to a particular song when she wanted, it was the loss of how certain songs brought people together or helped to define a moment. She'd never be able to mention those songs or bands or lyrics to anyone and receive understanding or a shared acknowledgment in return.

Just one more thing she would have to fake, wing, pretend. All day, she'd felt like an actor who didn't know her lines. She'd pretended to be a part of this world, but it had been hard not to feel like an alien. In her day, these people would all be dead and gone. Now, they were her peers. And it had happened so quickly, like someone strolling on a backlot at MGM, first walking down a modern city street setting, just to turn the corner and trip into a setting from a hundred years earlier.

Davis had said to *find your horizon.* Maude had inquired, *Got any ideas what you want to do?* What *would* she do now? She didn't even know what choices she had. Opportunities were scarce for women, and pay was minimal. That wouldn't change until World War II when women would flood the workforce to help the war effort. But, *this* didn't sit well with her, this carefree life. It was too foreign. Too without purpose.

If only Andrew were there. He was her husband and a part

of her life now. How could she make a decision about her future without him? She had no idea how or where they would live, so how could she make plans?

Then again, it was hard to think of herself as a wife, but even harder to think of herself as a widow. If only she could touch him, trace the lines of his upper lip, the indentation in his temple, the crinkles at the corner of his eyes when he smiled.

She pounded the bed with her fist. What *was* she crying about? Music? Work? Andrew? Her thoughts were so erratic. And, she'd acted like a fool with the sheriff. Was she falling apart?

She fell asleep thinking about all the things she would discuss with Andrew when he came back to her.

If he came back.

A RUMBLE OF thunder in the distance woke Libby the next morning. She climbed from bed and peered miserably out her lone window to find the sky filled with ominous gray clouds and drizzling rain. The sidewalks were slate-colored and the lawns glistened.

In such weather, no one would be about. At least not this early. She pulled on her jeans and boots, and tucked in the ends of the shirt she'd slept in. She needed to go back *there*.

Back to where she'd said goodbye to Andrew. Back to where her life had changed.

Through the drizzle, she walked to the Crystal Spring, passing an occasional puddle of collected rainfall that shivered against the breeze. She'd been right, no guests were out that early in the rain, and only a few uniformed employees moved about.

Distantly spaced wooden signs directed her way. The terrain was familiar enough that she was certain her path was correct. Within minutes she found the Crystal Spring, but it looked different, and not just because it was daylight. There was no low retaining wall. No signs that it had been prettied up for tourist purposes as it had looked when she'd used it in 2016.

Instead, the location was unadorned and more natural, the water dominant, its gurgle almost zen-like and tranquil, as though heedless of what it had done to her. The immediate area felt and looked timeless.

She dropped to her knees and with a trembling hand, inched her fingers into the cool water and waited. For what, she didn't know. A sensation, perhaps. A memory.

Nothing.

As she sat there, she didn't know how long, the rain strengthened, pattering in steady rhythm on the ground around her.

When she returned to the hotel later, the young man at the front desk stopped her, handing her two messages. The first was from Davis's broker, Thomas St. Clair, saying he planned to be there in three weeks and recommending they meet during lunch. The other missive from Maude suggested they get together for a swim.

Yes, she would meet with both, St. Clair out of necessity, Maude because she longed for companionship. After all, what else did she have to do? There wasn't a single person or commitment that wanted, needed, or commanded her time these days.

✖

THE RAIN CONTINUED into the next day. Following breakfast, Libby decided to collect more magazines from the lobby and return to her room for a day of reading advertisements to see what companies and products were available for investment.

Entering the lobby, she spotted a figure arriving at the same time on the opposite side of the expansive area. A pale, reed-thin man in ill-fitting clothing stepped from an exterior back door into the shadows.

It's not that she experienced recognition. His pale face was partially hidden by a hat brim turned down and a collar turned up as though against the rain, revealing only his eyes. Perhaps it was his posture that caused a quick electrical pulse to shoot through her heart. Hands tucked in his pockets. Head tilted. The slightly reckless stance made him look unhealthy and out of place. A premeditated meddler who had no concern about looking like the other guests. And that stillness! Between his stance and his glare, she felt stapled in place. His gaze, directly at her, was like a hatchet-glare, as if he was looking at her with such contempt he could easily bury a hatchet into her skull. For a moment, she didn't move, and neither did he. A porter emerged from seemingly nowhere pushing a luggage carrier stacked with cases at least seven feet high, and after it passed, no one was standing at the spot where the pale man had stood.

A vein pulsed in her neck and she looked right. Left. He was gone. She dropped into the nearest chair, waiting for her heartbeat to return to normal. *What just happened?* First the sheriff, now pale man. At least with the sheriff she hadn't felt threatened. Disoriented, uneased, perhaps afraid, but not threatened.

It was at least a half-hour before she conceded pale man was gone. She retrieved several magazines all the while reminding herself that she hadn't even been in 1926 long enough to have made an enemy. Either she had been mistaken, or he had mistaken her for someone else.

She turned to go but stopped short when she overheard a woman speaking French in a loud, panicked voice.

She watched a stylish woman descend the stairway, talking to a befuddled-looking Jarvis, her arms animated and her face streaked with tears. "Mon mari est mauvais." *My husband is ill.* She continued in French, "He brought medication with him, but we cannot find the bag."

Jarvis looked at her helplessly. "I'm sorry. I do not know what you want."

They stopped within two yards of her, so Libby stepped forward and addressed the woman in French. "Puis-je vous aider?" *May I help you?*

The woman's eyes lit up and she threw her hands on Libby's arms in a please-listen-to-me gesture. "My husband speaks English," she said in her Romance language, which to Libby always sounded like a song or an old-fashioned melodrama, "but he is ill. Until the water can help him, I need his medication. It was in a leather bag. I am sure we brought it. But when I searched for it, it was missing."

Libby touched the woman's arm, nodded and translated her concerns to Jarvis.

"A small leather bag?" Jarvis nodded hurriedly. "Yes, yes. Tell her we might have it. It must have gotten separated from their other belongings." He turned and signaled to a porter who had just come in the main entrance. "Paul. Did you hear? That unclaimed bag belongs to this guest."

Paul, a thin, grave young man of about twenty nodded and walked to a door behind the check-in counter, retrieved a bag and brought it to the woman.

"Oh, merci, merci!" She turned and hurried up the steps clutching it like it was a treasure chest.

Paul strolled back to his post outside the front door.

Jarvis turned to Libby. "You speak French." The way he said it wasn't a question, but rather an observation he felt obliged to make.

She pushed the pale man from her mind, and offered a curt nod, attempting to appear demure, poised. "As well as Spanish, Italian, German, several others. And, I'm well-educated and well-traveled, Mr. Jarvis." She hoped her voice sounded supportive, not pointed. "If you ever need my assistance again, let me know." She didn't wait for a reply. Why provide him with the opportunity to deny her civility? Instead, she turned and headed toward the stairs.

"Madame?"

She stopped and steadied her nerves before turning around. "Yes?"

"Thank you." He bowed with his head and walked away.

It wasn't his words that eased her mind, but rather the tone in his voice. One of contrition and kindness.

"You're welcome, Jarvis," she said although she doubted he heard her. It didn't matter. She said it because she wanted no more pandering or worrying what he thought of her. Mostly, she wanted to hear how the name rolled off her lips, the way the other guests addressed him, without the 'Mr.' honorific prefix attached.

It felt good.

LIFE TOOK ON a certain rhythm in the next several weeks. Libby spent her mornings with newspapers and magazines to learn current events and make lists of potential investments. Afterward she would swim, hike, play Ping-Pong, tennis or golf, or go horseback riding with Maude. Three times she played cards with Mrs. Beachum under the colonnade enjoying iced tea and the views of the rolling hills and distant mountains around them.

The colonnade walkway was edged by a series of columns supporting a flat roof which also served as a second-floor loggia and promenade sided with decorative railings, and ushered guests across an expansive lawn and Shobers Run. The ground floor, while a boardwalk also, sported tables, chairs, and benches for guests to enjoy leisure afternoons out of the sun or rain while still soaking in the surrounding vista. The landscape appeared familiar and ageless, and it comforted Libby. Others may find her new life monotonously repetitious, but she needed that predictability for now.

She also walked to town each Monday, Wednesday, and Friday, always careful to avoid the sheriff. She would shop, people-watch, and most enjoyable of all, meet with Hardin Lochery to discuss oils and herbs. He proved to be a delightful and self-educated man, enthralled with all things beyond the visual: health, religion, spiritualism, and supernatural. Libby enjoyed the walks but often felt like someone was watching her. She would catch herself looking over her shoulder. She thought of the pale man, but always, she shrugged it off. Her body was still healing, she reasoned. Her internal gauge for hunches and intuition were off because, as odd as the sensation was, it also felt inexplicably familiar as though it had been a constant in her former life.

Twice, Rose came to Libby's room with fresh linens while Libby was reading. The second time, Rose finally relaxed enough to talk fashion. Libby asked to see some of her designs and stitchery, then showered her profusely with praise days later when Rose brought several frocks she'd made. Libby ordered three dresses, paid in advance, and secured Rose's promise to coach Libby in all things fashion. As Rose turned to go, Libby again complimented her designs and stitching.

Rose blushed. "Thank you, ma'am. I always start with the styles by Chanel or Patou, then tweak them a little."

"Chanel? *The* Chanel, as in Coco Chanel?"

"That's her. The designer from Paris."

"Do you know if she's publicly traded?"

"Ma'am?"

Libby shrugged. "Never mind." Few people in 1926 could imagine how the fashion industry would grow in the coming decades. Libby made a mental note to add Chanel and the design industry to her list of possible investments.

One Tuesday evening, Oliver Kenton delivered a message that Sheriff Brogan Harrow was in the lobby and wished to talk to her. Instantly anxiety gripped her, so she feigned fatigue. She asked Oliver to extend her apologies and a promise they would talk some other time. Weeks went by, but she didn't hear from Harrow again.

Davis called twice each week. The conversations were warm but bland as both were aware that a switchboard filled with operators could be listening to their discussions. Her birth certificate arrived by special post, secured in an envelope with red sealing wax and accompanied by a brief letter typewritten on a machine with a faulty 'w'.

It read, *Thought you would enjoy seeing correspondence before the age of computers and printers. Regarding the enclosed: your new life begins. Live it well.* It was signed, *"See you soon, Davis"* in blue ink.

And through all this busyness and activity, a foreboding grew in Libby's mind, brought on by the briefest of encounters with Leon Martelli. For the most part, she was able to ignore or avoid him, but one evening on her return from supper she encountered him coming the opposite direction in the long, ground-level hallway.

He smiled that imperious smile he did so well and watched her pass by with only a curt nod and a snarky-sounding "Mrs. Shaw." Then, he stopped her in her tracks after she'd gone a couple yards beyond him when he said, "Your little friend Rose? I see she still travels that road alone. It's a shame you can't be with her all the time, isn't it?" She whirled around in time to see him turn his haughty look of triumph toward his destination and saunter away.

The next morning Libby told Rose to collect as many maids as she could for a self-defense training. Eight young, skeptical women joined her that evening on the lawn outside the pool building. After demonstrating several ways to handle attacks, she tutored their practice.

All seemed to be going well until she instructed them to hit the men in the gonads. Following several gasps, Libby explained what the results of such a move would produce. Only half the women acted pleased to learn of this crucial self-defense tactic; the others merely blushed and admitted they would never be able to do such a thing. Begging, reasoning, and more explanation wouldn't change their minds, so Libby suggested they always wear a long sturdy pin in their hats. That mollified their concerns, even titillated them a bit. By morning, three other maids pulled her aside sheepishly and requested the training.

In all, Libby held three sessions, with promises to provide practices and refreshers if the ladies ever requested. Rumor reached her after a week that Jarvis had learned about the classes. She waited for him to voice dismay or offer his opinion, but it never came.

AFTER A FEW weeks, Thomas St. Clair arrived. They met over lunch at the hotel, but carried their selections on trays to the outdoor patio to talk privately. He was a short, dignified man approaching sixty, with a round face, receding hairline, large nose, and heavy bags and other signs of age and stress beneath piercing eyes. Impressive wasn't the first thought that came to mind when one looked at the man, but his confidant carriage and impeccable clothing demanded a second perusal. His dark three-piece suit, highly starched white collar, and black tie were made of finest silk, and his shiny Italian shoes suggested success.

That morning and with the help of a hotel employee, Libby had retrieved most of her money from the guests' safe, kept in a locked room beside the lobby. Along with two hundred and fifty dollars, she gave him a list of investments she hoped to make. He wouldn't get rich off the commission on this small amount of money, but given its 2016 inflation value, she figured this was a good first-time investment and that St. Clair would see the future potential as her investments earned more money.

He donned wire glasses and studied the list with a thoroughness and scrutiny she appreciated. "General Electric, RCA, Kodak, Goodyear. You and Mr. Whitaker favor the same investments. He's a keen, astute investor. Everything he's favored has paid off handsomely, to say the least. I'm guessing that, like him, you are not interested in hearing about other possibilities? Say, Edison Records? They've been doing rather well."

Not a chance. Ever. They close their doors because radio proves more popular. "No, not this time, but thank you."

St. Clair finished reading the other companies on the list and looked up. "Mrs. Shaw, a couple companies you prefer have not gone public yet, but you can trust that I will otherwise follow the priorities you have outlined." He signed his name to a receipt and a contract, and handed them to her.

After reading and signing the contract, she handed it back. "Thank you, Mr. St. Clair." She bit her lip as she sought for words to another request.

His eyebrows pulled together. "Is something wrong, Mrs. Shaw? That is my standard commission—"

"It's not that…" *I need fast money to help my friend Rose.* "I have an urgent matter that demands a swift payout, faster than what I suspect these investments will bring."

He frowned. "Are you saying you've changed your mind?"

"No, I'm talking about…well…a wager, I guess. A gamble." She slouched back in the chair and looked away feeling defeated. In doing so, a stack of carefully ironed newspapers caught her eye. "Hold on…" she said, a tone of hope in her voice. "Bear with me a moment."

The papers represented varied cities and dates. She snatched a few, returned to the table, and flipped through them. *Brazil Leaves League of Nations.* So what? Nothing there on which to place a wager. *Mordecai Johnson Becomes First Negro President of Howard University.* Again, not wager-worthy. *College Board Administers First SAT Exam. Traffic Lights Slated for Piccadilly Circus in August. Gertrude Ederle May Become First Woman to Swim English Channel. Isadora Duncan Back in Paris.* No, no, no, and no.

As she scanned the headlines, Mr. St. Clair was aflutter with the proposition of gambling. She ignored his "couldn't" and "wouldn't" declarations.

Then she saw it, an update on the progress of the Tour de France. It began June 20, and would end July 18. One week away. *Perfect.*

"I've got it. Mr. St. Clair, do you know a good place to wager on a sporting event?"

"What? No, I do not…that is to say, yes I do, but no I will not." He took off his glasses and polished them fiercely with a spotless white handkerchief he pulled from his lapel pocket. "I'm here with you on official capacity, Mrs. Shaw. I could lose my job, my reputation, if—"

"Our official meeting has ended. Let's say we're talking on an unofficial capacity right now."

"If it's quicker money you need, then perhaps commodities—"

"I don't want commodities. I want to place a bet on the Tour de France."

"Mrs. Shaw, that is impossible. I simply could not—"

His words had a refusal, but his eyes flickered as though he also were rapidly calculating odds and potential payoff in his mind, so Libby added a finality to her next statement: "Mr. St. Clair, I'm going to place a wager on the Tour de France. Someone is going to earn a carrying fee and transaction fee for this wager whether or not I win. Now, it can be you, or you can let someone else have it."

When he said nothing, she went in for the kill. "Say, double the commission?"

He assessed her. Inhaled. Exhaled. Looked around them. Leaned in. "What do you have in mind?" His voice was hushed.

She pulled another one hundred dollars from her bag and handed it to him. "This, on a Belgian named Lucien Buysse to win."

He stared at the money a moment, then Libby saw a flick in his jaw the moment he decided to do her bidding. "He's riding with his two brothers. Do you want me to spread—"

"Just Lucien Buysse," Libby said. "The whole lot."

Two weeks later, Mr. St. Clair brought Libby her winnings of sixteen hundred dollars and a box of Belgian chocolates. She took six hundred and asked him to invest the rest for her.

Three days later, a stoic and resigned Jarvis agreed to let Libby move, and stay through the winter, in one of the ground-level rooms that offered a private entrance and heat from a steam radiator, and for the young maid Rose to live in the room next door. For agreeing to that arrangement, he secured more than the going rate on the rooms, and a promise that Rose would continue her work and be discrete in her comings and goings.

Chapter Twenty-Two

2016

ANDREW STEPPED INTO the cool dampness of the cave and smiled. It was good to be out of that furnace of a city. Washington D.C in July was miserable. By late morning the weatherperson had tagged the temperature at ninety-eight degrees, but Andrew doubted the perfectly coiffed meteorologist on TV took into account how much the marble and blacktopping that held the city together absorbed the sun, elevating the heat index to brutal proportions.

Why people chose to live in such temperatures was beyond understanding. Cool-weather locales were best. What he was used to. Most importantly where he would return. *Soon.*

For now, though, he was content: back in Bedford, back at the cave, and looking forward to a night of pampering at the spa in the Bedford Springs Resort.

He looked at the wall one last time. *L.S. 1926.* He exhaled a long-building breath of relief.

She survived! He knew where to find her.

The *Z.H. 1922* etched near her initials, however, made him pause. *Z.H.* Yes, he was a good man. Pragmatic. Bit of a roughneck, that one, but good. Would it be possible they might meet? Probably not, given the four-year difference, and knowing what he did of Z. H. That man was too hardheaded to stay in Bedford, or even Pennsylvania for that matter. He'd probably gone west, maybe south, by now.

Libby. His beautiful Libby. Was she adapting? Meeting people? He frowned. How would she make a living? Too bad the bureau in those days didn't take women. That could provide long hours of interesting conversation if things worked out, given what they knew about the country and the FBI in future years. But no, there were no possibilities for her in the bureau in 1926. Or, in audio translation, for that matter.

And, certainly no Matryoshka Project.

Heck, there weren't even Matryoshka tapes *in 2016* anymore. Another agent had discovered them missing right after her departure.

And now *he* was being followed from time to time. He'd had a hard time shaking the tail today. What was really going on? Why was the bureau spending money, especially taxpayer dollars, on what seemed like organized chaos? Didn't one department talk to another, or was everyone out to protect their own turf?

Thank goodness he'd removed Libby from this.

Now his dilemma was: could he, *would* he join her?

Chapter Twenty-Three

1926

B Y EARLY AUGUST, half the guests were different than those who had been at the Springs Hotel when Libby arrived. Of the familiar faces that remained, it was clear from the flushed skin, stooped shoulders, raspy voices, or chronic fatigue as to why many of them remained. The hope of the medicinal power of 'taking the water' seemed to spring eternal.

The healthier among the collected guests participated enthusiastically in the many activities the hotel provided. Besides golf, tennis, swimming, and horseshoes tournaments, the hotel held picnics, riding expeditions and competitions, dances, bonfires, and a revolving door of musical and theatrical entertainment.

Maude Berger had returned to Cleveland, but said she'd be back after Labor Day with a different patient. Unfortunately, Leon Martelli remained, but so did Mrs. Beachum, much to Libby's delight, particularly after the old woman pulled her aside and announced that her granddaughter had unexpectedly decided not to marry because her fiancé refused to leave Germany. Seems a young British officer had already caught Lena's eyes.

Davis continued to call dutifully, each time expressing regret he couldn't get away due to work.

August also ushered in sweltering hot days, prompting Libby to purchase a blue Hawthorne Flyer bicycle and switch her visits to town from afternoon to cooler mornings.

Plus, there was the presence of Brogan Harrow, but she denied to herself that he had anything to do with her change in routine. She had narrowly escaped several encounters with him in the afternoons. After a little spying from around street corners, she discovered he spent most mornings in the office, and afternoons on patrol around town. Each time she saw him, he was helping someone: a farmer loading a truck-bed of animal feed, two children attempting to cross the street, an old woman loaded down with heavy groceries, a young man working on the engine of his car. He'd even stopped two bored teens who had been kicking a can and passing a cigarette back and forth, to offer them a coin each for cleaning up the main street through town. Many of his efforts were rewarded with an invite to dinner, or a Sunday afternoon baseball game. She overheard him decline each as though his involvement extended only so far, that helping was appropriate but getting involved was more than he wanted to offer.

No doubt his kindness was just an act anyway. *That harsh scar on his face told the real truth, didn't it?* Served as a warning to others—*Caution: Interaction may lead to mortal danger.* Yes, that had to be why she was so in tune with his whereabouts.

ON ONE PARTICULAR Wednesday morning she stood shoulder to shoulder with Hardin as he taught her how to mix a sleeping aid with herbs.

"When it comes to plants you have to know what to use," he said, his focus on the counter where he was busy separating the harvest he'd grown. "Sometimes a root will do, other times you need a leaf or only a stem. It also matters how you use it. This particular plant can be ground up, but others you might have to boil."

"It's so fascinating," Libby said, and meant it.

"I ought to use it myself," he quipped as he picked up a glass bottle and held it to the light while using an eye dropper to add lavender oil to his concoction.

"Are you having trouble sleeping?"

"Sleep? No, I sleep like a baby no matter where I am. The problem is restfulness. My sleep is not deep. It is filled with pictures. Images that demand attention."

"Perhaps they're simply vivid dreams," Libby suggested. "Or memories that haunt you. Some that weigh on your heart and others that you just can't seem to grasp."

When he didn't respond, she turned to see him studying her. He lowered his work to the counter never breaking his gaze. "You are talking from experience about these memories that haunt?" His voice was pitched low, his brow furrowed in puzzlement. "This troubles you?"

How had this turned around to be about her? She couldn't tell him the truth, but perhaps if she talked in vague terms, she could empty herself enough to feel better. "Hardin, I—" *Tread carefully.* She rubbed her forehead and shifted her gaze to the counter. The words began to fall from her lips before she could restrain them. "I've taken the water...*more* than taken it. I have changed...profoundly. I left behind a life that I can never get back. Everything about that life was different. I had to leave behind a career as a translator and an investigator. A city I enjoyed. Alexandria. A lifestyle. A husband." She heaved a heavy sigh. "And, my dearest friend and roommate, Colette Ma. I never got to say goodbye to her."

When she finished, she looked up to see Hardin's face, expecting him to offer her chipper words of hope, to say she could always work things out. How could she explain it would be impossible? Would he entertain the thought of time travel?

He straightened his shoulders. "I confess I do not understand your situation, nor the impossibilities you allude to, but I can tell you are certain this is a final change. I am sorry for your loss. If there is anything I can do to help, I will."

Libby stared at him several heartbeats, overcome by the warmth in his voice and the world of wisdom that shone in his eyes. She forced a weak smile. "Thank you. I promise the same to you."

"Ah well, I'm afraid no one can help me either." He ran a hand through his scraggly hair and it flopped and stayed out of place, across one eyes. "You see, Libby, my visions are filled with urgency, as though I'm running to find something or someone. I do not know if they are premonitions, or memories of other lives."

"Other lives? Like reincarnation? You believe you've lived other lives before this one?" Reincarnation didn't mesh with Biblical teaching, nor with what she'd experienced. But then again, she'd once never given credence to time travel either.

He raised his right hand to his chin, rubbing it while he reflected on her words. "Interesting. But no, I do not believe in such nonsense. In my situation, I wonder if my memories are inherited from my ancestors. Is it actually *their* sense of urgency? We inherit our ancestors' hair color, nose structure, phy-sique…why not their thoughts and memories?"

Startled, Libby stared at him. "That's amazing. I never thought about it." *I don't think anyone in the twenty-first century has given that serious research either.*

They returned to their work, but Libby was left to wonder about what he said.

LATE THAT NIGHT, as Libby made notes about the oil blends she'd learned from Hardin that day, a faint, shuffling sound outside her door stopped her cold. She had left the windows cracked to cool the room, as there was no air conditioning.

She glanced at the clock on her bedside table. Nearly one-thirty in the morning. No sensible, and innocent, person would be out at such an hour. An unnerving chill splintered through her core.

The sound came again.

Heart hammering, she turned off her desk light, shot to her feet and crossed the room to her purse. From it, she retrieved her pistol, all the while praying Rose had shut and locked her windows.

She crouched and inched to the window, peering out around the edges of the dark curtain. There was no sound, no activity anywhere on the lawns, except for a large dark silhou-ette hastening away from the hotel, moving through the low glow of moonlight, then lost in the shadows of the night. His size, the hat, the way the figure moved, she was certain it had been a man.

Convinced the intruder had been right outside her door, Libby shut and locked the window. Perhaps she should have given more credibility to those feelings of being watched that she experienced during her walks to town. Could it be the pale man? Or Leon? Waiting to catch her or Rose off guard. What about the goon that was with the mayor and Gilbert Harris in the woods the first night she arrived? The size and physique fit, and the mayor knew she witnessed him lying about Gil Harris.

She got little rest that night.

MAUDE RETURNED AFTER Labor Day in early September. On her third evening back, she accompanied Libby to a live performance of Shakespeare's *Macbeth,* performed by the Ben Greet Woodland Players on the hotel lawns.

By the time the play ended, the light was changing, darkening the vibrant green world that surrounded them. A small band began to play music, and Libby agreed to join Maude for lemonade on the colonnade loggia above the main entrance. The loggia area looked out on the stretch of grass and was aglow with hundreds of bulbs, strung for this purpose. As they neared the front of the hotel, Libby saw Rose approaching through the crowd of people, and was about to call to her when a voice interrupted.

"Good evening, miss."

She turned to see the handsome dark-haired police officer from town, the tall one named N.C. Instead of a uniform, he wore a dark gray suit and bow tie. Not for the first time, she recalled Davis's comment about how well everyone dresses in this era. In 2016, half the audience would have turned out in jeans for a lawn event at a resort.

"Good evening. N.C., wasn't it?" Anxious, Libby looked around him. "You here alone?"

"Yes, miss, on both accounts. We drew straws on who could come tonight." He grinned and Libby was surprised that it made him even more handsome, if that were possible. "I got the long straw."

She still needed assurance. "No Sheriff Harrow?"

"He got the short straw. But, I think he rigged it to lose. He does that for us." N.C shrugged and pulled out a pocket watch to check the time. "I s'pect he's home with his wife by now anyway."

"His...*wife?*" Libby's stomach clenched, surprised at her own reaction. By this time, Rose had reached their side and Libby caught her and Maude staring at her. "Oh, I'm sorry. Dr. Maude Berger, Rosella Morgan, this is N.C...I'm sorry I don't know your last name, or for that matter what N.C. stands for."

When N.C. saw Rose, his eyes widened, looking dazzled. He yanked off his hat and wedged it between his arm and torso. With a smile that stretched ear to ear, he extended his hand, hesitated, then wiped it on his pants and thrust it out again. "Pleased to meet you, Miss Morgan."

Rose's face pinkened and she reached to touch his hand for the briefest contact. "Rose."

He repeated her name like it was the answer to the Earth's problems.

From the corner of her eye, Libby saw Maude try to hide a smile by tilting her head and reaching up to scratch her hairline.

The moment felt awkward so Libby said, "I don't think I caught your last name."

"Oh well…" N.C. sounded embarrassed, and his hands worked around and around the black grosgrain edge on the perimeter of his felt hat. "My last name is Smith. My mother didn't want me getting lost in the crowd of Smiths that seem to be taking over the country, so…well…" He blushed. "She named me Nebuchadnezzar Charlton Smith."

Maude raised her brows. "That's quite a name."

"What?" He shifted his gaze from Rose long enough to make eye contact with Maude and say, "Yes, ma'am, it is," before looking back at Rose. "Are you a guest here, Rose?"

The girl appeared flustered by the attention. "No, I work here as—"

"My personal assistant," Libby said. It was mostly true. When Libby had moved her into the room next door, Rose argued and said she couldn't take charity. Libby countered that Rose was saving two hours each day by not walking to and from town, and suggested she use that time to sew them both "some smart frocks and hats. That way, it will all even out."

N.C.'s eyes widened as though impressed, or pleased. Libby couldn't tell which.

Rose stood taller. Perhaps she'd needed the boost of a new title.

Libby winked at Maude. "Maude and I were just heading to the veranda for refreshments. If you'll excuse us."

Several minutes later, Libby looked back to see N.C. and Rose still talking.

✕

LIBBY DIDN'T CLIMB into bed until after midnight, and fell into such a deep sleep that when she heard frantic banging on her door and a frightened voice trying, and failing, to whisper her name, she thought at first it was a dream.

But, the banging and the voice persisted. "Please, ma'am, wake up. It's me, Rose."

Libby turned on the side lamp, threw back the covers, and grabbed a robe. When she opened the door, Rose practically fell into the room. She looked anxious, weary, even disheveled, her blouse and skirt crooked, her thick wavy hair cascading over her shoulders and down her back. Libby hadn't even realized Rose had such lengthy hair, as she had only ever seen it atop her head or tucked into a hat or maid's cap.

"Are you alright? Were you with N.C.?" Libby gasped. "Was someone out there? It was Martelli, wasn't it?"

"No, ma'am," Rose said in frantic, rushed delivery. "Well, yes, ma'am. I was with N.C. for a few minutes before he left, and yes the problem involves Mr. Martelli. But it's not me. It's Dulcina."

Libby shook her head to induce clearer thinking. "I don't understand." The girl was shaking. She placed her hand on Rose's shoulders and steered her to a chair. The room was much larger than Libby's old room, and included a separate sitting area. Libby pushed her down into a sitting position. "Slowly tell me what's going on."

"Yes, ma'am," she said but climbed to her feet. "Oh sorry, ma'am." She sat back down, then jumped back to her feet again.

"Rose, I'm getting dizzy watching you bop up and down. And, we really must discuss your use of ma'am so often."

"I'm sorry ma'am, but there's no time to waste. It's Dulcina. She's dying, she is…" Her voice hitched and she flattened her hand over her mouth like she was holding in a barrage of despair.

"What are you talking about?"

Despite the poor lighting in the room, Libby could see Rose's flushed face, the panicked expression. "Remember I told you he attacked her, ma'am?" Rose's lower lip quivered and she clutched at the folds of her skirt. "Two and a half months ago, right when we opened for the season. She became…became…"

Libby grabbed her shoulders again. "What Rose? She became what?"

"With child, ma'am." She scrunched up her face.

"Pregnant?" Libby pushed lank strands of hair from Rose's eyes so she could see the girl better.

"Yes, well, no. She tried to…you know…" Rose whimpered, her eyes glistening.

Libby gasped. "She tried to give herself an abortion?" She hurried out of her robe and pulled on her jeans, hurriedly stuffing in her shirttail.

"Yes, ma'am. She's bleeding something awful. Lavinia stayed with her while I came for you."

"Where is she?"

"In her room, she is. The staff dormitory, behind the hotel."

"Come on. We'll get Doctor Berger on our way."

AN HOUR LATER, Libby, Rose, and another hotel maid by the

257

name of Lavinia stood in the dark shadows of a cramped and dimly lit room, their gazes riveted on Dulcina's dead body where it lay pale and prone on blood-saturated sheets.

Maude sat beside the body. "We got here too late," she said, rubbing a hand across her forehead. "Honestly, given the damage she did to herself, I don't think there is anything that could have been done to save her." She flopped her stethoscope into her doctor's bag as though she were mad at it.

Her eyes vacant, Rose stood silent, still, as though paralyzed by grief. She held the hand of a sobbing Lavinia.

Libby felt a numbing tightness in her throat as she assessed Rose. Was the girl in shock? She should comfort her. Pull her into an embrace. But she didn't have words of comfort to offer. Besides, it was presence that mattered most, wasn't it? Yet within, she acknowledged that wasn't the reason for her own silence. The truth was, anger seared through her. Mother and child. Both gone. Indignation swelled achingly against her ribs and rose into her throat, bitter-tasting. She didn't even know Dulcina. Was she angry at the senselessness of the situation? Fast-forward ninety years and this pregnancy would not have had this outcome. And what about the mineral water? Could it have saved Dulcina if they'd gotten her there in time? Could she have helped the girl? *Would* she have revealed herself to save the girl? Libby shivered despite the warmth of the room.

No, she was angry at Leon. He had raped the girl, gotten her pregnant. She needed to focus on that.

Maude stood. "Libby, why don't you and Rose go back to your rooms? I'll have to call the police and sign some medical reports. I'll stop by later." She reached into her bag and pulled out a container from which she extracted two pills. She handed them to Libby and lowered her voice. "Give these to Rose. They'll help her sleep. I'll tend to Lavinia and clean up here."

With a weight settling on her heart, Libby was only too relieved to oblige.

✕

AT 3:10 A.M., Libby answered her door to see a weary Maude holding two teacups in one hand, and a glass decanter in the other.

Maude held them up as she walked into the room like she was toting the cure for the world's ills. "Brandy. I prescribe it for thirstitis tonight. Figured we could use it."

Before closing the door, Libby peered into the darkness beyond. *Nothing.*

Maude dropped onto the brocaded couch, plopped the cups on the coffee table, and poured. She handed one to Libby and they both took a swig.

Libby felt the warm liquid burn a trail down her throat.

"Rose?" Maude inquired.

"Sleeping."

Maude nodded.

"The police took Dulcina's body?" Libby asked, folding into a chair opposite her.

"Just left. Sheriff Harrow and a medical examiner from town." Maude huffed a sound as she swirled the liquid in her glass. "The local police force sure is easy on the eyes."

Libby ignored the comment, recognizing it as a statement to ease the stress of the moment.

"The thing is," Maude said, then took another swallow before continuing. "This is why I went into medicine. To help people when they're hurt by things beyond their control. And yet, so often I can't." She went silent as though momentarily lost in her own chagrin.

Libby took a hefty swig. *And, I went into investigation so I could get the perp who did the hurting.* She couldn't tell Maude that. It was part of her other life. Maude had said she didn't want to know. Besides, she didn't want to share that with Maude. Didn't want her past to be there between them every time they got together. Libby wanted to be equal with her, not the object of pity or concern.

Libby looked at the liquid in her cup, fought against the anger. "There's nothing you could have done. You said it yourself, we got there too late." *But there is something I can do.* She had to stop Martelli from doing this again. No one could prove he attacked Dulcina. DNA was not an option yet. Even if laws would be conducive to going to a judge to order a test on parentage, it would be Leon's word against a dead girl's as to how she got pregnant. No, Leon Martelli had to be banished from here. *But how?*

"Mind if I smoke?" Maude asked. "Trying to quit. It's killing my taste buds, but I sure need one now." Without waiting for an answer, she removed a cigarette from an engraved silver case she pulled from her pocket. Once it was lit, she blew smoke rings toward the ceiling, exhaling long, slow breaths before speaking again.

"My patients are mostly war veterans. Men who returned from fighting an outside enemy, only to find themselves wrestling even harder with an enemy within. A force bigger than themselves." She took another drag of the cigarette and when she exhaled through her nostrils, it came out blue. "The same with Dulcina. She couldn't fight her fear of being scorned or judged. Couldn't control the life she led inside her mind. For the rest of us, that is the only life we *can* control."

Libby gulped the rest of her drink. *Control the life inside our own head.* Was that possible? She reached for the bottle and refilled her glass. She might not be able to control her own thoughts, but she was determined to take control of a threat by the name of Leon Martelli.

Chapter Twenty-Four

1926

FOR TWO WEEKS, Libby watched Rose robotically continue through the motions of her life, eating, reporting to work, even creating new dresses and hats. Only Rose's puffy eyes and red, raw nose each morning whispered of the mourning she endured each night in her room.

Libby was able to lift the girl's spirits when she persuaded Jarvis to start a shuttle service for the hotel staff that couldn't live in the employees' residence.

Jarvis had watched her pitch and defend her idea, making no comment, merely waiting her through, his hands clasped together on his desk. She had studied the work hours of the maids and with slight changes in scheduling, the shuttle—a 1925 Ford Model T Suburban "Woodie" Station Wagon capable of holding six—would only have to run to and from town three times a day to keep all shifts covered. The morning driver could be the gardener who didn't start work until the dew was gone each morning anyway. The afternoon shift could be manned by one of the porters during slow times in the afternoon.

Thereafter, Jarvis paled, brushed a hand down his cheek and across his lips, and shook his head in disbelief. "It's highly inappropriate for a guest to bring this suggestion to us, Mrs.

Shaw. But, I am sensible enough to acknowledge when I hear a good idea. Frankly, I can't believe this idea has never been voiced before."

None of this would have helped Dulcina, of course, because the girl had lived in employee housing, but it did buoy Rose's spirits to know her friends would be saved the long walk in the dark. Too, Libby noticed that the discussion with Jarvis had been cordial, almost pleasant.

While time from Dulcina's death brought Rose peace, it proved to work just the opposite for Libby. Her anger at Leon Martelli intensified. That, coupled with anticipation of fall equinox just days away, left her feeling anxious about Andrew's possible return, with extra energy coursing through her veins.

In the third week of September, as she and Maude headed toward the lobby after supper, a loud chorus of voices filtered from the piano lounge. Curious, they stopped and peeked inside. A radio, or wireless, as Libby learned they called them in that day, had been moved to the center front of the lounge. Men and women milled about everywhere, drinks and cigarettes at the ready as a haze of aromatic tobacco smoke clogged the air. An aura of excitement and expectation filtered through the room.

"What's happening?" Maude asked a portly pipe-smoking man standing by the door.

He grinned, gripped the upper lapel of his jacket with one hand, and pulled the pipe from his mouth with the other. "Boxing match. Tonight. Heavyweight championship. You follow it?"

Maude shrugged. "I read the papers. Dempsey and Tunney. Supposed to be a record-breaking crowd."

"That's right." The man smiled, pointing the stem of his pipe at Maude. "Tunney, the Fighting Marine they call him, he's only lost once in his career. But, Dempsey's held the championship since 1919. My money's on him." He said it with smug assurance that he already knew the outcome and couldn't wait to count his winnings.

Libby scanned the room. The guests who'd assembled to listen to the fight were jovial, animated, as though anxious for the match to begin. A loud, low roar came from the far right corner and she shifted her gaze to see Leon Martelli standing in the middle of that crowd, the guests around him laughing as if he'd said something amusing. Like the first time Libby had seen him, his stagger and slurred speech suggested he was inebriated again. The drink in his hand provided further confirmation, and the ashes dropping from his cigar to the carpet provided still more.

"Come on, good ladies and gentlemen," he prodded, finally bending to tap his cigar on an overflowing ashtray, managing to miss it by a good three inches. "We need to make this interesting. Who's brave enough to place a wager on Tunney? I'll put one thousand dollars down on Dempsey."

Gazes shifted down and away, anywhere but on him.

A voice called out, "Too rich for my blood." Heads nodded.

Another voice said, "You sure your father would approve, Martelli?"

Nonplussed, Martelli smirked. "I'm twenty-eight. Don't need my old man's permission."

Someone snorted a laugh and said, "But you need his money."

Martelli scowled and smooshed his cigar into the ash tray as though it was bearing the brunt of all his problems. "Tell you what, I'll leave my thousand in the pot and all you have to put in is five hundred."

A different voice responded, "Come on, Martelli. No one is going to wager that kind of money on Tunney."

Libby stepped toward the group. "I will."

An awkward hush fell on the room. All talk ceased. No glasses moved. Someone even turned the volume low so that their verbal exchange could be more easily eavesdropped. For the first time ever, Libby understood the expression, *you could have heard a pin drop.*

Despite the look on Martelli's face, disgust mixed with delight, she added, "But you'll have to throw in your car and a promise that you'll leave here tomorrow and never come back. *Never.*"

The crowd collectively gasped. A titter spread. Bystanders inched away, placing distance between them and this brewing scandal. They didn't want to be a part of it, but neither did they want to miss any of its scrumptious particulars and its final juicy disgrace. Tomorrow, the drama of tonight would be rehashed, reworked, and exaggerated over breakfast, only to be regurgitated again in magnified proportions when they returned home.

Rage flickered through Martelli's eyes and his free hand fisted, but he caught himself and glanced at the others quickly before restoring his smile.

"Mrs. Shaw," he said in a condescending sing-song tone, "Tunney is the underdog. I do feel obliged to tell you that Dempsey is known for chewing pine tar to strengthen his jaw, and soaking his fists in brine to toughen them. Are you sure you can afford this loss?"

"Conjecture," she said, meeting his gaze. However, what wasn't conjecture, for her anyway, was the outcome of tonight's match. Davis had said Tunney would win. She hoped he was right and that she'd heard correctly. But she was rather sure this was the fight Dempsey would lose after which he would say the famous words "Honey, I forgot to duck." Words which fifty-five years later President Ronald Reagan would quote to his wife Nancy after he was shot. She'd learned this from a documentary about the former first lady after her death in March 2016.

"Then you have a deal...with one exception." He smirked, looking around at the sea of gawking faces. "Since you are putting far less money into the pot, I have a condition of my own."

Her heart drummed. Was she certain about the winner? This was a bad time to doubt herself. She was uncomfortably aware that the others were paying rapt attention to everything they said. "What is it?"

He grinned and took another swallow of drink, making her wait. "If...*when* you lose, you must agree to return to Philadelphia with me and work for free, as my housemaid, for one year."

A low murmur spread through the room. Someone in a disgusted tone said, "Martelli, you go too far."

Libby loathed this man. Not only was he getting puerile and perverse delight in this negotiation, he also had managed to toss an insult into the wager, practically announcing to the group assembled that he thought her no better than servant status.

Maude stepped to her side. "Libby," she whispered, "not like this. It's too risky."

Libby studied Martelli and without breaking eye contact with him, murmured low to Maude, "I know what I'm doing."

In a louder voice, she said to Martelli, "No worries. Your man's strategy is all about tough-guy intimidation. My man's approach is discipline and intelligence, and I think that always wins in the end." She didn't know if what she said about the contenders was true or not. Seems she had read that once. But it didn't matter because the smiles and whispers from those watching told her they understood her double meaning, that she likened herself and her wager to Tunney. "I agree to the terms, but I want it in writing. I don't want your inebriated state to be reason to contest the outcome." There, his turn to be insulted.

Again, his eyes flicked disdain at her. He mocked a bow. "Certainly. Caruthers, old chap," he called to a man with a thin body and fat mustache, "you're an attorney. Put this agreement in writing for us to sign."

The crowd settled in and listened as Gene Tunny stunned Jack Dempsey with a right to the chin in the opening moments, followed by ten one-sided rounds in which Tunney out-boxed his opponent. Before 10:15 p.m. that night Tunney was declared the heavyweight champion, and at 10:30 p.m. a stunned and very drunk Leon Martelli downed his sixth glass of hooch, threw a fat wad of hundred-dollar bills at Libby, and stormed from the room. By 11 p.m., the news of Martelli's downfall had spread through the hotel complex.

When Libby rounded a corner at 11:15 on her way back to

her room, Jarvis, sporting an uncharacteristic smile, stopped her long enough to say, "Madame, I congratulate you on your winnings." Without waiting for a response, he gave a slight bow, this time from the waist, and walked away.

The next day the hotel provided Martelli with a courtesy ride to the train station. His 1925 Auburn motorcar was left parked out front, paperwork on the front seat.

LIBBY SPENT THE early morning in her motorcar sightseeing the countryside, getting used to the way the vehicle moved and shifted and hugged—or not—the road. The color of buttermilk and almost as tall as she was, the Auburn was a huge, four-door vehicle with pop-up leather roof, roll-up windows, and white-wall tires. The seats were a camel-colored leather and as deep and comfortable as any couch she'd ever sat in. She practiced with the clutch, memorized the dashboard—a simple task given only four gauges vied for her attention—and experimented with acceleration up hill, learning the motorcar's limitations in power and stopping distance. As with what she'd learned about most vehicles available in the 1920s, the braking systems were poor, and the tires were terrible, generally needing replacement every five thousand miles. Combine those negatives with poor roads, and only a fool would drive at excess speeds. This particular motorcar apparently had a top speed of sixty, but at forty-five it was working hard. By mid-morning, she stopped to refuel at a "filling up station," as the man on the corner of John and Richard streets called it when she asked for directions.

From the station she headed east out of town, journeying

about a mile when she saw two men walking. Drawing near, she recognized one as Oliver Kenton, the kind porter at the Springs Hotel. She pulled to a stop.

"Good day, gentlemen."

While Oliver tipped his hat and offered a greeting, the man with him whistled and circled the motorcar. "Ain't that a spiffy piece of metal, Ollie? That's no hayburner. Must give a nifty ride."

"Turner, Mrs. Shaw is a guest at the hotel," Oliver said through gritted teeth.

Turner went white and wrenched the hat off his head. "Oh sorry, ma'am. Didn't mean to beat my gums."

Oliver shook his head in dismay and directed his next comment to Libby. "Mrs. Shaw, this is Turner White. He works in the gardens at the hotel."

Turner seemed a simple, genuine sort, so Libby replied, "No worries, Mr. Turner. And it's nice to meet you. Where are you two off to?"

"Everett," Oliver answered quickly, "a town about eight miles that direction." He pointed down the road. "We both need a new pair of shoes, so we thought we'd do the walk together."

Libby swallowed that surprising bit of ambition. "You're going to walk eight miles to purchase shoes. But why don't you shop in Bedford? There are stores there."

Oliver looked a little flustered, but still responded with warmth in his voice. "Everett has a shoe factory with discount prices."

Libby held her smile, hoping Oliver wouldn't see that she felt bad for them. "May I offer you two a ride?"

Turner's eyes shot open. "Oh yes, ma'am. Much obliged."

Oliver, however, pulled Turner's hand off the door knob. "No, ma'am, it's too generous of you. We couldn't impose on you like that."

"Don't be silly. You'd be doing me a favor. If I go to Everett on my own, I might lose my way back." *She never would, but they didn't have to know that.* "Besides, it will take you all day to walk."

That logic convinced Turner that a ride was in order. He reached for the handle again.

Again, Oliver intervened and stopped him. "No, Turner. We haven't money on us to pay the lady. We agreed to walk."

"Tell you what," Libby said. "I seem to be collecting a lot of things and I do not have enough storage space in my new room. You said you were a woodworker, Oliver. How about some basic bookshelves—I'll supply the wood—in exchange for the round trip? Do you have tools?"

Oliver's delight at the offer showed on his face, his smile reaching his ears. "Oh indeed I do, ma'am. I haven't had an opportunity to work on anything in a long time. I surely appreciate it."

He looked at Turner, and Turner stared back, a puzzled look on his face.

"Well?" Oliver scolded. "Get in!"

Turner looked like he was ready to shoot back a retort, but thought better of it, opened the door, and climbed into the back seat.

They returned mid-afternoon. After they climbed from the car, Oliver leaned back into the car through the open window. "I surely do thank ya for the ride, ma'am. I hope you understand. Vera and I live on a budget. I could pay more for the shoes here in Bedford, o' course, but she's had a terrible cough and I just don't know how much it'll cost for a doctor's visit." His face flushed and he looked away.

"Smart planning," Libby said with a smile she hoped put him at ease. "Why waste good money? Say, why don't you stop by soon? I have an herbal concoction for coughing that Mr. Lochery showed me how to make. It's all natural. You'd be doing me a favor because I'm wondering if it works. Meanwhile, I'll ask Dr. Berger to look in on Vera. The doc owes me a favor." It was a lie. If anything, she owed Maude.

Oliver yanked his hat off his head again. "Why, thank ya, ma'am. I appreciate that. We're in the first house west of the hotel, down Sweet Root Road."

After dropping them off at the hotel, Libby found Maude and Rose and took them to town for an early supper where they toasted Leon's hasty and permanent departure. "Schaden-freude," Libby quipped as they clinked glasses. *German for deriving pleasure in someone's pain.* Maude shot her a knowing look, while Rose acted like the word meant cheers or good luck, because she repeated it and knocked on the wooden table.

Afterward, they stopped at the drug store, and Libby and Rose introduced Maude to Hardin Lochery.

When they departed thirty minutes and three chocolate floats later, Hardin stopped Libby, taking her by the arm. "Those two." His whispered voice was blunt and perplexed. "They are your friends?"

She gazed at him, wondering where he was going with this. "Yes."

"But, you—the three of you—are so different."

Libby shrugged. "Friendship doesn't always mean being alike. Sometimes it simply means enjoying your time together."

A frown stamped his face as he pondered her words. She had never considered before the aloneness of his life. Everyone that came into the shop was there for a transaction, a purchase, a need. She softened her voice. "They are my friends, just as you are my friend, Hardin."

"We are?" As soon as he said it he caught himself, shaking his head as though to remove the surprise he'd heard in his own voice. "Yes, we are. Of course." A pause, and then, "What...what is it that friends do for one another?"

Libby smiled. "Whatever they want. Activities. Conversations. Sometimes just doing things side by side."

He seemed to like that and he stood taller. "Then, we are friends."

She nodded. "Yes. And now I better go."

But as she turned, he still held on to her arm. "Perhaps you could stop by. Later, tonight. After hours. I plan to blend some oils for making soap. One with spearmint and patchouli, and another with orange and vanilla. You expressed interest in that once."

Libby hated to decline, hated to dash the eagerness she heard in his voice at this concept of friendship that was new to him. But, she did, with a promise to herself to make it up to him later. "I'm terribly tired. I had hoped to retire early tonight," was all she could offer.

The truth, however, was that it was equinox, and she planned to spend the evening at the Crystal Spring, waiting for Andrew's return. Earlier in the week, she'd purchased clothes for him during a trip to town, and told Davis when he called—

through abbreviated language due to potential unwanted listening ears—she would undertake the duty this time of watching the spring. Davis had hesitated, but when she assured him she would keep her pistol at her side, he agreed.

✕

ANDREW DIDN'T COME.

A few minutes past midnight—after four hours of sitting on the ground and keeping vigil by the springs, *and* hitching her breath every time the water gurgled differently or reacted to slight breezes—she wiped a lone tear from her face, collected the bag she'd prepared for him, and returned to her car.

She stashed her things in the Auburn and got behind the wheel, breathing deeply, quickly, willing herself to remain calm and accept the inevitable. If he was going to come, he would have by now. He would have taken the water as soon as nightfall hit.

Wouldn't he?

She vowed to shed no more tears, and started the car. She would not fall apart. He had told her he might not be able to make it back this soon.

The thing is, it had already been three months. What if she began to forget what he looked like?

She put the motorcar in gear and steered it away from the Crystal Spring, heading back to the hotel. The intense blackness of the night sky matched her mood. Sleep would be almost impossible. When she came to the first crossroads, she found herself turning right and heading to town instead. A drive might help. Maybe Hardin would still be up. There were no other cars on the road and the moon illuminated the outline of Bedford as she drew near.

The little town slept. Only the wan glow of the streetlights announced when she arrived at the edges of the hamlet.

A form wavering in the sky caught her eye and she leaned forward over the massive steering wheel. Something dark gray swirled and shifted like a ghostly entity against the star-lit night.

It looked like smoke rolling upward above the long row of buildings. She accelerated and hurried her car onto Juliana Street. Three blocks down, a jagged line of a yellow and red light danced about. She watched in horror as it flickered and jumped, fevered in its movements.

Fire!

Hardin's building was engulfed in flames. He had told her once that he lived above the store, reached via a stairway in the back. She honked her horn frantically as she hurried the motorcar down a side alley, pulling behind the row of stores.

Scrambling from the car, Libby screamed his name. Rats dashed along the foundation and vanished into the shadows. Faintly, above the crackling of the flames, she heard voices in front yelling, "Fire! Hurry!" Good, the alarm had been sounded, but that alone wouldn't save Hardin. If he was inside, she had to wake him and get him out.

She grabbed a towel from the bag she'd prepared for Andrew, wrapped it around her hand, and grasped the metal knob to the building's rear door, tugging and praying it would open.

It did, and she hurried in.

Around her, planks dropped from the edges of the ceiling and hit the ground, spreading showers of embers and sparks, and igniting other wood in its path. Wood crackled sending ash floating on waves of smoke. She snatched the towel from her hand and held it to her face to breath.

She sprinted in the direction of the stairway, but was impeded by a wall of flames, stretching right and left as far as she could see. When the flame danced down in its high-then-low jerky waltz, Libby saw, for one harrowing heartbeat, angry rolls of blaze and billows of smoke pouring down the stairway. Despite the towel, blistering smoke filled her lungs, and she coughed and gagged.

She zigzagged left in a frenzied rush.

Then right.

She squinted through the furling black air, her eyes watering and stinging, to where she saw the fire at its lowest. Perhaps she could jump through it. Make a mad dash and soar clear of it to get to the stairs.

But, a figure on the other side appeared, staggering zigzag toward her. She froze and in that second could see the figure was stocky like a man and that he was weak and blackened. The figure wailed incoherent sounds of pain and panic.

She yelled, "Hardin!"

He turned to her and howled, "Help me!" He staggered toward the door she'd come in.

She hurried to the left, trying to follow him but was stopped by more debris. She dashed right and leaped over more blackened wood, then hurried around another flame, dodging falling planks and embers that spread like confetti in a wind.

Through the wall of flames, she watched Hardin teeter several feet, exit through the door she'd left open, and fall.

"Hardin!" Her own raspy voice startled her from her stupor and spurred her to dash through an opening on the right to reach him. She dropped to the ground beside his upper torso.

Her lungs burned and her chest wanted to explode, but she focused on him. The flames behind her illuminated his body, and what she saw made her stomach lurch. Puffy, blackened scabs and angry red welts covered his upper body and arms. Severe third-degree burns. He could never survive this, and until he died, he would experience unbearable pain.

She had to do something to help him! But, what?

The water! It was equinox. Perhaps it wasn't too late. In that split second when a million thoughts can race through the mind, she pictured herself somehow getting him into her car and driving him there. But, if he died before taking the water or even in it, she'd be left with his dead body and probably accused of foul play. Maybe second-degree murder.

She shouldn't interfere with history!

But, how could she not? This man had wondered if people who feel as though they've lived lives before their own are inheriting their ancestor's memories. He had a theory to share with the world.

She sprinted to her car, and pulled it closer, repeatedly yelling for Hardin to hold on, and to fight! Once beside him, she opened the passenger side rear door and crouched down, lifting him by grasping under his arms from behind. He shrieked in pain. With adrenaline coursing through her veins and tears streaming down her face, she blubbered, "I'm sorry, Hardin. I know it hurts. I promise the pain will end soon."

She heaved and pulled him into the car, dragging him backward onto the back seat as gently as she could. She opened the opposite door, climbed out, and raced around to shut the first door, then climbed behind the wheel.

The trip took forever.

Hardin moaned, at times screamed, and she bit back her nausea and fear and horror to reassure him. Libby sobbed and, through tears, implored him to hold on. "I'm so sorry. I want to save you. I'm taking you to the water. It works Hardin! I know it does because it brought me here from 2016. Think about that when you're in the water. Go to the future, Hardin. Stay alive!"

Near her destination, she pulled off the navigable road and bounced the car across the rutted meadow to pull beside the Crystal Spring. She turned off the car, set the brake, and exited in a frenzy, wrenching open the rear door to extract Hardin. Grasping him as she had before, she pulled him out. He didn't make a sound. Was he unconscious? Dead? She dragged him backward, up the slight incline to the edge of the spring.

"Please, Hardin," she muttered as she struggled and heaved, her mouth near his ears. "Live, and, forgive me!"

She stopped at the edge, laid him flat, and said through her sobs, "I'm so sorry, Hardin, but this, *this* is what friends do," then she pulled him beneath the surface of the water. She fell as exhaustion overcame her, but scrambled back up and dragged herself out of the water. Thanks to the bright moonlight, she was able to see him. Her gaze seared into him despite the tears flooding her eyes.

In the stillness of the night, a sound of twigs snapping came from behind her and she pushed up with her hands to twist her gaze in that direction. She heard it again, near the copse of trees about thirty feet behind her.

"Who's there?" she called.

Panic struck. Had someone seen her? Would they try to

stop her? Was she in danger? She'd left her pistol in the car. Could she get to it? Who would be here this time of night? The pale man? Martelli? She'd been a fool to think she could get rid of him in the way she did, without repercussions. Or, perhaps the mayor had a goon watching her? Was this the prowler she'd heard outside her room late one night?

Could it be Andrew? Maybe he arrived before she got there and was standing back, unclothed and waiting.

She looked back at Hardin. His body still laid there in the water. He should have disappeared by now. She scrambled to her feet, jerking her gaze back to the trees. She was about to yell "Andrew" when two arms grabbed her from behind pinning her tight and dragged her backward away from the spring.

She struggled and flailed her legs, but the stranger's hold was too strong. All she managed to shake loose was her hat.

Despite her struggle she watched Hardin's body disappear before she lost sight of the water. *The water had taken him!*

Overcome by the many conflicting emotions coursing through her, she felt her body go limp and watched the world go black.

Chapter Twenty-Five

1926

S HERIFF BROGAN HARROW squeezed the steering wheel in a rigid grip as he glanced at the young woman seated beside him in the 1920 Chrysler police patrol motorcar. Moonlight poured through the side window, illuminating her features, but he didn't need light to recall that thick russet hair, those large, clouded milk-green marble eyes with their intriguing touch of blue, or full lips of deep cherry that had quivered when she stared at him in the alleyway in Bedford weeks ago.

Who was she? Her name was Libby Shaw. But who was she *really*? N.C. had once described seeing Rose and *Mrs.* Shaw at a play at the Springs Hotel. He'd distinctly said "Mrs." Where was her husband, and why did her marital status bother him?

Who was the real Libby Shaw? The unassuming concerned citizen who had coolly assessed the Gilbert Harris murder scene with an astuteness that startled him? Or the attractive, well-heeled visitor at the hotel—who, as his observations revealed, drove one of the finest motorcars he'd ever seen, preferred dresses in shades of blue, and played the violin (that tidbit purely by accident from N.C courtesy of a proud Rose)?

Or, was she the lady who, unlike the other guests at the hotel, *did* notice those who existed beyond her glittering lodging? The one who enjoyed simple homemade remedies, friendly conversations with the townies, salads for lunch, occasional chocolate ice cream, and countless acts of charity in which she would stealthily drop candy in children's parcels and money in the purses and pockets of the poorer townies? He'd arrested many pickpockets through the years, but until she came along he'd never seen this reverse scenario of putting money *into* people's pockets. Yes, he had observed it all, without her knowing.

He couldn't help but be aware of her when she frequented town. He hadn't sought her out. Certainly hadn't stalked her. He just somehow always intuited when she was there. Further, he'd never quite shaken that disturbing feeling he'd experienced when he'd met her in the streets of Bedford. She'd been unreadable, mysterious. Then again, she'd seemed as disoriented by their encounter as he had been. When she'd turned and left the crime site, he'd felt a sense of loss unlike any he could remember.

What in the name of all that's sensical did that mean?

Most disturbing, why had a man been watching her from the oak grove tonight? And, why had that scared him to death? When the man shifted his stance, Brogan had caught a metallic reflection in the moonlight. A gun. That prompted a flash of a memory to race at him, but veer away before he could assess it, decipher it. He wasn't sure why, but he had needed to remove the woman from the man's sight. He'd seen this stranger around town a few times, he was certain.

The woman stirred and put her hands on her forehead as though to stop it from throbbing. Or, was it to induce thinking? She opened her eyes and turned her head to look at him.

"You!" she said, her voice hoarse, her face awash with confusion. "*You* grabbed me?"

A tightness entered his chest. He shifted his gaze to the left where he steered the car to a crawl then off the road across gravel into a wooded area. They were almost there. He didn't want to alarm her further, but their conversation could wait. His experiences had taught him temperance and the dangers of speaking and acting too soon.

A large opossum scurried from the glow of the headlights and disappeared into the dark. Once Brogan would have shot him and happily brought him home for dinner. Now, the thought of opossum on his plate turned his stomach.

"Are you taking me to jail?" Her voice cracked.

He didn't answer, instead maneuvering the motorcar to a stop. After turning off the engine, he reached into the back to retrieve the lantern he kept there. He pulled matches from his pocket and lit the cloth wick.

"Where are we?" She peered into the darkness beyond the car, but he was aware she could see nothing. No people. No buildings. Certainly no jail. "Why did you bring me here?" A new fear settled in her voice. The light was too dull for him to read her face.

He clenched his jaw. Did she think him an unscrupulous kind of sheriff who determined to swap certain favors for her freedom? She had no idea how important her safety was to him. *Especially after what he'd just seen.*

"What do you want from me? I didn't kill Hardin." Her voice shook. "He was burned beyond help. It's hard to explain. You have no right to bring me here."

He flinched. She was right.

She looked at him with a strength he found a little disarming, yet her tone wavered between annoyance and fear. "You don't say much, do you?"

"You're safe," he said. "We need to talk privately. I'll get your door," he said, reaching for his own door handle.

"Shouldn't you be at the fire?"

He slumped back in the seat. "My first responsibility is to victims. No one else was in danger. There is an alley on one side and an empty business on the other." *Why was he explaining himself to her?* "N.C. and Roscoe will guard and investigate. I'll return later. I wasn't certain of your status…" *but my heart pounded when I saw you in the middle of the blaze* "…or of Hardin's situation so I followed you."

She sucked in her lips as if she wanted to argue more but wasn't quite sure what to say. Ignoring his offer about the door, she shoved it open and scrambled out, heaving it shut behind her.

He shook his head at her stubbornness, then climbed out too.

"This way," he said. "Please don't run. You're safer with me than anything out there." He nodded at the darkness.

She followed him in barbed silence as he led her about fifty feet from the car, into a sloping grove of trees and around an outcropping of rocks. The trees thinned, opening into a small clearing. Stopping, he pulled another match from his jacket pocket and held it in the lantern flame until it caught. He took two more steps and lit a torch that rose from the ground at least four feet into the air. Then five more steps and lit another. He knew their location and height well because he had placed them there.

The new light revealed a stone fireplace standing alone, as

though a house once stood there, and the chimney was all that survived. He took off his jacket, draped it across a log positioned between the torches, and gestured for her to sit. She hugged her arms, moved to the log, and plunked onto the jacket.

Looking around, she wrinkled her nose, but didn't ask about the aroma.

"Fresh wood." He pointed into the darkness. "I'm building a cabin."

Her eyebrows arched a fraction, but she said nothing.

"You ought to take those wet shoes off," he suggested. "If you're chilled you could wrap your feet in my jacket instead—"

"It's warm tonight. I'm fine." She kicked free of her shoes and wiped her feet dry with her hands. "Why are we here?" She sounded resigned, and spoke in hushed tones, as though the still of the darkness demanded mute voices.

"I know you put Hardin Lochery in the water." He folded his lean frame a comfortable distance from her onto the log.

She took a deep breath, as if marshaling her forces, but said nothing, shifting her gaze to the ground. Thanks to the torches, he could see her better. *At times.* At others, the wavering lights created more shadows than they dispelled, and that annoyed him.

"But," he continued, "I know you probably gave him a new life by doing so."

Her head snapped up and her gaze met his, but she remained silent.

He pulled off his hat, placed it on the log between them, and ran a hand over his head. "You're a traveler as well, aren't you?"

Her rigidness unfurled and relaxed like a plant seeking the sun, understanding dawning on her face. She covered her mouth with both hands. Finally, she said, "A traveler," like she was testing the word. "Do you mean as well as Hardin or…are you saying…"

"As well as me," he clarified, leaning forward to park his elbows on his knees and clasp his hands together.

"So…by traveling… you mean…"

"Taking the water and going to another time," he finished.

They stared at one another, and he watched any remaining guardedness melt.

"When did you—" Their voices collided with the same question.

A startled pause fell.

She studied his face. "Three months ago. From 2016. You?"

Only three months? Her husband was back in 2016? "Nine years ago. From 1769. I was born Nathan McKenzie in 1743."

Confusion or disappointment crossed her face. But which? It was there, but quickly gone.

She closed her eyes. "Incredible…This whole time-travel thing, do you ever wonder if we're being punished?"

"Punished?" He cocked his head. "No, just the opposite."

She shot him a look of curiosity.

"I think we've been blessed." He shrugged. "God made the mineral water, right? So, it's because of Him we have a new start."

"A new start," she echoed, but with a tone of dismay. "What if we were okay with our old start?"

He shrugged. "I don't think the point is how long you stay

in a place. More important is what you do while you're there. To make it a better place. It's a new chance. Like you gave Hardin tonight."

She remained still, staring at him.

He whistled an exhale, fighting the thought that while there was complete surprise in this development, there was also a comfort in not being alone in this twisted time journey. Since Ista's departure, he'd grown lonely as a castaway, seemingly the sole survivor the water had deposited on foreign terrain.

He chose his next words carefully to nudge her to relax. "Twenty sixteen. I can't fathom that year. But, I'm not surprised. You seem very…independent. This women's movement for equal everything, it's successful then?"

She exhaled a shaky breath and shook her head, as though this wasn't the conversation she anticipated. "It may seem successful to you, but women in the future would argue with that conclusion."

He considered that. "My secretary Jean says women want equal pay for meaningful work."

A slow smile grew on her lips and inched to her eyes. "She sounds like a smart lady."

He shrugged. "Perhaps. I'm a little stifled by it all. When I'm from, everyone worked. Man, woman, child. It was a matter of survival. Women dreamed of *not* working. But always, women were to be cherished and protected. Respected. It was a code of conduct a gentleman followed. I'm not much understanding these changes and what women want."

She raised a brow. "Wow."

Was that fascination he heard in her voice, or consternation? He looked at the ground. *Best to change the subject.* He didn't want to upset her or make her feel like this was an interrogation, but there were things, random things, he needed to understand and he found her intriguing. "Why didn't you scream back there? When I grabbed you?"

She studied him, as though trying to determine the reason for his question. "A scream would dull my senses momentarily, and it wouldn't stop you if you intended to hurt me." To his dismay, her tone grew serious. "If I'd thought there was help within earshot, I would have. But, I heard a noise in the woods right before you grabbed me. I figured someone was with you so my best bet was to be quiet so that he'd have more trouble catching up to us." She shrugged. "I thought I could get away from one, but not two men. Now, I assume he wasn't with you."

"No."

Another silent beat fell.

"You thought all that," Brogan said, "in one moment? That's...astonishing. You sound like you've been trained to react."

"I have been. At least," she looked away, "I've come to believe I have."

"Your memory isn't restored yet?"

She looked back at him and shook her head. "Yours?"

"Memories still elude me. The person who took care of me when I arrived said I should continue my healing by drinking a lot of the mineral water. That it would help me remember. But, some of the memories that came back to me were so painful, I stopped."

Her face flattened of all emotions. In a hushed tone, she said, "Me, too."

When she spoke those two words, that same strange current passed between them, the one he'd noticed at Gil Harris's murder site in town. He liked it so much, he felt a compulsion to stay right there forever. After she'd lost her hat at the spring, her hair had come undone in their struggle and it now caressed her shoulders. He watched the flickering light dance on her locks, illuminating and turning them the colors of low-burning flames. He had the strangest urge to touch it, to see if it was as thick and soft as it looked.

She disturbed his thoughts by pulling her knees close and wrapping her hands around them. "You said someone helped you after you came forward in time?"

He nodded. "She's not here anymore."

"She? But, weren't you naked?" She bit her lip.

He could swear she found humor in that picture, and he grinned. "It was a bit hard making eye contact with her after that. But, she was like a mother to me." He reached down and picked up a twig and picked at its bark. "What about you? You must have been…unclothed as well."

"He's not around either."

He? *Why had he hoped it would be a woman that helped her?* He shifted position on the log. "When I first arrived, I returned to the spring several times a week. Just sat there and stared into it. Wondering how all this was possible. I was flabbergasted."

She chuckled. "Flabbergasted? I wouldn't have thought that would be a word used much in the seventeen hundreds."

He liked her smile, her laugh. "It wasn't. I've had to change my vocabulary quite a bit. Adopt contractions. Drop the thees and thous."

She nodded. "I'm well-versed in languages, but I had to

hear the term 'boiled to the ears' several times before I figured out what people meant."

"I'm glad to hear certain phrases don't last."

She chuckled and nodded, but said nothing.

A cow mooed in the distance, echoing in the still of the late summer air, a reminder of the world beyond this spot. The night was so still, so calm. Brogan breathed it in, liking the moment. He should be discussing Hardin, but he wanted, needed, to learn more about her. It was almost an inherent need. And, he wanted to keep her looking at him in that pleasant way.

"When I saw you at the edge of the spring tonight," he said, "then saw that same man hiding in the trees and something metal in the moonlight…I experienced a memory, or déjà vu, or something. It was as though I had experienced this before. With you." He watched her closely. "Does any of that evoke a memory for you?"

She looked like she was giving it effort, trying hard, real hard, to draw upon such a memory, but that it eluded her. "No, I'm sorry."

He exhaled a sound of futility and plowed a hand over his head again.

Once more, silence fell, and Brogan tracked her gaze to the moon, wondering if she felt the same comfort in familiarity that he felt when he looked in that direction. It was the only constant companion he'd ever had. Everything, and everyone, else had been temporary. Around them the torch fire snapped and responded to gentle breezes, and an owl and a coyote called their lonely sounds.

Libby broke the silence. "You said, 'that same man' as

though you'd seen him before."

He nodded. "In town."

"Who is he?"

Brogan shrugged. "I don't know. Probably just a familiar face. It is a small town, practically impossible to cough without your neighbors bringing you chicken soup."

She reacted with a smile, but it came and went quickly. She didn't appear to be afraid anymore, only puzzled, as though she had a thought. "Still, why would he be there?" she asked, almost to herself.

Yes, why *would* he be there? That quickly Brogan experienced a clarity. "When I saw him before in town, you were there, too. I'm sure of it."

"Was he tall or short?"

He thought about it. "I wasn't close enough to tell. But, judging by the other men that walked near him, he was taller than most."

Libby looked disappointed. "I had to leave my husband Andrew behind. In 2016. He's not very tall. You're certain you saw this man before tonight?"

When Brogan nodded, he could swear her disappointment gave way to a quiver of fear, but it disappeared instantly as she gathered her wits. When at last she spoke, the tone of her question suggested wonderment more than inquisitiveness. "You saw me in town?"

"Several times. I also came to the hotel to see you once. To let you know we caught the guy who murdered Gilbert Harris. Your assessment of the victim was startling. Instrumental in helping us focus our investigation."

She smirked. "I'm guessing the mayor is not behind bars."

"Mayor Drenning? He didn't do it. A man named Ambrose Talbot confessed. Turns out, Harris had been trying to blackmail Talbot over several crimes he discovered that Talbot committed. Talbot confessed to those, too."

"But the mayor lied about knowing Harris. He withheld evidence."

"He told me later that day that he knew Harris. The three of them worked stills together. Wanted to avoid the public's ears." Brogan smiled. "Drenning's a bootlegger and an opportunist, but that doesn't make him a criminal. Half the country is making moonshine and bathtub gin. If I jailed everyone bucking prohibition, there would be more people incarcerated than on the street. Besides, he's a politician. Are you saying they become more honest in the future?"

She rolled her eyes. "Point taken."

He flattened his lips. "The mayor has power around here. Powerful men are often careless when it comes to their pursuits."

"That doesn't change with time either," she quipped, stretching out her legs, looking more relaxed. She gazed back at the dark night. "You said seventeen sixty-nine? Before the Revolutionary War. I guess politics were pretty bad in those days. It must actually seem better now."

"Somewhat."

"What has surprised you? About this era, I mean."

He liked her questions, her hushed tone. They seemed to close the two of them together in this spot, and he endeavored to answer her question, but his head was aswarm with thoughts of so many changes. How could he list them all? "How the women dress. How forward they are. Dating instead of courting."

"Courting?"

He nodded "It was more intentional. Purposeful. Like you had identified your desired future and were going after it."

She offered a half-smile, so he continued.

"Everything is noisier and more expensive now. No more British rule, that was a good surprise. No more Indian raids and scalpings...sorry to be graphic. Motorcars. Airplanes. A country that spans from ocean to ocean, amazing. Oh," he clicked two fingers together, "indoor plumbing and wringer washer."

She chuckled. "Wringer washer?"

"We used to catch rainwater in a log trough under the cabin eaves, or haul it in pails from the creek. Then, we heated it in a pot over an outdoor fire, before beating the clothes on a rock to get the dirt out. Drying was on the fence or hung from rafters in the cabin. Now we have wringer machines and clothes lines."

Libby laughed harder and he liked the sound of it.

"The most startling change though, is the free time everyone has. Where...*when* I come from, every minute was spent working or hunting or preparing a meal. If there was any time left, we would sleep, then get up and do it all over again."

"I can't imagine that life." She pulled her brows together and twisted her lips as though wrestling with something beyond comprehension. "And yet, I don't know why, but it feels familiar. Perhaps it's the way you describe it."

Brogan studied her. *What would she think of the world he left?*

"For me," she said, "it was the poverty. I've driven the countryside and observed how people live. In the future, the poorest people we consider poverty-stricken still live ten times better than these people. They have their own cars…motorcars, and dish satellites, cell phones and televisions. Most at taxpayer expense, no less."

He thought about that. He knew what a dish was, but not a satellite. He wasn't sure what a cell phone was either. He repeated the word that struck him as most intriguing, "Television," he said as if he were trying the sound of it.

"You've seen a moving picture show?" she asked with a lop-sided grin.

He nodded.

"Imagine that with sound. In your home, twenty-four seven."

As fascinated as he was with the concept, it was the "twenty-four seven" verbiage he cataloged in his memory.

"So, everybody is exactly the same in the future?"

Libby rolled her eyes. "That's what society is pushing toward."

"That's not what God intended. He created us all different-ly. Different goals, talents, ambitions, purposes, outcomes."

She planted a crooked smile on her face. "Things change." She gazed at the sky again.

He wished he could read her mind.

"This place seems familiar." Her voice was laced in perplex-ity. "Like I've been here before."

"I felt that too. Something drew me here." He looked around. "I have flashbacks, visions when I'm here. Moments of peace…other times, odd discomfort. I've been trying to figure it out."

The truth, and what he wouldn't tell her, is that the good

memories involved a female…he was certain. When the conflicting visions surfaced, he forced himself not to linger, or to think about the pull he felt toward *her*, the woman in his visions. Decidedly he did not try to remember whether or not the woman reciprocated the feeling or became a part of his life or, indeed, what happened to her. Because, always, if he stayed too long, the vision turned to one of phantom screams. His chest tightened now as he savored the peaceful memory of the woman in his visions—*her* warm grin, the deep dimple in *her* cheeks when *she* smiled at him. And yet, above the grin and the dimples, the face was a blur.

"Mr. Harrow?"

He shook his head to dislodge his thoughts, and discovered she was looking at him expectantly. "It's Brogan. Sorry, what did you ask?"

"Why are you building here if it makes you uncomfortable?"

Because the good visions are so wonderful, they far outweigh the bad. "I'm building beside it. Not right here. Besides, during the day the view of the mountains is worth every effort." He needed to change the conversation. "May I ask why you wouldn't see me when I came to the hotel?"

She swallowed and looked away. "You unnerved me. I guess it was that sense of recognition I experienced when we met in town. You seemed frightening, yet familiar. Not exactly a memory though." She massaged her forehead. "When you said your name, I heard 'Broken Arrow' and I saw myself—a sort of ghosted version of myself—with you."

His heart gave a dangerous, unexpected flutter. "That was my name. My Mohawk name. When I told the former sheriff, he heard me incorrectly. Thought I said Brogan Harrow. When he retired two years ago and I became sheriff, he arranged identification papers for me before I could correct him."

"Why would you give him your Indian name?"

He shrugged. "I didn't want to lie."

The edges of her lips rose. "Of course. So, Brogan Harrow. Broken Arrow. You don't look Indian. I thought you said you were born Nathan McKenzie."

"The woman who helped me, she said I once was called that, but I don't remember. So, I never use it."

She laid a hand at her throat. "In the street, you whispered ohon…ohote—"

"Ohonte, oròn:ya." He swallowed against his embarrassment. "I'm not even sure what it means. For some reason, I felt it was important to say. Does it sound familiar?" *Why was hope surging through him?*

She repeated the words as she climbed to her feet and turned away from him. He watched her move, watched her shake her head as though she were pondering the words and decided they made no sense. She dropped her shoulders and turned back to him.

"I don't know what it means." She threw her palms up, a gesture of giving up. "Shakespeare wrote that the past is prologue. Maybe I'll figure it out eventually."

Hearing the quote, his body experienced an instinctual reaction, robbing him of equanimity. Something stirred, growing in the graveyard of his past. That quote, in *her* voice—the woman in his visions. Familiar. Too familiar. Achingly and poignantly familiar. Memories surged. He had stood with *her* once, at this spot. He was younger. So was she.

Another man was there as well. She called him "Pa." He told her to go inside so they could discuss the tracts of land. She had hesitated, instead stood there smiling at him in that way girls do when they're experiencing their first infatuation. Another memory nudged in. Something faintly disturbing. Unease prickled around the edges of the memory and burrowed in quickly. The same man lying across a wooden barrel. Scalped! Brogan smelled burned bodies, felt the residual heat of the embers. Panic for *her*. But why? The overwhelming feeling came that he would have hunted her to the ends of the earth if he had known. But she was here…

But, what about Gretchen, his wife? Gretchen, the descendant of the woman he'd abandoned to go in search of Elisa, who became Morning Meadow. And now, Libby. He remembered now! That girl-turned-woman had lived right here, at this home site. The Macay home. Libby was *her*—Elisa and Morning Meadow. The woman in his visions. He saw *her* face clearly now.

Then, his mind emptied and he felt like he was falling off a cliff. Trying to hold the memories, to process them, brought an ache to his head, his heart. He searched his mind, grasping for an explanation. Nothing came.

"Brogan? Are you well?"

"I…" He looked intently into Libby's distinct eyes, searching. And there she was. Morning Meadow! Ohonte, oròn:ya. *Green with blue. Together.*

But Libby didn't remember Morning Meadow. He rubbed a hand over his chest, trying to calm the knot developing there. "I need to leave." He needed to extricate himself quickly. He stood, looking around, confused. "I must get back to town. To the fire." To anywhere but here. "I'll drop you at the hotel. Best if you get your car tomorrow in the light of day."

Her brows pulled together, her gaze intensified. "Of course." She grabbed his jacket and handed it to him, then picked up her shoes. "I can put these on while you drive."

He extinguished the torches, and they returned to the car in silence. In his peripheral vision, Brogan could see her studying him, concern written on her face.

After they'd driven a few minutes, she broke the silence. "What now? Regarding Hardin, I mean."

Good. She was asking questions. He appreciated that. He took a deep breath, tried to concentrate. "I listen. Try to find out if anyone else saw him at the fire. I'm sure my deputies did not. He had no family around here. If no one else saw anything, I announce he must have left town. Case closed. Meanwhile, we pray he finds a better life in another time."

The rest of the trip unfolded in silence. When they neared the Springs, she pointed out her room. He pulled the motorcar to a stop at the bottom of the small slope that ascended to her door. He turned off the engine, and in the briefest moment of awkward silence that followed, he listened to the faintest of ticks as the motorcar cooled down, all the while trying to decide what to do and say.

She ended the awkward moment. "I'll be fine from here," she said, putting her hand on the door handle.

"I'll walk you." His tone was firm, his movements brisk. He climbed out, walked to her side of the motorcar and offered his hand to assist.

She took it and climbed from the car to stand beside him, but neither of them moved, as if the touch, though feather-light, had paralyzed them. He breathed her in. Did she feel it too? His knees weakened. He felt like he was swaying. The moment elongated, scintillated. And then it was over. She exhaled and stepped back, putting an arm's length between them. It took all of his restraint not to reach for her again. Abashed, he looked away and headed toward her door.

Somehow, he deposited her at her room, returned to the car, and headed back to town. As he drove, the memories came, one by one, piling on top one another, like a snowball at the top of a hill rolling down with a thunderous speed, picking up more and more flakes as it travels. Libby once had been Elisa Macay. Her family was murdered. *At that site!* She was taken by the Lenape and traded to the Mohawks. He'd gone after her. Found her. Fought for her.

Married her!

Watched her die.

Hadn't he?

Ista! She was there when Morning Meadow died…*and* when he had found her five years before that. Ista had lived alone, just outside the Indian camp because of her newfound faith. She had taken Elisa in, renamed her, loved her like a daughter. Later, Ista saved her life, by placing her in the water…at least four years before he took the water. This is what Ista had meant, later, when she'd left him in 1921! She had said, "Wait for her." He hadn't listened. Hadn't understood.

The memories were coming so fast and so complete, he thought he might be violently ill. He pulled the motorcar to the side of the dark road, kicked open the weighty door, and wretched. He sat back into the motorcar and held a hand to his aching head because it wasn't just memories pouring into him.

With those visions and flashbacks and recollections, came recall and comprehension, and all the searing emotions that accompanied the realities back then. All the feelings of anguish he'd felt at her family's deaths, the intense love he'd developed for Morning Meadow among the Mohawks, the joy at their marriage, the despair when she'd been shot.

He had thought she died in 1765, but here she was.

Alive!

Gaelic belief says love and friendship is not measured by space or time, but rather by the force and capability of the soul. It was true, he still loved her. He needed her back in his life.

But, their five years together had ended thirteen years ago. They had changed. Experienced different things. Grown in different ways.

Most concerning, they both belonged to someone else now.

Chapter Twenty-Six

1926

A WEEK HAD passed since Libby last saw Sheriff Brogan Harrow, yet their conversation, and the flashbacks it generated, was stuck on a repeat loop in her head. She had lost count of the number of times she had turned the facts and her questions inside out. Studied them from every angle. Weighed likelihoods and impossibilities, chances and odds.

And, the visions! They exhausted by day and prevented sleep at night, propelling Libby to pace her room, the hallway, the grounds, as if movement could drive her closer to understanding these teasing, taunting individual pictures of moments that refused to be caught.

The visions played in her mind like the reel of an old-fashioned silent flick, but were made up of unlinked stills without context. Snapshots without connection. No before and after explanations for clarity or continuity.

They inhabited her room like an unwanted roommate who shared and used her air. They peaked in the windows. Gathered in the depth of the drapes. Spread out in waiting on her bed, sofa and chairs.

Emotions surfaced as well. Intense feelings unlinked to the fleeting images. Feelings that meant nothing to her. She couldn't cutline, code, or catalog them. An agitation built inside her from an offense she couldn't identify. An abuse she couldn't describe. An injury that left her breathless. A rage that confounded. A love that ameliorated.

"Idiot!" Libby pounded her head with the back of her right palm as she paced back and forth the length of her room. Why can't she remember?

Brogan Harrow had once been Nathan McKenzie, then Broken Arrow. Why did that name leave her breathless? Bereft? His descriptions of living life so close to the land had sounded so raw, basic—why did that call to her? She was a woman who cringed at a life without plastic! And yet, the site he'd taken her to had intrigued her. She'd fought all week against finding her way back there.

Needing a bit of that raw element now, she barreled to her exterior door, yanked it open, and stood there breathing in the crisp autumn air. The mid-morning sun blanketed the area in a shower of golden warmth. October had ushered in cooler days, but temperatures remained unseasonably warm for that time of year.

She gulped in the air, determined to clear her head by re-placing thoughts of Brogan Harrow with anything else. She should be mourning Hardin's departure, not thinking about the sheriff.

Why then, was she trying to activate her memory by chugging the mineral water every chance she got? She'd consumed a gallon a day since the night with Brogan.

Ghostly spectrals surfaced again. Jolts of recognition. Unfamiliar faces. Yet, somehow not. The memories gamboled frustratingly just out of reach. A man, bare-chested, in a forest, raising a rifle. An old woman, her face covered by the angle of a hat, kneeling by the water. Brogan, holding her hand as they stood by a lake, the moon their only companion. Indians, painted and pierced, with stern faces, their tomahawks raised.

The only vision that came with a modicum of understanding was that this was the man who had haunted her dreams back in 2016. It was *him*. She remembered now. Before she'd even taken the water, with Andrew at her side, she'd seen this Sheriff Brogan Harrow, vivid and alive in her dreams.

He'd said, "Come back to me." Here, without intending to, it seems she had done just that. And, he'd come forward. But who was he and what did it mean? Why wouldn't these random images piece the story together in a coherent way?

She turned from the open door and returned to pacing, determined steps about six yards in one direction then back again across the jeweled carpet.

He had said a woman helped him when he came from the water. Who was that woman, and why did she care?

Who had followed her, watching as she placed Hardin in the water?

Her mind continued wrestling, returning full circle to thoughts of Brogan. She'd acted stupid. Muddled! When he'd brushed his hair out of his eyes...*oh my*. His hand was rough and slightly calloused. A true man's hand. Strong and solid.

What was she thinking? Prior to last week she'd been afraid of him.

She was losing her senses.

It was no use. All she saw when she closed her eyes was Sheriff Brogan Harrow. The spill of cocoa-colored hair across his forehead, the twisted grin that drew the eye away from the scar and dropped it on the dimple to the left of his lips, the way his gaze burrowed into her when he was about to be serious. He'd been bigger than he had appeared in Bedford when she'd first met him, and though he was lean, there was a compact strength to every inch of his six feet. His bearing was smooth, quiet, self-contained, powerful.

How could she be drawn to him? He wasn't sophisticated like the men of the future.

Yet, he was one of the most discerning and competent people she'd ever met—not formally educated like Andrew or her colleagues at the bureau, but insightful and sagacious with a mind that studied and adapted to his circumstances and fit pieces of knowledge together to tackle what life tossed at him, and then mastered it.

Would the men of the future have survived and adapted as he had? Doubtful. Clearly, this man Brogan was made of sterner stuff.

At his brief touch she'd felt safe and removed from harsh reality, yet terribly vulnerable, and that had launched a new fear. An anxiety for her heart. She took a deep breath, remembering his scent, all male, mixed with a faint underscore of soap and musk. She'd been close enough to feel the heat of his body. See the pulse jumping beneath his jaw. Notice the smooth skin of his neck and end-of-the day beard stubble. It had taken all of her restraint not to lean into him. To bury her nose in that hollow beneath his chin that was all chiseled bones and angles, and to relax in his strength. It would feel so natural.

But, what he must have thought! After he left that night, she had been mortified when she walked into her room and saw her reflection in the mirror that night. Her wrinkled, smoke-stained clothing had looked charred, black. Her hair had been disheveled, and her face smudged with soot.

Despite that, he had looked at her as though she was a memory he wanted back…until she quoted Shakespeare. Then, he had unexpectedly stopped. He could barely look at her. Like he had a thought he couldn't share. One that consumed him. Scared him. What had it been? She needed to know.

Why did she care? She intoned a sound of frustration and fisted her hands. The shoes she'd worn that night were still on a towel on top her bureau. She grabbed one, whirled around toward the opposite side of the room, and threw it, cursing as she did.

As it soared through the air, Libby watched Maude appear at the open door, and duck. Her friend watched the shoe land on the door stoop, then clapped. "Good show. Whatever it is, get it out of your system."

Libby rolled her head back with a groan. "Sorry."

"All's hunky-dory. It missed me." Maude retrieved the shoe, walked into the room, and plopped down on a chair, propping her feet on a small table. "So what have I missed? My guess is a man is involved."

"Why would you say that?"

"What else would cause such passion? Besides, you've been preoccupied all week. So who is it? Jarvis getting to you again?"

Libby hadn't seen much of Maude in the past week, and when they had gotten together their outings involved an activity like horseback riding or tennis which precluded much conversation. Maude knew nothing of her involvement at the fire. But, she did know Hardin was gone. Three days earlier, at breakfast, with others around them, of course, they had read about the fire in the local newspaper and about how it had been attributed to faulty wiring.

Libby shrugged. "I miss Andrew. It seems like forever since he...died."

"And?"

"What do you mean 'and'? Isn't that enough?"

Maude tilted her head. "Typically, yes. But you've never talked much about him. I would think his memory would evoke tears, not fits of anger. So, who else?"

Libby exhaled. *Just say his name.* Maude didn't have to know the details. "Sheriff Brogan Harrow. He's so...so..." Libby flailed her hands.

"Ahh."

"What's that supposed to mean?" Libby crossed her arms.

"It means ahh, that's all."

Libby groaned again. "Sorry. I don't know what's gotten into me." She rubbed her forehead.

"I do. You're attracted to a married man and you're annoyed by it."

Libby closed her eyes, struck by Maude's words. "That sounds so awful and scandalous and—"

"Normal. It sounds normal, Libby. What you do or don't do about it is what makes the difference."

"I suppose."

Maude continued. "You know...you've never asked me about my past. About any men in my life."

Embarrassed, Libby dropped into a chair and studied her friend. "I didn't want to pry. I figured if you—"

Maude chuckled and showed a stopping hand. "It's alright. And, it's one of the things I like about our friendship. It's not stifling." She pulled her silver case from her pocket, extracted a cigarette and lit it. "I was in love once. I told you I volunteered for the Red Cross in the war, right? 1917. Before America got involved. Ended up in France. Met another doctor. Fell in love. He was British. Brilliant, funny, full of life. We had three months together. Busy moments working side by side. Down times filled with passion. When you're caught that close to war's ugliness, you tend to live life on the edge. Like it's your moral duty to grab every available pleasure before death claims you."

Libby grabbed the gold velvet cushion from behind her, and hugged it against her chest. "Must have been surreal."

Maude nodded and drew a long breath on her cigarette. Exhaled. When she continued, her voice was low and husky. "One night he acted different. Came clean about being married. I was devastated. Furious. Began calling him all sorts of names. Suddenly, our compound was being bombed. In seconds, dead and injured lie everywhere. We raced to the surgical tent and did what we could. I lost sight of him at one point. Next thing I knew, his body was placed on my operating table. He died there. I was left wondering what more might he have told me about the marriage? Would it have mattered? And why had he suddenly told the truth? Did he suspect he was going to die? And, of course, did I do everything I could to help him?" She inhaled again and tipped her head back to exhale, her gaze moving to the ceiling and halting there, as if she were staring at something that challenged her.

"I had no idea." A choke rose in Libby's throat.

Maude shrugged. "Now you know why I work with people damaged by the war. I understand the experience, and the guilt of survivors." Her voice was tight with emotion.

"Why are you telling me this?"

"Point is, many people, especially men, are good at omitting information. At telling you only what it takes so they get what they want from you. Libs, you're a beautiful woman. Now that you're a widow, you need to practice caution. Don't trust or believe men so readily."

Libby's gaze ranged over the pillow to the patterns on the carpet, at a loss for words. Perhaps Maude was right. Then again, Andrew had been painfully honest with her. She could trust him. And Davis had been honest. She was certain. No, Maude was from another era. She didn't know that women in the future learned about the battle of the sexes at a much younger age.

Maude moved her feet from the couch to the floor, sat forward, and smudged the remains of her cigarette in an ashtray. "Enough of that. The train leaves at four—"

Startled, Libby asked, "What are you talking about? Where are you going?"

"Back to Cleveland for the winter. I told you the other day. You really have been distracted by the sheriff, haven't you?"

Libby waved the comment away. "I've had a lot on my mind."

"In case you didn't notice, autumn has arrived." Maude winked. "Most of the hotel closed this week. Folks have gone home. My patient left yesterday. Not everyone has a heated room and plans to stay here, like you."

"I hadn't realized. I'm going to miss you."

Maude tilted her head. "Look here, why not come along? Even if only for a few weeks. Now is a good time to go before the cold weather arrives with a vengeance. We'll have a swell time."

The idea both scared and titillated Libby, but she couldn't leave now. "Thanks, but maybe later."

Maude studied her. Libby waited for her to ask what in the world she might have to do, but bless that sweet woman, she didn't inquire. Yes, theirs was a good friendship. Instead, Maude said, "Then ride along as far as Pittsburgh. You could do a little sightseeing. Some shopping. We'll take in a show. Getting away would probably do you some good."

Libby liked the idea. Davis was in Pittsburgh. She could talk to him about Brogan, and report that Andrew hadn't returned yet. She ought to let him know that someone had been watching her, too. Still, she was about to decline, because greater than her desire to talk to Davis was her need to spend time with Rose and learn what N.C. had said, if anything, about the sheriff. But, she had a thought. "Would you mind if Rose came, too?"

Maude's smile grew. "Jolly idea. The more the merrier." She put her hands on her knees and pushed herself to standing. "It might be good to get Rose away from that deputy anyway."

Libby's eyebrows rose. "N.C.? You've seen them together?"

"Quite a bit. Haven't you?"

Libby cringed. She'd been too preoccupied to notice.

Maude headed to the door. "I'll arrange for two round-trip tickets. You two can decide later when you want to return. The hotel shuttle leaves for the train at two o'clock. Will that give you enough time?"

"We'll be ready."

"Eat something before we leave. The food on the train is limited and ghastly. And, pack something smart. There's a vaudeville show in Pittsburgh you might enjoy." With that, she was gone.

✕

A HALF-HOUR LATER, Libby stood in Jarvis's office holding a borrowed suitcase and a small wooden hand crate large enough to hold several containers of water. On a hunch she'd gone to his office to ask if the hotel had any abandoned luggage she could use on short notice. Her thought had proven correct and she became the proud temporary owner of a handled crate and a brown leather case, the perfect size for an extended weekend trip. Unfortunately, it didn't come with wheels and durable lightweight fabric like luggage in the twenty-first century, but she planned to tip porters to tend to her needs on this trip anyway.

The transaction complete, Libby turned to go, but Jarvis halted her with his next statement. "Madame—"

"Libby."

"Libby," he said her name like it was the hardest thing he'd ever had to do. "I've been meaning to talk to you. About a position."

"You mean for Rose?"

"No, you." He rubbed his chin, stood and came out from behind his desk. He leaned against the edge of it and folded his arms. "Does that insult you? You seem like an independent, modern young woman so I thought you might be interested in more than..." He swept a hand through the air as though gesturing toward the privileged life outside his office.

"The boring rut of a socialite?"

He tried to hide a grin. "I wouldn't have worded it quite that way, but yes. You see, Mrs. Henderson, my coordinator for the maids and the restaurant staff, will not be returning. You strike me as a...problem-solver. You've displayed a talent for scheduling and finances, as well."

Because she won a bet and got rid of Martelli?

"The staff likes you."

But you won't admit you do too?

"You seem to appreciate the work they do and how arduous it can be. You also have a skill with modern devices, like the telephone."

This one she couldn't let go by. "That's considered a skill?"

Jarvis unfolded his arms, flattened his hands on the desk, and drummed his fingers once. "Perhaps that's not much of an accomplishment, but you'd be surprised how many of the staff are daunted by the task." He cleared his throat. "Oliver Kenton tells me you interact well with individuals from all social levels. And, there is your skill with languages. It's proven quite handy on a number of occasions."

Foremost, you haven't seen Davis around here so you know your initial thoughts of me being a mistress were unfounded.

"The position wouldn't begin until next year. We train in May, open in June. We operate on a skeleton staff during the winter as there are so few guests. Since you will be living here, it will give you several months to become familiar with the establishment."

Libby's thoughts raced again. How could she promise availability when Andrew could return at any time? In that instant, that moment of worrying about him, she suddenly wanted to be cured of the need to continually watch for him. After all these months, she had no energy left for the emotional hope-disappointment-then-hope-again struggle.

She gripped the suitcase handles tighter. "Thank you, Jarvis. May I think about it?"

"Certainly. I'm not going to search in earnest until January. If you have any questions, let me know."

Libby turned to go.

"Oh, and madame, a telegram arrived for you this morning."

✕

LATER, LIBBY KNOCKED on Rose's door. The girl had earlier agreed to accompany Libby on the trip.

"You might want to use a larger case, if you have one," Libby said, assessing Rose's small gray valise and her progress in packing.

"This will hold everything, ma'am," Rose said. "I don't have much to pack. I am usually in a maid's outfit, I am."

"I meant for your purchases. We'll be shopping at millinery stores and haberdasheries." Libby sank on the edge of the bed near Rose. "Of course, we can always buy you another bag in Pittsburgh I suppose."

Rose grimaced and diverted her gaze to a small wooden four-leaf clover that hung from the valise. She began to rub it as she spoke. "I don't have that kind of money, ma'am. I surely can't be spending what I have on fabric for myself. I'm coming along to help you, I am. After we get back, I'll have to make some changes. Maybe get a job in Bedford—"

"A job? You have a job."

"The hotel has closed for the season."

"Why does everyone keep telling me that? I don't mean that job. Yes, you'll have your position again next year, but meanwhile you have a job as my assistant. My personal companion. You know that I—" She stopped mid-sentence as comprehension hit. "Good gracious, Rose. I forgot to tell you that I'm going to pay you, didn't I?"

"Ma'am, you don't have that kind of money." Rose's face pinkened.

Libby looked at the telegram clutched in her hand. It was from Thomas St. Clair, saying her investments thus far had more than doubled. General Electric had done particularly well. "Rose, I *do* have that kind of money. Let me be more clear this time. I would like to pay you to work for me. Like a lady's companion. You would live right here. I'll pay for that, of course. I'd expect you to make us both some smart outfits, run errands, look after our rooms, accompany me. If that sounds good to you, then I will pay you the same wages you make as a maid. You'll get two days off each week. And flexible leave anytime you want it. How does that sound?"

Rose's jaw fell open and she dropped on the bed as though needing support. "Ma'am, you'll pay for my room, and pay me, *and* I get two days off each week? That's too much, it is."

Libby twisted her lips. She probably could have offered one day off per week and secured just as much interest from Rose, but no, she wanted to be fair. "You can use them to visit your mom."

"Me mum! I can't wait to tell her about this. I'll do that as soon as we get back from Pittsburgh, I will."

"Does she already know we're going?"

"Yes, ma'am, I paid the front desk earlier to telephone the

pastor of our church. He promised to drop by and tell her."

Libby was quiet a moment, startled by how many people had to be involved in delivering a message to Rose's mother. She couldn't change that situation much on the receiving end, but she certainly could make it easier on this end. "Make that your first task when you get back. Look into having a telephone installed. For our use. There's no sense going in search of one every time we want to place a call."

Rose's sprang to her feet. "Oh yes, ma'am, I'll cross me fingers for luck on it, I will."

"If this works out, you may have N.C. call you here. It might be easier to make plans that way." Libby eyed Rose closely to gauge her reaction.

Rose blushed even more. "He's just a friend, ma'am."

Libby grinned. "But you enjoy his company?"

Rose looked away and busied herself by stuffing her folded clothes into her valise. "He's funny. A gentleman." She brightened. "He has cold hands."

"You say that like it's a good thing."

"Oh, it is. Warm hands, cold heart. But cold hands, warm heart."

"Ah." Libby couldn't think what to add to that bit of superstitious logic. She leaned closer and helped Rose fold the few items she had yet to pack. "Does he ever say anything about Sheriff Harrow?" She gave it her best effort to sound nonchalant.

"What do you mean?"

"You know… what sort of man he is. I know he has a wife. Any children?"

"Not yet, but she's with child now, she is. Due in six

months."

Libby looked away. "I see."

"But, it's such a sad situation." Rose buckled the strap on her valise.

"How so?" Libby forced a blank face.

"It's just that N.C. speaks so highly of the sheriff. Says he can't do enough for people. Always helping out, he is. Knows everyone by name. Polices the town fairly. Treats everyone equal. But..."

"But?" *Goodness, would Rose never get to the point?*

Rose looked around which struck Libby as odd since they were alone in the room. When the girl spoke again, it was in a whisper. "Well, ma'am, it's his wife. Gretchen's her name. She's much younger than him and, well, I guess she's not very happy. Not exactly faithful, if ya know what I mean." Rose's eyes grew big and she thrust a hand over her mouth, looking like she wished she could stuff the words back in.

So the handsome sheriff had married a much younger woman, a hot little number that didn't like being tied down? Libby noticed Rose's discomfort and deduced the rest of the saga in her head. That the paternity of Gretchen's baby was uncertain. Rose was just too sweet and circumspect to voice it.

Libby tugged Rose's hand from her face. "Don't be silly. It's just me. I'm paying you for your honesty and discretion."

Rose thought about that and visibly relaxed. "'Course it don't matter much anyway 'cause she's been sick lately. Real sick. So she's not been healthy enough to do much running around."

Libby left the room feeling dizzy.

FIVE HOURS LATER the three women stood outside the station as a low hum sounded and grew, finally turning into a roar when the train rumbled in from the east. Once the engine had passed, the line of four passenger cars slowly came to a halt, bracketing the platform. Behind the string of carriers, a half-dozen boxcars extended down the track, beyond the edges of the station.

"They're putting our luggage on," Rose said as she stretched to look down the line to the last compartment.

Maude and Libby turned to look, too.

"I can't believe how much water you packed," Maude quipped to Libby when she eyed the bags again. "They do have water in Pittsburgh, you know."

Libby shrugged. *I need my memory back.* "I have a sensitive stomach right now."

At ten minutes until four, the three women boarded, found their seats, and settled in. It smelled of disinfectant, tobacco, and stale heat. Libby could feel the vibration of the train beneath her feet, see the dust mites dance in the sunlight streaming in.

After the departure whistle sounded, the train pulled forward with a shudder, its iron wheels squealing. Maude leaned sideways and peered past Libby through the window. Her gaze sharpened in focus, graduating from a glance to a glare. Libby was about to comment when her friend spoke. "Do you know that man?" Maude pointed toward the east end of the platform. "The one in the black hat?"

Libby caught the briefest glimpse of a figure turning his

back to them. From the distance it was hard to judge height before he disappeared into the shadows.

"Oh! He left," Maude said. "He must have seen me pointing."

Rose emitted a sound of disappointment. "I missed him. Sorry ma'am."

"Me, too," Libby added.

Maude said, "I couldn't see his face. He wore his hat low and hid behind a newspaper."

"Hid?"

"That's what it looked like. I saw him watching you earlier, too. I didn't think much of it, men being men, but when you went to the ticket counter, you know, when Rose and I stayed with the luggage, his gaze tracked your every movement."

Libby shifted in the lumpy velvet seat as the train cleared the long platform roof and moved into the sun-filled landscape. She tried to act nonplussed, interested in the moving tableau outside the window. Could this be the man outside her room late one night? Or, pale man? He was about that size. And, had he watched her deposit Hardin in the water? She gripped her small purse, careful not to let the other two women know she was feeling for confirmation of the pistol within.

In her peripheral vision, Libby saw Maude staring at her with expectation as the train picked up speed. "I guess I have one of those faces that look familiar," she quipped. "Now, let's talk about our plans for this trip."

PITTSBURGH WAS BOTH a surprise and a disappointment.

Libby's first impression was of a city of hills and rivers, with a metropolis—at least, compared to Bedford—tucked in between. The streets were alive with porters blowing whistles, hawkers shouting prices, shoppers patronizing businesses, newspaper kiosks, street vendors, shoeshine stands, and drivers disregarding the few (and new-looking) traffic lights. Large motorcars and even larger trucks fronted with protruding bugeye headlights pushed past horse-drawn buggies and farm carts. The downtown buildings were four and five stories high, and surrounded in all directions with train tracks and one- and two-story houses. By far, the establishments advertised names suggestive of Scot-Irish and German origins.

The city was also a hub for coal mining and steel production. Unfortunately, this meant factories and smelters, both *in* and around the city, cranked out coal dust and smoke and grit that had long sense dropped a layer of black soot on the city, and waste was flushed into the rivers. Other odors—garbage, sludge, sulfur, and horse manure—assaulted their senses. The streets were noisy and the factories noisier still as they clanged in the distance and shook the ground beneath them.

Rose began sneezing. "Goodness, ma'am, me mum always said the country has the freshest air. I had no idea."

"Your mother is a smart woman," Libby mumbled as she and Maude hurried Rose into their hotel.

The next three days were spent frequenting stores, restaurants, and a museum. The three women also attended a vaudeville show starring the Lester Hope and George Byrne team, a singing baseball pitcher named Petey Pete, and eighteen-year-old Siamese twins Daisy and Violet Hilton who played saxophone and clarinet duets and danced with Hope and

Byrne. Wherever they went, the nightspots were filled with jazz music filtering into the street.

On their third day, Libby and Rose shopped at three millinery stores while Maude visited a former patient. At the third store, Rose echoed Libby's thoughts as they assessed the merchandise. "Just like the hats we saw in the first two stores, they are."

"Indeed. Let's go."

"May I help you?" The voice came from behind them, interrupting their departure. Libby turned to see a short, demure-looking woman of about sixty, her hair pulled into a tight bun, hands clasped at her waist.

"No, thank you. We were just leaving."

"Madame, your hat is divine," the woman said to Libby, studying her cream bead-studded cloche. "May I inquire if it is from New York? Chicago, perhaps?"

Libby got an idea. "Thank you, Miss…?"

"Mrs. Tucker."

"Mrs. Tucker, it is from an upcoming young designer. Perhaps you've heard of Rose's Designs? No, well, I'm not surprised because her creations fall into the category of custom-made, rather than mass-produced," Libby swept a hand past a long shelf, "like these. However, she's gaining popularity and is indeed collecting a following."

In her peripheral vision, Libby saw Rose's jaw had dropped.

"How delightful." The woman sounded intrigued.

"And, she just happens to be with me today." Libby dramatically flourished a hand toward Rose. "Rose Morgan."

"Gracious." The woman's eyes grew large. "It is an honor to meet you, Miss Morgan."

Rose nodded, but looked flummoxed at what to say.

"And I am Libby Shaw," Libby continued before Rose could say anything to thwart her plan. "One of Rose's investors. We are looking for a shop that might want to seize on the exclusive rights to sell her creations in this fair city. They are, as you can see," Libby said rolling her head and touching her broad-brimmed cloche so the woman could get a better look at it, "original designs. And, might I add, much better quality than these factory headpieces." *It didn't hurt to point that out twice.* "Ah, no offense, Mrs. Tucker."

Mrs. Tucker shook her head furiously. "None taken. I assure you."

"But, of course, we could only promise city rights. After all, we are pursuing similar contracts in other cities."

"Of course," the woman responded as though she would never think of arguing.

"Splendid. Shall we step into your office to discuss an arrangement, Mrs. Tucker? Or would you prefer a competitor to secure the business?"

Forty-five minutes later, Libby and a ghostly pale Rose exited the shop.

"Say nothing," Libby whispered as she set off at a brisk pace, "until we turn the next corner."

On the next street they found a pharmacy, climbed onto tall stools at the shiny counter, and ordered two root beer floats.

"Ma'am! I don't know what to say," Rose gushed as though she was going to explode if she didn't get that out.

"It's only one client. But, you should start slow. See if you like the arrangement. Figure out how much you want to do, or not. If you like it, you could go to Harrisburg or Baltimore next. Pick up contracts for those cities. It can be a part-time gig. Or a full-time job, if you work it right."

Rose bit her lip. "I don't know about that. I don't much like being in cities or away from home."

"But you can expand. Become a success."

Rose looked at her float, "Ma'am, I feel like I already am a success. If I let other people assign my success, then couldn't they also take it away? I'd rather define it. For me, creating as I wish is success, it is." Rose's lips turned up as her gaze lifted to Libby. "Besides, I enjoy being your assistant. I've learned a lot."

Libby stared at her, at a loss for words as to how her pupil had profoundly turned the tables on her. She had thought herself wiser because she came from the future, with its infinite amount of information. Perhaps that was mere knowledge, and some of the true wisdom had been left behind through the years in the name of progress.

When Libby spoke, her voice was hoarse. "I've learned from you, too, Rose." She cleared her throat and patted Rose's hand. "Work at it and see how you like it. You have her address. Once we get our own telephone, you'll have a contact number for business cards, if you want. If nothing else, it will be an extra source of income."

Rose's eyes grew big. "It will! I can't believe she agreed to the terms. The price of the doo-dads I use—"

"Raw materials, Rose."

"Yes, ma'am, the raw materials. My costs will be only a quarter of the price she will pay."

"And she will mark it higher than that to collect her profit. Welcome to the world of retail. Which reminds me...after this, we need to do more shopping. See if we can get raw materials at low, wholesale prices."

"Ma'am?"

"The ribbons, feathers, flowers, jewels, knickknacks, what-ever you use…and especially the basic frames of the hats. We'll make inquiries about getting those at discounted prices."

Rose dropped her shoulders. "I don't know how to thank you."

Libby swiveled her stool to make eye contact. "I'll tell you how." *A Depression is coming. Banks will fail.* "Promise me that for every dollar you reinvest in your business or put in the bank, you will stick a dollar in your mattress." A vision of Hardin's building burning seared through Libby's mind. Money could burn, too. "On second thought…we have a stop to make before shopping for hat trinkets."

After leaving the pharmacy, Libby steered a confused Rose into a general merchandise store where she selected two shoebox-sized metal boxes, a thin brush, and a small can of white paint. *Definitely lead-based.* Seeing no other options, she added a pair of rubber gloves to her purchases. Finally, when she caught Rose eyeing a new rabbit's foot, she threw it into the basket and headed to the counter. She'd have to paint their names on the boxes while outdoors wearing gloves. Then, she and Rose would put money inside and bury them. Rose, no doubt, would want to add the rabbit's foot to hers.

That night Libby and Rose decided to call it quits and re-turn to Bedford the next day. They were tired of the city and had purchased enough hat knickknacks that they now had four times the number of bags to drag back to Bedford as what they came with. The remainder of their purchases would be deliv-ered by post. Libby would have bought even more, but if she had to hear Rose apologize and promise payback one more time, she thought she would scream.

Maude agreed to their departure plan, and after the three shared a final dinner together, she announced she wanted to retire early, mumbling something about the rest of her journey involving a 'horrendous train ride' back to Cleveland. Rose busied herself sketching new designs on the limited stationery in the room.

Libby seized the opportunity of solitude, removing from her purse the card Davis had given her. She headed to the lobby. Following a porter's directions, she hurried beyond the arched stairway and through double doors with triple brass bars across panes of frosted glass that read, "Telephones and Telegrams."

Five wood-paneled telephone booths stood side by side. She entered the first unoccupied booth she saw. The phones were built into square boxes and attached to the wall. She lifted the earpiece from the left of the telephone and cranked the handle on the right. As she waited for an operator to pick up, she told herself she would not engage Davis in conversation over the phone. Instead, she would ask to meet with him. She didn't want to make matters awkward for him at home or work.

She first had the operator try the office number, but the line rang endlessly. Not surprising, given it was late evening. After trying the house number, the operator announced it was an incorrect number and offered to look up the party's name. A minute went by before Libby heard a click, and the operator announced the call was connected.

A soft voice said, "Hello. Whitaker residence."

Had a maid answered the telephone, or could this be Darcie?

Libby asked, "May I speak with Mr. Whitaker?"

After a few seconds—*a hesitation?*— the voice said, "Who is this, please?" The woman's tone suggested guarded politeness.

Libby gripped the earpiece tighter. *Be calm.* "Tell him it's an acquaintance from the Springs Hotel in Bedford."

A taut silence fell. Then: "Who are you?" Curiosity and doubt had crept into the voice.

What to do? If she hung up now, she would make things worse for Davis. She took a breath and persevered. "My name is Libby...Grey. My husband"—she emphasized the latter word—"and I met Mr. Whitaker at the hotel several months ago. We just wanted to say hello and tell him we looked forward to meeting him again."

"How nice. I am Darcie, his wife." *The voice now sounded cordial, trusting.* "But, he's not here. If you're in Bedford, Mrs. Grey, then you ought to look him up there."

Libby swallowed. Took a breath. "He's in Bedford? Right now?"

"Yes. I believe the Springs has closed for the season, so he's probably staying in one of the other hotels in town. He's been there for two weeks this time, so he probably won't be too hard to track down."

Two weeks? How could that be? She'd talked to him last week when he called, and he distinctly said he was calling from the office. The Pittsburgh office. What was he doing? Perhaps he was meeting with Mr. St. Clair. But, why lie about that?

Libby rubbed her temple as she asked, "Did he say with whom he was meeting?" *Careful Libby.* "You see, there were several people in our group. If it was a name I recognized then I... *we* might be able to find him."

"Oh, I see. When he packed he mumbled a name. Let me think...what was it...Matrusky...no Matryoshka. Yes, that's what it was. Matryoshka. Is he part of your group?"

Somewhere in the darkest, bleakest corner of Libby's mind, a warning bell tolled. She sucked in her breath, almost undone by the reminder of the project she'd worked on.

In 2016!

Libby sensed a shift inside her core, felt the future collide with the present and meld together like two parts of a broken teacup.

"Hello? Mrs. Grey, are you still there?"

One perplexed heartbeat, then two, passed before Libby could respond. "I...I'm here. No, Matryoshka isn't part of our group." She struggled to calm her breathing, restore her even tone. She had to get off the phone. "Mrs. Whitaker, I'm sure I...my husband will be able to find Mr. Whitaker. Thank you for your time." She hung up the handset and stumbled back to her room.

Davis was in Bedford and lied about it. And, he was somehow connected to the Matryoshka Project. She had never mentioned the investigation to him, she was certain. But, he wasn't the man that had been following her. How did all this fit together?

Libby left Pittsburgh the next day without answers, but with one driving determination: when she got back to Bedford, she was going to send a message to Sheriff Brogan Harrow that she needed to talk to him.

For some reason, the man who daunted her most and the one she ought to stay farthest away from, was also the man she needed most right now.

Chapter Twenty-Seven

1926

BROGAN PULLED THE police patrol motorcar as close to the old Macay homestead as he could, as had become his routine. He climbed out, dried leaves crunching beneath his feet and thick, warm air heating his face, air too warm for November.

Seven o'clock in the evening and already dark. The buttermilk moon cast dim light, but enough to confirm he was alone. *Good.* He hated the thought of Libby waiting here alone in the dark.

Then again, he hoped she would hurry. An old thrill of anticipation swept through him. Being with her was like emerging from a dark hovel into the sunlight.

When she called that afternoon and asked that they meet, she said she'd gotten a good bit of her memory back. He wasn't certain what she meant by *a good bit*, but he was anxious to find out.

Please let her remember us.

This would be the fourth time they met at this spot, not counting that first night when Hardin Lochery had taken the water.

At their first meeting after she returned from Pittsburgh, she spent considerable time voicing concern about being stalked, and describing the people she had met thus far in 1926. The thought of her being in danger had made his heart race, so he suggested they meet again to discuss developments.

A week later, they had done just that, but neither had anything to report so they talked about life in the 1700s. No people. No specifics. Just day-to-day life.

The third time, they discussed the 2000s, again without names and specifics. They talked for hours, accomplishing little in the way of figuring out who was watching her, but Brogan didn't care. He valued his time with her. He may be known around town as a quiet man, but around her, he couldn't stop talking. Always, they laughed, relaxed, and questioned one another about their other life. Unfortunately, there was so much she didn't remember.

Him, for example.

He had forced himself not to encourage more emotional closeness. Another man claimed her now.

But that was wrong, wasn't it? His marriage to her had never ended. Death had not parted them. Yet, here they were. She, someone else's wife, and he, someone else's husband. He didn't want to think about those legal bonds. Didn't want to put a face to Andrew, or think about Gretchen.

He most certainly did not want to think about Gretchen's baby. That's how he thought of the child. *Her baby*, because it wasn't his. Of that, he was certain. Still, he told himself the child needed a father, so he would fulfill that duty.

When he had called home and said he would be late tonight, Gretchen screamed at him, accused him of ignoring her, and wailed that black demons were after her and intended to punish her. She was almost five months along in her pregnancy.

And, she was ill. Convinced, in fact, she would die from the sickness if the demons didn't kill her first. Doc Henshaw had run several tests. Said her delusions were unrelated to the pregnancy and all in her mind. Brogan knew he'd become the subject of gossip around town. A man who'd married a shrew, a maniac. And now, a jezebel, an adulteress. He'd overheard it all. But, she was his wife and he would honor his commitment to her, praying each day she would heal. He couldn't stomach the thought of institutionalizing her.

As he lit his lantern, he heard the sound of tires cutting through hundreds of leaves and he turned to see headlights drawing near. A calmness settled through him. At that moment, he felt like the children he saw in town. If you asked them what they wanted behind the candy counter, their desire would fly out of their mouths without hesitation, without thinking. In his heart, he wouldn't hesitate either if asked what he wanted. His instant answer would be freedom to be with Morning Meadow. Libby.

That wasn't good.

He walked to her motorcar, opened the door, and held up the lantern to light the way. Libby climbed out. He smiled. Her head was uncovered and her hair cascaded to her shoulders. She wore men's jeans with a work shirt—the sleeves rolled up—flopped over them.

"Cotisuelto," he whispered to himself, but she heard it and smiled. *Cotisuelto.* She'd said it was Caribbean Spanish, for *wearing the shirt tail outside of one's trousers.*

She had worn the same clothing the last time they met, and apologized for her unusual attire. He had assured her it looked comfortable and practical. In truth, the clothes simply added a mystique to the disconcerting allure of her femininity. *He liked that.* He liked how she smelled too. Different each time, depending upon which herbs and concoctions she may have worked with that day, but always there was that undertone of a feminine flowery essence.

He reached out his hand and, without hesitation, she reciprocated. He was certain she, like he, told herself the link was a matter of practicality against stumbling in the darkness.

It was like an unspoken understanding that they said little until the torches were lit and they settled in their secret spot. And such it was tonight, even though Brogan could sense her heightened state of excitement, see the lighter rhythm of her stride.

"So?" he asked, taking off his hat and setting it beside him on the log.

"I remember! Well, not everything…but I was Elisa Macay. Lived here. Helped my mother bake bread. Beat the rugs. Tended to our livestock. Walked to neighbors' homes for school lessons and church services. Your momma and mine would get together when it came time to make butter. Your daddy would bring his horses to my daddy for horse shoes." That quickly, her joy disappeared and confusion crossed her face. "Horse shoes. He was a blacksmith, not a mechanic." As if dazed, she stood and began pacing, her shoes crushing the leaves. "All this time…" Her voice faltered, but she kept moving.

Brogan said nothing. He didn't move for fear of distracting her. She must have been so pleased her memories returned that she forgot about their context.

She continued. "I thought he was a mechanic. I remember

him holding tools and working with metal. I must have transferred that into a life as a mechanic. Something more palatable, given the 2000s. And my mother! She wasn't a botanist. She was a pioneer woman." She gasped. "That's it. That's all she could have been because that was full-time work. She had a huge garden, and loved plants. She was fascinated by the plants in this area, always in search of new ones for medicines. She made teas for stomach ailments from juniper and goldenrod. Slippery elm for sore throats and witch hazel for rashes and poison ivy. I remember her being so excited to find blue flag." She spoke in even, measured tones, as though she were informing herself, not just him. "She made a poultice from it. For sores and bruises. That must be how I gave her a false identity as a botanist…I never had parents in the future."

He watched the graceful way she moved, even as confusion and turmoil gripped her. Lively intelligence and spirit glittered in her eyes. She was determined to sort this out.

She shook her head, stopped pacing, and cupped her upper arms as if from a chill. "This afternoon, Oliver—a porter at the hotel—brought me a bookcase I asked him to make. With it, his wife sent a vase filled with purple asters. When I saw them, my memory was triggered. They bloom in late autumn. My mother…my birth mother used to say they were God's little smile on us before the winter. She loved seeing them at a time when other plants were beginning to die."

She rubbed the back of her neck with one hand and shook her head, but kept moving. "The memories came back and stayed and linked together and I couldn't wait to tell you. I was so excited about capturing them. I failed to take that next step, to figure out what they meant. Before, they'd always been just wisps of visions or threads of recollection that teased me but couldn't be trapped. Now they're staying and I'm having to face them." She stopped moving and whimpered. "I'm so confused. How could I have lived in the past *and* in the future?"

Hurrying off the log, he pulled her into an embrace. He felt her pulse quicken. Memories of loving her under the moon's beams flooded his senses. Holding her felt so right.

After a moment she looked up at him, still wrapped in his arms. He saw his surprise at this unexpected moment briefly reflected on her face.

He reached up to touch his palm on her cheek, and she tilted her head into his hand and fixed her gaze on his lips. His heart raced.

Clearly he hadn't thought this through before he'd hugged her. The energy between them had a distinctly magnetizing edge to it and delightful sensations cascaded through him. He longed to explore her mouth and those curves he remembered so well.

No! You'll scare her. She doesn't remember us. Try to refocus.

He fought against the moment, and dropped his hand. "Don't try to remember," he said softly. "Don't force it. Just tell me what you *do* recall."

She blinked, took a breath, and stepped back quickly, stumbling. She would have fallen but he caught her arm and steadied her. She mumbled a breathless thank you and took another step away. "I...I remember meeting you the first time. I was nine and you were already fifteen. You were so tall."

"You teased me about that."

"Because I had a crush on you. But, you weren't interested

in a child. You only had eyes for Anabelle Fisher. A year or so later we heard you two had an understanding. Figured you'd shortly be betrothed. Ah, listen to me." She jolted her hands to the sides of her face. "Betrothed. In the future we say engaged. Regardless, you two were planning to get married and it broke my heart." She chuckled, but it sounded forced. "So did you? Marry her, I mean?"

Startled, Brogan opened his mouth, but words wouldn't come. She didn't remember his engagement ended when he came looking for her. Or that the Indians kidnapped her. She remembered no deaths, no Mohawks, no interaction with him after age nine. No feelings for him.

She didn't remember *them* or their marriage.

"My last memory of childhood is incomplete," she continued, unconcerned about the question she'd posed to him and oblivious to the timing of the events in their pasts. She began pacing again. "I had been at Naomi Bennet's. I must have been about eleven years old. I'd taken a bag of chestnuts there, on Sage. Remember that smart, old mare? As I got close to home I smelled a fire before I even saw our cabin. It was such a strong odor I thought my daddy was burning stumps again and that it got out of control. And poof! There, the memory stops. On top of that, certain memories that I had in the future, I see now they're wrong...or incomplete..."

Brogan wanted to ease her anxiety. "You said you had an aunt Isabel, right? She was real. You remember her."

Confusion tightened her brows. "Yes, but she died when I was sixteen. I remember being placed in foster care at that age. Then, shipped directly off to college." She stopped, dropped back onto the log, and rubbed her temples. "But that can't be right either...if my parents weren't who I thought, then how could I have an aunt in the 2000s?" She gazed up at him. "Five years of my life are blank. I don't know if I belong to the past or the future."

Brogan walked to the log, sat beside her, but said nothing. He wanted to touch her again, but didn't. A breeze swept through, negligible in its strength but enough to send a couple leaves summersaulting over his feet.

"You know what happened to me, don't you?" Her voice was a whisper.

He cringed. "Somewhat."

"Tell me. Please."

He took a deep breath. Released it. "I can't. I learned that from the woman who helped me. She inadvertently would make a reference to my past or drop a tidbit of information that came before, and it would turn something puzzling into an obsession. It slowed my progress. I got confused by what was real and what had been suggested to me." His voice was steady, betraying none of what he longed to say.

She closed her eyes as she took a deep breath, then reached out to squeeze his hand where it rested on his thigh. "I understand." She returned her hand to her lap. "It has to mean I've taken the water twice. But why then, this second time, when I came to 1926, was I so frightened of climbing into the water? The whole idea sounded mysterious—and crazy. I had never even heard about mineral water before...well, I'd heard of people using mineral springs a long time ago for gout and rheumatism and such, but I never gave it much credibility. Yet, it turns out I've taken it not once, but twice. What can't I remember? What prompted my first time in the water? And how did I know to try it?" She waved a brushing-off hand. "Never mind. It's—"

A sound of rustling and crackling came from off to the right. Weight applied to dry leaves. Familiar, because they'd just done the same moments before. He touched a staying hand on her arm and put a finger to his lips. They froze and looked into the darkness, but saw nothing.

Brogan slowly reached under his coat and pulled out a pistol. "Stay here," he whispered, and hurried toward the source of the noise. He heard a steady strumming, almost like the cadence of a gallop, but it was in the distance. After progressing several more yards, he caught sight of an opossum scurrying under the brush.

"An opossum!" he yelled. He returned to Libby. "Blasted creatures. I ought to shoot that thing. That's the second time it startled me."

Libby bit back a laugh and Brogan recognized it as a release of tension. "Maybe he's my stalker," she quipped, but in it, he heard an edginess in her voice.

"If you feel threatened, I can—"

"What? Follow me everywhere? No, I'm careful. I keep my pistol handy when I'm not with you. Besides, I'm used to it again."

"Again?"

"During the timeframe I can remember…from about age sixteen on, until I took the water with Andrew's help, I thought that feeling of someone watching me was normal. But, I had nothing to compare it with. Then, after I took the water and came to this timeframe, the feeling went away. Again, I rationalized. Thought it was part of the healing process. I didn't experience the feeling of being watched again until after moving into the hotel."

A pause fell. He didn't want to say the wrong thing.

"Brogan," she said in a tone that told him she had a different topic on her mind again. "This right here, this ground, this chimney, *this*...is where I lived, isn't it?"

He hesitated, but could not lie to her. "It was. The Macay place."

She wrinkled her brow. "How did I become a Shaw?"

He shrugged. "Must be locked in your memory."

"What do you mean?"

"In Scotland, the Shaws were part of Clan Macay. So were the the Adamsons, Essons, Shays. Others as well. Your father and mother came here in 1741, two years before you were born. Things were bad for Highlanders in those days. The Jacobites wanted the return of the Stuart kings to the throne. Neil, your father, was convinced a final battle was coming between the Brits and Scots. Most of the Highlanders wanted to fight the Brits, but the Macay Clan disagreed. That didn't sit well with your father, so they left Scotland. He was right. An uprising did occur. In 1745 Jacobite forces were slaughtered at the battle of Culloden."

"Was my father a blacksmith in Scotland before he left?"

He nodded. "Yes, but he often talked of farming, rather than toiling over hot coals every day. He saved his money. Kept trading and bargaining for parcels of land until he was able to secure a huge tract of land from a drunk Brit in Baltimore."

Libby blanched. "*Secure?* You mean swindle, don't you? My father was a swindler?"

"Your father was a good man. His goal was to outsmart the

Brits and their tyranny."

She heaved a sigh, remained quiet.

He was afraid she would suggest they call it a night, so he asked about the topic hovering foremost on his mind, but what he least wanted to hear. "Tell me about Andrew. What sort of man is he?"

She shrugged. "Intelligent. Old-fashioned, but works with modern technology. Likes to read. Enjoys music." Her tone sounded matter-of-fact and that surprised, but pleased, him. She continued. "He's dark-complected, not real tall, and his eyebrows do this weird little flick up and down when he hears something he doesn't like. And oh…" She clicked two fingers. "…he has a bad knee which he hates to acknowledge, but it's quite obvious because there's a scar there."

A scar. He didn't want to feed her a memory, but he couldn't stop himself. Perhaps it would help her recall. "You have a scar." He touched his upper chest. "In this area. Depending on what you wear, it shows at times."

She touched the spot. "It's from a bad time in my life, when I was with Aunt Isabel in Africa and we…" She paled, pulled her brows together, and looked down. "But that can't be," she whispered. "It couldn't have been Africa…it must have happened here…" She rubbed the sides of her face. "Do you mind if we leave? I'm not feeling very well."

Yes, he minded! "Of course not."

They extinguished the torches and headed to their motorcars. Brogan holding the lantern in one hand and Libby's hand in the other. As they neared the vehicles, Libby uttered a nonsensical sound as though startled. "Wait, what is that?" she asked, pointing at the ground.

He moved the lantern to see a piece of cloth. Lifting it carefully by one corner, he held it closer to the light. It was faded white with cross-stitched flowers around the edge, and finished in lace.

"A woman's handkerchief," Libby said.

Brogan's mouth went dry. "Gretchen's."

Libby gasped. "How do you know?"

"I recognize it, her initials in one corner."

"How did she know to come here?"

His gaze moved from the handkerchief to her. "I bought the land several years ago. Gretchen knows I come here to be alone. To think. To build." He lowered the lantern closer to the ground and saw hoof prints. "She must have ridden here on old Bess."

"Brogan, I'm so sorry. She must have listened to our conversation. But, we weren't saying anything very personal. It was mostly about my memories and being ill and taking the water—"

"The water." Dread snaked through him.

"I don't understand."

"She's been ill. Terrible pain. Several times she has said death would be better. She wanted to get away from demons. What if she…"

Libby grabbed his forearm. "You think she left here and went to the mineral spring? We have to stop her. She'll drown. It's the wrong time of year."

As he spoke, he hurried toward his motorcar. "What are you talking about? You can take the water any time. I've got to go stop her if that's what she's thinking."

Libby raced to her car, yelling as she moved. "I'll follow

you. Don't worry, she's on horseback so we can get there faster."

As Brogan climbed in the car, he rejected what Libby said. Given the switchbacks in the hill trails and the condition of the roads, a horse could easily get to the spring faster than a motorcar.

And, Gretchen already had a lengthy head start.

BROGAN RACED THE patrol motorcar across the jarring terrain, pulling as close as possible to the Crystal Spring. For most of the trip the roads had been little more than rutted dirt paths that switched back and forth to make it easier for drivers to maneuver around steep hills and mountain slopes. Easier, but slower.

As he slammed the motorcar to a stop he realized he'd forgotten to pray for Gretchen. He'd spent the trip continually calculating and recalculating in his head how long the trek would take him on foot, all the time ready to abandon his ride if he determined foot travel was faster.

He grabbed a flashlight—no time to fiddle with a lantern— and ran, calling Gretchen's name. Several yards from his destination he saw a large silhouette of black in his peripheral vision and shone the light toward it. Old Bess! Gretchen had to be here. He bolted to the spring where his light illuminated something horizontal in the water. Moving closer, he discovered her lying on her back, eyes closed, body fully submerged. For the briefest moment he thought she might still be alive and transforming. The next second, however, sent a cognition through his brain and a horror through his core.

He climbed into the spring and dropped to his knees, the water rising to his waist. With gentle movements he lifted her and carried her away from the spring. The water reacted with a whooshing sound as it filled the void he created. He placed her on the ground and checked for a pulse. Nothing.

Gretchen was dead.

Grief swelled hard against his ribs and rose into his throat, bitter-tasting. A tear trailed down his face for the loss of this beautiful life, this young woman he had called his wife. That tear was followed by one more, this one prompted by a mixture of guilt and remorse for the life they had miserably shared together. He had married her to save her from unhappiness and tragedy and certain early death. In the end, that's exactly what he had delivered *because* he had married her. Would she have gotten ill if she hadn't been with him? Probably. Or pregnant? Most likely, given the path she was on. But, he was supposed to protect her, and if it hadn't been for him, she would not have hurried here in such a frenzy and been so reckless.

He heard footsteps behind him. He hadn't heard a motor-car or noticed lights, but he intuited from the lightness of the steps it was Libby. A moment later, he heard a gasp and a small whimper.

She touched his shoulder. "Is she…" Then, "I'm so sorry."

He heard grief, distress, anguish in those three words. Or, was that all *he* could feel at the moment?

"She didn't understand the water," he said hoarsely. "Didn't take it correctly."

He heard Libby exhale a weary breath, chest deep. He assumed it was a sign of resignation, but when he saw her reach for the flashlight where he'd dropped it on the ground and watched her move to the other side of Gretchen's body, he realized it had been a sign of determination and valuation as well.

She scanned the light around Gretchen's body. "No ground disturbed. No other footprints. No signs of a scuffle. No reason to believe anyone else was involved. The horse seems calm. She wasn't thrown off. Didn't stumble. It looks like she entered the water willingly."

As the husband in Brogan agonized, the sheriff in him tried to listen. This assessment of the circumstances surrounding a death was vital. He trusted what Libby said. The Indians' ability to assess a trail and navigate the forests was legendary, and *real*. Together, he and Morning Meadow had learned to pick up a trail from a slight indentation here, a broken twig there. They could distinguish between the paw print of a wolf and a dog. A twig gnawed by an animal and one broken by a man. *Morning Meadow was with him at that moment and she didn't even know it.*

Libby dropped to her knees on Gretchen's other side, and inched the light from the dead woman's feet to her head. When the light illuminated her face, Libby heaved another sound of shock. "Anabelle Fisher! Is it…but you said her name was—"

"Gretchen. Anabelle's descendant."

In the dim residual illumination cast by the flashlight, Libby studied him expectantly for several moments. She was waiting for more, he was sure, but he couldn't offer anything.

She nodded a couple times and restored her resolve, moving the light again and, this time, hovering it at the side of Gretchen's face. "These rocks…terribly rough and jagged. If she was distraught and frantic, she might have fallen and hit her head as she went in." She leaned in closer, toward the light. "But, there's no blood. Not even redness." She lifted her gaze to his. "You said she was ill. It looks like she willingly stepped in…drowned in a few feet of water…"

Brogan smoothed a hand down his cheek and across his lips. Shook his head in disbelief, attempting to shift his brain into sheriff mode. He reached under Gretchen to pick her up.

"Wait!"

Brogan sat back, startled.

"Don't move the body until I take pictures and call—" Libby broke off, shaking her head. "Sorry, I'm thinking of the future…"

"There's no one to call. Nothing to do. We know what happened."

"Okay, but I'm going with you. I'm your alibi—"

"Libby, go home." His tone was measured. "There's nothing more you can do."

"You said she was deranged. They might blame you for this."

"So what?" He chuckled derisively. "Some people already think I killed her father." No, he hadn't pulled the trigger, but he had handed Jasper Hudd a gun with one bullet in it so the man could do it himself. So, yes, he was guilty. His chuckle grew crazy, almost frenzied at his thoughts. "And the previous sheriff immediately rewarded me with a recommendation for his job when he retired. Can you imagine?" He shook his head, closed his eyes for a moment, and took a deep breath. He knelt closer to Gretchen and put one arm under the back of her knees and the other at the top of her back. He shifted her gently so her head rested against his chest, and stood.

"Please. No one will believe she drowned alone in such shallow—"

"Libby—"

"You'll need me there—"

"Don't you get it?" He blazed as he stood looking at her, Gretchen's body cradled in his arms. "God help me, but *you* are what I care about. It's best you're not involved. The only thing I can do is make sure you are safe. Besides, if we say we were together, that makes me look even guiltier. Now, go home." He yelled with an anger and a finality that brooked no further argument.

He turned and carried his dead wife to his car.

Chapter Twenty-Eight

1926

A T 10 A.M. the next morning, Brogan suspended himself from his position as sheriff for the indefinite future. The mayor agreed it was for the best.

"For now," he added, "until another scandal hits town and folks forget what came before. Then we'll slap that badge back on ya."

The mayor led him to the door, and with a wink, said, "I'll wiggle the accounts, shake the right hands, to keep you on the payroll."

Brogan flinched. "No, I—"

The mayor smiled. "You don't have a choice. Besides I'm not doing this out of generosity. I want you to watch over N.C.'s shoulder. Make sure he's doing things right."

"But, you shouldn't—"

The mayor clapped a hand on Brogan's back. "Son, I'm not askin', I'm tellin'." He sniggered a sound so hearty it shook his fat belly.

Too numb and shaken to argue further, Brogan returned to his office.

N.C. underwent an hour briefing during which time the young deputy repeatedly interrupted to say, "This is so wrong. You're the sheriff, not me."

By noon Brogan got word that Doc Henshaw, as makeshift undertaker, had finished preparing Gretchen's body for burial. The doctor helped lift the loaded pine box onto the back of a borrowed horse-drawn wagon, then put a hand on Brogan's shoulder and said, "Son, my sympathies. I never did think her life would end well. And the baby's heartbeat was irregular. Just a matter of time, it was. For them both."

Around one-thirty Brogan, his deputies and secretary Jean, and the pastor of the Presbyterian Church on Bedford Square laid Gretchen Hood Harrow to eternal rest beside her ancestor Anabelle Fisher Wallace in the neglected little cemetery on the north side of town that Brogan had discovered years earlier. A warm wind rustled through the fallen leaves as they said a brief goodbye. Around them, several weathered, vine-covered headstones marked the graves of other individuals long forgotten—people Brogan didn't know.

Afterward, N.C. insisted on giving him a ride home. Brogan no longer had rights to drive the patrol motorcar. He would drive his farm truck instead.

When they got to Brogan's house N.C shut off the engine. "Mind if I come in a few minutes?"

"Suit yourself."

N.C. followed him onto the porch. Brogan gestured to one of the rocking chairs before folding into the other one.

N.C. sat, removed his hat and stared at it as he ran his fingers along its rim.

"Something on your mind?" Brogan asked. He longed to be alone.

"Well, sir, I know I said it before, but I'm real sorry. You're a good man—"

"Everything I've heard today has been about me. What a good man I am. How people hope I'll find peace. How I should move on. What about Gretchen? Even the pastor wasn't sure what to say."

N.C. said nothing.

"And yet," Brogan continued, "people are questioning if it was an accident, aren't they?" He'd told people Gretchen drowned. That he found her dead. The doctor said he saw no signs otherwise and left it at that. But, no one asked Brogan where or when or why.

"I'm not." N.C firmed his jaw.

Brogan nodded. "I know you're not. But Gretchen was young. With a baby on the way. A sudden death like this makes people wonder."

"Well, folks know she was...trouble." N.C. stretched his lips wide in obvious regret.

"What's that supposed to mean?"

N.C. shrugged. "You know. Her reputation and all."

"Wanna clarify that?"

"Come on, Sheriff. You know what I mean. Heck, half the men in town have been with her." His face reddened and he continued in a hushed voice. "Some, after she married you."

Brogan swallowed that realization. He'd suspected, but he hadn't *known*. He looked into the distance. "I guess I look like a fool."

"No, sir. You look like a good man who gave someone a chance."

"Maybe." Brogan stood. "If you don't mind, I think I need to be alone for a while."

N.C. popped out of his chair. "Sure thing. I understand.

But, I didn't really even say what I came here to say."

"And that is?"

"We need you, Sheriff. You're the right man for the job. I admit it…I was sore that you were selected for it instead of me, but I realized early on it was the right decision. I still have a lot to learn from you. You were…still are, the best man to be sheriff."

Brogan wondered about that, but as with his exchange with the mayor, he didn't want to discuss it. "Thanks."

N.C. settled his hat on his head, and said goodbye. When he reached the motorcar he looked back to where Brogan sat. "If there's anything I can do, anything at all, just let me know."

THAT AFTERNOON AROUND three o'clock, a knock sounded at Brogan's front door. He climbed off the couch where he'd been lying for the past hour staring at the same spot on the ceiling, and pulled the door open to see two men standing on his porch. They were dressed in tailored clothing, bore sober expressions, and looked vaguely familiar.

"Sheriff?" the older of the two men asked.

Brogan shook his head. "Not right now. You'll find the interim sheriff in town," he said and began shutting the door.

The same man who spoke reached out his hand and stopped the door. "We know that. That's *why* we're here. We'd like to talk to you about your deceased wife and what we may have…seen."

The other man added, "Maybe strike a deal with you."

As a man of law, Brogan loathed, but understood the benefits of, deals. Still, he would have shut the door in their faces had they not said it pertained to Gretchen. He wanted to hear what these men had to say. He pushed the screen door open to let them enter. "You are?"

"Thank you for your time." The older man extended his hand. "My name is Davis Whitaker."

Brogan raised a brow. Libby had mentioned the name. "What's this about?"

Davis smiled. "Ever heard the word Matryoshka?"

It was near five o'clock before Brogan's two visitors left his house, the time stamped by the distant chiming of the church bells in the village. He walked them to their car where nods and firm handshakes were exchanged, a strategy approved, a corroboration confirmed.

Davis had already opened his door when he turned back to Brogan. "You're a good man for having heard us out. You won't regret this."

Brogan looked at the horizon before gazing back at them. "That's about the tenth time today I've been called a good man in association with something that's not that good."

Davis frowned and looked down.

"But," Brogan continued, "in this job I've learned that if I do *not* break a law once in a while, then I don't achieve justice. Odd how that works."

Davis nodded. "Indeed it is."

"But remember, gentlemen," Brogan added, "as soon as possible. If what you said is true, then we have to move quickly."

The other man tipped his hat. "We'll be talking real soon." He climbed in the passenger side.

As Brogan watched them leave, he wondered about these men and what he'd heard. Despite being alone, he spoke aloud. "Well, N.C., maybe I can use your help after all."

Chapter Twenty-Nine

1926

L IBBY GROANED AS a knock sounded on her door and a
familiar voice called, "Ma'am it's me, Rose." It was late
morning, the day after Gretchen's death, and Libby wanted to
be alone.

Blast it. She climbed from the bed and looked in the mirror. A haggard, wrinkled, puffy-eyed woman stared back. She
still wore her clothes from the night before, and she'd skipped
breakfast. She finger-combed her tousled hair, pinched her
cheeks, took a deep breath, and opened the door, forcing a
smile.

Rose held a large box filled with hats in a rainbow of colors.
The excitement on her face faded as she scanned Libby's attire.
"You're not wearing that today—" She caught herself and
shifted her grip on the box. "I'm sorry, ma'am. I'm forgetting
my place, I am."

"No, Rose," Libby said with a tone of annoyance. "I've
asked you to coach me on fashion so it is your place to tell me.
And yes, I probably would have worn this all day, so I deserve
the reprimand...although we're going to have to figure out
something for me to wear besides dresses and jeans. Now, come
inside before your arms break."

Rose entered, eyed the new bookcase but said nothing, and

placed the box on the bed. When she spoke, her voice was meek, like she'd been punished. "I wanted to show you the hats I finished. I have two that would match your—" Rose tilted her head, studying Libby. "Are you ill, ma'am? You don't look well."

Libby seized on the suggestion. "You're right, I didn't sleep well last night. I apologize for my tone a moment ago."

Should she mention Gretchen? Almost a month had passed since she and Rose had been to Pittsburgh. They had spent much of their time together, securing exercise each day, eating meals together, talking about design. They'd even written their names on the metal boxes they brought back, and each had placed an undisclosed amount of money in them; Libby, a generous amount because she'd received another positive telegram from Mr. St. Clair. Then, they'd hiked into the steep mountainside behind the hotel, found a severely sloped spot below huge elms they believed would never be disturbed, and buried their treasures. Libby told Rose they would add to their boxes from time to time, but otherwise leave them alone. "They're merely security in case the worst ever happens," she'd said. To Libby's delight, Rose voiced intentions of filling up her box.

Through all this togetherness, Libby had learned enough about Rose's character to know the girl was loyal, trustworthy. Despite that, she couldn't get herself to discuss Gretchen's death. Not yet.

Instead, Libby walked to the box of hats and gazed in, admiring the satin and running her fingers over the silk. "They're beautiful, Rose. But, could we discuss them after I get a bath? Maybe after lunch?"

"Of course." Rose headed to the door, but hesitated. "Oh, and ma'am? There's a newspaper tucked in the side of the box. Mr. Jarvis was looking for you last night, he was. He asked me to give it to you. He said to say it's an old paper, but he thought you should see the headline on page four." Rose left, closing the door behind her.

Libby snaked her hand into the box, freeing the paper. *The Pittsburgh Post*, dated more than three weeks earlier. She opened it to page four and read the headline, top, center: *Shipping Heir Found Beaten, Near Death.* The article was about Leon Edward Martelli of Philadelphia. The police had no leads, and the family had no idea why he was there.

Her hands began to shake. She threw the paper on the bed and went into the bathroom to run water.

While she soaked, she thought about the excruciating night before. Somehow, she had returned to her room, turned off the lights, and laid awake in the darkness. Silence had cloaked the room, but the voices in her head had refused to let her sleep. Judging by what she'd just seen in the mirror, she might have been better off if she hadn't even tried.

By two a.m. she had climbed from bed to pour mineral water from a metal jug into her tortoise shell mug. As she drank, the shadowed shape of wilting asters caught her eye. Without turning on the light she'd walked to them and filled the vase with the rest of the liquid in her glass. As she stood there, frustration coursed through her. She had snatched the flowers from the vase and deposited them in the garbage can.

She didn't need asters or mineral water to prompt her visions anymore. Seeing Gretchen's face had unleashed a cascading plethora of memories. One right after the other, like dominoes…no sooner had one activated than it touched another which touched another, and on and on.

She remembered her slaughtered family and being captured by the Indians. An Indian woman named Ista saving her from rape, starvation, and the life of a slave. Ista named her Morning Meadow because she would often find Libby lying in the surrounding meadows at dawn, having fallen asleep staring at the moon, relishing the tranquility and constancy it provided. She remembered Nathan's bloodied body being dragged into their village. He was tortured and humiliated for months after that. Once traded to the Mohawks, they were taken north where he was forced to run the gauntlet as spears pierced into his side. He survived to earn the Mohawk's respect. They'd named him Broken Arrow, as a sign of peace, they'd said, but she and Nathan had both known it was also a nod at separation, distinguishing his birth as a white man from theirs.

Foremost, however, she remembered marrying him. He had undergone so much to claim her. She was, by then, used to her new extended family of Mohawk brothers and sisters, and she loved Ista. Both Ista and Broken Arrow had hastened along a wedding before a warrior laid claim to her.

After the wedding, she'd fallen in love with Broken Arrow. He had suffered far worse physical pain and loss than any of the Mohawks, yet he was the most peaceful and the least angry. His smile and his laugh had been contagious. He would read to her every night from a book of plays by Shakespeare that a warrior named Running Bear had pulled from a dead white man. Broken Arrow had treated her with a respect and devotion that surpassed any she saw by the other warriors toward their wives.

When they were banned from the tribe due to the ending

of the French and Indian War, they had said heart-wrenching goodbyes with the Mohawks and headed back to their white families. He had held her under the stars, loving her with such tenderness that she would forget her fears about returning to people she barely remembered. Near home, she'd been shot, falling with him from the horse, his arms around her. Suddenly, Ista had been there, having followed them in silence. It was Ista who put her in the medicinal water.

Libby remembered now. All those tangled moments that heretofore had intersected freely without context were now coming together. Everything was sharper, crisper now. *Almost* everything, that is, but not select *who* and *why*. Who had led the raiding party that killed her family? She remembered seeing someone that was different than the others, but she couldn't put a face to that person. And, who shot her five years after that when she and Broken Arrow returned? Why did someone wish her harm?

After tossing her flowers, and without turning on the lights, she had turned a chair toward the window, opened the drapes, and stared into the darkness. The same moon that hours before shone down on Gretchen's dead body was in a different place now, and so, too, were she and Broken Arrow.

What a difference a moment can make! Children can be snatched, vehicles can collide, wars can begin, relationships can end. In their case, a young wife can die, and an escalating closeness rendered forbidden.

Last night, Brogan had pulled her close, steadying her. She'd been inches from his face, felt the steady rise and fall of his chest pressed against hers. Felt the hardness of his rippling, muscled body. Longed to touch the scar that marred his cheek.

She'd looked into his eyes, waiting to be kissed in that way—she now remembered—that only Broken Arrow could. Instead, she'd seen an unspoken question poised on his lips. She couldn't answer such questions, so she'd pulled back. Her blood was on fire now, reliving each sensual moment.

And at this moment, he ached because of her. If she hadn't been there with him, hadn't talked about the water, Gretchen would be alive. What had seemed so right and so natural between them last night now seemed horribly wrong.

Through the early pre-dawn hours she had cried for those turning-point moments, for being stupid and selfish, for Brogan's pain and the hurt she may have caused him, and for the young woman who looked so much like Anabelle. She cried for Hardin, Dulcina, and the loss of Colette from her life. She mourned anew the loss of her white family and Ista, the woman she now realized had put her in the water to save her.

More painfully, she had cried because she no longer loved Andrew. Perhaps she never really had. She understood now that what she had felt was infatuation. Such feelings were bound to change in an absence this lengthy, weren't they?

Besides, how could she ever think she loved Andrew after the passion she had shared with Broken Arrow? It had been so raw and real and pure, bringing a truth to that concept of 'one true love.' Nothing would ever match it. She knew with a sickening in her gut that she'd never be happy with anything less than what she and Broken Arrow had together. But, Andrew—wherever, *whenever* he was—was still her husband. Her relationship with Brogan could never be consummated.

Yet, she had been Elisa Macay, Morning Meadow, Broken Arrow's wife, Libby Shaw, and Libby Grey. The question was, who did she want to be?

In one more of those momentous, turning-point moments, while staring at the moon the night before, she had instantly answered her own question, and the awareness and the relief were so enormous she felt weightless and unshackled. But with it a guilt settled deep in her core.

She pushed the memories aside obstinately, for now, and climbed out of the now-cold bath water. She would have to think about all of this later. Rose was waiting.

LIBBY ATE LUNCH with Rose in the hotel's kitchen—which served as the rather unglamorous winter replacement for the dining room since there were no other guests and only a handful of staffers for the season—then passed several hours oohing and awing over Rose's hats and sketches, before climbing on her bicycle and pedaling toward town. Rose said she wanted to work on more designs, so Libby decided physical activity and the warm sun on her face might help her harness the anxiety she felt in waiting to hear news about Gretchen's death. She'd long since mastered the tricky combination of a dress on a bike, and the challenge of pedaling on dirt roads. Once near town, she steered away from the town's hub, not wanting to see familiar faces.

On her return, around half past five, she surveyed the darkening landscape skimming by on either side. She smiled at the raw cry of a predator bird in the distance, and goose bumped at the wind feathering through the wild grass. In 2016, she'd been too busy to stop and appreciate. Too caught up in collecting, and hurrying, and doing, and proving. She'd forgotten to just *be* in the moment. Landing here had been like coming from a techno-cramped place to somewhere she could breathe. It was much the same feeling she'd always experienced when camping. Why had she stopped?

As she rounded a twist in Sweet Root Road about a quarter mile from the hotel, she spotted a man to her left stepping off one of the many mountain trails the hotel created for guests to hike. Nothing out of the ordinary because many locals hiked the trails, too.

Her heart sped up, but wasn't sure why. She hit the brakes, bringing her bicycle to a bumpy, sudden stop, knocking the chain off its track. She dismounted, but kept her gaze on the man. Daylight was fading quickly so the figure was distorted by long shadows cast from the wooded hills that blocked the setting sun. Perhaps it was the way he walked, the distinct firm line of his shoulders, the angle at which he swung his arms. She watched until the man looked up.

Andrew!

"Libby!" An exuberant smile crossed his face as he jogged to her. Before she could collect her thoughts, he reached her side and pulled her into his arms. The angle was clumsy, given the bike between then, so she let herself be wrangled free of it and heard it crash to the ground.

"Andrew! What are you…how did you get here?" Silly question that. Of course she knew how he got there.

"I saw the 1926 on the cave wall, but I wasn't sure where I'd find you. You haven't moved on from this place?" He chuckled. "Well, I'm here now, babe, and the world is our oyster. It's so wonderful to see you. I wanted to surprise you."

"You have. I'm overwhelmed." *Then why did her voice sound shaky and underwhelmed? And why had someone—Davis?—added her initials in the cave?*

He looked thicker and less muscular than she remembered, and his black hair too short for this timeframe. But his face was the same, dark and mysterious with smoldering black eyes that demanded attention. Then again, there was a twitch around his eyes that wasn't there before. She sensed nervous energy. Her heart plummeted. He loved her and must have been anticipating an exuberant welcome.

She *was* glad to see him. He was a good man, and he had saved her life. She moved into him for another embrace. "It is so good to see you. I have missed you, too." Their lips met briefly and he pulled her tight again. She stroked the tweed jacket feeling his strength beneath, smelled his maleness, a mixture of sandalwood and soap.

Sandalwood? Tweed jacket? And, hadn't she noticed spit-shined leather shoes?

She pulled back. "Why are you dressed?"

He grinned. "Really, sweetheart, I don't think this is the place—"

"And you've bathed. Groomed. When did you get here?"

His head inched back and he hesitated. "I've learned so much. Turns out, you can take the water at any time. I arrived last night and I—"

"Last night?" She swayed a little, confused, unsteady. "At the Crystal Spring?"

"Yes," he said the word as though he were talking to a child. "I hoped to surprise you so I took a bath in town first and got some clothes. Libby, I did it for you. I didn't want to see you for the first time in months in my birthday suit. I have been here before, you know. I do know my way around." His voice trailed away and he looked undecided, as if hesitating over what he should and shouldn't say or do.

The look on his face unhinged her. She was instantly consumed with remorse. She cared about him and he deserved better. He was her husband. She stepped closer and put her hands on his chest. "I know, I'm sorry. For so long I had a visual in my head of how I would be there for you when you returned." She flattened her face on his chest and inhaled his essence.

His embrace was firm, hearty, and when he spoke it was with such tenderness she decided he could not possibly know she harbored ambiguity. "It's alright," he said. "We need to take things slow. Come on. You're still at the Springs Hotel? Let's head back and relax."

As they walked—Andrew pushing the bicycle—Libby did not know what he was thinking so she chattered on about the hotel, and her friends, Maude, Rose, and the Kentons. She was afraid Andrew would ask about her experience arriving in 1926. She wasn't ready to discuss Davis. She wasn't certain yet if she wanted him to know how she'd let Davis deceive her regarding his whereabouts. She schooled her face not to react to his comments about their future.

As they neared the hotel, she heard Rose yell, "Ma'am. Over here."

Libby turned to see N.C. and Rose strolling down the sidewalk toward them, Rose's hand resting in the crook of N.C.'s arm.

She swirled back to Andrew. "That's Rose. Please don't say

who you are. She thinks I'm a widow."

His shoulders drooped and the tips of his lips with them. He looked crestfallen. "Babe, really? A widow?"

She felt the sting of his admonishment. Wondered if her emotional betrayal clung to her like lint on her clothing that he could see. "I wouldn't know how to explain your sudden appearance. We can work on a story later. Please."

He hesitated, then gave her a quirky nod that suggested he didn't like it, but understood the need to avoid the awkwardness. "Alright. For now."

As they approached, N.C. tipped his hat and Rose said, "Ma'am, did you have a good ride?" But, Rose's gaze kept darting to Andrew.

Libby conjured up a smile. "This is Andrew Grey. We've... known each other a long time." *That would have to suffice because that's all she could offer.* "Andrew, this is Rose Morgan and N.C. Smith. Rose is my friend and lady's companion, and N.C. is—"

"A friend," N.C. interrupted. "Of Mrs. Shaw, and Rose, of course."

Libby blinked. She'd never known N.C. to be so concerned about status that he wouldn't want Andrew to know what line of work he was in.

N.C. pointed to the bike. "Trouble with the chain? My dad had a bike shop. I can fix that in a jiffy."

"That'd be great," Andrew said with a forced smile and turned the bike over to him.

"I'll just move it into the grass where I can sit," N.C. said, wheeling the bike a couple yards away.

Andrew followed. "I was going to fix it later. Once I could

wipe the grease off my hands."

Libby listened to the exchange. *Testosterone. Competition. Men would never change.*

Rose whispered, "It's the strangest thing, ma'am."

Libby wondered why the whisper. Still, she acquiesced in kind. "What's that?"

"We've been strolling up and down here several times. He seems anxious. Like he's waiting for something." Her eyebrows scrunched together in concern. "I'm afraid he's going to propose."

Libby raised a brow. "Does he have reason to believe you would accept?"

Rose shrugged. "He knows I want to get married. One day. But, it's too soon. I want to be more independent. Like you. Not just a wife. I want to have my own work."

"Maybe he's nervous about your ambition. Wants to stop your career aspirations while he can."

Rose didn't respond because Andrew and N.C. had finished, parked the bike, and returned. N.C. pulled a handkerchief from his back pocket and wiped grease from his hands.

Without warning, Rose made a loud exclamation and turned to Libby. "I almost forgot! The most terrible thing, ma'am. The sheriff's wife died last night. Tripped and hit her head at the river. Fell in and drowned." Rose shivered.

So that's the story being bantered through town? Libby steadied herself. "How awful."

Andrew asked, "The sheriff?"

N.C. nodded. "Brogan Harrow."

Rose continued. "N.C. was at her funeral. It's so sad."

Libby startled. "She was buried already?"

"Doc Henshaw got her ready," N.C. explained. "He was heading to Harrisburg tomorrow for a medical conference so he went ahead and prepared the body. She had no other family. There was no reason to delay."

"I wish I'd known." Libby's voice was hoarse. When three sets of eyes gazed at her, she added, "To pay my respects."

"Say," N.C. said as though he'd just gotten an idea, "Rose and I are going to a concert up the mountain tonight. Why don't you two join us?"

Rose's "Oh, yes," overlapped with Andrew's "No, I don't—"

An awkward moment followed their crashing answers, and Libby said, "That sounds lovely." Rose didn't want to be alone with N.C., and she didn't want to be alone with Andrew, so that made it a three-to-one vote.

Andrew raised his brows at Libby, but turned to N.C. with a chuckle. "I guess we're joining you."

N.C. looked pleased. "It's just a fiddler playing Appalachian mountain music. At one of the trail cabins. They'll have a campfire. You may want to wear hiking gear."

Rose shifted her stance. "Odd they planned a concert in November though. It's bad luck to assume the weather will cooperate you know."

N.C. shrugged. "I just heard about it today. I guess it's a last-minute affair." He touched Rose's arm. "I'll be back in an hour and a half and we can head up the trail. I need to check in at work first."

Libby watched N.C. exchange such an adoring, comfortable look with Rose, that she suspected he loved Rose more than the girl realized. He was a caring, considerate man, and Libby sensed he would tolerate any career aspirations Rose had in mind.

✕

AFTER N.C. LEFT, Libby suggested the three of them meet for a light meal before their nighttime excursion hiking up the mountain. Rose hurried off to her room to change her clothes, and Libby straggled behind with Andrew. She didn't want Rose to see them enter her room together.

Once there, Libby felt nervous. Was it her imagination or was the room suddenly cramped and intimate? She wished she'd left it in disarray, less welcoming.

She toyed with the notion of going into the bathroom to change, but that would be silly. Instead, she turned her back to him as she unzipped her dress. He came up behind her and put his hands on her shoulders. She wished the urge to lean back and rest her body against his would wash over her. But, it didn't. His hands caressed her shoulders, before sliding her dress down her arms, then to her hips. The dress fell to the floor. He made a gruff sound, something between desire and frustration. She reminded herself that he was her husband. And a red-blooded man. And, he had a right to touch her. She felt his effort to turn her around. She acquiesced.

He studied her gravely through eyes dark as unburned coal chunks, and she realized he wore no glasses. Perhaps the water had healed his eyesight this time. She tried, but couldn't force a smile.

Andrew frowned and dropped his hands. "I'm guessing you don't want me here right now?" He flexed a hand into a fist and released it.

She stared at him, this attentive, caring man who just five months ago had made her feel safe and valued, who taught her to love classic literature again, and to dream of sharing a life with someone. As recently as a few weeks ago, she'd begun to believe she would never see him again, so she'd closed that door.

"Andrew, I'm sorry. Rose's room is right beside mine, and—"

"I know." He shook his head and huffed. "Look, tomorrow, we'll leave here. Finally have a honeymoon. There's no reason to stay. This," he made a sweeping gesture to encompass everything around them, "isn't our life."

But it was her life. Her friends. Her home. Perhaps, her future. She'd even toyed with the prospect of buying a Sears Roebuck house. Of accepting the job Jarvis offered. He'd called her a problem-solver. She'd hope to explore that designation. Perhaps even help Rose build her business. Would Andrew understand these desires? She wished she had foreknowledge now, about her and Andrew's future.

He placed his hands on the side of her face and forced her to lift her chin. His touch was gentle. "Let's just get through tonight, then figure out what we want to do."

She reached out to touch his arms. "Thank you. For understanding." *For this reprieve.* "Thank you," she added again as if her gratitude bore repeating.

BY SEVEN O'CLOCK that night, the four headed to the dirt and stone trail, blankets and flashlights in their hands. Without the sun, the air cooled considerably. They hiked forty-five minutes, nothing strenuous, but ascending with almost every step. At one point, Rose spotted a black cat and insisted they alter their path, but otherwise, most of the hike passed in silence, leaving Libby free to soak in the sounds of leaves skittering on a breeze, shoes scraping over rocky paths, and squirrels scrabbling around tree trunks. She liked those sounds.

Finally, N.C. shined a light on a cabin made of mud-chinked logs, tucked into the side of the mountain and perched beneath a canopy of aged maple trees. It was fronted with a deep porch. A fire pit sat off to the right, a wood pile to the left. "There it is."

"Finally," Andrew huffed with a heavy breath. He bent to rub his thighs as though he suffered fatigued or burning muscles.

Libby had become familiar enough with the area and the terrain that she recognized the cabin as located one steep ridge away from the Crystal Spring and at least two ridges and a gully from the cave where Davis had tended to her.

"It's dark," Rose offered, stating the obvious. "There's no one here yet."

N.C.'s voice sounded in the darkness. "Maybe we're early. There's no electricity, but there are extra lanterns in the shed 'round back. Beside the outhouse. I'll get a couple. Maybe we can get the place lit and start a fire."

He ducked behind the building and was back in less than a minute. He took matches from his pocket, lit one lantern and handed it to Andrew, then lit the other. The wicks grew in strength, enveloping them as a unit in an amber glow. "Come on, let's go inside and get the best seats."

He led the way to the door. "It's warped. It'll take a shoulder," he said before proceeding to prove himself correct. With a strong heave, he thrust it open, and the door creaked and scraped over the floorboards. He waved for the others to enter, but reached out for Rose who was directly behind him and pulled her to his side. "Help me get a couple more lanterns." He looked back at Andrew and Libby. "We'll be right back."

Libby entered the cabin, followed by Andrew. It smelled of aged wood and earthy mustiness.

In the next instant, so much happened that Libby later would be hard-pressed to say what occurred in what sequence.

The door slammed shut behind them.

Someone slid a bar across the door.

She heard Andrew say, "What the—" as he held the lantern aloft, allowing the glare of the flame to dart into the shadows.

Chapter Thirty

1926

L IBBY GASPED WHEN light fell on the faces of Davis Whitaker and a man she'd never seen before.

"Surprise!" Davis donned a wide-tooth smile and spread his
arms wide. "Welcome back, Andrew!" He wore a field jacket
atop familiar casual clothing, attire Libby hadn't seen since her
first few days in the cave with him.

Beside him, on a wooden table—a board propped on two
barrels—sat a cake, a glass jar of what looked like lemonade,
and several metal plates, cups and utensils. Behind the food, a
sign half the size of a door leaned against the wooden wall. On
it, someone had written in red paint: *Welcome back.*

Jolted, Libby summoned what she hoped was an apprecia-
tive smile. "How nice." *And, odd.* "Isn't it Andrew?" She turned
to gauge his reaction.

His gaze darted between the two men before he spoke.
"Nice, yeah," he said, a flat tone to his voice.

Libby watched Andrew's rapid blinking. She'd never
known him to be unfriendly or daunted by anything. He was
agitated. Did he know some revelation about Davis she had yet
to learn? Perhaps Andrew had learned something sinister about
David and that's why…. A new suspicion crept through her,
unbidden, and it confused her, but she shrugged it off as non-

sense.

The other man lit four more lanterns hanging from rusty hooks and perched on make-shift sideboards along the cabin's two longer walls. The illumination bathed the cabin in a golden glow, revealing uneven wood plank floorboards, a stone fireplace against the back wall, and a scattering of weathered, backless benches strewn about. Toward one corner, the distinct lines of an alcove appeared, and beyond that, the light faded into darkness as though it led to a small space or back door in that direction. The cabin looked like it had been built for venues such as nature lectures or small-scale festivities.

"The place is crude," Davis smirked, assessing the structure, "but we didn't think it wise to celebrate in a public setting." He turned to Libby. "So good to see you. Sorry you haven't been able to reach me. Been busy with work." He gestured toward the other man. "Where are my manners, I don't think you've met Zachary Hayes."

"How do you do?" Libby smiled, and it was genuine. She recognized the name as a fellow traveler from the future, arriving in 1922. Davis had mentioned him in the cave. There was a certain comfort in meeting more birds of a feather, even if the circumstances were confounding.

"Zach," the man offered with a nod, but otherwise didn't move. He was unshaven, mid-thirties, with a wide brow and deep-set eyes that were heavily lashed and looked gray in the shadowed room. He wore casual clothing too, with a dark wax jacket, boots made of leather, and a Stetson hat. Controlled and ruggedly good-looking, Libby decided, but aloof, with a demeanor that suggested every expense of energy was deliberate, every moment watchful, and that he preferred being in the background.

She turned to Davis. "Andrew just got back. How did you know he was here?" *And why were you in the area without contacting me, and what do you know about Matryoshka?*

Davis's brow rose for an instant and his gaze flicked to Zach and back, but he chuckled heartily. This animated, jovial Davis was unfamiliar to her. "Worked out well, didn't it? Zach happened to be back in the area to replenish with the water. Saw Andrew by accident this morning. Isn't that right, Zach?"

A muscle ticked in Zach's jaw before his lips twitched into a half-smile, looking as loathe to don it as he might a clown outfit. When he spoke, however, his voice was encouraging. "We were afraid you'd leave before we could see you, Andrew. To thank you, of course."

Davis clapped his hands together and rubbed them. "How about some cake? Then we'll talk. Get caught up."

In the brief silence that followed as Davis cut and dished pieces of cake onto the metal plates, Libby spread their blankets over the top of the dusty benches and said, "It was nice of N.C. to help with the surprise. I didn't know you knew him." She didn't bother mentioning Rose because had the girl known she wouldn't have been able to keep it secret. After collecting her cake, Libby followed Andrew to a bench and sat beside him, opposite where Davis and Zach plunked down, before sampling the rich dessert. Zach removed his hat and placed it on the bench. Libby noticed his hair was longish for the timeframe and pulled together with a thin black leather cord. Davis had described Zach as a cowboy who didn't care about fashion.

"I met Deputy Smith on one of my trips here," Davis said. "About a year ago."

"He's a deputy?" Andrew glowered, looking up from his plate at Libby. His cake was untouched. "You didn't mention."

She winced at the whisper of annoyance in his tone, but kept her response light. "It never came up. Besides, it doesn't matter." Her chest tightened. He looked at her as if she had purposely deceived him, and she sensed there was a storm brewing in him. Or, was it her imagination?

Davis smiled again. "She's right. It's of no importance. What matters is we're all here now. A reunion of sorts. Safe and sound, and," his smile grew. "Might I add healthier, thanks to Andrew? If it hadn't been for his intervention and that doctor's confirmation...what was his name?"

"Dr. Kuzmich," Libby said, and took another bite of cake.

"That's it. Kuzmich. I knew it was of Russian origin." Davis took a swig of lemonade. "Good man, too. I was lucky he could drop everything to see me." He took another bite of cake then quickly pulled his shoulders back as though he had a thought. "Come to think of it, wasn't he the doctor you saw, too, Zachary?"

"That's right," Zach drawled.

Davis looked at Libby. "And you?" He didn't wait for an answer. "Isn't that odd? We all three saw the same doctor. And, we all three had no time to get a second opinion."

Andrew stiffened and sat his plate to the right on the bench, never breaking eye contact with Davis. He still had not touched his cake.

Libby had been about to take another bite, but instead lowered her hand to her plate. Where was Davis going with this? And, why was a disturbing, new energy emanating from Andrew?

"You know, come to think of it," Davis said, jabbing his fork into the air, "as I recall, there was another similarity as well. Zach and I both worked on the Matryoshka Project. What about you, Libby?"

She froze and, sensing Andrew had done the same, slowly dragged her gaze to him. He wore a sneer as thin and threatening as the edge of a sharp blade and his eyes were narrowed, glaring at Davis as if he wished he could kill him with a look. She steered her gaze back to Davis and saw the glare mirrored there.

With shaky hands, she set her plate to her left. She pressed the flat of her hands against her thighs to still them.

"Well, Libby?" Davis persisted. His voice, so jaunty an instant before, was suddenly curt, almost demanding. "Were you involved on the Matryoshka Project?"

She nodded, then said a meek, "Yes, I was." She shuddered and clasped her hands into her lap. They were so cold. "Interpreting. That's all. I had to leave the project undone, because of…my health." She swallowed again, each time harder. Her mouth was so dry.

When no one said anything, Libby's unease propelled her to continue. "I know Matryoshka means nesting dolls, but I have no idea what it had to do with the investigation. I…I thought it involved a mole in the bureau, but," her voice grew hoarse, "I wasn't briefed on it fully."

"That's right," Zach said, shifting his gaze from her to Andrew. "A mole. An infiltrator. Someone with layers within layers." The look in his eyes was as intense as the firmness of his jaw, and revealed a kind of remoteness or disdain.

Davis cocked his head. "Remove one and underneath you

find the same thing again and again." He set his empty plate on the ground. "Isn't that right, Andrew?"

When Andrew didn't respond, Davis continued. "Or, should we call you Andreii?"

"What?" Libby startled. She looked at Andrew again, then back at Davis. "What are you talking about?" She turned to her husband. "Andrew?"

His chin was high, his nostrils flared. *Caught. Cornered. Furious.*

Libby put a hand over her mouth as though to hold in a dawning realization. Her hand shook as it fell back to her lap. "Is that why you were so insistent we meet that night? You knew I was listening to the Matryoshka tapes. You thought I might learn something damaging?"

His eyebrows flicked up and down quickly in that quirky way she remembered. That way in which his body betrayed him by reacting to information he didn't like.

Andrew ignored her, and spoke to Davis. "I don't know what you're talking about. You've mistaken me for someone else."

Davis studied him. In a loud voice, but still with his gaze locked on Andrew, he said, "Heard enough, Sheriff?"

From the alcove area Libby heard the sound of a match being struck. She turned to see hands light the wick of another lantern. When the flame grew to cast a wide oval, Brogan's face came into view. For the briefest moment, her heart skittered.

Brogan loomed large in the light, his jaw set firm in unyielding lines, his height exaggerated by the dark shadows. In smooth strides, he moved to the group, his gaze, like Davis's and Zach's, never leaving Andrew. "That's him. Andreii

Grebenshchikov. The man who shot Morning Mead-ow…Libby. Four years later, he did the same to me. Left me to die."

Shocked, Libby touched her scar. Is that how she got it? She tried to form an image of Andrew carrying out these murderous deeds. She looked at him, desperate for him to deny everything, but afraid of the answer. "Andrew…?"

He flexed a hand into a fist and looked back at her with such contempt it made her heart race. *Restrained fury.* He wanted to kill someone, or perhaps everyone in the room. She could see it in his eyes. And in that instant a new memory streaked into her mind with the speed and roar of a locomotive. She braced herself against falling by gripping the splintered bench beneath the slight overhang of the blanket. "I remember now. I was ten. 1759." She spoke at Andrew. "You came to talk to my father." Her words emerged slowly, in synch with her unfolding memory. "About a tract of land in his possession. I was hiding behind our wagon. I heard the conversation. You rode away, but left very angry, vowing to come back."

A heinous sneer contorted the lines of his lips. Smugness laced his voice when he said, "And the next year I did."

Her body quivered with indignation. "Yes, you did." *And killed my entire family.* She wanted to reach out and slap him across the face, but she couldn't get her hands to move. She composed herself. Licked her dry lips. "Why?"

"I can answer that," Brogan said, moving the edge of an empty bench to angle it perpendicular to where the others sat. "Land. Power. Wealth. Delusions of grandeur. Take your pick." He sank his muscled length onto the bench. "But I'm not the one who can answer that best." His gaze moved to

Davis. Libby watched the two men hold a conversation without even saying a word.

"Then who?" Libby asked. "What's going on?"

Davis leaned forward, placed his elbows on his knees and clasped his hands. "This afternoon Zach and I paid a call on Sheriff Harrow. Set some wheels in motion. Then, about an hour ago we introduced him to a young woman that was able to put the puzzle pieces together. She first appeared to us a few weeks ago." Davis extended his hand to touch Libby's arm, a gesture of concern, but his tone carried a forewarning, the way dogs' ears jerk back before they leap. "Libby, Colette is here."

As Andrew cursed, Libby blinked. "Colette? My roommate? Here?"

Before Libby could digest her astonishment, she heard a familiar voice from the back.

"Hey, Libs."

Libby stood and swirled to see her roommate walk forward, out of the darkness. "Sorry, roomie," Colette said, "we didn't know how to spring me on you. We were afraid—"

Andrew seized on the distraction, jumping to his feet and leaping forward to apply a full head slam into Brogan's body, knocking him backward. They fell to the ground, arms and legs tussling.

In a flash Zach was on Andrew, yanking him to his feet, pushing him into a spin, then slamming his fist into Andrew's jaw, and another into his gut.

Andrew fell to his knees, but held himself upright with the aid of a bench. He slowly wiped his bloody lip with the back of his hand. After several gulps of air, he climbed to his feet. In one step, Brogan was beside him, placing the barrel of a pistol snug into his right jawbone. "Give me a reason."

Breathing heavily, Andrew attempted to regain his cavalier bravado by straightening his shirt collar and brushing at his sleeves as if he'd been touched by something unclean. His darting gaze suggested he wanted to ignore Brogan's warning. Depravity searching for an escape route.

Brogan put his free hand on Andrew's shoulder and pressed him down onto the bench. He circled behind Andrew and yanked his hands behind him. The click of handcuffs sounded.

After the scuffle and while the four men secured Andrew and brought their composure and the seating back to normal, Libby noticed Colette's wide eyes tracking Zach's movements. Libby murmured, "He's so…intimidating."

Colette pulled Libby into an embrace and murmured, "I know. Isn't he hot?"

When she pulled back, Colette wore an unabashed grin, leaving Libby flummoxed.

Could this evening get any more surreal?

Brogan holstered his gun into a leather sling stretched perpendicular across his chest and under his jacket. He folded onto a bench to the left of Zach, raked tousled hair from his forehead with a thrust, and fastened an ice-blue stare on Andrew, locking gazes like sabers.

Davis cleared his throat. "Thank you, Andrew, for that confirmation." He sat also. "Ladies, please take a seat and let's see what we can piece together."

Libby sat beside Colette. "Wait, Davis…" She held up a stopping hand, then rubbed her temples, trying to understand it all. "First, is there anyone else back there? Any other surprises?"

"No."

She looked at Colette. "How long have you been here?"

"Three weeks. But, I had been following Andrew for a long time. After I saw him take the water, I did the same."

"But how?" Libby asked, incredulous. "You weren't even ill."

Davis grunted. "You weren't either, Libby. Brogan was the only one of us who went into the water physically impaired."

She shook her head. "But...I was dying." She looked at Davis and realization dawned as she read the truth in his eyes. "That's why you said we all three had the same doctor. Isn't it? So I...none of us, needed to take the water to live, did we?"

"We believe you were healthy," Davis said. "We all were. Andrew simply had to get rid of us." He shifted on his seat. "But, make no mistake, to take the water successfully, we believe a person has to be in a dire situation. Desperate, ill, half-crazed, physically or mentally wounded—"

"With one exception," Brogan clarified and all heads turned his way. "The Indians know how to take the water without suffering pain or risking death." He dropped his gaze to the floor before adding, "Someone special taught me that."

"Interesting," Davis said in a tone that affirmed he meant it. "But, without that knowledge, it's a harsh risk. You either climb out the same, or drown. For each of us, we were desperate. But, we could have died."

Libby thought of Gretchen, and with a sigh closed her eyes and ran a hand over her forehead. When she opened them again, she looked at Brogan. In a quick moment, their gazes locked, acknowledging their memory of the young woman who had tried to take the water and drowned. Libby felt unsettled as he gazed at her, commanding her attention with his look of concern. She forced herself to refocus, and turned back to Davis. "What about Colette? She wasn't desperate," Libby said.

"That's not true, Libs." Colette's face scrunched in deep regret. "I was crazed, panicked that you disappeared on my watch. I've never lost any assignments, and I sure wasn't about to lose my best friend."

"What do you mean, on your watch?"

"Seven weeks ago, a man came to me claiming to have taken the water, thanks to you. He looked like a homeless guy, but when he spoke he was brilliant—"

"Hardin Lochery!" Libby jerked her hands to the sides of her face. "He made it?"

"That's it. Hardin. I was ready to close the door on him, but he said you were sorry for not having said goodbye to me. I had nothing to lose, so I talked to him. He told me the wildest story I ever heard. That you helped him take the water and told him to focus on the future. I kept cross-examining him, but he never broke or veered from it. He told me..." Colette paused, tilting her head as though she wanted to remember the message exactly as she'd heard it. "He told me to tell you, 'This is what friends do.'"

A warm thrill raced through Libby and she covered her mouth with her hand, lest she react out loud with delight that Hardin had heard her, even as he lay dying. She'd been right to put him in the water!

Colette continued. "So my next step—"

"Wait, what happened to him?" Libby asked.

"The bureau began setting him up in a special program."

Zach nodded knowingly. "Like Witness Protection without

the protection?"

"Similar." Colette smiled at Zach with open admiration, then looked back at Libby. "He was on track to get a new identity and help finding work. But, I changed all that before I left, which I'll explain in a moment." Colette turned her gaze to the others. "His story was so unbelievable that it *had* to be believable. Once we accepted that possibility, we decided that if Hardin could do it, then so could others, particularly Andrew." Her eyes glinted in the artificial light.

Davis had stood and retrieved more lemonade as Colette spoke. "You mentioned something about the steps you took?" He walked back to the others, but remained standing, putting a foot on a bench and leaning to prop his forearm on his thigh as he took a swig of the drink with his free hand.

"From the tapes, we learned he spoke Russian. So there was a connection to the Soviet Union. We started with the assumption that, as an immigrant from long ago, Andrew probably shortened his name, but otherwise didn't change it that much. We fed our data into the—"

"Fed data?" Brogan interjected.

Zach inclined his head, leaned toward Brogan. "Like a mechanical brain. It's fed, or given billions of pieces of information, and it can search and pull things together for you."

Brogan whistled under his breath. "Amazing."

Colette continued. "We began researching the entire history of the country, back to when it was considered the New World. We found a man, in 1760, dispatched by Empress Elizabeth of Russia to come to the New World. His name was Andreii Grebenshchikov. Born, 1738. Sent back here at the age of 21 to promote trade, build relationships, generally give Russia a presence."

Davis held out a stopping hand. "You said sent *back*."

"Yes, he was here before, as a boy. I'll get to that." Colette took a deep breath. "We focused on Andreii, in a frenzied manner I might add. Fed his picture into the system. It brought up a rendering of the man dispatched. The resemblance was undeniable. We were convinced it was the same man, and that we had a fugitive, perhaps a revolutionary, traveling through time. One, we believe, with greater plans for Russia in the New World than what the empress ever intended."

"The New World," Zach murmured, shaking his head as if in awe. "Unreal."

Colette nodded. "That's what we thought. Especially when it took us back even farther in time."

Davis asked, "How far back?" He straightened, removed his foot from the bench, and stepped over it to sit again.

"In the period of European exploration, from 1492 to the early-to-mid 1600s, there was a lot of activity in North America. The English, French, Spanish, Dutch. All competed for a foothold on this continent. Even Sweden was a European great power, and a major military force during the Thirty Years' War. By the mid-1600s, the Swedish kingdom included part of Norway, all of Finland and, key for us, stretched into Russia."

"Remarkable." Davis swiped a hand across his face. Andrew, meanwhile, sat quietly, head cocked with a smirk on his face.

Again, Colette bobbed her head. "In 1637—I might be off a year or two, my research was destroyed in the water—Swedish, German, Dutch and other stockholders from the

Swedish kingdom formed the New Sweden Company to trade for furs and tobacco in North America. More than 600 Swedes and Finns reached what are now the mid-Atlantic states." She swept a hand through the air. "Including Pennsylvania. But the British were gaining in numbers. In 1682 a Quaker settlement began after William Penn gained control of the territory from Charles II. Twenty-three ships carried in hundreds of Quakers. The Swedes and Finns were quickly outnumbered and required to be naturalized as English subjects. Many were promised lands elsewhere in compensation."

Davis leaned back, folded his arms and crossed his ankles, "So this is where Andrew's ancestors come in?"

"Bingo. His grandfather was one of the Russian-New Sweden citizens, but with allegiance to Russia. His compensating land exchange, or so he claimed, was here, in western Pennsylvania and eastern Ohio."

Brogan said, "Unexplored land at the time."

"Correct. We know land shifted and changed hands a lot during this time as the country became settled. France started claiming land, too. The French formed New France and expanded it into western Pennsylvania. We believe Andreii's grandfather made a pact with the French to restore what he felt was his rightful claim."

Colette spoke in a steady stream, a quiet dignity in the way she delivered her research. "Even William Penn lost control of the land several times. Three years after one of those incidents, it was restored to him by the British, so Penn met with Czar Peter the Great during a brief trip to London. It's quite likely they discussed any Russian holdings. That meeting gave us reason to believe that Andreii's grandfather felt he had a legitimate claim, and may have tried to secure it through the French to pass to his descendants. Andreii's father, then, was born in 1698 to a very young mother, and Andreii followed, in 1738, as I mentioned earlier."

As though a signal was given, the group reacted through sighing, nodding heads, adjusting positions, and, as it appeared to Libby, generally digesting the overwhelming story physically without saying a word.

Colette clasped her hands around her knees. For the first time, Libby noticed she wore trousers and an oversized shirt exactly like—and probably the same size as—the one Zach wore. "And that takes us into a time when the French and British battled for control during the French and Indian War."

"Part of which," Brogan said, "Libby and I lived through." He leaned in, resting his forearms on his thighs. "This is all making sense now. You said Andreii's grandfather believed he held a claim to a vast amount of land and tried to secure it through the French. Meanwhile, Libby, your grandfather was granted a sizable tract through the British."

Colette pointed her index finger at Brogan. "Exactly. The same land."

Brogan laced his fingers and shot Colette a pensive look. "But, as we know, the British won the French and Indian War and drove the French out."

Colette nodded. "And, in 1760 when Andreii killed Libs' family, we think he was not only trying to get them out of the way, but perhaps trying to find documentation of the land."

Brogan said, "Because Libby's grandfather never filed it. Never claimed it."

Libby looked at him. "You're right. I remember Papa talking about it. He said his father didn't believe one person should have so much. He agreed. Of greater concern to him was that the territory be settled by people who sought religious freedom from tyrannical government rule."

Brogan took a deep breath. "You came home in the midst of the house burning and found your family dead." His voice was laced in sorrow. "Andrew's band of Indians took you. I arrived too late."

Davis asked, "That was 1760?"

Brogan nodded. "Libby…Elise was 11. I was 17. I left, searching for her right after that. We returned five years later."

Married. We came back married. Libby didn't voice it. Didn't need to. She and Brogan knew it and that's all that mattered. She looked up to see him staring at her.

As if he could read her mind, he said, "Tiakení:teron." Mohawk, for *wife/husband.*

Startled, her eyes grew, but she said nothing, prompting him to ask, "Sa'nikonhraién:tas ken?" *Do you understand?*

"Hen." *Yes.* She bit her lower lip, trying to suppress an ardent and ill-timed smile in front of the others.

His face softened, his gaze intensified. "Konnorónhkwa." *I show you I care. I love. I am concerned.*

Overcome with emotion, she uttered a joyful syllable, immediately flattening her palm over her mouth to keep her emotions silent. She darted her gaze to the others to find them shooting curious looks at her and Brogan. Andrew's glare, however, was filled with contempt.

"Anyway," Colette murmured, pulling her gaze off Libby, "we believe Creases…err, sorry, that's what I used to call him…we believe Andreii thought the claim would be awarded to a Brit if Libby died. So, he instructed the Indians to take her. He probably intended to go after her later. To lay claim to the property."

Andrew's brows snapped together and he sneered. "*Thought* it would be awarded? I knew it would be given to an undeserving British imbecile." He looked at Libby. "It was a British officer that authorized me to kill your father in the first place. Seems Papa"—he said the word mockingly—"verbalized his displeasure with how the Brits treated settlers."

Libby bulked at Andrew's words. "My *father*?" Her voice revealed fury. "What about the rest of my family? Was killing them *your* idea?"

Andrew's eyes blazed. "I searched that house high and low. No deed. By then, everyone in your family had seen me. They had to die. We burned the place. You showed up at the end. I figured you might know where the deed was. But, we heard people coming so I instructed two of the Indians in the raiding party to take you. We all scattered. The idiots that took you kept going west. I started searching, but after a while, I gave up. Assumed you were dead."

Nettled, Libby glared at him. "Nathan…Brogan found me." She sat taller with as much dignity as she could muster and said in a cold, ridiculing voice, "He did what you could not."

Andrew glowered at her, his eyes shimmering with outrage.

A palpable tension hung in the air.

Davis cleared his throat. "Colette, do you know more about Andrew's travels through time?" He looked at the others. "I'm hearing much of this for the first time, too."

Colette said, "When Elizabeth's reign ended in 1762, Peter

III ruled for such a short time, that by the time Andreii left the colonies and made the grueling trip back to Russia, Peter had been murdered. His wife Catherine II became empress. We doubt she had any idea what Andreii's nefarious intent was, but she funded his return. Like, Elizabeth, she wanted an emissary here to establish good relations for trade. We assume Andreii saw much more opportunity. If he could change the power here, then Russia would benefit. Or, perhaps he wanted power for himself. As far as we know, neither Catherine nor Elizabeth shared that sentiment for Russia. Andreii returned here in 1763, but it gets sketchy after that. Historical records are far from complete. We found one document that suggested he was ill on the trip back. Perhaps that was the first, of many, times he took the water."

Brogan said, "It was two years later, 1765, Morning Meadow...Libby...and I returned from living with the Mohawks. That's when he shot her. But at the time I didn't know it was him."

A shiver coursed through Libby. "That's when I came forward to 2003. That time, the water did save me from death."

Andrew scowled. "You two were spotted returning from the wilderness. Word reached me. I had to shoot you. You could have identified me before I could find out about the deed."

Brogan gaped at him, shook his head in disgust. "After that you disappeared? I don't remember seeing you until four years later when you joined the Black Boys and shot me."

Andrew snorted. "I took the water several times. Traveled back and forth, learning about the future. Makings plans. And what do I learn in 1769 on one trip back? That you finally stopped mourning, enough to reunite with Anabelle. That's right, Libby, your Prince Charming couldn't wait to take up with Anabelle again."

And then Brogan married Anabelle's descendant. Libby forced that from her mind. She couldn't think about it now. "What happened to the deed?"

Brogan said, "I destroyed it. Your father didn't want anyone to get their hands on it."

Davis drummed his finger on his thigh. "Then why didn't *he* destroy it?"

"Things were so uncertain in those days," Brogan said. "Land constantly changing hands. Countries vying for control. We tended to hold on to things, just in case."

Andrew inclined his head and asked, "When did you destroy it?"

Brogan responded, "Not long before you shot me."

Andrew looked into the air, as though he was calculating. "So between 1760 and 1768, an 8-year timeframe, it was hidden. The Treaty of Paris was signed in 1763 and the Brits got that land. So there's a three-year span where the deed was waiting to be found." His gaze ranged over the faces as he spoke, then slid to the exit and back.

Brogan grimaced. "And you think we'll give you the chance to go back in time again to get it?" Andrew said nothing, so Brogan asked, "Why did you shoot me? And Richard and Anabelle?"

Andrew shrugged a shoulder. "I hadn't intended to. I had two horses at the fort because I thought I might need a hostage. The fact that it became you played so perfectly into my hands. Later, it became necessary to kill Richard and Anabelle. One night, in a drunken stupor, I spilled the beans, as we say in the future, about shooting both of you. When I sobered up, I had no choice. Richard was easy. As a soldier, he was always out and about. It took me a while to find Anabelle alone."

Brogan's face reddened with fury. "The court records say Anabelle was with child when you attacked her. The child barely survived."

Libby watched Andrew roll his eyes and look away, his demeanor suggesting he could not have cared less.

How could she have loved this man? She forced down the sickening thought that she was still married to him.

She tuned back into the conversation to hear Colette answer something Davis had asked.

"This was the first time the bureau ever dealt with such a situation. Previously we've had people globe-trotting from country to country to evade us, but not through time. This was much more problematic. We couldn't figure out any other way to resolve this than to follow him closely. Day after day I tailed him. Sure enough, he finally headed here and took the water. So I followed."

Libby bulked. "Colette, that was too much sacrifice."

"I had to, Libs." Colette reached out and clutched Libby's hand.

"I am so sorry," Libby said. "I was scared and angry when I left. I didn't explain. I found the gifts for your mother. I assumed you'd lied."

Colette flinched. "Yeah…that was a lie, Libs. I don't even have a mother. The gifts were fake. Part of my role. My parents have both been dead for eight years. When we moved in together, it was so I could watch you."

"Me?" She froze, aware the others were paying rapt attention to everything.

"We had been investigating Andrew long before you joined the bureau. During one of the few times we got into his apartment, we found a picture of you. We tracked you down. Recruited you. We wanted to pull you as close as possible. That's why I made sure to be with you the night you met him."

"I had no idea."

"You kept your cell phone too close. So did he. I couldn't do anything with those. But, our apartment was bugged, Libs. When I left, saying I was going to my mom's, I relocated around the corner to a hotel. Unfortunately, after that La Cicia dinner date you had with Andrew, you didn't say much of anything in the apartment."

Libby furrowed her brow, remembering. "You're right. I always went out on the balcony."

"I had a bug in your purse too. But you took a different one to the restaurant. And, left it at home the rest of the time. In the end, I failed you when you and Andrew left D.C. That horrendous D.C. traffic."

Libby tried to blink back tears that pricked at her eyes. She pushed off the bench and rubbed her forehead as she began to pace. Perhaps expending energy would help her muddled mind. The others remained quiet as though grasping her need for a moment to think.

She had sat in on interrogations before, providing interpretation when necessary. Sometimes suspects would crack from fatigue, or guilt, or when overpowered by the sheer weight of evidence against them. But, there were a few who were never tortured by guilt. For them their only regret was getting caught. She knew that look. She saw it in Andrew's eyes now.

How could she have married this man? He'd told her his friends loved him, his family adored him. But, she'd never met any friends or family. She'd fallen in love with the man he said he was, not the man he actually was. A weary ennui overcame her and she felt the center of her heart go hard.

She came to a halt and whirled to confront him. "The calla lilies... blue is my favorite color... you were aware of all those things because you had studied me from the future, didn't you? All those things you said and did were just lies. You knew I wouldn't go forward in time when I took the water, didn't you?" She shook her head and continued without giving him a chance to respond. "You were so familiar to me when we met. But it was born of a horribly bad familiarity that I didn't comprehend. And you were so deceptive about your feelings. Why did you bring me back? Marry me? Why not just kill me?" Her questions came out with the cool crispness of an inquisition.

Andrew exhaled dramatically, dropping his chin and shoulders as though bored. "You were getting too involved in the investigation of me. Those tapes. But I wasn't ready to carry out my plan yet. So, it was either kill you, or marry you and have you take the water. This way you'd be bound to me and more likely to cooperate. Besides, in 2016, a body is much harder to dispose of than it was long ago."

Libby cringed and Brogan's nostrils flared. She saw his hands fist.

Zach glared at Andrew, his eyes brimmed with contempt. "You're twisted."

Libby put her hands on her arms as she assessed Andrew. She didn't see the faintest flicker of regret on his face. "You never cared about me at all, did you?"

Andrew blew out his cheeks as he studied her dispassionately. "Frankly, no."

She suppressed a cynical retort. "Then why did you tell me to stay at the Springs? Near the water? And why lie about the nuances of taking the water?"

Davis said, "Control. To make sure he could find you when he was ready. He was weighing his odds with his thumb on the scale. Isn't that right, Andrew?"

Andrew tensed his jaw, but said nothing. His small, black snake eyes glinted like icepicks in the lantern light.

After a moment of silence, Colette cleared her throat. "We, the bureau, had a hard time isolating and classifying this. We couldn't call him a mole or double agent because he's not really feeding anything of any worth to either country as far as we can tell. Nothing of significance."

"Just providing enough," Davis said, "to keep both countries believing he's loyal."

"That was our conclusion," Colette said. "He's not trying to change the present or the future as much as he's trying to collect data to change the past which, in turn, will change the future. He's trying to learn a lot about the evolution of both countries, predominantly where resources are discovered, and the development of wealth in this country. There's quite an empire to be made in oil and steel. If he could own that particular land…if he could go back in time and change that land grant on behalf of Russia or, just himself, then he could become an extremely wealthy and powerful man. Particularly because he knows how history unfolds in advance. We believe Andrew may see himself as a time-traveling revolutionary."

Zach exhaled in frustration. "In the future, Winston Churchill describes Russia as a 'riddle wrapped in a mystery inside an enigma.' Just like a nesting doll," he said glaring at Andrew. "Just like Matryoshka. And just like you."

"This is ridiculous," Andrew snarled.

Davis plowed a hand down his face and spoke in a hushed tone, almost as if to himself. "The coal and steel industries evolve in Pittsburgh, with plenty of railroad and river accessibility." His voice grew louder. "Right in the middle of the territory we're talking about. And, Ashtabula Harbor, in northeast Ohio, at one point in history, became the third largest receiving port in the world. It served as the most direct source of iron ore to feed the booming steel mills in Youngstown and Pittsburgh." He grew quiet a moment and turned his gaze to Colette. "How many people in the future know about this?"

"Only two at the bureau," Colette said. "Also, Hardin, and whoever Andrew was working with. Presumably Dr. Kuzmich. Hardin knows his survival depends on being quiet. The two at the bureau are rather far up the ladder." She smiled sheepishly. "I ignored the chain of command. Went right to the top. They were astonished, to say the least. In that room, the three of us realized the possibilities of time-travel and what it could mean to national security and stability."

Davis interjected, "People could go back in time to sway elections, invest in stocks, sabotage company empires, win lotteries. Generally commit murder, theft, and fraud, and get away with it."

Colette's voice took on a hesitant, sobering tone as she continued in a near-whisper. "I'll be honest, their fears about time-travel threats were so all-consuming, I became afraid for my own life. For what I now know. So afraid, in fact, that I'm not returning to the future."

All gazes darted to her, eyes blinking against this sobering statement and what it meant for them.

Chapter Thirty-One

1926

AFTER COLETTE'S STUNNING declaration, a silence fell and lingered.

Libby frowned. "Hardin. He's still there. In danger—"

"No, Libs," Colette said. "When I got scared, I realized he might be in danger too for what he knows. You trusted him, so I helped him."

"What did you do?"

Colette's gaze flicked around the room before returning to her. "Let's just say it involved staging an escape, a middle-of-the-night flight, and a one-way ticket to Brazil. He's interested in the plant life in remote portions of the Amazon. He'll be fine."

Libby shook her head in disbelief. After a moment she looked at Davis. "Did you know about Andrew? When you helped me in the cave, I mean."

"Know? No. Suspect? Yes. For a while I thought you might be involved. As you healed you said things in your sleep that didn't jibe with the story you delivered once awake. I assumed you were lying. So, Zach followed you, until Colette showed up, that is."

Colette smiled. "When I climbed out of the spring...naked, I might add..." She looked at Zachary. The corner of his mouth curved slightly, hiding a smile. She ventured a smile in return. "… Zach was right there to help me. He took me to the Arandale Hotel and I met Davis. The bureau was too big for me to have known them. They turned the tables on me, and interrogated me."

"Zach spent much of his time nursing Colette back to health," Davis said, smoothly picking up the story. "I checked in when I could. Thanks to Colette, and watching your different interactions, we began to understand Sheriff Harrow might have been a time-traveler as well. So, we approached him this afternoon."

Libby looked at Zach. "*You* followed me? I thought it was a man named Leon Martelli."

"It was at first," Zach said. "Then I began to tail you, and it turned into me following him following you. On your last night in Pittsburgh, he acted agitated, tired of waiting to strike. And, I was tired of him. Tired of the threat he held over you. Tired of the concern you'd get hurt. So I pulled him into an alley and took care of him."

Libby gasped. "You tried to kill him?"

Zach shook his head. "If I had *tried*, he'd be dead. But, I admit his recovery has taken longer than intended. I forgot how behind the times medicine is in these days. Besides," he waved a dismissing hand, "I know he has a future ahead of him filled with countless mistresses, two scathing divorces, and death by alcohol. Why would I want to deprive him of all that misery?"

"What do you mean?"

"My first-ever assignment with the bureau was in Philly. I needed to know how the city worked. I read about his supposed greatness in a series of biographical articles. 'Course he's long dead by then."

"But who then," Libby wondered out loud, "was the pale-looking guy with the unkempt look?"

"A pale guy? I don't—" Zach's eyes grew wide. "Wait a second. I do remember seeing a guy like that once. He was sickly pale. I'd almost forgotten. Initially, I thought too that he was watching you. But I ruled it out because he was so sloppy about his attire. He stood out too much."

Davis asked, "What do you mean?"

Zach shrugged. "His clothes. They didn't fit. Too short, and too big. Like he'd stolen the clothes off a line somewhere. If you're trying to spy on someone the last thing you do is stand out yourself, right? I mean, who would do that?"

Davis frowned. "Someone from the future who had to hide his nakedness quickly."

"And, who was especially sick from the water and trapped here with no money," Colette added. All gazes shot to her. "Carter. Dash Carter. He disappeared at the same time as Libby."

Libby's heart hammered. "Are you saying another agent followed me back?"

Colette tilted her head. "I'm saying it's possible. Remember, the bureau suspected Matryoshka involved a mole. So, they had two groups work on it. Separate investigations. A sort of checks and balances."

Davis rubbed his lower chin, clearly agitated. "So it's true. We could have someone from the future out there already."

Libby listened to the others talk about what this might mean. The uncertainty. The jeopardy they could be in. But, she couldn't take her gaze off Andrew. This man she married was a murderer. The reasons she'd been separated from Broken Arrow. She circled the nearest bench and sank onto it, looking at the others. "Now what?"

Zach sighed. "There's nothing we can do for now, except deal with our most imminent threat." His gaze bored into Andrew.

Andrew looked around, snorted. With a condescending tone in his voice, he said, "You can't prove any of this. It will never stand up in court."

"You're right." Brogan pulled a folded piece of paper from his inside jacket pocket. "That's why we have the signatures of two eye witnesses saying you killed my wife, Gretchen Harrow, last night."

Andrew's eyes narrowed. "That's a lie. Who signed that?"

Brogan unfolded the paper. Slowly. He read from it. "Davis Whitaker and Zachary Hayes."

Andrew blazed, tension escalating in his voice, "You're framing me for her murder? I never even met her. I guess that makes all of you as guilty as me, doesn't it?" Sweat broke out on his forehead like dew.

Brogan remained calm. "It would be rather hard to prove you murdered Libby's entire family, and Richard and Anabelle Wallace. Or, that you shot both Libby and me and left us to die. Or, that you manipulated three other people's lives by—"

"Son of a...you can't do this. I'll ruin all of you." He turned beat red, looking like a man gone mad. The madness that comes from lustful dreams and delusions of grandeur destroyed.

Davis raised his brows at Andrew's cold warning. "Andrew, I don't think you understand."

Libby sucked in her breath. She watched the three men exchange looks. Another nonverbal conversation.

Andrew snarled with contempt for the group and launched a freight train of words at them. "I'll tell people Zach killed the sheriff's wife. He's a stranger in town with no links to anyone, whereas I will look familiar to the townies. Davis, the fat cat over there, I'll say he was colluding with the sheriff to cover it up." He whirled to Colette. "And you! You're just a freak in this time with that height…"

In her peripheral vision Libby could see Zach posturing loathing and rage at Andrew's cocky attitude and his snide words.

Yet Andrew continued anyway, speaking in a steady stream and pouring his derision on Colette like syrup. "You'll be easy to track. You'll stand out everywhere. Be very afraid because I will hunt you down no matter where you go!" He smirked with what could only be considered cold, diabolical triumph, then continued ranting, delivering impudent, revolting, provocative jibes and threats about what he'd do and what he'd say about them all. "And I'll tell—"

In several efforts that blurred together as one fluid, frenzied movement, Zach cursed, sprang to his feet, pulled a pistol from his backside, and shot Andrew in the chest.

The sound roared and echoed in the small cabin.

The shot hit Andrew hard and flung him backward off the bench, his hands still cuffed behind him. He howled one animal cry of pain, flailed his legs and shuddered. Then, a final inhuman sound gurgled up from his throat, and he went still.

It happened so quickly Libby later thought if she had blinked, she would have missed it.

By then, Davis and Brogan had leapt to their feet yelling unintelligible exclamations.

Libby and Colette pulled together, locking arms. Tears welled in Libby's eyes even as a chill of relief streaked down her spine. The tension in her shoulders dissipated and she could feel her limbs relax. She flinched against the cold, almost uncaring feeling of ambivalence she had at his death.

For a harrowing moment all eyes darted from Andrew to Zach and back again. Everyone appeared stunned at the speed with which Zach had acted. But, Libby supposed he had taken just about all he could. Andrew's mistake had been to attack Colette.

The silence that descended was particularly pronounced, coming as it did immediately following Andrew's growled oaths of retaliation and vile insults.

Brogan crouched to check the body. He rose slowly. "Dead."

Davis still gaped at Andrew's body, his mouth hanging open, a dazed look in his eyes. From the stunned expression he wore, Libby surmised that killing Andrew this quickly, in this way, had not been part of the plan. If they had planned to kill him at all.

Zach's cold eyes dwarfed to slits as his gaze slanted down to assess what he'd done. It was clear that anger still burned in him. He lifted his gaze and in a cool, smooth gesture, spun the pistol around on one finger, like a true gun slinger, and handed it to Brogan. His voice was flat, serious. "You going to arrest me?"

Brogan stiffened and looked at the gun, then Zach. He took a breath but didn't take the gun. "No." He looked back at

Andrew. "He took your life. Now you've taken his. Sounds like justice to me."

The two exchanged a look of understanding, then nods of agreement.

"Then I'm outta here." He placed the gun on the bench closest to his knee, donned his hat, and turned to Colette. "You coming?"

Colette stared at him a moment, her eyes wide. He extended a hand. She smiled and reached for it as she stood.

Startled, Libby scrambled to her feet. "Colette, wait!" *What in the world happened in the past three weeks between these two?*

Colette looked back at her. "I'll find you. Leave a bread crumb trail." She turned to Zach.

Zach looked at Davis. "You know how to reach me."

Davis said nothing. He looked lost in a stupor, his face red and his gaze locked on Andrew's body. His shocked look confirmed he hadn't anticipated this turn of events.

Zach turned to Brogan. "How do I get back to my bike?"

Brogan gestured. "Left out the door. Straight up the hill. Over the top, the trail veers to the right. Follow it to the Arandale."

Zach pivoted to Libby and tipped his forehead.

Colette gave Zach an expectant look. "Bike?"

"A 1924 version of a Harley," Zach said. "Built for one, but if we move as one and lean in unison, we'll be fine till we get a sidecar."

Her smile grew and she picked up a lantern. "Let's go, cowboy."

They hurried out the door, not bothering to shut it behind them.

Dazed, Libby followed after them several steps before stopping a couple yards from the exit. She stared at the darkness beyond the open door. When Zach had thrust it open, the sound had been unnaturally loud in the stillness of the cabin. Libby thought now how apropos the whole departure was, how it punctuated movements that were so Colette-like, jumping right into the unknown in search of adventure, but leaving doors open for a return.

In the lull of the moment, she heard a frog croak, and a gentle rush of warm, humid air carrying an earthy scent wafted through the opening. She breathed in the lush fragrance, feeling her anxiety subside. It had taken her a while not to see the *less* that she saw in 1926, and to achieve what Brogan saw, the *more* of life here. Colette had seen it almost immediately.

Libby knew all along that Andrew had been able to take the water more than once. She hadn't considered doing the same, telling herself she was staying because she was waiting for him. Or, because taking the water was so painful. Or, because she didn't know where she'd end up. But, she realized now, the truth was that the rhythms of life at this time felt right for her. And Brogan had been right about this being a second chance. She wanted this place, this time, to be better off for her having been there.

Brogan came up behind her and placed a hand on her shoulder. She really didn't even know him, yet their lives were forever entangled. They'd lost so much time together, but if— as the French novelist Marcel Proust said—"Love is space and time measured by the heart," then perhaps their story was still young. *Han. Korean for the state of feeling sad and hopeful at the same time.*

Libby touched Brogan's hand on her shoulder and nodded in confirmation that all was well. "Ohonte, oròn:ya."

They turned to see a pale Davis pointing the pistol at them. "No one else is leaving this room," he growled.

Chapter Thirty-Two

1926

A CHILL CREPT down Brogan's back as he assessed Davis, and more frighteningly, the gun. The flickering light from the lanterns danced on the sleek metal, sending his memory back to that other time Libby had been shot. Heart thundering, he reached for her and tried to move her behind him but she wouldn't have it.

"Davis, what are you doing?" Libby cried, stepping toward him and raising her palms, as though posturing disbelief and a have-you-gone-mad look, all in one. "We're your friends."

"We agreed earlier about Andreii," Brogan reasoned with the man. "I won't let you alone with his body. We'll wait until N.C. returns and—"

"It's not that." Davis's gaze dropped to Andrew's body on the floor, and back. "I can't let anyone else leave. Don't you understand?"

Brogan bristled, but calmed his voice. "Perhaps you should explain it to us."

Davis rubbed his temples with his free hand. "I should have stopped Zach and Colette. Now I'll have to hunt them down. All this time we thought Andrew was a communist, plotting against the United States. Turns out, he didn't care about any country. Just himself."

"But he's dead," Libby said. "It's over."

Davis shook his head. "Don't you see? Zach was right…about killing him. That *is* the only way."

Libby asked, "What are you talking about?"

Davis looked at her like she was daft. "He wanted to change this country to his own advantage. I can't let that happen. All of us who understand time-travel can use this to our personal gain. I took a vow to protect this country."

Brogan said, "We pose no more of a threat than you." Heck, if anything Davis was the biggest threat in the room. He clearly felt remorse, whereas Brogan refused to. The gunshot that took Andrew's life had stilled Brogan's hammering heart, restored it to a steady, comfortable pace for the first time in a long time. If he allowed himself to feel guilt or regret, then even in death, Andrew would eclipse him again.

What's more, in the greatest of ironies, all the justice and reasoning benefitted Andrew, because a person should be innocent until proven guilty by a jury. Andrew had been denied that. But, Brogan didn't care. The culpability and responsibility he felt for nine years had spread so thin, in so many directions, for so many of the wrong people, like Anabelle, Jasper Hudd, and Gretchen, that it had become invisible and impalpable. He'd lived several deaths of the man he had once been; it was time to choose life. He took a deep breath. "If you think—"

Davis snapped, "I'm entrenched in this life now. You're not. I have a wife. Children. I'm not going to time-travel again to change the country. I don't know about you two."

Libby shook her head as though Davis's logic escaped her. "I'm not going anywhere, Davis. And neither is Brogan," she said, shooting him a hopeful look.

Brogan returned her gaze as he spoke, hoping she'd ascertain his full meaning. "Of course not. Everything I want is right here."

Libby stared at him a heartbeat and he watched her soften. Then, as though catching herself, she turned to Davis and squared her shoulders. "Besides, Davis, there are others out there. People like us who have traveled. Think about it—if we figured it out, then they could have, too. We already suspect that pale-looking guy is out there."

Davis's hand began to shake. "I'm sorry. I really am. You have the potential to travel through time again and change the whole course of our country."

"Do you mean," a voice from the open door said, "change it *before,* or *after* your people changed it by removing mine from this land?"

All gazes darted to see a short woman standing there. She was dressed in pants made of hide, and a fringed jacket. Beneath her wide-brimmed hat, a long dark braid dropped at least eight inches past the smirk on her face.

"Ista!" Brogan said at the same time Libby uttered, "Aunt Isabel!"

Brogan and Libby looked at one another as they each digested the other's words. He composed himself quickly and yelled to the woman, "Don't come in! He has a gun."

Ista tilted her chin and looked at Davis from the top of her eyes. "He's not killing anyone," she said with a leisure delivery as she entered, her steps slow and lithe. She embraced Libby and Brogan as though she hadn't a care in the world. Holding her cheeky, confidant look intact, she sank down on a bench.

Davis beetled his brows and wavered the gun between Ista

and where Brogan and Libby stood. "What's going on? Who is this?"

Libby hurried to sit beside the old woman. "Ista." *My Mohawk mother.* "My aunt Isabel."

Davis paled. "Aunt…from the future…?"

Ista grinned. "And the past." She patted Libby's knee as she spoke to Davis, indulgence in her voice. "You are not killing anyone. If you do, then you will have to kill your pretty wife, too."

"What are you talking about?" Davis sounded stunned. His hand began to tremble. "How do you know Darcie?"

Ista's grin grew. "Ask her about 1814. When the British burned Washington."

"What…" Davis began, but fell silent. He ran his free hand over his head. "It can't be. My Darcie? How many people have you seen take the water?"

Ista shot him a wicked smile. "Fourteen. Perhaps more when I could not be there." She pulled off her hat and brushed back loose wisps of hair with her hand before parking the hat back on her head. There was nothing hurried about this woman, Brogan remembered, as she continued. "Probably many more before my time. For years, campfires were built beside the spring. Tubs and buckets…kept there so people could heat the water in winter, too."

Davis's eyebrows arched in two perfect, black apostrophes. "So…so there could be dozens?" His question smacked of defeat, not curiosity.

Ista gestured to a bench. "Sit down, Mr. Whitaker. If someone in time wants to harm the country, there is nothing you can do about it. Besides, they cannot hurt it more than what your politicians have done already."

Davis uttered a heartfelt groan and lowered his hand. A man defeated by overwhelming odds. He passed the pistol in slow delivery to Brogan, and sank onto a bench. "Forgive me," he said, defeat and remorse lacing his voice. "I just want to do what's right…"

Brogan parked the pistol in his holster. Davis looked contrite, resigned, so Brogan knelt beside the old woman, but kept Davis in his peripheral vision. "Ista, I have missed you. You must forgive me." He swallowed hard. "I thought Morning Meadow was dead. That I'd never see her again. I didn't understand when you said to wait for her…"

Ista touched his cheek. "I know, yen'a." *My son.*

"All that time I lived with you, I never remembered it was you who saved her when Andreii shot her. In the wilderness, I had only ever heard you speak Mohawk…but that day when you took her body, you spoke to me in English. It didn't become clear to me until—"

"I know," Ista said. "It does not matter."

Brogan studied her lined face, the stories of hundreds of worrisome moments written there. "It matters to me. You bandaged me which kept me alive until other people got there. Years later when Andreii shot me again, you found me and pulled me from the water into 1917. Gave me a new home."

Libby looked from one to the other. "It was Ista that nursed you?"

Ista's eyes moistened. "I did my best to travel between you two. Tried to watch over you both until you could be together again."

Libby gasped. "You took me to 2003! I remember

now…living with you outside the Indian village until Nathan arrived. I thought I remembered traveling with an Aunt Isabel in third-world countries, but it was with you in the wilderness. Somehow, I created a false history, changing the natives and the crudeness of the wilderness to be the natives in Africa and the Australian Outback. The people I imagined attacking me were Indians attacking my family. And my scar…it was from Andreii's bullet, not a harrowing moment in Africa."

Ista nodded.

Brogan wanted to reach for Libby. Hold her. But, now wasn't the time. He focused again on Ista. "Andreii said he was in this decade once before. That's why you left in 1921, isn't it?"

Ista frowned. "I couldn't let him see you. *This* is when you belong. I stole into his room. Added something to his drink. To make him ill enough to take the water again. Then, I had to follow him to make sure my girl was okay."

Libby let her breath out in a ragged exhale. "In the future, I often felt like I was being followed. That was you, visiting, watching over me, wasn't it?"

Ista smiled.

"I never knew." Libby's words came out scratchy, but clear. "All this time lost."

Ista shook her head. "Not lost. Sometimes God takes people from us. If He gives them back again, then they're even more precious than before." She looked from Libby to Brogan. "Did you read Romans?"

Embarrassed, Brogan uttered a sound and looked down before meeting her gaze again. "Not until this afternoon."

Startled, Libby said, "Ista, I remember you mentioning

Romans, when you put me in the water. What does it say?"

Brogan ran a hand over his head, embarrassed. "That hope is everything, and waiting does not diminish us. The longer we wait, the larger we become, and the more pleasurable our expectancy."

Ista placed a hand on each of their cheeks and grinned, that grin that always made her look as though she knew something others didn't. "The best things take time."

"But why here? The 1920s, I mean?" Libby asked. "Why guide us to this timeframe?"

Ista shrugged. "The water did it. Not me. Maybe because what happened here tonight…" Her gaze shot to Andrew's body and back. "…that kind of justice could not have been done in the future. Too much forensics and technology."

From outside the cabin Rose's voice sounded, carried on the still, night air. "But N.C., I know we didn't leave anything behind. Everyone knows if you start to go somewhere and come back for something you will have bad luck."

Brogan stood quickly, crossed to the door, and pushed it shut. "N.C. knows nothing about time-travel, but he believed the story that Andrew was involved in Gretchen's death. He won't be too surprised to see his body."

Ista stood. "I will go now. No point in trying to explain me, too. I will be gone a while. Watch the water for me. Help others. They bring their problems with them. They need your help."

Libby scurried to her feet. "No, don't go! I just got you back."

Ista kissed her cheek. "Time has changed both your lives. Now let it make you a new and better life, my children."

Libby clung to her arm. "Ista, please."

"If I stay," Ista said, "I will be a crutch. But, I will return." She smiled sheepishly. "Save the crumbs for Colette. I need no trail. I will find you."

Davis stood and stepped closer to Ista. "I've heard enough to know you are an amazing woman, ma'am. God speed."

Ista nodded at Davis, kissed Brogan's check and walked out the back door.

"Sheriff?" N.C. called, the volume of his voice suggesting they had arrived.

"We're fine," Brogan yelled, "but I'll need your help." He turned to Davis. "We stick with our plan?"

Davis inhaled deeply. "That Andrew killed Gretchen? Yes. Let's put this to rest. I need to get back to Pittsburgh. To work, and to have a long talk with Darcie. If the future does come looking for us as Colette suggested, we better all be in sync."

DAWN WAS BREAKING by the time N.C. and Roscoe transferred Andrew's body to town for burial. When N.C. had gone back to Bedford to retrieve a wagon, he dropped Rose at the hotel. Upon return, he informed them that Rose was anxious to see for herself that Libby was well.

"She's mighty upset Gretchen was murdered by a man you used to know," N.C. said to Libby. "She'll be glad to see you in person."

"I'll check on her," Libby assured him.

"I appreciate that, ma'am." He blushed. "I'm kinda sweet on that girl."

After watching them drive off, Davis shook hands with Brogan and kissed Libby on the cheek. "Again, I'm sorry about what happened here tonight. I panicked."

"It's forgotten," Libby said.

Davis nodded. "I'll be in touch." He turned to go. "Oh," he swirled back to them. "Remember, if the future, or the pale guy, or whoever comes knocking, we can always take the water again. But, telephone lines being as public as they are, we'll need a code word in case you see any concerning activity. Think about it. We'll talk soon." He headed down the trail.

Brogan watched him go for a moment, then looked back at the cabin. They had cleaned the blood splatter with cloths and water N.C. brought from town. The log dwelling looked peaceful again.

He turned to Libby and gently touched her cheek. "Those eyes! How I've missed them. Green with blue."

"Together." She smiled and kissed him.

When they pulled apart, he said, "My motorcar is parked over the ridge. At the Crystal Spring. Why don't we hike over there?"

She bit her lip as though pondering a deep thought. "Alright, but I'm not letting you anywhere near the water." She pursed her lips into a lopsided grin, her eyes sparkling.

Brogan reached for her hand and brought it to his lips. "Why would I want to do that when my future is standing before my eyes? I meant it when I said everything I want is right here." He hitched his breath, almost afraid to ask. "What about you?"

She pulled his hand to her lips, repeating his gesture. "Where you go, I go. *When* you go, I go."

They extinguished the lanterns and set out, walking side by side despite the trail being narrow. After a few steps, he reached out for her hand and tucked it in the crook of his arm. His chest tightened. It felt right to walk freely with her. To love her. To look forward to a future. *Finally.* He sighed, feeling peace and contentment pour through him for the first time in a long time. Glancing toward the sky, he spotted the distant moon. He could swear it smiled before tucking away for the day.

"So," he said, "I guess I better learn more about this women's movement, eh?"

"Definitely," Libby said, her voice firm. Then, she donned a mischievous smile. "But first, tell me more about courting."

The End

A Word from the Author

I grew up in Bedford County, Pennsylvania. Our family farm was tucked into the rolling foothills of the Appalachian Mountains about 15 miles from the Bedford Springs Hotel (now, the Omni Bedford Springs Resort).

On each shopping trip I took with my mother to Bedford, I would beg her to drive by the hotel. Occasionally, she indulged my request, and the quick drive-by would always set my mind to wondering. That joy and the scintillating notion of "if this place could talk" stayed in the recesses of my mind for decades. Further, the Bedford area is rife with rich history, and filled with stories of rugged, intrepid men and women who settled the frontier in the push to move west. Sadly, history books don't give the area much attention.

As I grew, I turned into an ardent lover of history. As such, my novels tend to blend historical intrigue and modern-day suspense, with romance, and a touch of supernatural.

In *What the Moon Saw*, I changed a few aspects of the Bedford Springs: there was no manager named Jarvis, porter named Oliver Kenton, nor maid named Rose Morgan. Further, I tweaked the hotel's décor, and altered its access to telephones, electricity and heating, for the sake of the story. I also took liberties in describing the location the Crystal Spring in relation to the hotel.

However, the history of "taking the water" in Bedford for medicinal purposes for centuries is actual, as is the list of presidents and dignitaries that frequented the hotel. Presidents Thomas Jefferson, James Polk, Zachary Taylor, Thaddeus Stevens, and several others stayed there. President James Buchanan made the Bedford Springs his summer White House. While he was there, the first trans-Atlantic cable message was sent to his room from Queen Victoria in 1858. The hotel also housed the only Supreme Court hearing, in 1855, ever to be held outside of the capital.

With one exception, none of my characters were real people; the lone exception being James Smith (James "Black Boy Jimmy" Smith). He was a frontiersman, farmer and soldier. Through the 1760s, Smith coordinated an unofficial band called the "Black Boys" (so called because they blackened their faces while engaged in their activities) to protect settlers in western Pennsylvania and eastern Ohio from Native American ("Indian") attacks. The settlers wanted to live in peace with the natives, but the British were intent on allowing tradesmen to sell arms and ammunitions to the Indians and inciting them to kill. The settlers considered it licensed murder.

On March 6, 1765, the Black Boys stopped a pack train and burned illegal goods, including rum and gunpowder, that British official George Croghan sought to trade to Native Americans. British authorities supported Croghan's illegal trading, and this led to the Black Boys Rebellion in armed resistance to British rule in North America. In 1769, Smith and the Black Boys did surprise Fort Bedford, the first fort taken from the British by the colonials, freeing prisoners being held there.

Earlier in his life, in 1755, Smith helped work on a road built west from Alexandria, Virginia in support of General

Edward Braddock's ill-fated expedition against the French. Smith was captured by Delaware Indians and brought to Fort Duquesne at the Forks of the Ohio River, where he was forced to run a gauntlet before being given to the French. He was adopted by a Mohawk family, ritually cleansed, and made to practice tribal ways. Eventually, he escaped near Montreal and returned to the Bedford area. You will find parts of his experience in the character Nathan McKenzie.

Also based on an actual event was the description of Indian uprisings in 1764 when four Lenape Indian warriors entered a settlers' log schoolhouse in Greencastle. Enoch Brown, the schoolmaster, pleaded with the warriors to spare the children. Nonetheless, he was scalped and killed. The warriors tomahawked, scalped and killed nine of the children, and took four others as prisoners. As described herein, two other scalped children miraculously survived to describe what transpired. The slayings of Susan King Cunningham and her unborn child by warriors are part of recorded history, too.

Finally, the discussion in *What the Moon Saw* is true about the English, French, Spanish, Dutch and Swedes competing for a foothold on this continent in the 1400s, 1500s, and 1600s. And, it's true that Empress Elizabeth of Russia did dispatch representatives to come to the New World in the mid-1700s to promote trade, build relationships, and generally give Russia a presence. From this historical tidbit came my character Andreii Grebenshchikov.

As for the time-travel aspects in the story…well, that's the touch of supernatural I mentioned. The beauty of the supernatural is that you can choose to believe as much as you wish.

Thanks for reading.

If you enjoyed *What the Moon Saw*, you'll love these next stories from Tule Publishing…

The Farrier's Daughter by Leigh Ann Edwards
Book 1 in the Irish Witch series

Blood Bound by Traci Douglass
Book 1 in the Blood Ravager's series

Animal Instincts by Patricia Rosemoor

Available now at your favorite online retailer!

About the Author

An award-winning author and former journalist, D. L. Koontz writes about what she knows: muddled lives, nail-biting unknowns and eternal hope.

Growing up, she learned the power of stories and intrigue from saged storytellers on the front porch of her Appalachian farmhouse. Despite being waylaid for years by academia, journalism, and corporate endeavors, her roots proved that becoming a writer of suspense was only a matter of time. She has been published in seven languages.

D.L. (aka Debra Roberson) is a mom, step-mom, rancher's wife, animal lover, and busy bee trying to write intriguing suspense novels one extraordinary day at a time.

She loves history and research, so her novels blend historical intrigue and modern-day suspense with romance, and a touch of the mysterious. D.L. is passionate about words, photography, health, yoga/exercise, her porches, and barn preservation.

Visit D.L. on her website at DLKoontz.com

Thank you for reading

What the Moon Saw

If you enjoyed this book, you can find more from all our great authors at TulePublishing.com, or from your favorite online retailer.

TULE
PUBLISHING

Made in the USA
Middletown, DE
31 March 2018